PRAISE FOR
THE INHERITOR

"Wither's debut novel and first in a series creates a
chilling world in which mass-scale terrorism and
dangerous military operations are the norm. The
narrative provides plenty of mind-numbing twists
and turns along the way. Military buffs and fans of
high-stakes action thrillers will find a lot to like."
— *Publishers Weekly*

"Vivid, terrifying, and all too possible,
Tom Wither's novel sets a high bar in the
darkest speculative corner of the political thriller niche."
— Larry Brooks,
USA Today bestselling author of *Darkness Bound*

"*The Inheritor* is a spectacularly good thriller—
banging with action, filled with absolutely fascinating
and authentic details from the world of military
intelligence—fans of Tom Clancy will love it!"
— Max Byrd,
author of *The Paris Deadline*

AUTUMN FIRE

AUTUMN FIRE

A NOVEL

Tom Wither

TURNER

Turner Publishing Company
424 Church Street • Suite 2240 • Nashville, Tennessee 37219
445 Park Avenue • 9th Floor • New York, New York 10022

www.turnerpublishing.com

AUTUMN FIRE

Cover design: Maxwell Roth
Book design: Kym Whitley

Library of Congress Catalog-in-Publishing Data

Wither, Tom.
  Autumn Fire : a novel / Tom Wither.
     pages cm
  ISBN 978-1-62045-498-5 (alk. paper)
  1. Special forces (Military science)--Fiction. 2. Terrorism--Prevention--Fiction.
  3. Suspense fiction. I. Title.
  PS3623.I8647A95 2014
  813'.6--dc23
                         2014019212

Printed in the United States of America
14 15 16 17 18 19 0 9 8 7 6 5 4 3 2 1

For the dedicated NSA/CSS professionals, both military and civilian, who defend our nation while upholding our Constitutional principles under the law—it's an honor to have served alongside you.

ACKNOWLEDGMENTS

Thanks are due to Steve, David, and Jimmy for the security reviews, my friends and family for their support, and my agents, Roger and Betty Anne, for their continued enthusiasm.

AUTUMN FIRE

CHAPTER 1

· ·

November 2018

ELECTRICITY WAS FIRST EXPERIMENTED WITH around 600 B.C., when Thales of Miletus conducted his study of static electricity. In 1600, the English physician William Gilbert studied electricity and magnetism, recognizing the difference between magnets found in nature and the static electricity produced by rubbing amber. In the eighteenth century, Benjamin Franklin conducted extensive research in electricity. In June 1752, he was reputed to have flown a kite in a storm-threatened sky to find proof for his theories.

In 1800, Alessandro Volta's voltaic pile, constructed from layers of zinc and copper, provided a more reliable source of electrical energy than the electrostatic machines then in use. Hans Christian Ørsted and André-Marie Ampère discovered the relationship between electricity and magnetism by 1820, followed quickly by Michael Faraday's invention of the electric motor in 1821, and Georg Ohm's mathematical analysis of the electrical circuit in 1827.

The greatest progress in the science of electricity occurred during the late nineteenth century through the efforts of Alexander Graham Bell, Thomas Edison, Lord Kelvin, Ernst Werner von Siemens, Nikola Tesla, and George Westinghouse. More than 2,400 years of effort turned electricity from a scientific curiosity into an essential tool for modern life.

In short order, the lightbulb, gramophone, wireless radio, and cinema became commonplace in American life. Refrigerators, stoves, clothes washers, dryers, heating and air conditioning, and traffic lights quickly followed. By the 1970s, semiconductors had replaced the vacuum tubes of the early electronic devices, turning a simple radio from a thirty-pound block of metal and wires into a solid-state device that could fit in the palm of your hand. Semiconductors led the way to microprocessors holding the entire functionality of the room-filling ENIAC or UNIVAC computers on a tiny silicon chip a quarter of the size of a thumbnail.

The natural outgrowth from the microprocessor was the micro-computer. The microcomputer's mass production, coupled with the advent of the Internet, led to desktop and laptop personal computers in every home as the digital age, and then the information age, took shape in the 1990s and early twenty-first century. As technology continued its unabated march toward the future, electronics manufacturers, telecommunications, and Internet service providers coupled the telephone network with the Internet, a phenomenon commonly termed "convergence." This led to the introduction of mobile telephones, and then smartphones, allowing people to carry the Internet in their pocket, making near-instantaneous communication anywhere and anytime a practical reality—all underpinned by a moving stream of electrons that essentially never stop coming out of an outlet in the wall or of a battery.

Until now.

NO ONE EVER EXPECTED THE power to be out for this long. A couple of hours was tolerable, and even expected from time to time, as were outages lasting a day or two after major storms. But three straight weeks without any power at all? For that entire time, the majority of the population in the Northeast and mid-Atlantic United States were living in the world of the mid-1800s. Not an ampere flowed nor a volt of potential existed in any electrical socket of any home and business from Maine to Virginia.

Without electricity, no modern convenience could function; buildings, offices, and homes were dark at night, chilled or ice cold. Electronic bank transactions ceased. Electronic payment for goods and services was nonexistent—the ATM and debit cards of modern banking instantly became useless. Cash was the only acceptable form of payment, with each transaction recorded by hand. People now had to interact directly with bank tellers to obtain cash, as long as they didn't mind waiting in a long line in a cold bank lobby, lit only by sunlight and under the watchful eyes of local police officers stationed within, since the holdup alarms could not function without power.

U.S. government agencies still functioned, but not at their usual pace. Their diesel and jet engine–driven turbine generators still provided the megawatts of power needed to keep federal government buildings and U.S. military bases heated and lit, and their computer networks functioning.

Inside the National Security Agency complex at Fort Meade, the lights were on in every window. The squares of light were tinted green by the glass in the two office towers built in the 1980s, and a smoky gray in the old headquarters' tower and three-story operations complex building erected in the early 1950s.

Dawn was still more than an hour off in the cold, late fall morning, but the parking lots were already half full. This was due in part to the patriotism and work ethic of the NSA employees, and also because of the recent attacks the United States had suffered at the hands of an enemy not yet fully identified or understood.

David Cain, Chief of NSA's Counterterrorism Shop, a twenty-year veteran employee of the NSA, leafed through the black three-ring binder containing the hard copy of the CTS Daily Briefing Book. He was of medium height and build with dark hair, and a deeply ingrained habit of not wearing a tie despite his senior position.

The Daily Briefing Book's front and back covers bore the red-and-white-striped cover sheet marking the contents as highly classified material, most of which was considered Sensitive Compartmented Information.

SCI access was one of the most coveted clearances in the U.S. government, but as Cain had learned in his twenty-plus-year career, it was only the starting point for even more sensitive accesses. The cover sheet itself was a special visual indicator that the briefing book contained something very few people would ever see: Special Access Program information. Anything using the word *special* within the Department of Defense usually meant one of three things: nuclear weapons, special operations activities, or very closely held intelligence operations. The material in the folder Cain held had nothing to do with nuclear weapons.

Outside of those in the military and intelligence communities directly involved with it, only the president and his national security staff, the secretary of defense and his senior staff, and the senior leadership of Congress, along with a few members of the various intelligence and military affairs committees, knew about the Special Access Program called CAPTIVE DRAGON. The CAPTIVE DRAGON SAP protected the tightly coordinated operations between certain unique elements of the intelligence community and a special operations unit known as the 152nd Joint Special Missions Unit, known informally as the Wraiths.

This morning, Cain was just returning from a mandatory seventy-two hours off he had placed himself and his entire watch team on following three weeks of almost nonstop duty after the first attacks. He and his people had been beyond tired four days ago, their judgment suffering from the continuous extended shifts, stress, and lack of sleep.

Cain lifted his eyes from the binder and looked over the two-tiered CTS watch center. Large video displays formed a semicircle in front of the lower tier of the watch center, where the liaison officers from the various intelligence community agencies had their desks arrayed before them.

The left screen showed a mix of real-time news network feeds, and the right screen displayed the main INTELINK web pages from the CIA, DIA, and NSA. Each page displayed that agency's real-time intelligence feed, including summary articles addressing items of interest from around the world, as discovered or reported by the intelligence sources controlled or managed by each agency. The pages automatically updated every few minutes as each agency reported new information. Some conspiracy-minded Americans actually thought the agencies spied on U.S. citizens around the clock, Cain silently smirked, understanding the depth of their ignorance. It took every resource the U.S. intelligence community had just to keep an eye on the foreign threats and adversaries the agencies were lawfully empowered to monitor. Keeping an eye on 350 million Americans would have been impossible, not to mention illegal and unconstitutional.

Alongside the intelligence updates burned a sectional map of the mid-Atlantic and New England coastal states, with a smaller inlay for Texas and Louisiana. The portion of the sectional map from Virginia to Maine was shaded to represent the size of the current power outage, with much of it covered by multicolored symbols representing the geographic location of a specific security-related event.

Scanning the symbol key in the lower right corner of the map, Cain took in the magnitude of the damage done to his country. Red explosive symbols represented the car bombings in San Antonio, with larger ones showing the attacks on the Strategic Petroleum Reserve and the Home Heating Oil Reserve. Yellow lightning bolts showed the locations of damaged main electrical power distribution stations, and red generators represented power plants that had suffered damage from the attacks.

Cain shifted his eyes to the watch floor, and noted that a few of his Alpha shift personnel were starting to trickle in and relieve the Charlie shift team that had covered the night watch. They were no doubt swapping stories about the difficulties each of their families was having dealing with the extended power outage while also getting up to speed on the previous shift's events. To stay as current on the events as they were, he needed to finish reading the briefing book before the formal handover briefing he would co-lead with the Charlie shift team leader.

Returning his attention to the binder the CTS team leaders were using in the event of a sudden power loss, Cain took a sip from his coffee cup. He had started by reading all of the AUTUMN FIRE situation reports from the beginning, even the ones he had released, bringing back to mind all the events that began this nightmare.

It had started with the horrific car bombings in San Antonio. He and his people had watched on live TV, along with the rest of America, the attacks on that great city as a group of car bombs exploded in the midst of the morning rush hour. More than 200 were dead and 300 wounded. Even the historical site of the Alamo, revered as a symbol of American courage in the face of hopeless odds, had suffered damage during the random bombings.

The next attack was a series of unsolved murders two days later in Atlanta, Chicago, New York, and Washington, D.C. Within a two-hour period during the morning rush hour, more than twenty-five men were shot to death, mostly from long range, while waiting at commuter bus stops or train stations, or just sitting in their cars at stoplights. There was no solid evidence that these attacks were part of the overall plan in motion against America, but Cain did not think it was a coincidence. Local police forces were investigating, backed up by the resources of the FBI, but so far, there were no investigative leads or even evidence beyond the victims' bodies and the bullets recovered at the scenes or during the autopsies.

A FEW DAYS AFTER THE murders, both the Strategic Petroleum Reserve in northeastern Texas, near the Louisiana border, and the Home Heating Oil Reserve storage tanks in Connecticut and New Jersey were attacked by a combination of suicide bombers in cars and armed gunmen. In hindsight, it became clear that the assaults on the SPR and the HHOR were intended, beyond the initial economic impact, to compound the damage from the next attack.

The next night, the power grid serving the mid-Atlantic and northeast states was struck through cyberspace. From what the Department of Energy experts had pieced together so far, one or more computers under the control of a hacker had masqueraded as at least two, and possibly three, different control computers managing the electrical energy production and distribution network, issuing false and ultimately damaging commands.

Commonly called the SMART GRID by politicians and energy companies and more formally known as an Electrical Power Supervisory Control and Data Acquisition network, the network connects all power generating stations, the power distribution network, and the smaller electrical substations. By simply masquerading the hacker's computers as the network's control computers, orders issued electronically caused the major components of the system to self-destruct, not merely turn off in the way Hollywood usually depicts.

If it had only been an order to turn off, restoration would have been much simpler. Instead, generators ran at excessive output voltages beyond the distribution network's capacity. Safety breakers at transformer stations that should have disconnected as the voltage rose had their upper-limit voltages raised to ensure that they would never disconnect. Transformers heated, melted down internally, or exploded, while the massive electrical generators continued to ramp up their output until they suffered internal damage. Making matters worse—and diagnosis and restoration even more difficult—the power plants received orders to shut down completely.

Across the northeast and mid-Atlantic states, complex nuclear-reactor automated-control systems sent neutron-absorbing control rods deep into the hot cores, stopping the controlled fission reaction, as external steam loops vented into the atmosphere, starving the turbines of their motive force. Automated coal conveyers and oil feed lines into the fossil-fuel plants stopped, pilot lights sputtered out, and in less than four minutes, twenty million people in America found themselves in the dark on a frigid autumn night.

The cyber-attack successfully damaged the power grid's infrastructure beyond immediate or even near-term repair. While a power plant's heat-producing engine—be it coal, oil, or nuclear—could be repaired if needed and restarted within two or three work shifts, the damaged generators and transformers had to be rebuilt, or worse, manufactured elsewhere and brought in for replacement. The surge of high voltage throughout the electrical distribution system damaged or destroyed many of the generator systems, heavy-duty transformers, and other equipment, rendering the power grid itself incapable of supplying electricity to commercial and residential customers from Maine to Virginia.

Cain sighed as he stopped reading and looked up again. Catching the eye of the Charlie shift supervisor, Al Combers, he said, "Have you gotten any word on how long before we get electricity back up?"

Like Cain, Combers was a veteran intelligence officer. Midforties, graying, and a taciturn observer of world events, his eyes told the tale before his voice did.

"Not anytime soon. DoE is coordinating the response, and power restoration crews from the western states and Canada are on-site all over the affected areas, but they expect it to take another week or two at least before they even think about bringing the grid back up for what they call a 'bootstrap start.'"

"What's that?" Cain asked.

"When the power grid is completely dead, they bootstrap it back up, using smaller power plants that don't need electricity to start them, like a hydroelectric dam."

Cain nodded his understanding as he took another sip of coffee, and Combers continued. "So once the smaller power plant at a dam is operating, it will provide power to larger-capacity oil or coal plants, so that they can restart. Then the oil or coal plants will power the much larger capacity nuclear plants, so they can come online. Once enough of the big megawatt producers are back up and running, they'll start energizing the grid for commercial and civilian use. It's like starting the electrical system in your car with a battery. Use the battery's power to start the motor, it drives the generator, and power flows."

"Got it," replied Cain, rubbing his eyes with both hands as he absorbed what Combers told him. If the Department of Energy said it, Cain would need to chop some more wood when he got off shift. He and his wife would need more for the fireplaces in their house. Maybe he could try ordering a truckload of wood from somebody. That thought quickly brought a frown to his face. He and his wife would probably have to pay a fortune for it at this point.

Cain shook his head and reached for his coffee again. "I'll be done reading in a few more minutes, and then we can do the shift-change brief for my people."

Looking down, Cain flipped the page and scanned the last AUTUMN FIRE summary report. He had approved its release, and he knew what it said, but it helped him to pull everything together and bring him back into his role as a senior member of the intelligence community ready for his duty shift.

SECRET
PRECEDENCE: IMMEDIATE
DTG: 0200Z 05 NOV 18
FM: CTS WATCH
SUBJ: AUTUMN FIRE Situation Update 05-18
TO: CTS/ALFA TWO FIVE

1. FBI forensics teams continue to investigate the wreckage of the al-Qaeda safe house in Chicago, gathering evidence for the future prosecution of the individual or individuals responsible for the murders of the FBI Hostage Rescue Team and the Chicago SWAT unit who died while attempting to apprehend the suspects at that location. This safe house was positively determined to be the ori-

gin point of the attacks against the U.S. power infrastructure in the northeast and mid-Atlantic states. Computer and other equipment recovered from the site have yielded no information thus far, and forensic examinations of the storage media are continuing. Two unidentified bodies recovered from a shallow grave within the wrecked building are not members of the Chicago SWAT unit or the FBI's HRT. Initial autopsy findings indicate that both subjects were murdered at least six months ago. Cause of death in both cases was a single gunshot to the head. The FBI and Chicago police department are leading a joint investigation into those deaths.

2. A letter recently published in open press claimed responsibility for the attacks and subsequent fires at the Strategic Petroleum Reserve in Texas, and three separate components of the Northeastern U.S. Home Heating Oil Reserves in New Jersey and Connecticut. The FBI obtained the letter from a U.S. newspaper and subjected it to forensic analysis. No fingerprints or usable DNA from the envelope seal or stamp was recovered, likely due to the use of a damp sponge on the seal and the use of a self-sticking stamp. Analysis of the printed characters has identified the printer as an inkjet printer from a U.S. manufacturer. The letter was postmarked from the Chicago metropolitan area seven days prior to the mass power outage and attacks on the Home Heating Oil Reserves in New Jersey and Connecticut. The letter is judged to be credible due to its allusion to future "incidents that will take place in . . . the whole of the Northeast . . ." Based on preliminary review by the CIA of the form and content of the letter, the letter is adjudged very similar to those issued by former members of al-Qaeda senior leadership. The signature at the bottom identifies the writer as "The Rightful Successor to the Warrior Bin Laden and the Ruler of the Returned Caliphate." The CIA assesses this to indicate that the drafter is claiming or believes himself to be Bin Laden's successor and intends to continue to pursue al-Qaeda's previously stated goal of establishing a Caliphate spanning Eastern Europe to Southeast Asia.

3. The subject believed to have knowledge of, or to be potentially coordinating, these recent attacks against the United States is

likely Aziz Abdul Muhammad al-Zahiri. Recent information from the FBI, obtained via Saudi Arabian Internal Security Forces, identified seven bank accounts that held, according to bank records, more than $200,000,000. These accounts, believed to have been controlled by Osama Bin Laden prior to his death, are now empty and closed out. The money was transferred out of these accounts early in 2012 to unknown countries/banks. The FBI is continuing its investigation into the money trail and any domestic activities by Aziz al-Zahiri under the investigative codename INHERITOR. A partial phone number associated with the subject is 98 21 333 (NFI). Open source information confirms that the phone number belongs to a landline geographically located in the Tehran, Iran, area. Additional information from Saudi intelligence services reported Aziz al-Zahiri at a home in the suburbs of Tehran, Iran. A team from the 152nd Joint Special Missions Unit raided the house to capture Aziz for questioning. The raid was accomplished with zero Blue Force casualties, six hostiles KIA, and no collateral damage, but the subject was not at the location. The 152nd JSMU team gathered what intelligence it could from the site for document exploitation and successfully exfiltrated the area with the hostile KIAs to Iraq. After refueling and rearming, the assault team was ordered to return to the United States after Saudi Arabian government protests/inquiries.

4. U.S. State Department and the FBI report polite but insistent queries from Saudi Arabia's Ministry of Interior officials strongly urging that the U.S. provide a detailed explanation for the mission into Iran. Saudi Arabian officials are concerned, on behalf of the king, about the use of Saudi Arabian territory to launch an invasion into a sovereign nation, apparently without sufficient cause.

5. CURRENT ANALYSIS/RECOMMENDATIONS: It appears likely that Aziz al-Zahiri is a senior leader or operational planner for a resurgent al-Qaeda or an unspecified al-Qaeda faction that has considerable financial resources available for use and has been able to consolidate and reassemble sufficient operational elements among AQ affiliates to enable the recent attacks. Informal assessments by intelligence community experts, FBI investi-

gators, and Homeland Security personnel reveal that fewer than 60 people have likely been required to carry out the recent attacks within the United States. The Chicago safe house location points to this city as a nexus and a potential base of al-Qaeda operations within the United States, although other potential bases of operation within the United States cannot be discounted. Further attacks within the United States and against U.S. interests abroad are likely.

S E C R E T
//EOT//

Placing the binder back on his desk, Cain rose and took a quick visual attendance. Most of his people were here now, except for Thompson. Stealing a look at the clock, he nodded to Combers, "One of my people is running a little late, but let's not wait. Let's get the brief started."

Combers nodded once in agreement and turned toward the two shifts' worth of people now crowding the lower-level watch floor area before the immense screens, raising his voice to be heard over the group's chatter.

"Okay, everyone! Huddle up! We're going once around the horn."

Everyone drew closer to the semicircle of upper-level desks, forming up by tradition and practice into pairs of oncoming and outgoing desk officers. As incoming shift leader, it was Cain's job to start them off. Once they sorted themselves out and quieted down, he began.

"Okay, everyone. My team is coming back from a seventy-two-hour stand-down, so this might run a bit longer than usual if we don't keep it brief. So, as they used to say in the seventies, 'hit it and pass it,' let's keep this moving or we'll be here all morning."

Only a few of the watch standers smiled at the joke. They were either pop-culture buffs or actually had a joint or two in their formative years and got the reference. Combers was old enough to get it and just smiled and shook his head at the joke he knew the "kids" on his shift would be calling Cain an "old fart" for later. After a beat or two to notice who did get his early morning attempt at humor, Cain started.

"CIA?" Cain asked.

"NTR," responded the Charlie shift CIA liaison.

Nothing to report. Well, that's an easy way to start, Cain thought, looking over the heads of the watch standers for Thompson. Where the hell was she?

"DIA?"

EMILY THOMPSON KNEW SHE WAS late—and that was only half of it. The power was still out, and she had awakened to her infant son Jeff's crying only to look at her watch in the cold darkness of her bedroom to realize she had not programmed its alarm properly.

Rising from her bed, she wrapped herself in the long wool coat on the bedside chair, grabbed the flashlight off her night table, turned it on, and went to Jeff's room. He was sitting up in his crib, wailing. She picked him up, and took him immediately to the changing table. After she had cleaned him up and put a fresh diaper on him, she snuggled him to her chest beneath the warm wool coat for a few minutes and he quieted down.

Frustrated, she went back to her bedroom with Jeff in her arms. Jerry, her husband of four years, was deep under the covers, oblivious to the baby's cries. She whacked him in the shoulder less than gently.

"Waaaa?" he mumbled, still half-asleep.

"Wake up!" she said quietly, trying to keep Jeff from crying again, and swatted her husband in the shoulder once more. Jerry finally opened his eyes and looked out of his warm cocoon to see a very unhappy look on his wife's face.

"What?"

"Are you deaf?" Emily asked him sotto voce. "Jeff is crying and you know I need to go to work. Get up!" Emily gently kissed her son on the head and carefully put him in his father's arms beneath the covers, then headed to the bathroom. Fortunately, she had taken a warm sponge bath the night before with water heated on the camp stove in the kitchen, but there would be no time for makeup today. She would even have to make do with her hair, pulling the blonde tresses back severely and knotting them up hastily, before braving the chill in the room to strip and put her camouflage uniform on.

Emily headed back into the bedroom, frowning at the sight of her jobless husband, still snuggled under the covers with Jeff, warm and dozing in the bed. He got to stay home—albeit a cold home—with their son, and didn't have to go to work. She, on the other hand, had to go back to CTS. Back where she had failed. Back where she had killed those men. *Damn him anyway.* She was the sole breadwinner for now, and with the power out in half the country, there was no sense in his trying to schedule interviews or do any job searching today.

She went back to the bed and bent down to kiss her son gently on the head. How would she explain to him one day what she had done? Jerry stirred and leaned toward her for his usual kiss, but she backed away. The surprise and pain in his eyes was easy to see. So was the worry.

"Baby, what's wrong?" Jerry asked.

"Nothing," she lied, then added an excuse. "I'm just running late and I didn't brush my teeth. I'll grab a mint in the car so I don't offend anybody at work. I'll see you tonight."

She left the house quickly, climbed into the car, and drove out of the family housing area on Fort Meade as quickly as the speed limit would allow.

After passing through the multiple vehicle checkpoints to reach Operations Building Six on the East Campus of the National Security Agency, she found a little luck in an empty parking spot in the underground garage near the elevator core. She passed through one of the retina-scanning "man traps" and then the metal detector. She bypassed the elevator bank and jogged up six flights of stairs. Turning left out of the stairwell into the third-floor corridor painted in the standard government-issue "Calming Sand" color, she reached the keycard-controlled access for the CTS watch floor, slipped her badge into the slot by the door, punched in her nine-digit code, and breezed through. The first thing she heard was Cain's voice.

"Thanks, everybody. Alpha shift has the floor. Charlie shift is relieved. See you tomorrow morning."

Shit. The shift change brief was over. She would need to find her counterpart, apologize, get the brief, and then apologize to Cain. Emily looked toward her desk on the watch floor, seeking the Charlie shift NCO working the Remote ISR and Weaponry Desk, or as the team called it, the Drone Desk. Seeing the desk again brought to mind an image of the explosions in Chicago, causing her to close her eyes briefly as an invisible hand squeezed her heart. Her fault. No one else's. She thought she was so smart, yet she couldn't even find the right set of floor plans for a building in the middle of America.

Opening her eyes again, she saw Cain walking toward her. He was an attractive man, dark hair with some silver at the temples, with a few extra pounds more from middle age than lack of exercise, and since she had worked for him, she noticed his dark brown eyes didn't miss much. Looking at his face, all Emily saw was a mask of disappointment, and she sighed. Being chewed out for coming in late would not improve her mood. This was not going to be a good day.

"SO WHAT'S GOING ON, SIR?"

FBI Special Agent Dave Johnson was not used to questioning people as senior as Special Agent in Charge Steven French, but the morning pleasantries were out of the way. Plus, he had been central to getting the INHERITOR investigation started, so he thought he could afford a little leeway.

French was not surprised or annoyed by the inquiry, but he knew how to remind a practically brand-new special agent of his place. Johnson had been out of the academy for only two years, and the tall, brown-eyed, baby agent still had a great deal to learn, particularly about dealing with senior agents.

"Well, Dave, surprisingly enough, that's why I asked you to report to *me* this morning."

Using his first name as opposed to his title and the slight emphasis on the *me* got the point across. Johnson may have been young, but the FBI Academy training was ingrained. By reflex, he sat up just a little straighter in his chair, and he actually had to stop himself from reaching up to ensure that his tie was straight in his collar. French was a senior-level agent with more than thirty-four years of service in the Bureau, and Johnson had not even finished his probationary period yet.

After noticing the change in Johnson's body language, French took the opportunity to swivel his chair around to the dark wooden credenza behind his desk and load the automatic coffeemaker with one of the little premeasured cups, slide his favorite FBI-logoed mug beneath the spigot, and punch the button to start the brew cycle. As the coffee streamed into his mug, French kept his back to Johnson and did not speak. Forty seconds of silence while the cycle completed punctuated his earlier comment. Retrieving his cup, he turned back to his desk, took a sip, and placed the mug in its customary spot. Naturally, he did not offer to make a cup for his subordinate. Fixing him with an intent look, he began.

"The INHERITOR investigation is proceeding, but isn't yielding much at the moment. The trail on the money went cold after it routed through a bank in Kuala Lumpur. We suspect our friend Aziz had a banker friendly to al-Qaeda cover up the records of any further movement, possibly by converting it to securities and other financial instruments that are usually bought and sold in large volumes in the course of a routine banking day. This banker probably also falsified the paper trail as needed to cover his tracks. Our 'follow-the-money' people are working the international banking angle hard, but the bankers in Kuala Lumpur operate in a pretty permissive environment in terms of what they don't have to disclose to the government, so our Legat there is not getting a lot of help from the locals."

Johnson nodded. He couldn't do anything to help the Legal Attaché from here. "Yes, sir. What do you need me to do next? With the Saudis putting Sadig on trial, I'm not sure what my next move should be. Am I going to be assigned to help out the 'follow-the-money' agents?"

French shook his head. "No. I've gotten a special request for you."

"Sir?" a puzzled Johnson asked.

"Your Saudi friend Akeem wants you to return to the Kingdom, and I'm inclined to let you go."

"What does Akeem want me back in Saudi for, sir?" Akeem ibn Dabir ibn Farid al-Haddad was a special assistant to the Saudi Arabian Minister of the Interior. His real title within the ministry was a bit more nebulous, but what mattered more was his close friendship with the minister. A prince of the Saud family, or at the very least a trusted cousin, usually ran government ministries in Saudi Arabia, to ensure personal loyalty to the king. This naturally created a patronage-like system, allowing trusted friends outside the royal family to gain jobs based on their friendship with the right people. In the Interior Ministry, Akeem handled all the delicate or sensitive matters for his minister. The man had also proven himself not only a help to Johnson, but also a decent teacher of Saudi culture and the Arabic language during Johnson's very first overseas assignment.

When Johnson traveled to the Kingdom as part of the INHERITOR investigation, Akeem helped cut through the red tape and find Sadig al-Faisal, the former Taliban Finance Minister, and welcomed Johnson into his home and allowed him to meet his children and, very briefly, his wife. It was an offer of friendship that Johnson was very flattered by, and it created an informal back channel of communication to the minister and eventually the king that Johnson had leveraged to allow the Wraith Team to stage from Saudi Arabia into Iran on its covert mission to capture Aziz.

SAIC French had chewed his ass for leveraging that channel, but it had worked. The Saudis approved the mission and the president did not suffer the embarrassment of being told no when he asked the king through more formal channels. Being a conduit for that level of communication between his nation and the Saudis was thrilling, but it had also contributed to his overfamiliarity with French a few minutes ago. Lesson learned.

"Akeem has placed a formal request on behalf of the minister for you to return to the Kingdom to be present for Sadig's sentencing before a Sharia court."

In spite of his friendship with Akeem, the long flight and more time away from his newly expectant wife did not exactly thrill him, which motivated his response.

"Are you ordering me back to Saudi for the sentencing, sir?" As much as he thought he was hiding it, Johnson's tone actually said, "Am I really needed there?"

The look in French's eyes and his almost feral smile told him how taking this direction would go. This youngster was about to be reminded again that he was not in charge of anything in the FBI, and that duty came first in the Bureau. More important, it would be good to keep the back channel open, especially if the young agent remembered that all his back-channel requests or messages from Akeem went to French first for a sanity check. God help him if he tried to call the secretary of state or president directly.

"Yes, Agent Johnson. Go home and pack."

CHAPTER 2

NAVY LIEUTENANT SHANE MATHEWS WAS starting to sweat, but it didn't last long. As soon as his temperature rose two-tenths of a degree, the microchip controlling the thermal control suit under his battle dress uniform began circulating cool water around his body. His breathing was something the computer could not regulate, though, which was what constant physical conditioning helped with. That physical conditioning gave his shoulders the breadth and depth of an NFL running back, which he thought went well with his close-cropped sandy-colored hair and blue eyes.

He had just ordered his team to run toward the target house in the broad daylight of early morning, trying to cover the empty space between their jump-off point to the entry door as quickly as possible. The men moved single file, with Mathews' senior NCO, Air Force Master Sergeant Terry Simms, in the lead.

Normally, Mathews would have wanted to lead the team as a good naval officer should, but in a tactical situation like this, the commander went second and the most experienced NCO took point, using his years of experience to evaluate the situation and ensure that the initial stages of an entry were handled smoothly.

Team Four was stacked on the door now. The team had broken into two sub-teams within yards of the door, each sub-team stacking in a long line parallel to the outer walls on either side of the door. The last two men in each sub-team now faced out, eyes and weapons scanning for unexpected threats from the direction they had just come.

Mathews' breathing was rapid but slowing quickly. He felt the chill over his skin as the cooling garment did its work beneath his black combat uniform and the high-tech body armor he wore over it. His sub-team was now stacked to the left side of the door, and his Executive Officer's sub-team was stacked to the right, waiting for the final orders.

Keeping his Heckler & Koch M8 rifle pointed at the ground just to the right of his sergeant's shoulder, he turned his head left and slowly scanned the wall of the building. From the vantage point of an observer, it would have looked strange, but Mathews couldn't have cared less. The helmet he wore not only provided ballistic protection, with its impregnated Kevlar weave for his head and neck, but also gave him a set of adaptive optics and an augmented virtual-reality view of the world everyone else in the U.S. military would give vital body parts to have.

Keeping up his scan, he noted that the new millimeter band radar sensors placed around the target building were working as advertised. The latest thing in high-tech sensors, they literally allowed an observer to see through walls. They were not good enough to provide facial details, just rough shapes of humans. Telling men apart from women was damn near impossible, but the best part, as far as Mathews was concerned, was that you could also see the outline of something being carried by the human shape. Deciphering concealed weapons, however, was a problem, but he supposed the eggheads would work on that and a few other things for the next upgrade. The processing power of the local sensors was just too limited, and keeping the sensors man-portable was important.

Completing his scan, he spoke, the voice-activated radio clipped to his ear inside the helmet relaying his words to the team.

"This is Lead. Four Tangos in sight, room number one, left side. Other rooms appear clear, but remember, I can't see deeper than 20 meters or so given the type of walls. Watch for surprises. Stealth entry is a go."

With that, Mathews tapped Master Sergeant Simms on his left shoulder. Simms pulled a lock-picking gun from the tactical webbing over his body armor and worked the lock. It clicked open in seconds. As he pulled back toward the stack and readied his own M8 rifle,

Mathews laid his hand on Simms' shoulder and held on, as each man behind him did the same. The shared contact helped to synchronize their initial movement into the space beyond the door on entry, and provided the psychological reassurance that they were one unit with a mission. Each man on the sub-teams was ready. Lives would depend on how well they did what came next.

Mathews kept his head turned toward the wall, his eyes on the four Tangos. They were not moving. He gave Simms a gentle shove, and in one smooth motion, Simms opened the door with one hand and moved into the target building, Mathews hot on his heels with the rest of the sub-team. The building was lit only by the sunlight streaming in, but it was enough so that their enhanced vision systems would not be needed. The men already knew their positions based on the pre-mission briefing, and they flowed into the structure like an onrushing tide.

Simms and Mathews were to clear and hold the entryway, and then move into the first room on the left if the entryway was devoid of threats. Both men had their rifles up and tracking as they moved into the room he had seen the four Tangos in, Simms covering the left sector of the room, Mathews the right.

Simms' rifle coughed six times, two suppressed three-round bursts that caught the two Tangos in his sector of the room dead center in their chests, felling them instantly. Mathews' rifle only coughed twice, one shot exploding the head of each target. Neither man made any radio calls. On this mission, radio silence meant success. Only unexpected events warranted radio traffic.

Behind them, the other members of their sub-team moved swiftly into their assigned areas, followed quickly by the second sub-team. Mathews could barely hear the suppressed shots the other team members took. Clearly, there were more Tangos than the new PICTURE WINDOW sensors had shown him. They would need to put the sensors closer to the target building next time. At least the new loads for the rounds in the M8 rifles were working as expected. Much quieter, but no serious reduction in stopping power.

"Lead, this is Omega," whispered the radio in his helmet. "Entry secure, all team members in."

Mathews waited for five seconds. He didn't much like performing a breach-and-clear operation under radio silence, but they were trying it. He preferred the "clear" radio calls that were routine as each room within the structure was secured and the threats eliminated. The problem in using them, however, was that the radio traffic could become very garbled with multiple simultaneous calls and it became difficult to keep track. Nothing heard. All done then.

"Team, this is Lead. All clear. Exercise concluded. Put 'em on safe and let 'em hang."

The FBI agents monitoring the facility known as the "Kill House" of the FBI's National Academy, deep in the woods of the Marine barracks in Quantico, turned on the interior lights, raising the illumination level. Mathews and Simms removed their helmets and examined their handiwork.

The four man-shaped dummies were worse for the wear to begin with, having been subjected to this kind of abuse before, but Mathews' two simulated targets were a bit worse off than normal. His two head shots had left the dummies themselves standing, but the "heads"—which had been beautifully sculpted halves of watermelon—were in dozens of smashed pieces all over the floor.

"Your idea?" Mathews asked, gesturing to the nearly pureed watermelon bits.

"Yes, sir," Simms answered with a wide grin to go with his Midwestern cornfed looks. "I needed to know how the new loads would perform, and I knew you were going to hot dog this one."

Mathews smiled in return. This was the fifteenth time they had run this exercise over the last several days. The FBI guys were great, and they kept giving the team a new floor plan or challenge every time they came in for practice. Colonel Simon, the Wraith unit's Director of Operations, had arranged to let the team "borrow" the FBI's high-tech, rapidly reconfigurable Kill House every morning and afternoon so that they could maintain their close-quarters combat skills since they had returned from the Middle East.

Mathews supposed that was a good sign. General Crane was not very impressed with Mathews' performance in Iran. Crane did not initially see the wisdom in bringing out the dead bodies to deny the Iranian authorities any forensic evidence that would point back to the

U.S., and Mathews thought he'd done a good job explaining his reasoning, but he could still be on the general's shit list. *I'll probably go down in the record books as having the shortest Wraith Team command ever*, he thought.

"Ell-tee?" Simms asked, seeing the look and figuring the younger man was beating himself up about Iran again.

Mathews looked up from the little red bits of watermelon on the floor to see his NCOIC holding something out to him. "What's this?"

"It's our unofficial unit patch, sir. With everything that's gone on since you were assigned to our team, I didn't get a chance to give it to you. I asked Colonel Simon to get one of the patches out of my desk. He sent it FedEx last night for you."

Mathews looked at the patch. It had a matte black background, with a stylized hooded figure in dark gray. The only recognizable features were the hands reaching out toward him. The figure had only two blood-red points for eyes peeking out from under the sinisterly curved hood. They matched the red number "4" centered on the figure's amorphous body.

Mathews looked up and smiled his thanks at the older man. Who cared what the commanding general thought? To command men like this, who welcomed him as one of their own. Clearly, they did not think he had screwed up in Iran.

"Welcome to the Wraiths, Ell-tee."

THE WHITE GULFSTREAM G550 GLIDED through the warm, dry air rising from the desert south of the city of Jeddah, toward King Abdulaziz International Airport's Runway 34 Right. The plane was one of the largest private aircraft types with transoceanic range and a cruising speed near Mach 1.

As the jet continued its descent over the southern portion of Jeddah, it passed over the small homes and apartment houses in the less wealthy portion of the city at 900 feet.

Still holding the plane's control yoke to maintain the slightly nose-high descent angle, the pilot, a former Saudi Air Force Colonel named Hamzah, reduced the throttle another 15 percent to increase the descent rate by 100 feet per minute to ensure that he'd place the main gear on the runway at the optimum landing point.

Hamzah, whose name meant "lion" in Arabic, prided himself on the technical proficiency of his flying—and knew almost instantly he had made a mistake. The sun had risen nearly nine hours ago and had heated the more than 2 miles of bare ground between the housing developments and the runway threshold, creating a strong updraft from the desert floor. The effect of the increased descent rate and the powerful updraft caused the jet to bounce as it entered the more turbulent air. The former 767 cargo jet pilot winced at the impact. As the senior pilot of his employer's small fleet of aircraft, he knew all too well that he did not like turbulence.

During the last mile of the approach, the G550 violently rattled twice more in the turbulent air before Hamzah placed the main gear down on the runway precisely between the thick pair of painted white lines marking the ideal touchdown point. Hamzah pushed forward on the yoke while simultaneously pulling the throttle back to idle to trip the spoilers and engage the thrust reversers. The nose of the aircraft rotated down to place the nose wheel on the asphalt, and the G550 began to slow to a speed more fit for driving.

After retracting the spoilers and flaps, Hamzah turned the aircraft left, off the runway, allowing the last of the landing speed to carry the jet onto Taxiway A. He set the throttle just above idle and "drove" the G550 west for half a mile, and then turned north onto Taxiway B, heading toward what first appeared in the distance as a large group of tall, off-white tents. As the G550 got closer to the north terminal, the "tents" resolved themselves to be the roofline of one of the largest airport terminals in the world.

Known as the Hajj Terminal, it was designed to accommodate 80,000 pilgrims at once during the annual Hajj to the holy city of Mecca. Its largely open-air architecture of large tentlike canopies was supported by huge concrete-and-steel-reinforced central poles that covered nearly 210,000 square meters of floor space. The canopies provided a shaded place to wait for the buses that took the thousands of pilgrims passing through during a typical day from Jeddah to Mecca. Large international airports would naturally not be built in the holy city.

Hamzah guided the G550 to its assigned parking slot on the ramp near the Hajj Terminal and then locked the brakes.

Casting a knowing look at his copilot, Zaki, he said, "Complete the post-landing checklist. I'll speak to him about the landing."

Zaki, another Saudi Air Force veteran, gave him a look of sincere sympathy, reached down for the computer display in the center console between their seats, and began bringing up the engine shutdown and post-landing checklists on the flight computer's screen.

Hamzah unbuckled his seat belt and rose to unlock the flight deck door and then proceeded aft. His employer had already lifted his 6-foot-tall frame from the plush leather seat and was not happy.

"Have your skills fled?" Aziz asked hotly, his bearded face stony.

Hamzah froze. The look in his employer's dark eyes was not a pleasant one.

"My apologies for your discomfort, Sayyid. The updraft from the desert today was stronger than predicted by the local weather forecasts. Such is the will of Allah."

Aziz continued to stare at him as the male cabin attendant opened the G550's cabin door, and hot, dry air spilled into the cabin. After a long pause, he spoke again.

"This is true. Allah's will is always present. Come with me. I have another task for you."

"Yes, Sayyid." Hamzah breathed a quick sigh of relief as he stood aside to allow Aziz to pass him and exit the G550 first. Hamzah was usually permitted to call him by name, but had instead used the Arabic honorific of *Sayyid* to convey his understanding of Aziz's displeasure and his continued respect. It seemed to help calm Aziz, Hamzah thought.

Aziz led the way down the jet's steps, Hamzah in tow. Naturally, there was a small group of men awaiting Aziz's arrival. Two of them stood in the unrelenting sun in well-tailored, dark, lightweight suits and wore dark sunglasses. The remaining four wore the more traditional long white *thawb* and *keffiyeh* head covering and remained in the shade of the terminal canopy. Aziz motioned to Hamzah to wait near the jet and proceeded forward to speak to the two men in the dark suits. Both men inclined their heads briefly toward Aziz and listened intently. After a few minutes, Aziz beckoned Hamzah forward.

"Yes, Sayyid?" Hamzah inquired.

Gesturing to the men, Aziz explained, "These are my assistants, M'an and Saqr. Saqr will help you get through customs and immigration and then drive you to the southern terminal to a jet I intend to purchase. I need you to assess the aircraft, check the flight logs, and make note of anything you feel is deficient. I do not wish to pay for shoddy goods."

"I will be happy to, Sayyid. Let me get my bags from the plane."

"No need. Saqr will get them for you."

Aziz looked at Saqr and nodded his head in the direction of the G550. Saqr immediately walked over and headed up the stairs.

"I did not know you had assistants, Sayyid."

Aziz smiled. "I have assistants in many parts of the world, my friend. Up until now, I have not had a need to have them close to me. Recent business events have necessitated a change."

"Is that why you are buying the new aircraft?" Hamzah asked. "Does it have better midair communications than this one?"

Aziz's smile did not change, but if Hamzah had looked closely, he would have seen his eyes harden a little.

"Among other reasons, yes. Ah, Saqr has your bags."

Turning, Hamzah saw that Saqr had descended the steps of the G550 carrying his black flight case with his air charts, logbooks, and manual navigation tools, as well as his two-suit garment bag. Passing Hamzah, Saqr led the way into the Hajj Terminal. Hamzah threw his copilot a wave, which he saw returned through the G550's cockpit window, and then followed Saqr under the broad canopies into the terminal.

Saqr obviously knew where he was going, and his employer's wealth apparently greased the wheels at customs and immigration. His bags were not inspected, and the Saudi customs official gave his Saudi passport only a brief look before stamping it and waving him on his way.

Exiting the terminal, Hamzah was not too surprised to see a car and driver waiting. The driver opened the trunk for Saqr to deposit the bags and then held the rear door open for him. Hamzah settled himself in the backseat, the air conditioning blowing cool air into his face. Saqr and the driver exchanged a few words that were muffled by the air conditioning before they both got in and sat in the front, as was proper. After all, they were only assistants, and Hamzah was Aziz's personal pilot.

The driver put the car in gear and pulled away from the curb, passing a few Saudi National Guardsmen on foot patrol as they headed north away from the main terminal.

"Why are we heading north?" Hamzah asked the driver. "Aziz said the plane I was to look at is at the south terminal."

The driver glanced into his rearview mirror to make eye contact with Hamzah.

"Do not be concerned. The Hajj Terminal roads do not connect directly with the south terminal. We must loop around the Hajj Terminal, and then we can head south."

"I see. *Shokran.*"

"Think nothing of it."

Saqr spoke up next, "Aziz tells me you were called 'Lion' in the Air Force."

"Yes. My name means 'lion' and my fellow pilots chose that as my call sign after I completed initial training, may Allah bless them."

"Now I understand."

"Understand what?"

"Why he said I should tell you, 'Even the strongest Lion starves when he cannot make a kill.'"

Hamzah belatedly understood the depth of his former employer's viciousness as he saw Saqr raise the unusually long muzzle of a silenced H&K P2000 SK pistol up over the edge of the front seat in one smooth motion. Two quick, muffled shots later, Hamzah was able to speak to Allah more directly.

"AH, I SEE SAQR HAS returned," Aziz said, seeing his other bodyguard walking through the terminal. "I told you his errand would not take long."

While he waited, Aziz had been chatting amiably with the four other men in the shade of the Hajj Terminal, while M'an stood at his shoulder, alternately watching the four men and the people passing by in the terminal. The four men managed business interests for Aziz in Jeddah, and it would have been very impolite for them not to welcome Aziz after he had arrived.

Aziz addressed the four men again, dismissing them, "Shokran, my friends. It was very kind of you to meet me before I begin the Umrah. I will see you all again soon."

Walking back toward his G550, with Saqr and M'an in tow, he waved to the copilot to join them on the tarmac. The copilot hurriedly left the jet and stood warily before Aziz, having a much better sense of the man he was than Hamzah had.

Aziz looked at him carefully. "Zaki, you have flown as copilot for many years. Today is the day Allah has willed you to be promoted."

"Promoted, Sayyid?" A puzzled look crossed Zaki's face.

"Yes, promoted," Aziz smiled. "Hamzah has decided to retire from my service and he has been given a just reward for the quality of his skill. I have chosen you to succeed him."

Zaki was stunned by this because Hamzah had said nothing to him about it, and then he realized Aziz was looking at him expectantly. He quickly decided to save his speculation and curiosity for another time and put his thoughts on the present.

"Thank you, Sayyid. You are most generous. But who will fly with me as copilot? The aircraft is not certified to be flown with only one pilot."

"That is your first job as my new chief pilot. I will be spending a few days on the Umrah, so you will have time to identify candidates. Until you choose a competent one, I will trust you to fly me anywhere, no matter what the certifications may require. Am I understood?"

The menace in the question was certainly apparent to Zaki. Pick a good copilot, and until you do, fly me where I tell you to whether you have someone in the second seat or not.

"Yes, Sayyid. It shall be as you wish, Sayyid."

"Good. Naturally, your salary will increase with your responsibilities. I will leave you to them."

Aziz turned on his heel and strode back toward the terminal, Saqr hurrying ahead a little, anticipating his next destination, with M'an keeping pace on his left side. Reaching into his thawb, Aziz grasped his special cell phone and slid his finger across the screen to unlock it. Dialing the number from memory, he waited as the call went through and the ringing began.

"Yes?" The voice spoke English with a Pakistani accent that Aziz knew from his time in Peshawar, a believer in his old mentor's cause who was trusted with sensitive transportation needs.

"How are things going?"

"As expected. We are about two days away from our destination. If everything goes well with the people we hired, then we should pick them up when we arrive and leave shortly thereafter. The weather seems favorable."

"You are prepared to pay them as we discussed?" inquired Aziz.

"Absolutely. They will be paid in full, as we discussed."

"Excellent. I will be out of communication for a few days. If anything goes wrong, leave me a voicemail at this number and I will make other arrangements."

"I hope that will not be necessary, but it shall be as Allah wills."

Aziz smiled. "Yes, it shall," he replied and broke the connection. Save for one more thing, he could clear his mind of other concerns and prepare for the Umrah.

REPIN THOUGHT THAT FALL IN the Mid-Atlantic was very pleasant. The late autumn sunshine filtering through the branches of leafless trees, the crunch of dried multicolored leaves underfoot, the sound of the wind moving through the evergreens, and brisk, cold air in his face—what could be better?

It was not completely like fall in Novosibirsk, where he grew up—there was usually snow on the ground this late in the year there—but it would have to do. He had parked his rented sedan in the park's paved lot about thirty minutes ago, donned his pack, locked the car, and started hiking the well-marked trail east. He had followed the red blazes on the trees since he left the car behind, and as long as he'd chosen the correct trail from the painted map of the state park, he would be there after another ten minutes of hiking.

Before flying out he had looked at the overhead imagery of his targets on Google Earth as the first stage of this reconnaissance trip. He took a commercial flight from his new home city to Columbus, Ohio, and then a small twin-engine plane to the municipal airport in West Virginia. Landing there necessitated a long road trip in the rental car from the municipal airport in West Virginia, but that was preferable.

The airports in the mid-Atlantic states were running at severely reduced passenger capacities, and he did not want to risk any additional scrutiny from the Transportation Security Agency screeners with less than their normal workload to occupy them.

The imagery had shown him the overall view, but he still wanted some handheld imagery and firsthand observations to complete the final intelligence package for the assault teams he would send against these targets. Besides, it had given him a chance to drive past the nearby plant's main entrance a few times to assess the perimeter security. The plant was the first of the three targets he was interested in on this trip.

The uniformed guard force and the cameras at the main entrance were the most visible security presence, but the barrier on the roadway was a simple steel-pole design, and no concrete "flowerpots" or other vehicle barriers had been erected beyond the perimeter fence.

Given the direction he wanted the assault force to penetrate the plant from, the guards and cameras wouldn't be a problem, but he'd needed a good idea of the level of security the assault group would be dealing with. The guards certainly wore their uniforms well, which spoke of their professionalism, or at least of the receipt of decent paychecks, but they carried no shoulder arms like rifles or shotguns, just revolvers in holsters.

Taking a small risk, Repin had pulled to the side of the road across from the plant entry road and pretended to check his tire pressure while watching the entry point. He was fortunate enough to witness a vehicle approach it while he was playacting a search of his trunk for a pressure gauge. The on-duty guard had actually propped open the door to the guardpost and approached the car without a hand on his holstered sidearm. The guards were obviously in a more relaxed routine, at least during daylight hours, in spite of recent events. They would pay for that casualness in a few days.

The sounds of children ahead brought his thoughts back to the present.

"Catch me, catch me!"

"I can, I can!"

The two boys—he assumed they were brothers judging from their similar features—were probably about four and five, both dressed in jeans and warm winter jackets. The older brother was running away from his younger brother right down the trail toward Repin. The older boy was looking over his shoulder to be sure his brother couldn't catch him, oblivious to the nearly 6-foot-tall man right in front of him.

"Watch out, son!" Repin called in a friendly tone, affecting a Midwestern accent, and amused to see the boy pull up short in surprise as he turned back to the trail in front of him.

"Oh! Sorry," the boy said sheepishly.

Repin was about to tell him it was all right when his younger brother practically tackled him from behind.

"I caught you!" the younger boy cried.

"No fair, I stopped!"

Repin noticed a woman in her early thirties hurrying up the trail in the boys' wake and knew this was a situation best left to their mother to referee. He stepped around the two boys, who were now accusing each other of cheating in increasingly loud voices.

As he passed her, she said, "Sorry about that."

Repin smiled. "No problem. Good luck keeping up with them."

She smiled in return as she started to jog past him, calling over her shoulder, "Better this than having them cooped up in a cold house with no electricity!"

Repin could still hear the woman trying to distract the boys, and the older boy still claiming his brother had cheated, when he reached the small strip of beach at the end of the trail.

The stiff wind off the water of the Chesapeake Bay was cold, roiling the water into white-crested waves before blowing toward shore and cutting into Repin. Two powerboats and a sailboat were on the bay in spite of the chill, and Repin watched them move across the bay. After a few minutes of tolerating the cold air, mainly to assuage his male ego, he zipped up his heavy coat and donned his gloves.

Before he got to work, he paused to enjoy the view. In spite of the cold wind, the bright blue sky and the white wave tops stretching east out into the infinity of the bay was beautiful. After a few minutes, it was time for the trained intelligence officer to take over.

The sounds of the two boys and their mother had faded down the trail, and he looked back toward the trailhead briefly to make sure no one else was heading toward the beach. He was alone for now, so he had to work quickly.

Repin examined the beach first. The pale brown sand was well compacted by the tidal flows, and he walked the length of the relatively short beach area, looking at the sand. The only footprints he saw were the smaller ones of the two boys and a larger pair he assumed were their mother's. That was good, and about what he expected. It was too cold at this time of year for this isolated piece of beach to attract too much attention, and because the park closed at sundown according to the sign at the entryway, it should be empty during the expected time frame of the operation.

Three-story-tall crumbling cliffs of clay, topped by small stands of thick trees, reached out from the land at each end of the 50-meter stretch of beach. There were signs at both ends of the beach warning that the cliffs were not to be climbed. The evidence of multiple collapses was plain to see, and anyone who ignored the posted warnings and tried to climb them deserved to die in the resulting avalanche. Repin judged that the cliffs would provide good line-of-sight blockage to the north and south, and they would limit any approach to the beach to either the park trail he'd just come down or the waters of the bay.

Taking the pack off his back, he set it down on the packed sand above the current tide line and took a few sips of water from the integrated CamelBak water bladder's plastic tube, then pulled the expensive digital SLR camera from the pack. The target he came to see was more than a mile away from him, and he attached a 70–300mm zoom lens to compensate.

Checking that the settings on the camera were correct, he turned it on and began shooting. For the benefit of anyone who might be watching from the boats or the target, he started taking pictures of pleasure boats and ships on the bay, and then the target.

The target was more than 400 meters long and nearly 100 meters high, standing nearly a quarter-mile offshore, so he photographed it in segments at maximum magnification and then took some overall pictures at the lowest magnification. When he was done four minutes later, he had taken more than 200 pictures in total, bookending the photos of the target with pictures of the boats and ships on the bay.

Three minutes later, the camera was in the backpack on his back, a blank digital memory card in it, and the memory card with the target images rested in a protective plastic case in his jeans pocket. Taking one last look at the bay, Repin turned and hiked back into woods on the trail he had come down on, back to the parking lot.

DARKNESS HAD FALLEN NEARLY TWO hours ago, the light as always vanishing from the sky quickly behind the rocky hills and dormant volcanoes surrounding the city of Petropavlovsk-Kamchatsky. The major population center of the Kamchatsky Peninsula in the Russian Far East, it was home to more than 180,000 people of Russian and Ukrainian descent. Most of the population worked serving the port, the Russian naval base on Avacha Bay, or the tourists who came to explore the volcanic ranges on foot or who traveled via ATV to hunt elk and bear or to fish.

Sergey Prebin looked out over the bay, breathing in the damp chill deeply and then slowly exhaling into the slight breeze that caressed his pale skin and moved through his thinning silver hair. The temperature would dip below freezing tonight as was usual in the fall, and the cold, clear air did not bode well for the plans he and his five friends had made. Nearly 10 miles away, the faint lights of the once-secret base of the Russian Far East Fleet glimmered, outshone in the darkness by the much closer lights of the city shining in a circle around the shore.

The tourists hunting bear were mostly gone now or asleep in the hotels that in Western Europe would be considered no better than two-star establishments. But out here they were the best available, commanding 200 euros a night. Prebin's gray eyes shifted toward the port. He could see the ship from the doorway of the small warehouse nestled against the pier.

A sharp noise from behind him made Prebin look back into the warehouse. Two of his fellows had dropped one of the larger cases. Prebin almost walked back in to investigate, but his colleagues, all senior academicians from Khabarovsk's Lenin Institute, would certainly manage without his help. Each man had, at the very least, a graduate degree in his common field, and most had held doctorates for several years and split their time between lecturing classes and conducting research. As the Lomonosov chair of the department, he knew them very well. In fact, Prebin had handpicked each man for this effort, knowing that each shared his views and understood that while some lives might be lost in the next day or two, the benefit to humanity would be worth it. In any case, the State he grew up in did not teach him to believe in God, only the Party. That lie was exposed when the Berlin Wall finally fell, but he still did not choose to believe in a god.

Prebin believed in science, and science told him that what was going on was wrong, no matter the government propaganda, and it had to be stopped. He had spoken out in public rallies, lobbied the local and national government, and written opinion pieces and given interviews to what seemed like every news outlet at every opportunity. He stopped giving interviews when the two men in the dark suits came to his small office one morning. They explained, in some detail, how his academic career would be ending in the near future, and then how his body would be found in his small apartment a few days after his very public firing, forgotten, not even a footnote in the science texts he had found the truth in. In the new Russia, they said that the KGB, now known as the SVR, was no longer something to fear. They were wrong.

A few months later, he had taken a trip to Ottawa to attend the annual worldwide conference, where a man whose Russian accent spoke of the Baltic coast approached him at one of the evening cocktail parties. Initially, Prebin was afraid the SVR had followed him to Canada to kill him. Instead, it was a man named Repin who told him that his employer, a very wealthy man, was concerned about the same danger Prebin was. The wealthy, unnamed man was also willing to help Prebin show the world that danger in a way that would leave no doubts in the minds of the politicians. He would even ensure that Prebin and his friends escaped Russia in the process.

It had taken some time to arrange, but the day had finally come. Prebin and his colleagues had "borrowed" some of the equipment they would need and had come to the warehouse to load the trucks for the trip to the ship.

The sound of footsteps behind him broke into his thoughts.

"Comrade Akademician Prebin."

"*Da.*" He had to look up slightly into the face of his younger colleague. He envied the fifty-year-old with his fuller head of hair.

"We are ready. Everything is loaded."

"Excellent, Arkady. Let us go and meet our new friends."

Both men walked toward the two medium-duty Ural trucks and clambered aboard. After a couple of failed attempts, the Ural's engines coughed to life and they drove out of the warehouse toward the brightly lit port of Petropavlovsk.

CHAPTER 3

"WHERE ARE YOU GOING, *TOVARISCH?*"

The port guard was obviously one of the last Russians who remembered the old Soviet Union. He was on the far side of seventy, and his breath stank of vodka. Prebin had to restrain himself from leaning away from the man, even though he was 3 feet from the truck's passenger-side window, which was rolled down to admit the night air and allow Prebin to communicate with the elderly guard. Looking at the old man, he knew instinctively that he had spent his whole adult life at this guardpost, as much a victim of the old Soviet system of limited education and creative thought as he was a relic of it. The key here was to give him a feel for some of the system he missed.

"Ah, tovarisch, sentry! Good evening!" Prebin shouted in spite of the late hour. Dawn was only five hours away. His voice was full of the old exuberance he had learned to fake in his early teens at Communist Party meetings, his smile wide as he exited the six-wheeled Ural-4320.

"We are headed to the Capitalist ship at Pier Six. The trucks carry replacement parts for her electrical systems."

The old sentry's eyes widened, but Prebin could see that he still had trouble focusing. The old man must have indulged a bit more than usual tonight. But Prebin's attitude had the desired effect.

"Ah, tovarishhh, driver," the old man slurred, forgetting that Prebin was not driving. "I don't remember your delivery being on my schedule for the night."

"It's not," replied Prebin, his smile wider now. "The captain called in the request earlier this evening, and practically begged my manager to have the parts brought to the dock."

Putting his left arm around the old man's shoulders, Prebin turned him away from the trucks slightly and lowered his voice.

"He even promised to pay in euros. A premium, even."

The old sentry looked at Prebin. The smell of the vodka was almost overwhelming now.

"Eurosss?" he slurred, his eyes gleaming. Even through his alcohol haze, he felt his luck had changed for the night.

"Da." Prebin looked around casually, primarily for the guard's benefit to add weight to the fairy tale he was spinning for the man, then slid his right hand in his coat pocket and withdrew two 100 euro bills. Prebin moved his right hand across his body, holding the green-and-white bills under the old man's face.

"We are being well paid for meeting the Capitalist's needs tonight, and it is proper that all who aid us should benefit, da?"

The sight of the green-and-white bills caused the old sentry's eyes to widen. He began reaching for them even before Prebin had stopped speaking. It was more than he made in nearly a month of sentry work. Vodka made the long nights pass more quickly these days. Now it would be easier to obtain.

"Da. *Spasiba*, tovarisch."

"I will remember your comradely ways should I need to bring more urgent shipments to the docks in the future." Prebin released the man's shoulders and went back to the Ural. Climbing aboard, he waved Arkady forward through the open gate.

The old man watched Prebin signal the driver to move along, belatedly remembering that he was supposed to do that. With the two bills still in his hand, he waved them into the port.

The two Urals lumbered through the port, moving slowly to avoid attracting attention, but purposefully toward Pier Six. As they grew closer to their destination, Prebin got his first clear look at the ship.

The M/V *Sea Titan* was a middle-aged 'Ro-Ro,' or Roll-on/Roll-off vessel. Designed to transport all kinds of wheeled or tracked vehicles across the oceans, she was huge, a boxy steel block topped with a super-structure for the crew's comfort, nearly 200 meters long, with a beam of more than 25 meters. Painted in a two-tone blue-and-white scheme, she sat tied to Pier Six, a thin wisp of smoke curling up from her stack. Her rear-loading ramp was open, the end resting on the dock, the edges on the dock marked by orange cones. Several crew members in dungarees and reflective vests milled about checking the mooring lines, the loading ramp's hydraulics, and other moving parts with flashlights. One uni-formed officer stood near the end of the ramp, supervising.

Prebin surveyed the situation as the Ural approached. All was as he was told to expect.

"Pull up to the end of the ramp and stop, Arkady."

"Da."

Arkady drove the truck down the pier, warily eyeing the scene, pull-ing up just short of the ramp. The ship's officer noticed the two trucks the moment they began to drive down the pier and watched them carefully. As the lead Ural stopped at the ramp, the officer put his hands in the pockets of his heavy coat, gripping the Beretta 92 semiautomatic pistol inside the right pocket, and walked over to the passenger-side window.

Prebin rolled the window down again and examined the officer in front of him. He was Filipino, medium height, in his early thirties, with golden skin, jet-black hair, and dark eyes, features common to his ethnic-ity. In spite of the cold, Prebin began to sweat a little. Scamming the old man at the gate was simple, the nearly automatic application of a tactic he had learned as a matter of survival in the old Soviet Union. What he would embark on now would make him famous in the scientific com-munity if it went well. He leaned out the window. Prebin's English was heavily accented, but he knew he was close to fluent.

"I am Demitry. I was told by Vladimir that you would be expecting me."

The Filipino man nodded, his grip on the hidden pistol relaxing a little, and the hint of a smile tugging at the corners of his mouth.

"Yes, Professor Prebin. Who paid for your journey?"

"A wealthy industrialist as concerned about the environment as we are."

The Filipino's smile grew even wider. Prebin thought he saw

a shadow of mockery in it, but dismissed that as improbable. More likely, his unfamiliarity with Filipino body language was to blame for his misunderstanding.

"Drive straight up the ramp," the Filipino ordered, "then follow the red markings to the third level. Once there, follow the signs marked BOW until you reach a solid wall with three trucks parked facing it. Unload your equipment and wait. I'll be along in a few minutes to show you to your work area."

"Thank you. I'm sorry, you are . . . ?"

The man smiled again, and Prebin did not see anything other than the smile this time.

"Ah, forgive me, Professor. I am Angel Ramirez, First Mate of the *Sea Titan*, under Captain Manuel Esteban."

"Thank you, Mr. Ramirez. We'll be waiting for you. I can't wait until we show the world how dangerous these things are."

Turning to Arkady, he motioned forward. The two trucks headed up the ramp slowly, swallowed by the cavernous, well-lit interior within minutes.

Ramirez stood on the dock, still smiling, and watched the cars disappear inside the *Sea Titan*. He looked up at the night sky, facing west to see the high-level clouds that heralded the approach of the storm front that would aid them. Under his breath he said, "I can't wait, either, Professor. Insha'Allah."

JOHNSON WAS PACKING AGAIN. AS an FBI special agent, he always kept a tan leather bag in his car trunk with a spare set of clothes, including a dark suit coat, a pair of slacks, a couple of shirts, two changes of underwear, and a couple of cheap but nice ties, as well as some toiletries. Duty as an agent could take him anywhere on short notice, and he needed to be ready for the possibility that he would be handed plane tickets and find himself anywhere in the U.S. in less than six hours. For overseas trips like this one to Saudi Arabia, however, that bag just was not enough, which meant that he needed to pack.

For less businesslike settings, he kept another bag in the trunk, a slightly larger black canvas one that was never checked but always carried on board a plane. It had a rolled-up pair of black tactical fatigues, an FBI windbreaker, a change of underwear, a gun-cleaning kit, a spare SIG Sauer P226, two empty magazines, and a fifty-round box of .40 S&W ammunition. The weapon and the ammunition were in a locked aircraft aluminum case for safety. When he was home, he always brought the case in the house and put it on the top shelf in the closet, and it would stay there while he was gone on this trip.

That thought brought a smile to his face as he loaded some socks into his large suitcase. He would probably have to change that habit, maybe get a large gun safe for the garage and store it there when he was home. After all, he could never be too careful with a kid in the house, and he would have a year and a half or two to research a high-quality safe before his son was old enough to walk.

Imagining his son walking caused him to stop packing. The early afternoon sun was streaming through the windows in the bedroom, and he took a few seconds to look outside at the bare trees swaying gently in the cold breeze, the blowing leaves on the ground, and the bright blue sky. It would be nice to hold his infant son in his arms, bundled up against the cold, and let him touch his first fall leaf next year.

Sarah had announced her pregnancy just after he returned from his last trip to Saudi Arabia, and the thought of being a father was still new enough to make his heart constantly swell with a happiness even greater than when his wife said yes the night he proposed to her.

"Tough guy," he muttered as he went back to packing. Fortunately, his fellow agents could not read minds. If they could, the ribbing would never end. The smile lasted a few more trips to the dresser for underwear and socks before he remembered why he was flying back to the Kingdom tonight.

Sadig al-Faisal, the former Taliban Finance Minister, surely was not what the average person would call a model citizen in any country, but what the Saudis had done to get him to talk was not pleasant. He had watched it all, powerless to intervene, and not entirely sure he should have. He still wrestled with that, and kept reminding himself that the Saudis had their own rules, and they were not America's rules. In fact, they had just proven that again.

Sadig's conviction would never have been possible in a U.S. courtroom. The rules of evidence were very precise and unforgiving. Information coerced from a suspect was inadmissible under any circumstances. Any judge in the States would have tossed out his confession in about two seconds, probably during the preliminary hearing. Sadig would have walked free that very day.

Johnson supposed that Sadig was better off being tried in Saudi Arabia. His stay in prison would be a lengthy one, and Saudi prisons were not likely to be the sweet and kindly "social rehabilitation" facilities they were here in the States.

"David," Sarah interrupted his thoughts in a soft voice, standing in the doorway of their bedroom, "aren't you all packed yet?"

Uh, oh. She only called him David when she wanted something from him. Since he had been back, she had wanted a particular "something" a lot more often.

Looking at her as she walked toward him, though, he could not help but love her even more. She was covered in three layers of warm clothes, but she looked wonderful. Her hair was loose and flowing and he could swear she was already glowing.

"I'm almost finished," he said.

She slipped under his left arm and wrapped her arms around him, snaking one up his back and the other across his chest to clasp her hands together over his shoulder.

"Hurry," she said playfully, pressing her body against him. Even through the layers of clothes they both wore against the chill in the house, she felt good this close to him.

He slid his free hand down to her lower belly, gently pressing down. There wasn't even a tiny bulge in her trim waistline yet, she wasn't far enough along for that, but he was sure he could feel the difference.

She smiled up at him, "Still think it will be a boy?"

"Yep," he smiled back at her. "It's too cold up here for you to get undressed. Why don't we go downstairs near the fireplace?"

"Uh-uh. It's beautiful up here with the sun streaming in, and you can help me warm up the bed."

He protested halfheartedly once more as she pulled him closer to the bed. "My suitcase is in the way."

It took only seconds to find out that it wasn't.

* * *

"GOOD AFTERNOON, SIR." CAIN REACHED across the threshold of the conference room doorway and shook Air Force General Terry Holland's hand as usual.

"David," replied Holland, nodding at Cain in a friendly manner and looking him directly in the eye as he returned the handshake. The general was what people in the service called a "fast burner." Midforties, a little silver in the short dark hair, with a stocky build from his time moving weights around in the gym during lunch hours. He was a career intelligence officer, not a pilot, which made his meteoric rise through the Air Force even more remarkable. In a culture that viewed anyone who was not a pilot as being less capable than those who were pilots, his rank was surprising. His last posting was as the Chief of Intelligence for the Joint Chiefs of Staff, back when he was only a three-star general. He and Cain had seen each other at the daily intelligence community video teleconference over the last two years, and the men got along well.

Cain turned aside to let the general move toward the conference table first. The video displays were already up, the secure connections with all the intelligence agencies already active. On the two screens set up, Cain could see the multiple little windows on the right screen showing the corresponding conference rooms at each of the agencies, with the display on the left showing the full-screen view of either the current or most recent speaker.

Cain let out a long breath and took his chair next to Holland, the briefing notes before him. He was not normally nervous for these. Attending them was just another part of his daily routine. Today, it would be a bit less routine. Cain locked his eyes on the left display. It showed the dark wood and expensive leather chairs of the White House Situation Room.

Since the attacks, the White House Communications Agency had connected the Situation Room to the secure network, allowing the president's national security advisor to sit in on the daily VTC, asking questions and keeping the president up to date. She could be grating and abrasive when she attended, and often was. Her job was to keep the president informed, and she had not yet come to the realization that the intelligence community was not as omnipotent or as omniscient as people often thought.

For the moment, the chairs around the table at the White House were empty. Cain hoped they would stay that way for a change, but he knew that was probably unlikely. In the meantime, like any good intelligence officer, he would try to get some information from the general.

"I understand you've been summoned to appear before the Hip-See and the Sissy," he said, pronouncing the acronyms for the House Permanent Select Committee on Intelligence—the HPSCI—and the Senate Select Committee on Intelligence, or SSCI. These committees—one in each of the two houses of Congress—provided oversight of all intelligence activities.

Holland turned and gave Cain a look of exasperation mixed with the resigned expression of someone about to face a firing squad.

"Yes. Our friends in Congress need to be given a fuller briefing than what they can get off the cable news channels. Fortunately, it will be a closed-door session at the SCIF in the capital. That should keep the political grandstanding to a minimum."

Now Cain was smiling in agreement. "Yes. No C-SPAN cameras allowed in a SCIF." A SCIF, or Sensitive Compartmented Information Facility, was a specially constructed room or building intended for discussions of classified information. Designed to limit the amount of sound and electromagnetic energy that could escape from it, no recording or computing devices not specifically authorized for use in the SCIF were permitted inside. Happily, that prohibition included cameras and digital recorders from the news media—and journalists.

"That's right," Holland replied. "Usually these sessions are pretty tame. We brief, they listen, maybe ask a couple of questions, insist that we do more, and I assure them we will do all we can. The more experienced committee members usually ask better questions, like whether we need any enabling legislation."

"That's nice of them. Feel free to put in a request for a larger pay increase for my staff. As you know, the military folks are usually taken care of, but the civilian workforce often gets shafted. No cost-of-living pay raises in the last three years, and they are talking about extending it for a fourth. I noticed they haven't been shy about voting themselves a cost-of-living increase."

A resigned frown this time. "David, you know I can't do that."

"Yes, I know. But that doesn't mean we don't need one. All those stupid studies about the average civilian pay rate is such crap. Most of my people make less than fifty thousand dollars a year, a couple less than forty, and nearly all of them have families. Those cost-of-living increases help them keep their heads above water."

"David, I hear you. You also know I can't bring it up with them. I'll discuss it with SECDEF, though, although it won't be the first time. He has to sell it to the president for the next budget cycle, and right now, they have more important things to worry about, just like we do."

Cain caught the firm tone in Holland's last words. He knew Holland would indulge him and listen to his concerns, but he could only argue a point so far.

"I know, sir. And I appreciate it. You know I'm just venting a bit. Do you have everything you need for your brief to the committees?"

Holland considered for a moment. "Yes. I think we're ready. Let's see what comes out of today's VTC. The chairmen of both committees have called me a couple of times since this started and they've asked some pointed questions. I've pulled together answers and the time line of what we knew and when we knew it, and the video footage from the Op in Iran that Team Four executed. The video from the drone should be proof enough for them to see and appreciate what we are doing in response to the attacks."

"If you need anything at all, let us know."

At that point, the sixty-second warning tone sounded from the VTC. Holland began looking over his notes, and Cain returned his attention to the two monitors. What he saw on the monitor to the left surprised him. The Situation Room camera now showed a packed house. Every seat was full, and as he watched, everyone suddenly rose to stand.

"General," Cain warned, "we've got an unexpected guest."

"Oh?" Holland's eyes lifted from the briefing papers and shifted to the left monitor, just in time to see the president walk on camera and head for the chair at the head of the conference table.

"Were you expecting him?" Cain asked.

"No. Let's stick to the script. If he changes it, then we'll just go with the flow."

"Right." Cain heard the beeps starting the countdown on the last ten seconds before the official start time, and a single three-second tone at the top of the hour. Once the tone cut off, he unmuted the microphone at his end, and began.

"Good afternoon, Mr. President, everyone. Mr. President, since you are attending, I'll defer to you if you have something to say or direction to provide."

On the monitor, the president began speaking, but no sound came out of the speakers. Cain almost smiled, but he killed the impulse.

"Mr. President, we can't hear you. Your microphone might be muted at that end."

Cain could see the president look off-camera with that "Really? I'm the guy in charge here" expression on his face. A moment later, Cain could hear the background noise from the microphone being unmuted.

"Sir, I think we have you now."

The president looked back at the camera, and being old enough to remember the commercials said, "Can you hear me now?"

This time, Cain did smile. "Yes, Mr. President. We can hear you."

"Good. I have nothing for the group just yet. I've been listening to Dr. Owens briefing me for the last few days, and I wanted to sit in on one of these myself. Please proceed as you normally would and I'll chime in at the end, or if I have questions."

"Yes, Mr. President."

Cain paused for a moment and looked at his agenda to reset himself.

"All right, then. We'll start with the briefing from the Department of Homeland Security."

Cain muted the microphone at his end and then watched the monitors as he heard, "Good afternoon, Mr. President, and all the senior leaders online today," from the on-duty watch officer at the Department of Homeland Security. The VTC system automatically minimized the view of the White House Situation Room and moved it to the right screen, then selected the view of Homeland Security's conference room, moving it to the left screen and maximizing it. Cain didn't know who this man was, and he was obviously nervous enough that he forgot to introduce himself.

"Unless anyone has any specific questions, there are no major changes to the current status of the electrical grid in the Mid-Atlantic and Northeast. Repairs are ongoing at all major power plants focusing on generator/turbine systems, and associated transformer and local power transmission systems. Repair crews also continue work on the transformer systems throughout the grid that were damaged during the recent cyber-attack."

Cain waited with everyone else for a few seconds while the watch officer paused for someone to chime in with a question. Cain expected that the officer had mentally crossed his fingers that the president wouldn't ask a thing. He got his wish.

"Moving on, then," the watch officer continued. "Based on the recent sniper attacks on the infrastructure repair teams the electrical companies field, we've issued an advisory to all the states. National Guard troops now deploy to all electrical grid infrastructure repair sites twenty-four hours prior to the arrival of the repair crews and conduct patrols of the surrounding area before and during the repair efforts. Repair crews check in with the patrol on arrival and check out once the repair is complete. So far, we have not seen any additional sniper attacks, and infrastructure repairs continue. Overall, the major electric utilities are estimating that they will be able to begin restoring power in two weeks or so."

Even on the monitor's multiple smaller images, Cain could see from the body language of the people in the Situation Room that they were not overly pleased at that assessment. There was quite a bit of side chatter that he could see, but not hear. No one on the president's staff, or the president himself, chose to speak up, though.

"Other than those updates, DHS has no additional updates or threat data to share today. Are there any questions?"

Another pause. Cain checked his notes. State had something to share today, and their duty officer was up next. Time for Cain to move things along. He reached for the mute control.

"State?"

"Good afternoon, Mr. President, everyone. I'm Carol Miller, a watch officer at State Intelligence and Research. I've been asked to pass along some information to the community today. The Saudi Arabian Foreign Minister called the Secretary again yesterday morning to inquire about, quote: 'The mission into Iran, staged from the sovereign territory of the Kingdom of Saudi Arabia, is of concern to His Majesty. The objective of this invasion was obviously not what His Majesty was told it would be. The government of the United States needs to fully share with the Kingdom of Saudi Arabia the exact reason an invasion of Iran occurred. If this action is to become known to the international media, the Kingdom will lay the blame for it squarely at the door of the United States,' unquote."

Cain looked at Holland. This was not good. The last part was a direct threat to expose the operation to the media and let the chips fall where they may. The look on Holland's face mirrored Cain's concern. Holland started to reach for the mute control when the president interrupted.

"Ms. Miller, I understand you were told to pass that along, thank you. Who asked you to do that?"

The look on Miller's face was one of sudden panic. She was not expecting to get hit with a direct question from the president that was about to put her between two very senior-level members of the government. It was a tough position to be in for someone with a mid-level pay grade in the civil service. After quickly collecting herself mentally, she replied, "The Secretary stopped in this morning, Mr. President."

"I understand, Ms. Miller. Please pass on to your superiors that I will be calling Secretary Pierce immediately after this meeting."

The relief on Miller's face was undeniable. "I'll do that, Mr. President, thank you."

"General Holland, Mr. Cain; I'll speak to General Crane about this, after I've had a chance to talk to Secretary Pierce and the king." Crane was the Commanding General of the 152nd Joint Special Missions Unit. His Team Four had conducted the Iranian operation.

Holland tapped the mute button, activating the microphones in the room. "Understood, Mr. President, thanks." He hit the button again to mute the microphones.

Before speaking, Cain checked his notes again, giving the president a few seconds if he had more to say. Hearing nothing from the White House, Cain continued.

"Those are the only highlights to share this morning. Before we open the floor to general discussion, does anyone have any alibis?"

The silence lasted only a few seconds before the president's national security advisor, Dr. Jessica Owens, chimed in. Owens was as organized as she was intelligent, and her poise and economic movements reflected those qualities as much as her well-tailored suits and neatly arranged silver-frosted black hair.

"Mr. Cain, I'll need a fresh update of all the information the community has to date after this meeting concludes."

Holland hit the mute again, and Cain nodded his thanks.

"No problem, Dr. Owens. You'll have it in an hour or two after we conclude today."

"An hour would be better, Mr. Cain."

Damn, she could be annoying. "Understood." This time, Cain hit mute as the president started speaking.

"Ladies and gentlemen, I'll leave you to finish this meeting in a minute, but before I do, I want to pass on a few things. The first is that we will maintain the terror threat level at IMMINENT for the power infrastructure, and I'll be speaking to the DHS Secretary later today to continue the 'remain vigilant' messaging they've been putting out through the media and various social-networking sites. Please keep up the good work."

Cain watched as the president rose from his chair and exited the Situation Room. Shortly after he went off-camera, the connection to the White House went black.

EMILY SAT AT A TABLE alone in the Ops building cafeteria, just outside the Starbucks. She had always hated the U.S. government's cheap imitation European coffeehouse-like décor with the small conversation pits, low tables in scattered booths mingled with bar stools, and high tables. It seemed to her like a pathetic attempt at disguising what the room was—a 1950s cafeteria-style seating area with not enough room for the large lunch-hour crowds. NSA's employment rolls, while still classified, had swelled over the years, far beyond what the building's architects had originally envisioned.

The din from the small crowd in line at the Starbucks was lost to her. She needed to get away from the CTS floor for a little while and since she wasn't sleeping well, she needed some coffee to make it through the shift. This seemed to be the logical place to go to meet both needs.

She had no sooner sat down and taken a sip of her coffee when her mind drifted back to the Chicago incident again. Her fault they were dead. She should have known better. She should have made a more thorough check for the floor plans to the warehouse. Those men were dead because of her incompetence. They had families—she had asked the liaison officer for the FBI and he had told her that after it was over. Nearly all of them had wives and children. The few single men on the FBI Hostage Rescue Team and the Chicago SWAT element probably had special people in their lives, too.

All were in mourning now because she was incompetent and responsible for their deaths. The pit she was falling into was deep, and she kept going deeper. She stared toward the far wall, not really seeing it, a look of weariness on her face that sleep alone would never cure. Fortunately, she had not realized that just yet.

Cain found her there at the table, staring off into space.

"Emily?"

She was so engrossed in her own failure that she wasn't even blinking, much less responding to him. But Cain's mind was on the recent teleconference with Dr. Owens at the White House and he thought she had just zoned out for a minute. Besides, they were all a little tired, even after the three days off.

"Emily!"

That snapped her out of it. Looking sheepish, she replied, "Yes, David. I'm sorry. I was thinking about something else."

"That was obvious," he replied, his mind still on the VTC. Dr. Owens would need that summary and he wanted to check a few things with the DIRNSA before Emily finalized the draft.

"I need you to get back to CTS and pull together a summary of all the AUTUMN FIRE reports for Dr. Owens at the White House. I'd like to send it out in the next hour."

Getting up, then reaching for her still-full but now-cold coffee cup, she said, "I'll get right on it, Mr. Cain."

"Good," he replied, thinking about his upcoming conversation with the DIRNSA. "I'll be back in about a half hour to help you out."

Cain headed out of the cafeteria through the main south entrance, while Emily headed toward one of the side doors closer to the CTS watch floor. She was frustrated with herself, not thinking clearly in the early stages of the depression she was sinking into.

The last thing she needed right now was the Chief of CTS personally wandering the halls of NSA looking for her while she was on a coffee break. He didn't seem too happy about it, either. She hoped things would not get worse.

IT WAS COOL, BUT THE sunshine streaming through the windows in the car kept the temperature warm enough that Repin did not need to keep the engine running. Slouched in the driver's seat, he kept his eyes half closed and did his best to stave off sleep, glancing off to the right and looking through the passenger-side windows by moving only his eyes.

The vehicle entry point was guarded, and from what Repin could see, the guards appeared competent. They wore their uniforms properly, and they were equipped with semiautomatic sidearms and shotguns. Repin had been watching them for almost an hour now from the small picnic area outside the gate, cataloging his observations mentally. The guard shift change went smoothly. The oncoming shift talked amiably but briefly with the guards being relieved. Handshakes were exchanged, even with the female members of the team. A couple of the oncoming officers even took the shotguns out of the guardhouse to give them safety checks and then return them to their racks.

Repin guessed that the sidearms were probably Sig Sauer or Beretta pistols, either .40 or .357 caliber, the preferred type for short-range work with high kinetic energy stopping power, whether the target was a man or a machine. The shotguns were probably 12 or 20 gauge for the same reason, perhaps with single slug loads rather than buckshot. The guards on both shifts used proper technique, too. They approached all vehicles with their hands on their sidearms, and at least one of the guards remained in the doorway of the guardhouse within reach of a shotgun and the phone inside. They would probably respond well to a direct assault, but they would not likely survive one launched with heavy weapons or overwhelming force.

The other target would be a different matter entirely. Soldiers were assigned there now, and from what he had seen of their bearing and mannerisms, they were well trained with the AR-15s they were carrying. No matter, Repin thought. The men he was sending in wanted to die for their beliefs, and they would likely get their chance, whether they achieved the objective or not.

Repin kept watch on the checkpoint, but began working out approach routes and timings in his head. It took him another hour's worth of observation; he visualized the terrain and the potential obstacles, estimated the timing, and then considered what they would need in terms of weapons and equipment. Finally satisfied with his observations and his mental planning, he sat up and started the car. Twenty minutes later, he was driving north on Solomon's Island Road.

PREBIN AWOKE WITH A START. Running his fingers through his thinning hair, he took in the unfamiliar surroundings as his mind groped for fuller consciousness. Early morning light streamed through the single porthole, and through the dust motes suspended in the air he took in his cabin on the *Sea Titan*.

A deep breath brought the smell of the salty brine of the sea and the wool of the blanket he had slept beneath. Looking around, he took in the simple oaken desk and bookshelf bolted to the wall, and the swivel chair before it, its red upholstery faded and worn. The single bunk bed he lay on was also oak, the mattress far from luxurious, but just thick enough to keep him from feeling the plywood platform it rested on. He suspected that after his long workdays on board, he would not care how thick the mattress was, he would undoubtedly collapse on it with no trouble. Tossing aside the wool blanket and rough sheet beneath it, he rose from the bunk and rested his feet on the metal floor. He took another deep breath and sneezed from the dust, shivering slightly from the cool metal touching his feet.

Prebin usually rose early, although having been out late last night, he had hoped to sleep a bit later. His usual biorhythm would not be denied, however. Remembering why he was aboard this ship energized his mind, and all thoughts of sleep vanished with the small surge of adrenaline. It was finally time to get the recognition and acknowledgment he and his colleagues deserved. He relieved himself in the small private bathroom, then showered and dressed quickly before leaving his cabin and heading to the bridge.

The ship was a rabbit warren of passageways and cabins, but Ramirez had shown Prebin and the others to empty cabins in junior officer territory on the third deck after the trucks were unloaded. Clearly marked stairwells further aided navigation.

Prebin went up one level, and then walked down the central corridor bisecting the second deck's senior officer quarters toward the bow until he saw the narrow stairwell heading up. He emerged at the rear of the bridge and looked around to get his bearings. Sunlight flooded the entire bridge, the brightness muted slightly by the transparent darkening shades pulled down over the bridge windows facing east. Prebin had never been on a ship before, and he thought the shades were a clever, albeit obvious, solution. Naturally, the ship's officers would need to see all around the vessel, even at sea, but the bright sun in the morning and evenings at low angles would be a nuisance.

Continuing his survey, Prebin was surprised to find the bridge relatively open. There were multiple workstations clustered near the center, some of which had obvious functions. Chart tables and large glass computer displays for navigation dominated the center area, with a large compass suspended above them. A few feet forward of the navigation station, a console with levers and the ship's wheel served as the helm. To the left was a bank of radios, fax machines, and other communications gear, and to the right, a set of low cabinets with exterior markings for fire extinguishers, first-aid equipment, and other safety items. The remainder of the bridge perimeter was open, no doubt so the officers could circulate around the perimeter and keep watch in all directions around their ship.

Near the helm, Prebin spied the man he was looking for. Captain Manuel Esteban was deep in conversation with Ramirez. As Prebin moved closer, he realized he could not make out what they were saying. They were probably speaking Tagalog, a language native to the Philippines. Esteban noticed his approach.

"Good morning, Professor Prebin!" Esteban's smile was wide and genuine, and he looked Prebin in the eye as he took his hand, his English carrying only a small trace of his Tagalog roots. "I did not expect you up so soon. Welcome to the bridge."

"Thank you, Captain Esteban. I'm pleased to be aboard your ship, and thank you for helping us. I cannot tell you how much this means to me. It's a chance to finally prove everything I've been telling the scientific community for years."

Esteban's smile remained fixed. "We are happy to help you, Professor. Ramirez and I have long believed that such things are a threat to the safety of other people and an unacceptable risk to the environment." The smile faded now, replaced by a steady, grim look.

"You know that we may have to harm the security force guarding it." A hesitation as he saw Prebin bridle, then, "Naturally, we will do all we can to use nonlethal force, but they will not hesitate to fire on my men, and I cannot tell my crew not to defend themselves."

Prebin frowned and looked at the white vinyl that covered the steel deck. "I do not wish to have anyone killed, Captain, but these men agreed to guard one of the most dangerous and unpredictable pieces of technology on the planet. We must prove to the world that these things are dangerous, and I think this is the best way." Prebin looked the captain in the eye again, and his voice grew firmer. "Do what you must to protect your people, Captain. I expected this to be difficult, and I have made sacrifices. It is a hard thing, but we cannot let them stop us."

Esteban's smile returned, and he placed his hand on the professor's shoulder. "You have made a difficult choice, my friend, but this must be done if we are to prove that everything you've been saying is true. We will do what we can to avoid killing anyone, but such things may be unavoidable."

Prebin nodded in agreement. He would have to praise their sacrifice at the press conference when this was over.

"I understand, Captain. I inspected the facility you've built for us in the bow. It's exactly what I told our friend Vladimir I needed. The welding looks good. How thick is the plating?"

"Six inches. They did the work in Manila just before we sailed here."

"Good. The shower areas are also acceptable. We moved the nitric acid containers and other equipment into the work area last night before we retired to our cabins. When do we sail?"

Esteban motioned out the bridge windows facing west across Avacha Bay. "In a day or two, Professor. The clouds you see in the distance are the leading edge of a weather front that we will use for cover. The storm front will hide us visually, and the heavy rain will shield us from long-range radar."

Prebin looked dubious. "It will also make handling heavy equipment difficult, and the casings will be slippery. We don't want to drop any of them. I'll speak to my colleagues and see if they have any ideas."

Ramirez looked at Prebin indulgently. "No need, Professor. We have several sets of nonslip gloves for you and your men."

Prebin saw the same smug look on Ramirez as he had seen on the faces of politicians who had ignored him at one time or another. *Academics think they are so smart.*

CHAPTER 4

· ·

DRESSED IN THE IHRAM, A two-piece white garment representing his sacred state and designating him as a pilgrim to all, Aziz looked over the small breakfast buffet. The catering company offered this service to all who could afford the expensive price tag associated with its location so close to the Hajj boundary line. Many who came to the Kingdom for the Hajj used their services to ensure a more comfortable experience, taking the opportunity to rest in a cool place and eat well before starting out, since the Hajj was a potentially grueling test in the hot, arid climate of the Kingdom. In spite of one of the main tenets of the Hajj, that all were equal in the sight of Allah, which was exemplified by the fact that all wore the Ihram, those who could afford it were still more equal than others in the world of men.

The catering company had done a fine job this morning, laying out a tempting breakfast along the rear wall of the air-conditioned tent that stood outside the pilgrimage boundary. Yogurt, dates, apples, pears, cantaloupes, strawberries, and cereals, as well as three kinds of milk and fruit juices in glass carafes sitting deeply in a tray of ice, were there for his choosing. Once he crossed the boundary, Aziz would not eat; he would only drink water for the next few days on his al-Umrat al mufradah.

Known more simply as the Umrah, the lessor pilgrimage could be performed by Muslims at any time in their life and as many times as they wished, while every Muslim was expected to perform the full Hajj just once in their lifetime, if they were able. After breakfast, Aziz would turn his mind fully to Allah, cross the pilgrimage boundary through the Miqat station at Thaneim, and begin his third Umrah.

He was not yet ready to participate in the Hajj, but he had promised himself and Allah that he would perform it after the Great Satan had been destroyed. In keeping with proper tradition, he carried only a small, unadorned plastic bag for his possessions; some money; his passport; two cell phones; and the Holy Qur'an given to him by his mentor. He would read from it tonight after the rituals were complete.

He looked forward to circling the Kaaba seven times and kissing the Black Stone during the Tawaf, then praying at the Place of Abraham in the mosque surrounding the Kaaba, before running seven times between the hills of Safa and Marwah to reenact Abraham's wife Hajar's frantic search for water for her son.

He disliked that the Saudi government had "modernized" the performance of the rituals soon after the turn of the twenty-first century, but he begrudgingly accepted it. Stoning of the Devil during the Hajj no longer meant throwing stones at the three pillars; there was now a broad wall pilgrims could throw stones at with catch basins below, and multiple levels of pedestrian access to accommodate the ever-increasing number of pilgrims. Even running between the hills of Safa and Marwah was done indoors now, fully enclosed within the Masjid al-Haram mosque's air-conditioned tunnels, with special lanes for those with physical maladies.

Such was the price for having so many faithful throughout the world, Aziz thought with a glimmer of distaste. People should prove their commitment to Allah by suffering through what Abraham, Hajar, and Allah's blessed prophet Muhammad suffered. All in good time.

Aziz would perform the Umrah rituals as faithfully as circumstances would allow, leaving his two bodyguards at the Miqat's entrance. Saqr and M'an would rejoin him when he was finished. Allah would no doubt watch over him in the holy city, rendering his bodyguards unnecessary. For now, they kept others a respectful distance from him within the tent as he picked through the buffet, selecting fruit, yogurt, and pomegranate juice for his morning meal.

"The breakfast looks delicious, my old friend."

Mildly surprised at having his train of thought interrupted and wondering how someone got past his bodyguards, Aziz looked up and then recognized the man and smiled.

"Abdel! So good to see you, my friend. I'm glad you could come with me today."

Aziz placed his plate and glass in an empty spot on the buffet table and embraced his old friend. Abdel ibn Taweel ibn Zayd al-Maloof was a few inches shorter and a few pounds heavier, dressed in Ihram like Aziz. His faith in Allah and their cause was unquestionable. Abdel was a Pashtun tribesman who joined the jihad soon after Bin Laden's death. Now he was Aziz's chief recruiter in Europe, maintaining contact with the imams in certain mosques in major cities in that part of the continent, and using them to keep a wary eye out for potential new recruits for Aziz's growing army of jihadis.

"It is good to see you as well. May I eat with you?"

"Of course. Take your fill and join me. My friends will see to it that we can speak privately."

Abdel filled a plate with fresh fruit and poured milk from an ice-cold carafe into a fresh glass among the many set out, and then followed Aziz to a quiet corner of the tent where some comfortable cushions were arrayed in a circle. They both sat, while Saqr and M'an stood away from them, facing outward, their mere presence encouraging the others slowly trickling into the tent to look elsewhere for seating.

"All is well with you, my brother?" asked Aziz, before sipping his juice.

"Yes, my brother. And you?" replied Abdel, popping a slice of crisp apple into his mouth and munching on it.

"My latest endeavors have gone well so far, with only one minor setback," he answered ambiguously. They were still in a public place and it would be wise to be cautious.

A look of concern crossed Abdel's face. "Is there anything I can do?"

"No, my friend. You are doing exactly what must be done to aid me. In fact, I hope your latest efforts have borne fruit."

"They have. It has taken me many months, but I believe I have another small group you can use . . ." Abdel quickly ran his eyes over the area beyond the two bodyguards without moving his head, and dropped his voice to a whisper.

". . . for Allah's Chariot."

Aziz's eyes widened a little, and a broad smile came to his face, which did not match the frost in his next whispered words.

"Excellent, but please do not utter those two words again."

Abdel's heart skipped a beat at the menace in Aziz's tone, but he could not flinch from the conversation. He ate another slice of apple to give him time to recover his courage.

"Your pardon, my old friend, but surely Allah will guard our words here, so close to the Kaaba."

"Let us hope so. I trust you are not so free with your words elsewhere?" Aziz inquired acidly.

"I speak of this matter to you and you alone, my friend, and only face to face."

Slightly mollified, Aziz returned to his food. Taking a few minutes to consider what Abdel had told him, he finished his food in silence. Wisely, Abdel placed his attention on his breakfast as well and waited for Aziz to speak again.

"I would ask you to introduce me to the candidates you have chosen. I wish to speak to them myself before committing them to training."

Abdel was surprised—Aziz had never directly met any of the people he had recruited before. Although Abdel did not know specifically what Allah's Chariot was, it must be very important. Aziz had asked him to recruit men in their late teens or early twenties with great faith in Islam, who had suffered directly from Western hands, preferably American hands, and had a thirst for vengeance. Finding such young men was easy, particularly in Europe, where the assimilation of Middle Eastern immigrants into the culture of many European nations was problematic at best, but he never expected that Aziz would want to meet them before they began to train.

"As you wish, my friend. Where shall I meet you?"

"We shall travel together. Your passport is in order, of course."

"Of course," Abdel smiled.

"Where must we go to meet them?" asked Aziz.

"France."

"Good. Then let us go to the Miqat now and begin the Umrah."

"Praise be to Allah," Abdel replied.

* * *

"WELCOME BACK, MY FRIEND." JOHNSON shook Akeem's out-stretched hand warmly. The return flight to the Kingdom had not been nearly as good as his last flight from there on Emirates Air. The United jet was comfortable, but this time Uncle Sam was buying, which meant coach class. Even in a state-of-the-art Boeing 777, thirteen-hours-plus in a cramped seat from Dulles to Kuwait overnight, was never going to be described as comfortable or allow the passenger to arrive rested. To add insult to travel injury, there was a brief stop in Kuwait to deplane passengers and luggage, before an immediate departure to Bahrain for an eighteen-hour layover. Johnson, and any other government employee traveling on official business, marveled at the idiocy of it. You fly all the way from the U.S. to Kuwait, and rather than getting on a plane in Kuwait for the hour-long flight to Riyadh, the airline flies you farther south to another country to wait eighteen more hours for a scheduled plane to Riyadh. Johnson swore the government travel system picked the worst possible route and timing on purpose.

At least he had had a good night's sleep in the Bahrain Hilton before heading out to catch the Gulf Air flight to King Khalid International. The Airbus A320 was comfortable and fast, but when the cabin door opened, he knew he was back in the Kingdom. The arid desert air sucked the remaining moisture out of the cabin air in seconds, and as he descended the steps to the tarmac, the warm sun chased any remnants of the cool cabin from his thoughts. As usual, he did not feel himself sweat, as the dry climate caused his sweat to evaporate too quickly.

Akeem's genuine smile was a welcoming sight as Johnson walked from the base of the jet's stairway toward the terminal. The Saudi was a kind man, and had extended to Johnson all the hospitality both Akeem's strong religious faith and culture required of him. He had also appreciated Johnson's attempts to learn his language, which formed Johnson's response.

"As-salaam 'alaikum."

Akeem's smile grew wider. "Wa 'alaykumu s-salamu wa rahmatu I-Iahi wa barakatuh."

Johnson shook his head ruefully. "I'm sorry. I didn't understand any of that."

Akeem reverted to speaking English. "It's all right, my friend.

You've had a long trip and I responded in the most formal way. Translated it means, 'May peace, mercy, and blessings of God be upon you.' It is the most courteous way to respond and comes directly from the Holy Qur'an."

Akeem's English was excellent, and in all his dealings with Akeem, Johnson had never detected more than a moderate accent.

"Well, after I've another night's sleep, I'll ask you to teach me that one, too. Is there a formal response to it?"

"No. But I have refrained from kissing you on both cheeks after the handshake, which is customary here among male friends."

Johnson's mock horror merely reinforced the good judgment reflected in Akeem's respect for Johnson's culture. "Shokran. My Western upbringing isn't really ready for that, in spite of how much I value your friendship and that of your family."

"Of course. We've only known each other for a short time, but I know you to be a man of honor and I value your friendship as well. I also respect your culture in the same way you have obviously done all you can to respect mine. Which is why I will also avoid holding your hand as we walk to the cars."

Looking at Akeem's face, Johnson could see the knowing smirk of a man "yanking his chain." In Saudi culture, men who were friends did in fact hold hands in public to show the bond, and doing so carried none of the stigma that it did in Western cultures, which perceived it as being a sign of romantic or sexual involvement, primarily because homosexuality was unthinkable in the Kingdom and under Sharia law, punishable by death.

Reflecting on this made Johnson glad he was born an American. It was not a perfect country, but he definitely preferred the civil rights stance and laws in the U.S. over those in the Kingdom. Akeem broke into his thoughts a moment later as they turned and walked through the open-air terminal toward the exit.

"Are you staying in the Hilton again?"

"Yes. You know our government travel offices. They always book the same place in the same city. I lobbied for bachelor quarters at the embassy, but I'm not really senior enough for that."

"It's not a problem. I'll drop you at the hotel and let you settle in.

I have spoken to my wife about your return, and she will be pleased to prepare us dinner again while you are here."

"That is too kind of you and your family, Akeem. I couldn't—"

Akeem cut him off. "Of course you can. You are most welcome in my home. It will give my children a chance to practice their English with a native speaker."

"I would be pleased to help them, Akeem. When is the sentencing?"

"In two days, in the morning. I will come to your hotel and get you. We can have dinner and tell stories to the children tomorrow night."

"That might be a good idea. I'll need some practice telling them."

"Oh?"

"Yes. My wife and I will have a child next summer."

"Congratulations! I will tell my wife. She will be very pleased for you."

"Shokran."

The two men left the terminal and Akeem guided them toward a blindingly white BMW 750il sedan. The driver had already seen Akeem and moved to open the rear doors.

Akeem motioned to the car, "Here, my friend. Since you are now an official guest of the Kingdom on behalf of your government, the ministry will make a car and driver available to you for all official activities. We would normally make the car and driver available throughout your stay, but your country's ethics regulations . . ."

Akeem trailed off, shaking his head at American attitudes and "ethics." A politician would take a million dollars from a company for an election, look favorably on them when writing tax laws after he had won, and then deny a civil servant the use of a host government car and driver for a week because it would be "unethical." Such were the ways of Americans.

"There is a rental car at the hotel for you. The keys are waiting at the desk."

"Shokran," Johnson said, rubbing his tired eyes. Both men were seated in the rear of the BMW before Johnson remembered something he had left behind.

"I didn't get my bags!"

"It's already taken care of," Akeem assured him. "I had the airline pull your name off the manifest. They will identify your bags from the barcoded tag and send them via car to your hotel."

"Thank you again." The BMW set off smoothly, its turbocharged eight-cylinder engine pulling strongly but steadily. Johnson luxuriated in the smell of the leather and the feel of the comfortable rear seats. He had always wanted one of these cars but knew he couldn't afford the more than $140,000 price tag. He would have to stick to indulging his car fantasies by watching the British car show *Top Gear* while he spent his money on more important things, like his wife and baby.

Time to get back to business, he chided himself.

"So Sadig's trial is already over?"

Akeem nodded. "Yes. His trial was conducted under Sharia law. It was pointed and brief. He has admitted his crimes before the judges and expressed his regret for them. The judges have been considering his sentence for the last week and informed the ministry they were ready to pronounce the sentence a few days ago. Since this is a politically sensitive case, they accepted a request from the minister to delay until American representatives could be witnesses, since you were so instrumental in helping us capture him."

Johnson thought back to Sadig's screams as the Saudis tortured him. He wondered if the Saudis used anything he had said under torture at the trial, and then remembered that he wasn't in the States anymore, and that here, the U.S. Constitution didn't apply. He answered neutrally, his voice a bit more stiff than he intended.

"I'm pleased to be able to represent my government and that His Highness and the Court would allow me to attend."

Akeem looked at him, understanding the cause. "So formal, David? I know our interrogation disturbed you. If it helps you at all, you should know that Sadig admitted to everything freely in front of the judges. He could have remained silent, but he did not, and no one from the government introduced anything we learned from his interrogation. The judges asked how he came to be in the Kingdom illegally and things proceeded from there. He told them how he had worked for the Taliban, his abuses of women and men as he extorted money, his drug use, even his desire to foment jihad against American and other interests in the Middle East. He was quite specific."

Fruit of the poisonous tree, Johnson thought, recalling the consideration under U.S. law that if the first confession is coerced, every subsequent confession stemming from that coercion is considered tainted and inadmissible in court. But again, this wasn't America.

"I understand, Akeem. This is your country, and your laws apply," he said, just as the car was pulling up under the wide awning of the Riyadh Hilton.

"Yes they do, David, and I think you will be impressed with the swiftness of justice found under Sharia law."

REPIN CLIMBED THE STAIRS SLOWLY, looking for signs of anything out of the ordinary. Everything seemed normal, but it would be fatal not to be sure. This place did not have the kind of escape route he had had in Chicago, forcing him to rely exclusively on camouflage for protection. The stairs creaked enough that anyone ascending them could not do so unheard. The walls and floors, however, were thick, particularly on his floor. Approaching his door, he checked for the two telltales he always left on it, and seeing them still in place, he relaxed a little. Resting his pack, a small paper sack, and his traveling bag on the floor, he worked the two locks, then opened the door, keeping his body partially shielded by the thick exterior wall in the hall while he looked inside. The main room was clear, so he waited a couple of beats, listening for movement. Hearing nothing, he grabbed his bags, throwing the traveling bag over his shoulder, and headed inside. He relocked the door and then slid home the three heavy security bars with one hand. It would take several minutes to breach the door, even with explosives and a blowtorch. If it came to that, Aziz knew he would be arrested, but the thick doors and walls should give him enough time to wipe the electronic evidence, making it very difficult to tie him to any crime in a U.S. court.

Aziz had had the floor renovated months ago as part of the larger plan, consistent with Repin's needs. The new walls, floors, carpeting, utilities, and furnishings provided the level of comfort he desired, without being overly opulent. The downside was that he was now limited to a single TV and satellite television signal, complemented with

Internet connectivity, all with backup power supplies. The upside was that the entire floor was his, and all the other doors on the floor, although appearing to be normal apartment doors, were false fronts. This would prevent anyone from U.S. law enforcement masquerading as a new tenant and setting up long-term surveillance on his floor. The extra space also permitted the installation of a small exercise area with weights, a treadmill, and an open mat-covered area for stretching, yoga, or martial arts practice. Repin preferred the open air and sunshine for his daily runs, but if he was forced to lay low for a while, this safe house could accommodate his needs.

Turning his back to the door, Repin looked around once more, took a deep breath, let it out, and finally relaxed. Everything was where he left it, and everything smelled new and clean. He walked through the main room containing his kitchen, work area, and small sitting/living room, and just far enough into the bedroom to casually toss his traveling bag on the bed. He glanced toward the tiled bathroom and decided he could hold off on the shower until after his evening workout.

Returning to the main room, he put the paper sack on the dinette table and left his backpack on the floor. He washed his hands and face in the kitchen sink as the sun disappeared behind the mountains, dried himself with some paper towels, then retrieved a bottle of Sprite from the refrigerator before sitting down at the table to eat one of his favorite meals: a Quarter Pounder with cheese and fries.

After he finished his dinner, it was time to get to work. He pulled the memory card from his jeans and sat at his computer, hitting the TV remote to bring up the local evening news before entering his password to break the screen lock.

Repin inserted the memory card into the computer, and it automatically began downloading the card's images. While it continued, he brought up Google Earth and began zooming in to the target areas, reviewing the overhead imagery of the area he hiked through, and the small strip of beach along the Chesapeake Bay at the end of the trail. Zooming out, he moved the view southeast to examine the two primary targets one at a time.

When the images had completed downloading, Repin began uploading them to Google Earth via an anonymizer in Hong Kong, using the embedded geo-coordinates in the image metadata to fix them in the proper place on the overhead views and make them available to the public.

Repin then reached for the pad of paper underneath the computer desk and began sketching out rough diagrams of all the targets, looking at the handheld and overhead imagery as he worked. Once the basic diagrams were complete, Repin marked various ingress routes and attack points in red pen along with the places to plant the explosives for maximum effect. Pausing to examine his work, he smiled. The explosives would not do much damage to the last target, but the impact of an attack on it would create fear amongst the American public. Maybe the explosives would breach it, though. Then everyone would have more reason to panic, which was all according to plan. The Americans needed to have their attention firmly focused on what was happening at home for Aziz to achieve his primary goal.

Double-clicking the scan icon, Repin fed the diagrams into the attached scanner one by one. As the full-color images appeared on the monitor, he checked them for clarity. Satisfied, he opened a dummy account on a free public webmail service and uploaded the diagrams as attachments to a draft e-mail. He left the message in the draft folder on the server and logged out of the account. After setting up a second free e-mail provider account, he drafted an e-mail and clicked Send.

FROM: ASCEND@FREEMAIL.NET
SENT: THURSDAY, NOVEMBER 7, 2018 7:00 P.M.
TO: GABRIEL@FREEMAIL.NET
SUBJECT: RE: INFORMATION NEEDED

That information you wanted is ready. I expect project completion no earlier than three days, and no later than six days from now.

Good luck.
Abdul

After logging out of the e-mail service, Repin opened the images folder on his computer. He selected the scans of his hand-drawn diagrams and right-clicked to access the data-shredding tool from the menu. In a few seconds, the images were gone. A few minutes later, he stood over the kitchen sink watching the remains of his physical hand-drawn sketches curl into ash.

His work done for the night, he screen-locked his computer and took another Sprite from the refrigerator before changing the TV channel to ESPN. An American rules football game was just starting, the Denver Broncos versus the Oakland Raiders. It should be a good game.

EMILY WAS LYING ON HER couch, nestled up against her husband in the dark living room, her back to his chest, his arms wrapped comfortably around her. A single blanket covered them both. It was cool in the room, but not too cold. They had left their gas oven on at 300 degrees to get some heat in the small apartment. The thermometer had not dipped below 60 degrees during the night, and Jerry had even gotten a few battery-operated carbon monoxide detectors and scattered them in the rooms for safety. All they had to do was wear a sweater or two, and they were comfortable.

The little guy was asleep in his crib under three blankets so that Mom and Dad could spend some quality time together. Tonight was "grown-up" movie night; Jerry had recharged the laptop's battery earlier with the car so that they could at least watch movies online. Emily took her eyes off the glow of the laptop screen and checked her wineglass on the table. It was a little less than half-full, and there was no need to leave her husband's warmth just yet. She could feel his cheek against the back of her head, and she knew he was breathing in the scent of her hair. He had complimented her on it during their second date, right after their first kiss. Once his lips had touched hers, she had known he was The One. She decided then to use the same shampoo as long as it was made, so he would always want to smell her hair.

Breathing in deeply, and letting out a slow, relaxing exhale, she turned back to the movie. The leading men—very good looking—were just to the point where they ran the scam to steal the money from the three casinos. She felt Jerry shift his weight a little beneath her, and then tilt his head down a little, preparing to whisper something in her ear. He probably wanted to turn off the TV and take her to bed now, which she thought was a good idea. Warm, loving sex sounded like a great way to end what had been a lousy day.

"How is the new job working out? The hours are pretty long."

What the hell? Emily pulled away from him and turned to face him. She could feel her face heating, and her voice hardened.

"The hours are not a problem. You know I enjoy my job. The work is important and I'm needed there." Jerry looked confused, but that was not her problem. He brought this up. How dare he question the demands of her job! They agreed before they got married to keep their professional lives separate and be supportive of one another. She could see him getting ready to say something and she cut him off.

"We agreed that our professions were our own concern!" she shouted. "You don't even have a job right now, and I'm paying for your school!" Jerry reached out to her and Emily pulled away, rising from the couch, the movie forgotten. In the other room, Jeff started to cry.

"Now look what you did!" she screamed. *Damn him anyway.* Emily turned on her heels and headed for Jeff's room.

Jerry sat on the couch and watched her leave in stunned silence. What the hell had just happened? Ask a question to show your wife you're interested in her career and concerned about how much rest she's getting when she puts in long days, and she explodes. He could hear her cooing at their son, calming him down. Rising, he headed for Jeff's room and walked through the doorway, ready for an argument, only to find Emily sitting in the rocking chair, Jeff held against her shoulder and tears streaming down her face. His anger melted into deeper concern.

"Sweetheart, what's wrong?"

Emily just shook her head and cuddled her son while Jerry crossed the room and knelt in front of the rocking chair, reaching his arms out to her. She had been an idiot to overreact like that. Why did he have to ask about work just when she had managed to forget it?

She leaned forward and Jerry enfolded her and his son in a gentle hug. Emily buried her face in his shoulder, drying her tears on his shirt, imprinting two small blotches of mascara on it. After a few moments, he pulled back a little and looked at Emily's face and into her eyes, measuring what he saw against everything he knew about his wife of nearly four years.

"It's okay, honey. I think you're just a little overtired. You've been working very hard and I'm very proud of everything you do. I wasn't trying to criticize you." Emily saw the honesty in his face, and closed her eyes as the tears welled again. He was such a good man. He didn't deserve a wife who yelled at him for no reason. He didn't deserve a wife foolish enough to get people killed, either. That thought almost made her wail aloud, so she leaned into him and stood up with Jeff still cradled in her arms, burying her face in his shoulder again and letting the tears flow freely. Jerry closed his arms around them both again and slowly began to rock her and the baby gently.

After a few minutes, Jerry looked down at his son, sleeping peacefully again against Emily's shoulder, his little lips parted and his chubby cheeks relaxed in slumber. He rubbed Emily's back gently.

"Come on, honey. The little guy is out again. Let's tuck him in and we'll get some sleep, too. You need a couple of good nights' sleep and you'll feel better."

Emily leaned back to look up at him, and nodded. She kissed Jeff on the head, and put him gently in his crib and under the blankets. Jerry looked over her shoulder while she settled the baby in.

"The monitor is on and I checked the batteries earlier, they'll be good for the night. Come on," Jerry said, reaching out to take Emily's hand.

She let him lead her to their bedroom. Under normal circumstances she would change into the lingerie Jerry bought her last Christmas, but with the only heat coming from the stove in the kitchen, layers were the order of the night.

They both changed quickly into sweatshirts and sweatpants along with thick socks, and slipped under the sheets and two blankets. Emily lay on her side, and once he was in bed, Jerry snuggled up behind her and draped his arm across her body in the sleeping hug he usually held her in during the night. The warmth of his body spread from her legs to her shoulders, and in minutes, the bed was warm. A few minutes later, she could feel his slow, regular breathing against her neck and the back of her head as he slept.

Emily knew she really did not deserve him. She could never tell him what she had done. He would be so disappointed in her. What could she do? What would her son think when he was old enough to understand? She couldn't find an answer in the darkness and kept asking herself the same questions again, and again, for an hour. Then two. Then three.

CHAPTER 5

"CAPTAIN?"

"Yes, Professor Prebin."

"How long will it take us to get to the field?"

Sea Titan was making way nicely, heading southeast out of Avacha Bay at a steady 10 knots. The sky behind her was full of high clouds moving east, the herald of the storm front they needed for cover.

Prebin looked over at Captain Esteban, wondering why he had not received an answer to his question. Esteban was looking down from the open-air bridge wing the two of them stood on, checking the deck of his ship, measuring the sea and wind. Prebin recognized a professional at work, and did not interrupt further. He did not notice Ramirez watching him carefully from within the glass-enclosed bridge.

After a few seconds of examination, Esteban raised a short-range Motorola radio to his lips.

"Helm, Captain. Twenty degrees left rudder. Steady up on the pre-plotted course to the oil field."

Prebin felt the ship begin the turn, and the wind shift from the direction of the bow to the starboard side, moving along his face to press against his right check, tossing his hair this way and that.

"Captain, helm. Turn complete. Rudder zero, steady course zero four two," the radio squawked.

"Helm, Captain. Roger. Hold speed as is." Turning to Prebin, Esteban finally answered his question.

"We will move slowly and allow the storm to overtake us. Once it does, we will use our weather radar and the weather service broadcasts to match our speed to be sure we approach the oil field with the storm."

"How will we avoid detection by any surface radar from the oil production platforms?"

Esteban offered Prebin a sly smile. "The storm will help us hide. As we move with it, we will choose the heaviest band of rain or snowfall our weather radar shows us, and do what we can to keep the heavy precipitation bands between us and the oil production field."

Prebin nodded. "I see, Captain. You have given this a great deal of thought."

"Yes, Professor. A great deal of planning has gone into this." Esteban hesitated a moment, and added, "Just as you have planned a long time for your part in this. We wanted to ensure that we did not fail to do our part; otherwise, all your efforts over the years would be wasted."

Prebin's relief at working with people as dedicated to his cause as he was emboldened him. "I cannot tell you how grateful I am to you, Captain, and all your men. Without your ship and crew, and the thought you have put into this, I would never be able to realize my goal. I will be sure that when the time is right, the world knows your name and that of your ship."

Before the captain could answer, Prebin gave him a resigned, apologetic look, and added, "Although it may be several years before I can do that. I do not want the hardworking men of your crew, or you, to suffer prison or legal trouble for my goals."

Esteban nodded sagely. "We understand, Professor Prebin. I think it is best that way. I am content to know that I will have contributed to the great ecological awakening you seek. In fact, I think it would be better that no one ever knew my name. Being the mysterious friend of a famous man is sometimes better, yes? Certainly women will find my tales of courage and daring alongside you more appealing if 'only she' knows that I am the capable and trusted friend of a man such as yourself."

Prebin laughed heartily, fully understanding the meaning in Esteban's words. A few drinks in a bar. Some tales of adventure, mixed with compassion for the planet's ecology, and many women would likely fall willingly into bed.

"Just so, Captain. It will even be better when I can reveal your name and your ship after a few years. Publishers and newspapers will clamor for your story and offer you huge sums to tell it."

Steady rain suddenly swept across the ship as the storm continued to bear down on them. Esteban gestured toward the bridge hatchway and led Prebin to it. Like all sailors, Esteban loved the sea, but he knew enough not to be on deck in the rain unless he needed to be.

Prebin was equally happy to return to the dry warmth of the bridge, and as he approached the open hatchway, he noticed Ramirez watching them through the thick glass of the bridge windows. Prebin wondered if he had heard their conversation. Was the first mate concerned that he had discussed mentioning only the captain's name to the press and not his? No matter. Ramirez was aware of the plan; in fact, he would lead the initial boarding party, so there was no need for concern. Prebin concluded that Ramirez was probably just looking after his ship's captain, as a good first mate should.

"MATHEWS, HOW IS THE DAILY training going?" Simon asked.

Mathews was in the Kill House manager's office, with the door locked, and the STE secure telephone handset to his ear. The LCD display read "TOP SECRET SCI," assuring Mathews that no one could eavesdrop on their conversation. Even through the slight degradation in voice quality caused by the encryption process, he could not hear a trace of annoyance or concern in Colonel Simon's words. Regardless, he had to be just as pissed as General Crane was about Mathews' poor performance in Iran.

"Well, sir. I really appreciate you going out of your way to arrange this with the FBI. I've got the team sub elements competing against each other in CQB drills."

Mathews had come up with the idea yesterday at their makeshift dormitory in the hangar reserved for them and their massive C-17 Globemaster III transport at Andrews AFB. Use the same floor plan, the same set of simulated Tangos and hostages, and foster a little competition among the teams. It would keep the men from getting bored and help pass the time while keeping everyone's skills dialed in. The only hitch was the sniper team, Mellinger and Tate, but they had found their own fun.

These two men, known as "Sierra Team" in the field, had posted a sign at the long rifle range a few miles away from the FBI's advanced Kill House, inviting all challengers to shoot against them. They offered prizes to anyone who could shoot more accurately than they could at various ranges. It became competitive enough yesterday that they hunted down one of the airplane mechanics on-base and rented her millimeter-scaled ruler. Although Mathews could not get the details out of either man, the fee negotiated for the ruler was a dinner date at the base NCO club with the sniper of her choice. What criteria she was using to pick was a mystery to Mathews, but in any case, that was her call, and the younger of the two men seemed pleased with himself this morning.

"How are your men responding to the competition?" Simon asked over the encrypted phone line.

"Well, sir. They are earning points for each Tango killed and hostage saved, with massive deductions for any team member wounded or killed. I'm buying the winning team dinner tonight."

"Outstanding, Lieutenant Mathews. That's good thinking, and you're doing a good job looking out for your men. I'm impressed with you so far."

Simon couldn't see Mathews raise his eyebrows in surprise. "Really, sir? I appreciate that."

"Absolutely. You sound surprised."

"Yes, sir. I am. I thought that after the last mission . . ."

Simon cut him off. "Lieutenant, I think you did a great job during the last mission. Having your men grab the guard's bodies and extract with them was good thinking in my estimation. You denied an adversary vital intelligence about our operations, and you thought clearly enough on your feet to recover as much intelligence from the house as possible. You did well."

"General Crane seemed to think otherwise, sir. He chewed me out pretty well on the command aircraft before we left Iraq."

"Yes, I know. I spoke to him about that. He told me he was pretty hot about it at the time, but he's cooled off quite a bit. Trust me, if he really thinks you had screwed the pooch, he would have relieved you of command of your team. That is not going to happen."

Mathews was relieved. "Thank you for telling me that, sir. It felt like the right decision at the time, but the general's assessment has had me rethinking it ever since we got back."

"Don't dwell on it. Just remember what I told you and keep doing what you're doing. I think your instincts were right on the money. Keep it up."

"Yes, sir."

"How are your medical cases doing?" On the way back from the Iran mission, two of the Wraiths started showing flu symptoms. Mathews had placed them on light duty initially, but as the symptoms worsened, he ordered them to Walter Reed National Military Medical Center for treatment.

"The docs at Walter Reed say they are responding well to the treatment, but their fevers still haven't broken yet. Worse, two more of my people seem to be coming down with it."

"Didn't your people get inoculated?" Simon demanded.

"No, sir. We were supposed to, but the sudden deployment blew that out the window."

"Are they mission capable?"

"They tell me they are, but in the interests of their safety and the teams, I've ordered them to report to Walter Reed."

"Do you think you can function with an eight-man assault unit?"

"Yes, sir. Based on the results of the exercises so far, Team Four is still fully mission capable."

"Good. Keep an eye on your hospital cases," Simon instructed him.

"Yes, sir. Do you have any orders for us?" Mathews asked.

"No, not yet. We want to keep you and your team right there at Andrews as our East Coast rapid reaction team for now. If we can get the diplomatic situation with the Saudis straightened out, we'd like to post you back to the Kingdom. Failing that, we'll reach out quietly to the Qataris or Kuwaitis and see if they would be willing to host you. For now, we stand pat. You and your team need to keep your skills sharp. Don't push it, though. Keep training, but keep the pace easy and give your folks as much down time in the afternoons and evenings as you can. I'll be back to you with orders as soon as we have some for you. Did you get the secure cell phone I sent?"

"Yes, sir. The courier brought it to the hangar this morning."

"Any trouble using it?"

"No, sir. It seems straightforward enough. I used the secure app on it this morning and the test call worked just fine. I couldn't get the secure e-mail to work on it, though."

"No trouble," replied Simon. "I'll have one of the techs call you on the VSAT at 0200 Zulu tonight to help you troubleshoot it. Once it's up, you can e-mail me a daily situation report."

"Yes, sir. Do you still want the SITREPs by 0600 Zulu?"

"Yes, that's fine. You can shoot it to me before you hit the rack for the night. If anything happens overnight, I expect a call."

"Will do, sir. That reminds me, did we recover anything useful from the material we brought back from Aziz's house?"

"Hang on a moment. I'll check." Simon turned and clicked the e-mail icon in the taskbar at the bottom of his computer screen. "No. Nothing yet from CTS. Right after your team landed back at Andrews, all the hard-copy and optical media was copied and sent to the CIA, DIA, and NSA for translation and exploitation. I was expecting something from CTS pretty quickly, but nothing yet. The last e-mail I received from CTS said that the optical media was encrypted. They are probably still working on it."

"Okay, sir. Once I get my e-mail up, I'll shoot you a quick note."

"Do that. Oh, and Lieutenant?"

"Sir?"

"Let me know what the tab for dinner is for the first winning team. I'll split it with you."

Mathews smiled, completely assured now that the colonel had faith in his ability to lead the team.

"Thank you, sir. I'll do that. Out here."

EMILY WAS RUNNING LATE AGAIN and was frustrated with her-self. She finally fell asleep around three in the morning, still wrapped in her husband's arms, only to be rudely awakened by the battery-powered alarm clock at five thirty. Worse yet, she had dozed off again after silencing the alarm. The twenty extra minutes her sleep-deprived brain wanted meant no breakfast and barely enough time to dress. Fortunately, makeup was not exactly a requirement with the Air Force's version of the battle dress uniform of pale green camouflage. The downside was that the lack of makeup made her look even less rested than she felt, but she didn't have time to look in the mirror to see that, either.

The drive in, parking, and gaining access to the Ops building passed in a blur. Emily burst through the badge-controlled door to the CTS operations floor to find her colleagues already in the semicircle around Cain and the off-going shift team leader. *Oh shit,* she thought, *if I've missed the pass-down brief again, Cain will probably fire me.*

Looking up over the crowd from his vantage point on the raised desk area, Cain saw Technical Sergeant Thompson insinuating herself into the back of the crowd, trying to catch the eye of the sergeant she was relieving. "Okay, let's get started with CIA today," Cain intoned. "What do you have for us?"

Emily breathed a quiet sigh of relief. They were just getting started. She listened with one ear as the watch standers getting ready to go off shift briefed any significant items of interest, as she carefully wormed her way through the small crowd toward her counterpart. Her colleagues silently made room for her to move between them, a few of them, mainly the women, giving her appearance a second look, making her feel self-conscious. She would have to head to the ladies' room at the first opportunity and check her uniform and maybe fix her face a little. If anybody asked, she would say she had been up most of the night with her son. They would understand and sympathize. They were all such nice people.

When the "round-the-horn" pass-down was done, Emily took a few minutes to catch up on the night's activities with the sergeant she was relieving.

"Anything beyond what you mentioned in the pass-down?"

"No. Like I said, it was a quiet night, and you get to have all the fun today with the Global Hawk."

Emily brightened a little. "I'm looking forward to it." In the rush to get into work, she had forgotten that today was the day. The RQ-4D Global Hawk was an incredible machine. Built for long-duration Intelligence, Surveillance, and Reconnaissance, or ISR as the Air Force called it, the Global Hawk had a twenty-eight-hour endurance at a flight ceiling of 60,000 feet, nearly 12 miles up. She could fly her mission completely autonomously, or under the control of a human operator, and today was the day the operators from Beale Air Force Base in California were going to show her and a couple of the other drone operators how to manage her ISR systems.

She knew the operators from the other two shifts were as excited about it as she was, coming in on their off days for the training. They had to. The operators from Beale could only stay four days, and Emily and her colleagues would need to be certified before the Beale operators left, or they would not be allowed to use the Hawk's sensors for operational missions. The Department of Defense would never let someone use the sensors on an aircraft costing more than $140 million apiece without training. *You break it, you buy it,* she thought, as she headed over to the drone desk.

The drone desk was on the extreme left side of the semicircle facing the large monitors, and consisted mainly of a couple of very high-performance desktop computers, purpose-built for the government by Falcon Northwest, attached to a set of four 30-inch, high-resolution monitors arranged in a four-segment square. Directly below the monitors were the standard array of secure phones—one STE and one grey phone—and the plug for the internal private voice channel all the desk officers shared and used during operations. Below them, in a recessed tray, were the keyboards and mice for the computers.

As she approached, she took stock of the two senior NCOs wearing visitor security badges. They were standing next to her two counterparts from the other shifts, who were lucky enough to be wearing civvies this morning since they were not officially on duty. The guests' green "V" badges indicated that they had valid Sensitive Compartmented Intelligence clearances, but the red light was on because they were not cleared for the specifics of the CAPTIVE DRAGON compartment. If a Wraith Team operation was initiated on short notice, the two men would need to be ushered out of CTS as quickly as possible.

Both senior NCOs wore green fire-resistant Nomex flight suits festooned with the unit patches of the 10th Reconnaissance Wing at Beale. Emily smiled at that. The two men were not really fliers, but wore the flight suits aircrew usually wore. It was a silly Air Force cultural thing, in Emily's opinion. If you happened to get assigned to a flying unit, whether you actually were aircrew or not, and the unit commander authorized it, you could wear a flight suit. Even the Space Command assignees got green Nomex flight suits, and all they ever flew were desks.

In fairness, it was as much an ego thing as it was a comfort thing with some people in the service. The flight suit was loose, and had many convenient pockets. Even real pilots in the Air Force wore theirs on days they were not even going near a plane.

"Good morning," she greeted them, reaching out to shake hands.

"Good morning," replied the master sergeant, whose name tag read "Carmody." The other man, whose name tag read "Sarenson," just nodded. Carmody must be the senior of the two men, and would probably be doing the briefing, she thought. Her assessment was proven correct after Master Sergeant Carmody, having moved his coffee cup to a more convenient position, started talking.

"Good morning and welcome to Global Hawk One oh One," he said with a smile. Emily and her counterparts smiled in return. It wasn't a bad icebreaker.

He continued, "Today we'll spend some time showing you the Hawk's sensor suite and what you can do with it. Before I get into that, let me give you a few factoids about the aircraft." Carmody took a quick sip from his coffee cup, and then continued.

"The RQ-4D, Block 50 Global Hawk is a long-endurance ISR platform. It has a 130-foot wingspan, a length of 47 feet, and is powered by a single Rolls-Royce turbofan engine that produces nearly 8,000 pounds of thrust. Its service ceiling is 60,000 feet, and it can stay aloft for more than a day." Another sip of coffee.

"The sensor packages we'll be covering today are the electro-optical, infrared, and active electronically scanned array radar, which provides synthetic aperture radar along with ground moving-target indicator capability."

Emily interrupted, a puzzled look on her face. "What about the high- and low-band SIGINT sensors?"

Carmody was ready for that one. "We are not going to discuss the SIGINT sensors today."

"All right. Are we saving that for tomorrow?" she asked.

Carmody's face hardened, "No, Sergeant. We will not be covering them at all. Any details about the SIGINT sensors and their capabilities are classified by NSA. Since the CTS does not conduct a SIGINT mission, or have the legal authorities for one, we do not need to cover them."

Emily began to formulate a caustic response, but bit it back. He was right. Need-to-know still applied. CTS was not a SIGINT producer and had its hands full supporting the CAPTIVE DRAGON program. She nodded at Carmody and let it drop.

Master Sergeant Carmody took another sip from his cup to let the mildly tense moment pass before continuing.

"All right, then. Let's look at the electro-optical and infrared sensors."

She watched carefully as Sergeant Carmody ran through the standard control suite for the electro-optical and infrared sensors, more commonly known to normal human beings as the visible light and infrared cameras. The cameras were commanded through the software suite loaded onto the computer at the drone station. The software package was started up like any other application on a computer, and the graphical interface displayed the command console for the Hawk's sensors. She noticed a large section of the interface Carmody had brought up on the lower right monitor was completely blank. That must have been where the SIGINT sensor controls were normally. She surmised that they were using a modified software load that omitted those controls to ensure that no one was tempted to use them illegally.

Carmody began demonstrating the control suite, and brought up an image on the upper right monitor, zooming the picture in and out, then slewing the camera around, and finally switching over to the infrared camera. When he was done, he looked up at the operators clustered around the desk.

"Who would like to get familiar with the controls?"

Emily answered first, as eager as a kid on Christmas to open her toys. "I would."

Carmody stood to let her sit. "All right, Sergeant Thompson, go ahead and give it a try. It's not much different from a Reaper; I'm sure you'll get the hang of it quickly. The difference is mostly in the placement of the various buttons on the GUI."

As she moved toward the chair, she had a thought.

"Are we using test imagery?" she asked.

Carmody shook his head. "No. This is a live feed from a Global Hawk out west, on an extended orbit over the Arizona border with Mexico. We've temporarily taken control of one of the cameras for this training. The others are being used to surveil the border between us and Mexico in support of U.S. Customs and Border Patrol."

She was thrilled—a live feed on an actual Global Hawk. "That's great," she said as she started to collapse into the seat.

"Sergeant Thompson?" Cain's voice stopped her cold. She turned to look over her shoulder to see him approaching the drone desk.

"Yes, Mr. Cain." She knew he preferred David, but they had guests and proper decorum was required.

"I'm sorry to interrupt," Cain continued, "but I need to speak with you in the conference room for a few minutes."

She deflated, and nearly dropped into the chair. Her first chance to work with a cool new drone—well, new to CTS, at least—and he needed to talk to her. *Damn.*

"Mr. Cain, could it wait . . ." She stopped. He had cocked his head to the side, and the look on his face was clearly, "You don't ask me if it can wait. I'm in charge here, and I want to talk to you now."

Reluctantly, she excused herself from the training session and followed Cain into the conference room. He stood just inside the door and let her pass him.

"Please take a seat, Emily," he said as he closed the conference room's door. She chose a chair near the end of the table. Cain came over and sat at the end and looked at her.

"Emily, are you all right?"

"Yes, I'm fine."

Cain frowned as he looked at her, his eyes narrowing.

"Emily, I have to say this. You look terrible. Are you getting enough sleep?"

She started to tell him about being up all night with her son and he waved her off, continuing, "Before you answer, listen to me. We work a tough schedule, and the events of the last few weeks have been pretty tough. You look really rough. Tired. I'm worried you're getting a little burnt out. I want you to know that you can ask for some additional time off if you need it."

"Mr. Cain, I'm okay." Her voice made it more of a plea than a statement of fact.

"Are you sure? How much sleep did you get last night?"

Emily hung her head a little. "I'm not really sure. A few hours. I have some things on my mind."

Cain nodded. "It's been pretty rough lately. Seeing the aftermath of those bombings, the SWAT and HRT teams getting killed . . ."

Emily's head came up and she practically screamed, "That wasn't my fault!" Tears began to well in her eyes, but she resolved not to cry. This was business and she was a professional.

"Whoa!" Cain said, putting his hands up. "I didn't say it was. It was nobody's fault. Not in this organization, anyway."

Emily looked away and rubbed her eyes. Cain gave her a little time while he considered her reaction. Then he reached out and gently gripped her upper arm to regain her attention. When she turned back, she was under control again.

"Listen to me. We did everything we could for those men in Chicago. The terrorist bastard who planted and then triggered those explosives killed those men, not anything we did or didn't do. Do you understand that?"

Emily looked him in the eye and nodded. She did not trust herself to speak without losing it, and Cain just didn't understand.

"Look. It's obvious you need some rest. We have no Ops planned for today. I want you to take the rest of this shift off. Go home, spend some time with your son and husband. Go to bed early and get a solid eight hours and we'll see you tomorrow."

No, she thought. She could do her job. "I wanted to work with the Hawk. It's a great piece of technology and a tremendous asset for us to leverage."

"Yes, it is, but the guys from Beale will be here for a couple more days, so you won't really be missing out if you don't finish out this shift. You can complete the training tomorrow."

"Mr. Cain, please!" she pleaded, "I can do my job."

Cain was resolute. "Yes, you can, but not as effectively as you should be able to now. There is no crisis and no immediate need for you to be here today. Particularly when you are as wrung out as you are now."

Emily was frustrated with herself. How could she make him understand? She clenched her fists, feeling her nails dig into her palms. She wanted to cry. She wanted to scream at him. She wanted to scream at herself. To make him understand.

Cain watched her carefully. He could see the internal struggle playing out on her face. He had been working with her long enough to know she looked angry. At him? Some reassurance, maybe?

"Emily," he said calmly, reaching out to lay his hand gently on her forearm, "you are one of the best people I've ever had working for me. I'm responsible for making sure that you continue to perform at that level and grow beyond it."

Emily turned to look at him, and Cain saw a doubtful look . . . and something else. Maybe she thought he was dissatisfied with her recent performance.

"Emily. You do great work here and I want you to continue to do great work here. I've noticed you coming in late for your shifts." Cain saw her bridle before he continued.

"It's okay. We all can get a little burned out from time to time, or deal with sick children or just plain have a few bad nights. Everyone has a life outside of the mission we do here. I'm not upset that you've been late. I am concerned that you haven't come to me and told me that you need extra time off so you can be at your best. I admire your dedication, but if you can't be effective when you are here, you aren't any good to us."

Emily hadn't expected that. She leaned back in the chair, pulling back from his hand, and felt her fists unclench. Cain saw her face relax a little, so he continued.

"What I'm doing is giving you the chance to take some additional time off and come back fresh and ready to get the mission done. I also want you to know that if you need to talk about anything that's bothering you, you can come to me." Emily looked away from him, not sure what to say, tears of both frustration and appreciation starting to well once again.

"If you aren't comfortable talking to me, maybe a friend here that you can talk shop with?"

How could she tell him? He was her boss; he had probably never made a mistake that killed so many people. Maybe a half-truth, then. "No. It's not that. I really appreciate your offer. I just need to get some sleep. What we've been doing has my mind working after hours."

Cain nodded. "I understand. The same thing happens to me occasionally. I think people like you and I get very involved in our work and we sometimes have trouble leaving work here and not taking it home with us." Cain fixed her with an understanding smile, not knowing his understanding was not as complete as he thought.

"I've lost count of how many times I've lost a good night's sleep because my mind wouldn't let whatever the problem du jour go until tomorrow. In part, that's a mark of a dedicated pro. In part, it's the mark of what can be an unhealthy set of events. You need to find something to do, something to take your mind off things."

Emily nodded, keeping her eyes on the floor. She had avoided telling him, but the advice she was hearing seemed like a good idea. "Yeah. Maybe I should run more."

"That's an idea," Cain agreed. "The gym in the basement of the Ops Two building is still open if you don't want to run in the dark."

At that point, Cain's deputy stuck his head in the door. "Mr. Cain. DIRSNA is on the phone."

Cain looked over his shoulder. "I'll be right there." He turned back to Emily.

"You going to be okay?"

She nodded and looked up at him. "I'll manage. I'm off shift, right?"

"Yes. As of now."

"I think I'll go for a run, then." Maybe if she ran long enough, she would be tired enough to finally sleep.

CHAPTER 6

JOHNSON SLID THE BACK OF his hand across his sweaty brow and took a long pull on the water bottle. The air conditioning was on full blast in Akeem's personal Mercedes S63 AMG out of deference for Johnson, and he expected that Akeem was probably freezing in the driver's seat in his lightweight white thawb.

Akeem sliding behind the wheel after meeting him in the lobby was surprising. He was no run-of-the-mill gofer, but a high-level assistant to the Minister of the Interior. At his level, he rated an on-call driver and car for official duties. Culturally, however, it was a sign of friendship and respect that Akeem drove his personal vehicle for Johnson. It also did not hurt one bit that his car was an obscenely comfortable, diamond white metallic luxury sedan from the Mercedes high-performance AMG division. The sleek car was gliding down Al Washam Street at nearly 80 kilometers an hour, which seemed fast to Johnson, but that was mostly caused by Akeem's cavalier disregard for traffic lights and the 40-kilometer-an-hour posted limit. After all, what police officer would dare ticket a senior assistant to a government minister?

Johnson relaxed into the sumptuous comfort of the ivory leather seats and placed his faith in his friend's knowledge of Riyadh's roads and traffic patterns. It was not quite nine in the morning and traffic was light, with only a few pedestrians on the sidewalks.

"So where exactly are we heading?" Johnson asked in English.

"No Arabic today?" Akeem said without taking his eyes from the road, a smirk playing across his face.

Johnson shook his head. "Not today. Honestly, I don't think my vocabulary is good enough for any discussions of legal procedure under Sharia law."

"It's quite all right, my friend. I understand. We're heading to the Ministry of Justice building."

"What stage are the proceedings at?"

Akeem slowed to navigate one of the ubiquitous roundabouts in the Saudi road system, and once back on the dual carriageway, answered. "The court has already heard from all the witnesses, and reviewed the documentary evidence provided by the military and my ministry."

"Did the witnesses include the man who interrogated Sadig?"

"Yes."

"But he tortured . . ." Johnson began reflexively.

Akeem interrupted him before he could finish protesting. "My friend, I have told you before that this is not your country. Sadig debased himself before Allah, he used illicit substances; abused the faithful, including women and children; and chose to enter this country illegally after committing hostile acts against his fellow Muslims. He does not deserve your pity. We did what was necessary to make him speak. Moreover, in the eyes of the law, no statements were taken down during the harsh treatment, only afterward in the hospital, and Sadig signed them and testified to them under oath at the trial."

Johnson was not convinced. "I understand that this is your country and that my nation's laws do not apply here. What bothers me is that if we do such things to other human beings, we bring ourselves down to the level of those we despise. We in effect say, 'We will do anything to stop you.' At what point have we lost ourselves and what we profess to stand for in the pursuit of our enemies?"

Akeem considered that, and nodded. His American friend may be young, but he was obviously a man of good character. Akeem was not ignorant enough to think that just because Johnson did not share his faith, he was not a man with a moral compass. A man to be respected, particularly in that he had shown respect. Johnson had not acted the way many in the Middle East would expect of most Westerners or, more specifically, an American. In all the time Akeem had known the FBI agent Johnson had tried to learn Akeem's language, and was most respectful toward his beloved wife and even solicitous of Akeem's children when he had invited him into his home for dinner. In Akeem's eyes, Johnson had acted in every way as any Arab guest in his home would.

Since meeting Johnson and seeing his obvious respect for Arab culture, in spite of his differences with it, Akeem had often been reminded of the many statements in the Holy Qur'an that spoke of tolerance for those not of the Islamic faith.

The Holy Qur'an spoke of being respectful to the all the Ahl al-Kitab or the "People of the Book." In keeping with the teachings of the Holy Qur'an, Jews, Sabians, Magians, and Christians were tolerated and given autonomy within a society governed by Sharia law. Akeem accepted these tenets not just as the teachings to be found within the Holy Qur'an, but as a proper way to deal respectfully with all men. He was also worldly enough to know that most Americans shared that outlook, yet they approached it through a different lens of cultural identity.

He knew that in America, children were taught at an early age that the freedom to worship as a person chooses is a right enshrined in custom and law. In that learning, they internalize a tolerance for religion and other men that Akeem felt had closely paralleled what he had learned as a younger man in his study of the Holy Qur'an. The fact that two peoples, separated by a vast distance, with extremely disparate cultures, and holding very different political views about many issues, shared a common underpinning of religious tolerance gave him hope that all men could one day reach a point where peace was the order of the day.

In spite of this, the American view of civil rights sometimes seemed more like an impracticable high ideal when dealing with the vilest of men. They had chosen to prey on those who were weaker. They wasted their lives in the pursuit of dominating others to gather power, or imposing their own viewpoint or outlook on others when they disagreed. If their viewpoint was so righteous, Akeem felt, others would flock to it; they would not need to be forced. The people who chose the path of deceit and coercion were vipers in the world of peaceful men, and deserved nothing but contempt and harsh treatment.

"David, I understand why you look at what we did to Sadig with distaste. It does not please me to have witnessed it, either, but I understand the need. Sadig, by his own actions, chose his path. In spite of his lack of character, and what we already knew of his past crimes, we asked him to tell us what he knew at the beginning of the interrogation, and he refused. We were forced to compel him to tell us what he knew. He had to speak to us. We could not have it otherwise. He was a criminal, in the Kingdom illegally, and a member of an organization that had committed horrible crimes against the innocent people of Afghanistan and both of our countries."

Johnson began to interject, but Akeem continued. "Moreover, an honored guest of a friendly country came to us seeking aid. Our nations may have differences, and we will disagree on many issues like the need for a Palestinian homeland, but we still owe your country a great debt for protecting us from that lunatic in Iraq last century. We did what we had to do to learn what you needed to know. Without his information, your government would never have located this man Aziz and given you a chance to try to catch him."

Johnson considered that. Akeem was right about some things. Without what they had learned from Sadig, they would not have developed the leads that gave them an initial location on Aziz. The little Saudi interrogator had asked Sadig to answer his questions before they began beating him. The memory of watching that, helpless, as they eventually broke his leg before moving on to more brutal methods was not pleasant.

Seeing and hearing it all had affected him so much he had to step out and find temporary refuge in the washroom. Akeem had found him there, sickened and angered by what he had seen. Akeem had politely but firmly told him then that this was not his country and that U.S. law did not apply here.

Shortly after Johnson had returned to the observation room, Sadig's screams morphed into pleas to stop. But they did not stop. Eventually, he began begging to talk before he passed out. The Saudis cleaned him up and gave him medical attention before Johnson was allowed to "officially" interview Sadig in a carefully guarded room within a Saudi military hospital.

"Akeem, I can't deny the results, but I still think that using torture brings us down to the level of our enemies. We are supposed to be better than they are! We lose ourselves and break faith with our ideals when we sink to that level."

Akeem shook his head at his friend's naiveté. "I agree, David. If we arrested all persons accused of crimes and then tortured them to get confessions, then I would say we are doomed as a people. It should never come to that. We do not treat any but the worst offenders to what you witnessed, and only under carefully controlled circumstances. Also, no statements were taken during the harsh treatment, since they could not be used during trial. The colonel who supervised the interrogation sought permission for the more severe measures from his commanding general before he began. We are not uncivilized, you know."

Johnson heard the tolerant accusation in Akeem's last words and let out a long breath. This conversation was a lost cause. "I know, Akeem. I wasn't trying to imply that your people are; only that I believe torturing a suspect is wrong."

Akeem was conciliatory. "I know you weren't, David, and I know you believe what we did was wrong, and in your country, under your laws, it would be. I respect your viewpoint, but I must point out that I think in some ways, America can be very naïve. Ah, here we are."

Johnson looked at the building as Akeem braked and then turned the Mercedes S63 smoothly right, off the palm-lined Al Jamiah Street onto the gated side road that ran parallel to the ministry. The building was seven stories tall, built of sand-colored concrete and lined with windows on every floor. Johnson had no hope of reading the Arabic characters on the 20-foot-tall green sign on the corner, but the English lettering below them read: MINISTRY OF JUSTICE.

The two uniformed guards barely glanced in the car as Akeem tossed them a quick wave as he drove by, accelerating down the alley. Johnson was surprised by that, but held his tongue. Security at the ministry did not seem too tight. One more left turn later and Akeem slid the Mercedes into a parking slot alongside the building.

Both men alighted from the car and Johnson followed Akeem in through a side door on the ground floor, past another uniformed security guard who barely glanced at them when they passed. A few minutes and a brief elevator ride later, they were at the entrance to what Johnson assumed was a courtroom. Akeem had a brief conversation in Arabic with a man standing outside the door, and then led the way inside.

Johnson followed Akeem into the room and took stock. It was obviously a courtroom but a little different from what Johnson had expected. In America, courtrooms were heavy, imposing places with dark woods and leather. This courtroom was simple, but no less dignified. The woods were light in color, the bench with the seats for the judges was lower, and there was a 4-foot-wide rostrum centered before the bench, and rows of simple bench seating for the observers. One thing that struck him was the complete lack of tables and chairs on either side of the rostrum for the opposing councils.

Akeem guided him to an empty row of benches on the left and walked to the far end toward the left edge of the room, and bade him to sit. Once they were comfortable, Akeem leaned in close.

"The proceedings will be in Arabic, of course. I will translate for you so you can follow them. If I'm too loud, the judges will warn me, so lean close and I will speak softly. They know you are participating on behalf of your government, so I don't think we'll need to worry about it too much."

Johnson was hesitant. "I don't want you to get in trouble with the court."

Akeem motioned his concerns away with one hand. "We will be fine. They will be tolerant because of the political issues with this case. The session will start in a few minutes."

Johnson sat and looked around the room, noting that he and Akeem were not alone. A few other men had drifted into the court, taking seats well apart from one another. In a few minutes, the doors at the rear closed, and Sadig was escorted into the courtroom through a door built into the right wall near the bench.

His leg was still in a cast, and he used crutches to reach his seat on the bench directly behind the rostrum. Two guards escorted him in, seating themselves in the row directly behind Sadig. Johnson watched him for any sign of recognition, but saw none. Sadig seemed deep in thought, staring at the floor, and nervous, chewing his fingernails. He never once looked up or searched the room for a familiar face or friend.

Another minute or two later, the same door opened again. Five men entered, dressed in white thawbs. Johnson judged them all to be in their midfifties, if not older, and they carried themselves with the bearing of judges the world over. They moved with purpose toward their seats behind the bench and settled themselves. After shuffling papers for a few seconds, the senior man spoke. Johnson was pleased Akeem would translate. The senior judge spoke quickly, no doubt as fluent in his native tongue as his upbringing and long education and experience with Islamic law could make him.

Akeem whispered, "The senior trial judge told Sadig he need not stand because of his cast."

The judge continued speaking for a minute and then looked briefly at his colleagues, who nodded in assent. The judge then addressed Sadig, who responded. Johnson saw Sadig's expression change from resigned expectation to intense focus and wariness.

Akeem breathed into his ear again, "The judge told Sadig that the court has reviewed all the documentary evidence, and Sadig's own written statements he has affirmed under oath in this courtroom. He asked Sadig if he was a member of the Taliban government, a government known to support the terrorist organization called al-Qaeda, an organization known to conduct Hirabah—unlawful warfare. Sadig told him he was."

The judge turned back to his fellows and conferred with them quietly. Johnson's eyes flicked from their conversation to Sadig. He was starting to fidget in his seat, and the two guards behind him seemed to be leaning forward expectantly, their hands on the back of Sadig's seat, inches from his shoulders.

The judges stopped their consultation, and the senior man spoke at length. As he did so, Johnson saw Sadig's eyes open wide in horror. He rose, balancing himself with one crutch, and began shouting at the judges. The two guards stood behind him and moved to bracket him, each taking a firm hold of his upper arms. Sadig struggled briefly, but without the use of both legs, he could do little but bounce from side to side in the strong grip of the guards.

The judge continued to speak, raising his voice to be heard over Sadig's obvious protests. As the judge finished, Sadig's protests became screams, and the two guards began to pull him from the courtroom. He resisted as best he could, still screaming. It took three more guards called from the area outside the courtroom to drag him from the court.

Johnson looked at Akeem, surprise on his face. "What the hell happened?"

Akeem was grim. "The judge told him they were ready to pronounce sentence. The court has determined that Sadig is a Hirabi. Do you know what that is?"

"No," answered Johnson, completely perplexed.

"A Hirabi is a person who commits 'unlawful warfare' or piracy, which is called Hirabah. The penalty for Hirabah is death, and the sentence will be carried out immediately."

Johnson was stunned. "What about an appeal?"

"There is no appeal," Akeem replied, his eyes steady and fixed on Johnson. "He will be punished at noon. As the official witness for the American government, you will be there when justice is done upon him."

AT ONLY NINETEEN YEARS OF age, Saddam Haddad had seen more violence and death than most young men. He hunched himself forward against the chill in the wind blowing down the Rue de Champions on the outskirts of Paris and drew his light jacket closer to his body. France was much colder in the last months of the year than Morocco ever was, and he did not want to be late for his appointment with Imam Abdel. His words had brought enormous comfort after the death of his brother.

Karim had been sixteen and as boisterous and full of life as Saddam had been at that age. They both wanted to leave France and, against their mother's wishes, spent time with the older men in their small Islamic community in the slums of Paris planning demonstrations against the French government.

Their father had wanted to provide a better life for his family, and used his degree in economics to secure a position in a small company that could pay infinitely more than what he could earn in Morocco. Their parents had sold practically everything they had of value to afford the tickets, passports, and visas to get them to Paris and prepay the rent in a small apartment for three months.

Then their father died of a heart attack three weeks after they settled near Paris. Saddam had gotten what work he could, and in his free time had escorted his mother to the French government offices to beg and plead for the necessary travel documents to leave the country for Lebanon. They had family there and his uncle could take them in. Good man that he was, he had already sent money to his mother so the three of them could eat, but it wasn't enough. What they needed were opportunities to work. Opportunities the French government claimed they had aplenty for young people willing to work.

They were liars. Every time Saddam had gone to the government employment agency for work, they told him to "come back tomorrow." The best he could do was beg for work from the shopkeepers in the neighborhood. Some helped if they could. He could sweep floors, clean bathrooms, and move stock for a few francs, but it was never really enough to help his mother. He had shared his annoyance with some of the other young men he knew in the neighborhood, and they told him of the protest planning. Nothing violent, just a demonstration with signs and chanting. The plan was that the protest would draw the news cameras, and they would make all of France see the injustice of their plight.

On the day of the protest, Karim followed him. Saddam told him to go home and stay with their mother, but Karim was insistent, and eventually Saddam relented. The protest went as planned. There were dozens of young men his age, and a few his brother's age, all carrying signs and chanting, "Work! Work! Work!" It worked as planned. The police arrived after an hour or so, wearing riot gear and erecting barricades to keep the protest group from wandering at will in the streets outside of the slum. The television cameras were hot on their heels, setting up within minutes of their arrival to capture the protesters and the police barricades in the same shot.

Some journalists tried to interview a few of the protestors, but language barriers made that difficult. Few of the protestors spoke French beyond the basics, and none of the journalists on the scene knew Arabic. English sufficed as a common tongue, but the protesters' words seemed disjointed and feeble, making them look more like rabble on camera than serious men wanting a fair attempt to gain honest work. Even members of the protest filmed events with their cell phones and tried to upload the videos to the Internet to generate more interest and sympathy via social media sites.

Then someone in the crowd of protesters threw a Molotov cocktail at the police. The makeshift grenade exploded against a police officer's chest and turned him into an instant torch. His comrades extinguished the blaze and carried him off to a waiting ambulance, while the officer in command of the riot squad made the bad situation worse. He ordered the deployment of tear gas.

The officers threw the grenades into the crowd of protesters, and they exploded in vast clouds of noxious fumes. Saddam looked around for Karim through the wisps of smoke that were growing denser by the second and saw him standing next to a man lighting another Molotov. On the other side of the barricades, the French police officer in charge saw the cocktail flare into life and ordered the men nearest him to open fire on the man holding the cocktail, the rag stuffed in the neck of the bottle burning brightly.

No less than three officers opened fire with their Swiss-made SIG SG-543 assault rifles on the man with the burning Molotov. While it was difficult sighting through the tear gas clouds, the burning flame made an excellent target.

The rounds were only rubber bullets, and each officer fired only twice, as per their training, but in less than three-tenths of a second, the damage was done. Three of the rubber bullets missed entirely. Two struck the man holding the Molotov in the chest, just as he started to throw it, spoiling his aim and knocking him to the ground with the force of the impact. The last one passed straight through Karim's right eye and into his brain.

Saddam saw a puff of red mist in front of his brother's face, and watched, horror-struck, as he fell to the ground like a marionette with the strings cut. He raced to Karim's side and knelt down to see the black hole where his right eye used to be and knew he needed a doctor immediately. He scooped up his brother's body and carried his lifeless form toward the police barricade.

The officers followed him with their rifles but did not fire. The sergeant who had actually fired the shot that killed Karim stepped forward under the cover provided by his brother officers and examined the boy quickly, then hustled them through the police line to the ambulance. The officer, given the chaos of the situation and the lack of a completely clear sight picture, would never be certain he had fired the shot that killed the boy, but he did feel badly that the young man had actually been hit by a million-to-one shot from what was supposed to be a "nonlethal" round.

Saddam shook himself from the memories of that day, and the days after. The doctor in the hospital speaking the unintelligible French words to him, shaking his head sadly. The stark white sheet being pulled over his brother's head, blooming bright red where it touched the empty eye socket, his mother's screams when he told her that her youngest child was dead.

He could not find work, and his mother would not look at or speak to him any longer, so he spent his days at the mosque and found solace in the Holy Qur'an. In the quiet interior of the mosque he could sit, study the enlightening words of Allah, think, and pray for Allah's help. Imam Abdel had found him there one day, reading in a peaceful corner.

The imam listened to his plight and gave him several hundred francs for his mother, from a Zakat fund the mosque kept for such tragedies. The imam even let him work in the mosque, cleaning and helping others to repay the kindness. Saddam and the imam, an obviously learned man, had spent many hours talking about the injustice that had been visited on him by the nonbelievers in France.

Saddam could see the minarets of the mosque a few blocks away, and he hurried on, hoping he was not running late. He could not even check his watch to be certain; he had pawned it last month to buy some fresh chicken and vegetables. As he waited for traffic to clear before crossing the Rue de Triumph, he thought back on his conversations with Imam Abdel. Long and instructive, they gave him hope.

The imam had explained the real reason behind the French government's refusal to allow him to emigrate. Many young men who went to Lebanon did so only to join the struggle against the occupiers in Palestine. The French officials did not care if Saddam actually had relatives in Beirut, and was trying, as any honorable young man responsible for a family might, to care for his mother's needs and have the opportunity to earn a living.

The imam had even told him in strictest confidence that he knew of men of faith within the French government who had seen the diplomatic cables from America instructing French officials to deny travel to intelligent young men like himself. Doing so would keep the long-suffering Palestinians from gaining the manpower they needed to fight off their occupiers.

With this revelation, Saddam had found a new focus for his anger. The French, and ultimately their American puppet masters, were attempting to deny the Palestinians a homeland, and in doing so had denied him the chance he needed to succeed. Saddam asked the imam how this could be so, and the imam had answered him forthrightly. It was another kind of crusade. The Westerners were doing all they could to keep men like himself from fighting to protect their loved ones and families. Hemming them in, creating one set of rules for the wealthy unbelievers, while sending occupying armies to the Middle East to suppress and contain the faithful of Allah.

Saddam did not think them so bold, and had told the imam with great respect that he must be misinformed. Large occupying armies could not be hidden from the world; everyone would know! Imam Abdel had smiled and clapped him warmly on the shoulder, saying, "The young must often grow up quickly and leave the dreams of youth behind suddenly. American, British, and French armies are already in the Middle East, with large numbers in Kuwait and Qatar, and huge numbers of forces afloat on ships in the Persian Gulf, awaiting orders for an invasion."

Saddam had looked closely into the imam's eyes as he spoke, searching for any sign of a lie or fabrication. He could not find any. "Again, Imam Abdel, I do not doubt your word, but I must see this for myself to know the whole truth."

The imam had smiled, a trace of expectation on his lips. He rose from their comfortable place on the carpeted floor in one of the mosque's quiet alcoves and went away for a few minutes. When he returned, he held a small tablet computer in his hands. It was a new, black-cased iPad, normally kept in a secret place in the imam's private office. Saddam watched as the imam activated the video application, tapped the icon for the video file he wanted to start, then handed the iPad to Saddam.

Saddam could not believe his eyes and ears. The narrator began by praising Allah, the Most Merciful, and then provided commentary about the news clips that ran one after another. Israeli missile strikes on women and children in Gaza, amphibious troop landings in Kuwait and Bahrain by U.S. Marines, drone strikes by the American CIA in the defenseless villages of Afghanistan and Pakistan that killed dozens of children when they claimed they were targeting terrorists. The video went on for nearly an hour. How could it not be true? Saddam watched the bloodshed with his own eyes. The news reports from the Middle Eastern television stations were obviously real, and the commentator's words rang true, matching the horrific scenes of mothers wailing in the rubble of destroyed homes, fathers holding the limp forms of children, begging for help.

The last few minutes brought uncontrollable tears to Saddam's eyes. As he wiped at them, trying to appear more manly before the imam, he felt Abdel's hand on his shoulder.

"It is just that you should weep for the persecuted and the abused. It is worthy in Allah's sight. I believe that there is much a young man of courage like yourself can do to help."

Saddam lifted his eyes to meet the imam's. "Really?"

"Yes." The imam's eyes held his. "You have felt their pain, and have seen the pain of your own mother when the infidels took an innocent life. You can fight back. If you have courage, and if you wish to."

Saddam's gaze was steady. "I do."

SADDAM FELT THE CHILL WIND bite, but he ignored it as he approached the doors to the mosque. Today was the day he would take his first steps toward righting the wrongs the infidels had visited on his family.

Pushing the door open and entering the peace and serenity of the mosque, he paused to let the warmth soak into his body and caress his face. Making sure the door was closed behind him, Saddam removed his shoes and placed them in the alcove set aside for all worshipers to use, then passed the fountain for Wudu, crossing the rear portion of the carpeted prayer hall. He then passed through an arched doorway and turned right, heading toward the small meeting room the imam spoke of. As he rounded the corner, he came to an abrupt halt. There were two very imposing men standing outside the doorway to the room.

"Saddam! As-salaam 'alaikum." Imam Abdel came out of the room and shook his hand warmly, his Arabic warm and fluid as always. "It's all right," he reassured Saddam, noticing his uncertain glances toward the two men. "These are the bodyguards of a trusted friend. A man who can help you carry the fight to the unbelievers. Come in."

Saddam allowed the imam to draw him into the room and shut the door behind him. He was more surprised to see five other young men in the room, already seated on cushions in a semicircle on the floor, and it must have shown on his face. The imam patted him on the shoulder reassuringly.

"These are your brothers. They have all been wronged as you have been and wish to fight injustice. All are strong believers in Allah's word and His Prophet, praise be upon him. Come and sit."

The imam gestured to the empty cushion on the floor and Saddam sat. After settling himself, he noticed another man not sitting with the younger ones. Older than he was, the man was bearded, with strong features women would find appealing, and wearing a business suit that probably cost more than Saddam's father had earned in his entire, all-too-short lifetime. The new man looked at each of them briefly and then began to speak.

"I am Aziz. Like you, the Crusader's armies hurt me deeply. They took from me the only man I ever called 'Father.' I have seen their reign of terror with my own eyes in Afghanistan, Pakistan, Palestine, Egypt, and Iraq, and I have vowed to stop them."

Saddam was impressed. This man spoke with a deep conviction that was easy to see. Aziz looked at each of the younger men as he spoke, his voice firm and measured, his Arabic very literate, a mark of education and knowledge that always engendered respect in Saddam.

"My good friend Imam Abdel tells me that each of you wishes to reclaim your lives from the unbelievers who have stolen your future. Is this true?"

Each of the younger men nodded, but Saddam spoke. "*Na'am* Sayyid."

Aziz locked his eyes onto Saddam's and came closer to him, then knelt down to look directly into his eyes from a distance of about 1 foot.

"Only you spoke aloud what was in your heart. Your courage shows even in that simple act."

Saddam did not move or flinch from the examination; he merely looked into Aziz's dark brown eyes with equal scrutiny.

"What is your name, my young friend?"

"I am Saddam."

"Ah," Aziz smiled. "The 'one who confronts.' Will you fight for what should have been yours?"

Saddam's gaze did not waver. His brother should have had a life. His mother should not cry in the night. "Na'am."

Aziz smiled like a proud parent. "Will you risk martyrdom for what you seek? Will you choose martyrdom if needed and look Allah in the eye after confronting the infidels?"

Imam Abdel had discussed this with him. Seeing Paradise with blood of the unbelievers upon his hands would gain his mother peace and immediate entry into Paradise when her time came. "Insha'Allah."

Aziz nodded, and echoed his words. "Insha'Allah."

Aziz rose and addressed the others. "Will you follow this brave man's example? Will you choose martyrdom and look upon the benevolent face of Allah to crush the infidels?"

In unison, they cried out, "Insha'Allah!"

Aziz studied them for a few seconds more, as if to allow their hopes and expectations to build.

"Then you shall be trained."

JOHNSON SAT BACK IN THE feeling the firm cloth of the cushion press into his back, and closed his eyes. The bar in the hotel was practically vacant in the early afternoon. The bartender was the only other person in the room, and the three televisions mounted to the walls along the outer edges where patrons could see at least two of them from any vantage point were dark and silent.

The bartender was running his inventory behind the bar, making a list of items to order. Johnson was surprised that the hotel offered alcoholic beverages, but since it catered primarily to Europeans and Westerners, it was not a problem as far as the Saudis were concerned—as long as an alcoholic drink never left the hotel and no Saudi citizen was ever seen consuming one. Western or European women could even go without the hijab or abaya within the hotel, and the bartender and staff were non-Muslim Indians or Pakistanis.

Johnson soon discovered that having his eyes closed did not help anything. He reached for his scotch on the rocks and took another sip. The fire traced down his throat and warmed his belly, but it did not dispel the images in his mind.

Akeem had driven Johnson to Deera Square from the Ministry of Justice to see Sadig's execution. A crowd had already gathered, and Johnson wondered if the government Tweeted or texted notifications of some kind to the general public.

"Now what happens?" he asked Akeem.

"Now, my friend, justice will be done."

Akeem led him forward toward the crowd. Deera Square was perhaps 200 feet a side, surrounded by two-story buildings of almond-colored bricks with tall palm trees marking an inner square away from the buildings. The crowd, consisting of men and some older teenage boys, was only seven or eight people deep from the center, where a single man dressed in black and wearing a face mask stood waiting with a curved scimitar that glinted in the bright sunlight. There were no barricades or barriers of any kind to keep the people back; it seemed citizens were allowed to be as close as they wished.

Oddly enough, Johnson's next question was a bureaucratic one. "As the official witness, do I have to sign anything?"

Akeem shook his head. "No. All the formalities have been dealt with. All you must do now is witness the sentence being carried out."

As the two men approached the rear of the crowd, some of the onlookers noticed them. They began to speak in animated Arabic about Johnson's Western features and clothing, which made him stand out in the crowd like a hunter's blazing orange vest against a white snowfield. Johnson assumed they were just taking notice of the Westerner among them until the people in front of him began to move aside, leaving a channel for him and Akeem to walk closer.

"What are they doing?" Johnson asked, afraid he already knew.

"They are giving you a path to see justice done. Most of our people disagree with the 'enlightened' way Americans and the Europeans deal with criminals by putting them in jail and attempting to rehabilitate them. If a Westerner comes to Deera Square to see real justice, they make room and will often push the Westerner forward to ensure an unobstructed view."

Johnson frowned, hesitating. Akeem saw his indecision and reluctance.

"If you are not up to the task, we do not need to get any closer. You will see Sadig when he is brought in, and the body parts removed afterward."

Johnson looked at Akeem, and saw the implicit challenge in his eyes. This man was a friend, but clearly, he agreed with the rest of the crowd. Americans did not have the stomach for this kind of justice and that made them soft and weak.

Johnson's face hardened into a stern mask. "No. I am, in part, responsible for your government being able to bring this man to justice. I am also a representative of my nation. I must witness it."

Fighting back the urge to close his eyes and deny what he was about to see, Johnson walked forward through the corridor of bodies, with Akeem right behind him. A few steps later, he stood on the edge of the inner ring formed by the crowd. He could see the blood on the sandstones before the executioner. Someone else had already been put to death today. Johnson swallowed and stood his ground. This wasn't going to be pleasant.

Behind the executioner, the crowd made a larger space as a small white van backed in toward the center of the milling group of people, stopping short of the executioner. Two men in the military uniforms of the Saudi National Guard exited the vehicle and opened the rear doors. Johnson could see Sadig slumped forward on the bench. His hands were tied with black cord, and he made no sound as they led him toward the executioner.

Sadig looked around, but could not seem to focus on anything. He was pale and his gait seemed uncoordinated. He looked at Johnson, but there was no indication he recognized him. One of the guards spoke briefly to the executioner and then slipped a hood over Sadig's head before leading him forward a few feet and making him kneel on the sandstone to the right of the bloodstain. Then the guard backed away.

The executioner came forward and said something. Akeem translated for Johnson, "He told him to recite the Shahada."

Johnson knew that the Shahada was the declaration of faith that all Muslims and all non-Muslims wishing to convert to Islam made three times in the presence of an imam and witnesses. It was a verbal agreement to commit to Islam.

Sadig spoke haltingly at first, then more firmly as he recited the words, Akeem echoing them in English in Johnson's ear. "I testify that there is no god but God, and that Muhammad is the messenger of God."

As soon as Sadig finished, the executioner moved. He was obviously well practiced at his craft. The scimitar became a bright flash of silver, and Sadig's head came free, a fountain of blood spurting up from his neck. The severed head tumbled to the ground and bounced twice before stopping, blood pouring from beneath the mask. The body pitched forward, the open neck spilling blood onto the sandstones to mix with the blood from the other criminal.

Johnson found himself staring at the gaping opening that was the upper portion of Sadig's neck, his right hand on his waistband above his right hip. It took him a second or two to realize what he was doing—he had reflexively reached for his service weapon, normally at his hip but now 4,000 miles away. He let his hand drop and forced his eyes away from the corpse.

"Is that it?" he asked Akeem.

"Yes, David. That's it. Justice has been done upon him. May Allah grant him the mercy he did not show others in life."

Seeing the silver blur of the sword and Sadig's head come free from his body once more in his mind, Johnson reached for the glass again and took a longer sip of his scotch. After the beheading, Johnson had asked Akeem to drive him back to his hotel. During the ride, Akeem had explained the process. After the sentence had been pronounced by the court, Sadig had been given a strong sedative and then time to pray if he wished to. After a half hour or so, a doctor had carefully drawn nearly four pints of blood from Sadig's arm. The blood would be tested and if free of disease, used in one of the local hospitals to save lives. The combination of the sedative and the blood loss had the effect of keeping the condemned man calm and cooperative during the execution, and limited any excess gore and excessive cleanup afterward.

Upon reaching his destination, Johnson had bid Akeem a good day, saying that he needed to report to his supervisor. He then headed into the hotel and straight to the bar. He had witnessed a human being killed from a distance of less than 10 feet. All in accordance with the law, as this nation implemented it. Sadig's body was probably already mounted on a cross. The court had ordered that, too, as a warning to anyone else who might commit Hirabah within Saudi Arabia. *A lamb to the slaughter.*

Johnson wondered if the punishment was enough. Sadig's crimes had been numerous and committed under a regime acknowledged throughout the world as a terrorist organization's puppet. Johnson's own reaction at the execution surprised him. He had actually reached for his service weapon when Sadig was beheaded in front of him. Had it been there, would he have aimed at and possibly shot the executioner? Why? This was justice here. Sadig's case was tried under Sharia law; he was found guilty and then sentenced for his crimes.

Johnson's glass was empty, but he still did not have any answers. He briefly debated ordering another but decided against it. Johnson knew he would not find the answers in a bottle. Instead, the investigator within told him to examine the evidence carefully.

He thought back to the conversation he and Agent Pittman had in Guantanamo Bay. Would he beat the answers out of a terrorism suspect to save lives? He had already decided that particular gray area was one he could live in. If a suspect had knowledge of an imminent attack, he would not, could not, treat them with kid gloves; but could he do what the Saudis had done to Sadig? Break bones, or electrocute him slowly until he talked? No.

There had to be a line somewhere. Torturing a suspect would violate every principle he had joined the FBI to defend and protect. Sadig had been sentenced to death under the law in the justice system in this country, a system that allowed a man to confess as a result of being tortured. The Saudis should never have allowed his coerced confession into evidence at the trial.

Johnson took a deep breath and slowly let it out through his nose. Sadig's life was over, and as much as he disagreed with the process that allowed it, he also did not think Sadig was an innocent man or deserved to go unpunished. In the states, he probably would have gotten twenty-five years in prison, based on evidence uncovered in an investigation, not from a coerced confession that any judge would have tossed out during pre-trial hearings, if not the initial indictment.

Sadig would have spent his days in a cell, his afternoons exercising or getting some fresh air in the yard, or maybe attending distance education classes to get his college degree along with counseling sessions to help him understand the depth of his crimes until he was paroled in around ten or so years.

Johnson smacked his empty glass against the table, rattling the melting ice cubes inside it. How was that the proper punishment for a multiple rapist, murderer, extortionist, and blackmailer? Maybe he did need another drink.

CHAPTER 7

· ·

THE RAIN FELL STEADILY FROM the completely overcast sky, pelting the deck of the *Sea Titan* as the 2-foot swells of the North Pacific slapped against the steel hull. The sun had set four hours ago, and in the smothering darkness, Professor Prebin could not see beyond the bow from his position on the bridge. He was frustrated after a two-day delay at sea caused by the storm they were using as cover. The storm front had stalled due to a large high-pressure system to the east, before finally overpowering the block of high pressure and continuing its relentless march eastward toward their target.

In spite of his frustration, Prebin was excited that the time had finally come to begin showing the scientific community that he was right. He had dressed carefully before heading to the bridge. Long underwear, jeans, a black wool roll-neck, dark blue rainwear, and rubber-soled boots. The chill wind off the Pacific was biting, and his footing on the wet decks would be crucial during his part of the operation tonight. Slipping and then dropping something or knocking one of his fellows overboard would be detrimental. Prebin looked out again over the *Sea Titan*'s weather deck stretching before him through the thick glass of the bridge windows.

The ship had been darkened for the approach—every running light extinguished, every interior light in rooms lining the ship's exterior switched off, all portholes covered with thick curtains.

The bridge's lights were switched to red for night operations, and Prebin felt they gave the command center the feel of a ship of war going into action, as, in a way, it was. Although the radios were powered and manned, Captain Esteban had given strict orders that no transmissions be made or acknowledged, except under his direct orders. Even the navigation radar made only one sweep around the ship every five to ten minutes during the approach, stopping completely when they were within 20 miles. They would make every effort not to alert their target during the last hour of the approach. If everything went well, the first indication to the men on the target, or to its nearby companions, that anything was amiss would come after it was far too late to stop them.

Ramirez took a station on the bow with a radio and binoculars. It was his task to be the ship's eyes in the dark and the steady rain. He would issue single-word commands as needed when they were within a hundred yards or so of their objective. For now, the onboard GPS systems tracked the *Sea Titan*'s progress across the ocean, using two reference points from the previous radar sweep—the last positions of the target and the four massive structures near it—for the captain to avoid a potential collision.

The boarding team was already aboard the two launches on the port side, ready to swing out from the davits and head for the target as soon as Ramirez sighted it. Instead of the standard white-and-orange paint scheme, the crew had repainted the open-topped launches a dark gray, similar to the color most navies used. Repin's colleagues waited below, inside the ship, but near the watertight outer door nearest the launch they would use in the operation. Prebin snorted. At least advanced degrees taught a man enough to stay out of the rain.

The radio crackled and Ramirez's voice uttered a single word. "Deploy."

He had seen the target through the rain.

Captain Esteban issued an order. "Full reverse for two minutes, then all stop!"

The helmsman obeyed instantly as Esteban headed out to the bridge wing and used his binoculars. He could see the target now as well, its outline becoming more and more visible as the distance shrank. He took a small device from his rain slicker's pocket and pointed it at the distant vessel, then pressed a button on the case. A red laser, barely visible in the rain, lanced out toward the ship, and the device read out the distance on a small LCD display. The captain glanced at the numbers and raced back into the bridge.

"Hold the full reverse for three more minutes and then all stop." Glancing at Prebin, he said, "We've got plenty of sea room. We won't ram the target and we don't have to maneuver at all. We should stop right where we need to be for the recovery operation."

Prebin nodded his understanding and looked back out the window. He could see that Ramirez had raced from the bow to the stern quarter on the portside, already climbing into a waiting boat that lowered immediately on the davits down to the sea. In about twenty minutes, it would be his turn.

IN THE LAST LAUNCH, RAMIREZ braced himself as the waves began to smack the hull repeatedly. Fortunately, the launches they were using were equipped with remote releases for the davit lines. The helmsman hit the release control and gunned the throttle on the already running engine. The launch was buffeted by the waves, but cut through the water at a good 15 knots. Ramirez knew the other boats were about thirty and forty-five seconds ahead of him, but he had confidence in the leaders of each team and their men. All were longtime members of Abu Sayyaf, an experienced group of jihadis from the Philippines, and veterans of hard combat with the American-trained Philippine army and U.S. Special Forces.

Ramirez did not know all the reasons the Abu Sayyaf men owed their allegiance to Aziz, but he knew that the former leader of Abu Sayyaf had not been heard from in many months, and that Abu Sayyaf's operations against the Philippine army had been more aggressive of late. The men even came aboard the *Sea Titan* with brand-new assault rifles. Ramirez guessed that Abu Sayyaf had likely recently received a huge influx of cash to support their efforts, and perhaps a new leader.

As the small launch thrust itself through the waves, Ramirez could finally see the target clearly through the rain. The ship was more than 140 meters long and 30 meters wide, but only 10 meters high above the water line. Its superstructure was a large, square box with a smaller box, about a third of the size of the lower one, stacked on top of it. The entire upper structure was predominantly white, with a dark blue 2-meter-tall stripe running horizontally down the center of the lower box. The markings on the hull were all in Cyrillic, which he could not read, but that did not matter. He knew what ship she was. The Floating Nuclear Power Station *Laverenti Volkov*.

Ramirez could see the lights from the portholes in the forward section. That was where the personnel quarters were. The aft sections of the ship contained what his men wanted, but they needed to secure the forward section first, as most of the people were there at this time of night. He glanced around quickly, peering through the darkness. Through the heavy rain, he could barely make out the three massive shapes nearly 300 yards away, north of the FNPS *Volkov*. He could see their outlines, and a few discrete points of light, but none of the true bulk of the large crude oil production platforms.

Ramirez smiled and thanked Allah silently for their good fortune so far. The weather was perfect, hiding them from the surrounding vessels and their crew's prying eyes, and the *Sea Titan* was coming to a halt just to the south of the *Volkov*. The *Volkov* was not large enough to hide the *Sea Titan*, but the distance and rain would suffice to shield the ship from anyone on the oil platforms.

Ramirez's launch reached the *Volkov*, the other two gray-colored launches already bobbing in the ocean swells, locked alongside the *Volkov* by magnetic grapnels attached to mooring lines. He could see the bare heads of the pilots waiting in their boats, G4 assault rifles at the ready, guarding them as a precaution. The two teams of men were nowhere to be seen, already moving through the ship per the plan. Ramirez took a brief look at his team. The six men looked back at him expectantly, rain cascading off them, sheathed in heavy sweaters and water-repellent gear, gripping their suppressed Heckler & Koch MP-10 submachine guns tightly. This weather was far colder than what they were used to, but the desire to punish the infidels for their arrogance burned within them.

Ramirez waited until the launch was a meter from the *Volkov*'s hull, moved his own MP-10 to cover the *Volkov*'s forward deck, and then nodded at the man nearest the stern. Without hesitation the man turned and tossed a rubber-coated boarding ladder up and over a clear segment of the *Volkov*'s bow rail. It caught immediately. At the bow of the launch, another man on the team affixed the first of the magnetic grapnels to the hull, then pulled the mooring line through it and tied it off to a cleat on the launch. As the man in the stern did the same, Ramirez led the other men up the boarding ladder onto the deck of the *Volkov*.

Turning left toward the stern, Ramirez brought his suppressed MP-10 up to a ready position, and then began walking quickly toward the dark oval that marked the weather deck hatch on the forward superstructure. He could feel the Abu Sayyaf jihadis following closely behind him, but could not hear their footsteps on the deck in the rain. As he drew closer to the door, he slowed and then peered around the sill of the hatch carefully. He saw one jihadi, who was kneeling on the floor and pointing his MP-10 down an interior hallway, look at him and then jerk his head to the left, a "proceed" gesture.

Ramirez stepped through the hatch and glanced down the hallway before him, which ran across the beam of the *Volkov*. Three bodies lay on the white-tiled floor, bright red blood pooling beneath them. The dead men wore orange jumpsuits with reflective panels. *Ship's crew*, Ramirez thought. The officers wore merchant naval uniforms, the nuclear reactor team wore white, and the small security team wore red.

Ramirez took two steps deeper into the hallway and paused at the corner where another white-tiled hallway headed aft to the reactor area. Silence. The other two teams were doing well. No screams, no alarms. That probably would not last much longer. Ramirez turned left and briskly headed down a hallway stretching aft, stopping only briefly to inspect the two other hallways that ran starboard to port across the ship's width. He saw only open doorways and green *X*'s on the floor. The other two teams each had one man with a small paint can who marked the white-tile floor with an *X* when an area had been cleared. The men and women living in the cabins on this level were dead. Shot in the head as they slept with the suppressed MP-10s of the assault team.

Reaching the end of the fore-to-aft running hallway, Ramirez slowed, creeping up to the corner. He peered around the edge of the wall to check the last of the starboard-to-port running hallways. Another body. This time in red, laying before a hatchway marked with red-and-white signs in Cyrillic, a tightly grouped set of three bullet holes in the chest. Moving forward quickly, he ran down the hall toward the hatch, and skidded to a halt at the body. As he stared, the six men of Abu Sayyaf moved around him, opening the hatch and proceeding deeper into the ship.

The dead guard was a woman. Pale skin and dark hair tightly tied in a bun, her blue eyes wide open and vacant in death. The unbelievers had used a woman as a security guard. Ramirez would never believe that this woman had enjoyed her work or wanted to excel at it. Instead, he was mortified that the infidels allowed their women to do such a dangerous job. Wondering what her family would think when she never came home to marry and have children, Ramirez removed his rain jacket and covered her with it, even as he heard the screams starting from beyond the hatchway. He could do no more for her now. Maybe a prayer for her soul later.

Ramirez rose from her body, angry at the ignorance of a culture that would allow a woman to be exposed to the kind of danger only men should face, and headed through the open hatchway. He headed down a short flight of stairs and through the two open hatches that marked each end of the decontamination area and into the heart of the *Volkov*.

The reactor room took up the starboard side middle third of the superstructure, its outer edges crowded with catwalks and high-pressure water piping, steam lines, and electrical cabling. The center was occupied with what at first glance appeared to be an open-top, large square box. The open-top box was actually a 1-meter-thick lead shield that surrounded the two KLT-40S pressurized water nuclear reactors.

The two reactors sat lower in the ship's hull than the rest of the equipment in the room, the tops of their shining silver exterior cylindrical cases and cluster of control rods and sensors at the top barely visible above the walls of the lead barrier.

Ramirez's team had become bogged down clearing the reactor section. Two technicians in white jump suits were already dead near the inner door to the decontamination area, but the Abu Sayyaf jihadis were taking sporadic fire from a red-uniformed security guard in an aft corner of the catwalk. The lone guard had effectively pinned down the jihadis, since they could not simply open fire on the guard and risk puncturing any of the radioactive steam lines near him.

Ramirez looked around quickly and saw an access ladder to his left.

Slinging his MP-10 over his shoulder, he climbed the ladder quickly while the guard was preoccupied shooting at the other men on his team. Reaching the top, Ramirez unslung his submachine gun and faced aft toward the guard's position, just as the guard noticed he had company on the catwalks. The guard fired off two shots in Ramirez's direction, before retreating deeper into the aft area of the reactor compartment. Ramirez winced as he heard the two rounds ricochet off the wall and piping behind him, miraculously not hitting him or penetrating a radioactive steam line. Seeing the guard begin to shy away from him at the far end of the catwalk, Ramirez raised his MP-10, looked down the tritium marked sights, and waited, knowing Allah would aid him.

As the guard moved along the catwalk, he stepped between a 3-foot gap between two of the larger steam pipes. Ramirez saw the guard's head appear beyond his sight picture and pulled the trigger once. The three-round burst from the MP-10 crossed the reactor compartment at 1,800 feet per second, lancing into the guard's head, killing him instantly. The man's body dropped off the catwalk and hit the steel deck 10 meters below with a satisfying sound.

The Abu Sayyaf jihadis looked up from their positions at Ramirez and cheered.

"Allahu Akbar!"

Ramirez smiled. At least one infidel was now in eternal torment. More on this ship had already paid for the cowardly and unmanly use of a woman as a guard, and more would. Ramirez looked down at the jihadis.

"Quickly. Take the bodies to the crew quarters forward, make sure the generator room is clear, and that all the interior hatches in this area are open."

The jihadis rushed to obey. Two men shouldered their weapons and dragged the dead guard from the room, while the remaining four men made one final check of the reactor room before heading further aft toward the generator room.

Ramirez headed back down the ladder from the catwalk and returned to the forward section. He did not pause at the woman's body this time; he had done all he could for her. The corridors of the ship were vacant. He spot-checked a few of the passenger cabins on the first and second decks as he headed up through the crew quarter's interior. He found only a few bodies here and there in the cabins, and became briefly concerned until he reached the recreation room on the third deck.

At least fifteen men and women lay sprawled on the floor of the room. The walls were splattered with blood, and the floor bore rapidly congealing pools of red. Some of the people had been eating or playing cards. A television was still on in the corner, surrounded by three of the bodies. The other jihadis had done well.

Ramirez walked up the final flight of internal stairs to the bridge level. The *Volkov* was more like a barge than a ship, originally designed to be towed from place to place by an ocean-going tug, but at the last minute, she had been fitted with two Azipod thrusters to help with tight quarters maneuvering.

The leader of the initial Abu Sayyaf boarding team was waiting for him. He was in his late teens with an ugly scar down his right cheek from a jungle firefight with a squad of American Rangers a year ago.

"It went well."

Ramirez looked around. The ship's officers were on the floor, their hands tied behind their backs. There was no need to check on them or even watch them. Each man was missing a large portion of his head or face as the result of what any medical examiner would antiseptically classify as "penetrating trauma." In this case, caused by a three-round burst from an MP-10's .45-caliber rounds.

Ramirez looked at the boy. "The engine room?"

"Secured. Two of my people are waiting for your call."

"Good. Head back to the boats and wait for them. It will be a half hour or so."

The young man smiled, pleased with the night's work so far, and left. Ramirez headed over to the rear-bridge windows. *Sea Titan* was visible just to the south, a spectral outline in the dark night. Ramirez pulled a radio from his back pocket and checked that it was on.

He keyed the microphone, "Ready."

PREBIN HEARD THE RADIO SPEAKER pop and Ramirez say "Ready." His heart started to pound, now that his time had finally come. Captain

Esteban had been standing next to Prebin, watching the *Volkov* through binoculars when Ramirez called in. Letting the binoculars hang from the neck strap, Esteban put his hand on Prebin's shoulder and looked him in the eyes.

"Remember, move quickly, but not hastily. The ship is secure and you will not be disturbed, but we cannot linger more than we must."

"Da, Captain. We will return soon." Prebin turned to leave, but the captain called after him.

"Remember! Enter from the stern only. Ramirez and his people are on guard outside of the reactor room. No one will pass them while you work."

Prebin waved to acknowledge the captain's words as he headed down the interior stairwell. In minutes, he and the other scientists were bouncing across the waves in the largest of the *Sea Titan*'s launches, the Abu Sayyaf helmsman steering straight toward the *Volkov*'s stern. Prebin smirked, remembering Esteban's last admonition. How could he enter any other part of the vessel but the stern? He was not piloting the launch.

A short while later, the larger launch was also moored with two magnetic grapnels to the stern of the *Volkov*, with the rubber-coated boarding ladder hooked over the ship's rail.

Prebin led his small team of five fellow scientists up the ladder and onto the stern deck. When they were all on board, Prebin unhooked the ladder from the ship's rail and dropped it back into the large launch. The helmsman was already removing the grapnels from the hull. The next stage of the operation required the launch to move to the midship portion of the starboard side and wait for Prebin and his men to finish their tasks on board.

Moving as quickly as he dared on the slick deck, Prebin led the men forward toward the rear access hatch. He was sweating in spite of the chilly temperature and the cold rain on his neck and face. As promised, the access hatch was open, and he could hear the whine of the powerful turbines inside.

The two reactors produced a combined seventy megawatts of electricity, all of which was sent via heavily insulated cables to the three oil production platforms. The platforms used the power to drill into the seabed nearly two miles down and bring crude oil to the surface.

Crude oil that also contributed to poisoning the world in so many ways, thought Prebin. The Americans had learned how dangerous these platforms were in the Gulf nearly twenty years ago, but the lure of hard currency and one's own dacha on the Black Sea had increased the corruption of his country's business and political leaders. Worse, they used a mobile nuclear plant to power the platforms.

Prebin led the way into the small "generator alley" on the *Volkov*, passing quickly through the boxy superstructure and reaching the decontamination area adjoining the rear of the reactor compartment. He and his men immediately removed their bulky rain gear and coats and donned the white protective overalls hanging from the pegs in the "clean" area of the decontamination chamber. One of his men handed out personal dosimeters from the small pile of spares kept on a shelf, and each man clipped one on his overalls pocket.

When properly protected, Prebin led the way over to the inner door that led to the reactor compartment. Strangely, the door was open, a major safety violation. No matter. The generator room was never manned when the turbines were running, and the door had likely been mistakenly left open by some errant crew member.

Heading into the reactor chamber, and waiting for the last man to close the inner door properly, Prebin surveyed the reactor. It was just as the smuggled plans described. Two KLT-40S reactors in a paired configuration, judging by the control rod assemblies and the sensor arrangements he could see over the shield wall. Such folly. They were the most dangerous things in the world, and the Russians put two of them on a barge that anyone could walk onto with little effort and some assistance, as he and his colleagues had just proved.

"Vasily," Prebin said in Russian, motioning to the man who had just locked the inner door. "Go to the controls and commence a manual shutdown. Move as quickly as you can."

"Da," Vasily responded and set off toward the emergency manual control console on the far side of the reactor vessel. It was closer to the crew quarters portion of the ship to facilitate easy access.

Prebin looked at the remaining men, and continued. "Come with me, tovarischi."

Prebin led the way to the left heading for the port side, away from the reactor vessels behind their shielding and toward the large, roll-up doors that bisected the main wall separating the reactor vessel on the starboard side from the portside storage area. Prebin knew from the plans that the dividing wall was 1 foot thick, and composed of two 1-inch outer sheets of lead, welded to an inner steel support framework. In spite of what lay on the other side of the dividing wall, the security precautions were ridiculously easy to bypass. Prebin simply walked over to one side of the roll-up door and pressed the green button marked "vverkh" in the small wall switch, and the door began rising.

Prebin and his colleagues wasted no time. Once the door was high enough to allow them to slip beneath it, they crawled under. Standing still, they looked at what lay before them.

The pool was about 2 meters deep, lit by the glow of underwater lights around the upper and lower edges. Within the pool, suspended in a purpose-built framework that kept them separated by at least four inches in every direction, were the spent nuclear fuel rods from the two KLT-40S reactors. Even in the pool, long removed from the operational conditions of the reactor, the rods gave off the faint blue glow of Cherenkov radiation as the residual, low-level nuclear reaction continued within each rod.

The water in the cooling pool circulated constantly. Pumps moved the water, warmed by the decay heat from the fuel rods, through a closed loop to a set of heat exchangers deep in the hull, where the surrounding cold ocean water cooled it before returning to the pool. The water from the pool never intermingled with the ocean water, and sensors in the pool sped up or slowed down the pumps to hold the water temperature at a steady 100 degrees Celsius.

During normal operation, a reactor's fuel rods would need to be changed annually as the heat and fission reactions within the reactor vessel changed the uranium or plutonium fuel in the fuel rods to less useful by-products. Once the fuel rods were used, only about 3 percent of the fissionable material was left, but it was enough for what Prebin needed.

"All right, tovarischi," Prebin said. "Quickly and carefully, just as we planned it. We only need three of them."

The men began to split into two-man teams as yellow warning lights started blinking from within the reactor compartment. Prebin looked back over his shoulder as he heard the steady two-tone alert for a reactor trip. Called a SCRAM at a boiling water reactor, this rapid, controlled shutdown of the fission reaction in the reactor vessel usually occurred in response to an emergency or fault condition. It was often effected by immediately sliding the neutron-absorbing control rods, composed of silver, indium, and cadmium, deep into the core of the pressurized water reactor very quickly.

As Prebin watched, Vasily trotted around the corner from the forward section of the compartment.

"Nicely done, Vasily."

The younger man smiled. "You know as well as I do that the SCRAM button is so recognizable that even a junior technician would know which one to push."

Prebin returned the smile. "Which is why I sent you, tovarisch Academician. You are the most junior of us." Vasily took the barb with his usual air of unruffled calm, and then made sure Professor Prebin knew he was not totally witless.

"I also vented the accumulators. The sodium polyborate solution will aid in the neutron absorption, and it will take them a few days to drain it off before they can start up again."

Prebin smiled wider at Vasily's riposte and clapped him on the shoulder. "Well done, Professor! Join Arkady."

Vasily moved off to join his partner Arkady for the next and more difficult part of the exercise. Prebin turned and watched as Pavel, his partner for this part of the exercise, prepared one of the three handling cradles made specifically to hold and transport the 2-meter-long fuel rods.

Prebin and his colleagues were intimately familiar with the dangers of what they were about to do. One mistake removing a rod, and they might achieve criticality if it drew too close to others in the pool, causing a low-level fission event that would irradiate all of them with hard gamma rays. While it wouldn't cause an explosion, they would all be dead in a week. Drop a rod while handling or moving it, and the brittle outer casing might shatter, spilling the "hot" fuel pellets all over the deck. This would vastly increase their exposure to more beta and gamma radiation than they had calculated would be safe.

Radiation exposure was all about time, distance, and shielding. They all knew that bulky radiation suits were not possible given the time constraints, so time and distance needed to be managed as carefully as possible. A short exposure time at close range was all they could afford and survive. As a group, they had decided that each pair of men would be completely responsible for the removal and handling of one rod. If a mistake was made, the others would move away as quickly as possible and avoid any contamination.

When Pavel had the cradle in position and its tie-down straps open, Prebin moved to the control console along the aft wall, where he would move the rods with a remote manipulator arm. The rods within the pool were always handled by the arm, from the time they were placed on the support structure in the pool immediately after removal from the shutdown reactor, until they were off-loaded to another boat and taken to shore for reprocessing. Because radioactivity decay levels were measured in tens of thousands of years for the rods at this stage, the only thing that mattered in the short term was the actual temperature of the rods.

Once removed from the reactor, the rods were relatively cool, only a couple of hundred degrees Celsius. As they sat in the cooling pool bleeding off residual heat, they would be periodically rotated in the framework by technicians so that the hottest fuel rods, most recently removed from the reactor, were stored at one end of the pool, and the coolest rods at the other. The coolest rods were always closest to the operator's console, partly out of the innate human desire to keep dangerous things far away, and partly for practical reasons.

After removal from an operating reactor, the rods usually took a year or more to cool to a temperature that made them safer to transport and work with, which was why Prebin and his colleagues knew immediately in their planning for tonight's operation that they would take only the coolest fuel rods. What they were doing was dangerous enough without adding to their burdens.

Activating the manipulator control console, Prebin slowly guided the grasping arm over the pool toward him, and following Pavel's hand signals, lowered the grasper into the pool above the first rod. Within seconds, he saw a signal light on the arm change from green to red, and he knew he had captured the rod. Slowly moving the control joystick up, he withdrew the rod until it dangled above the pool, a 2-meter, dull silver lance, dripping water.

Sliding the joystick to his left, Prebin moved the arm over the cradle then slowly lowered the rod as Pavel gently guided it in with his gloved hands. Once it was in place, Prebin moved to the cradle and helped Pavel quickly strap it in place. When it was secure, the two men slowly moved the cradle out of the cooling pool area, through the roll-up steel door, and around the reactor's shield wall. Then they angled left, rolling the cradle carefully toward the starboard wall.

Set into the starboard bulkhead before them were two heavy cargo doors. Pavel kept his hands on the cradle to ensure that it was stable and still, while Prebin stepped away to activate the cargo door controls. In seconds, the larger door was moving upward, sliding smoothly on its greased track. Designed for access to the reactor room to support heavy maintenance activities or fuel rod transfer, having the door open during power on operations of the reactor or at sea was strictly forbidden. Prebin wondered briefly what the remaining crew would think of the alarms that were blaring throughout the control room, then went back to his work, knowing that if there was a problem, Ramirez's men would handle it.

WORKING WITH HIS COLLEAGUE, PREBIN maneuvered the cradle to the gaping opening in the superstructure left by the open cargo door. Aligning the cradle to be parallel with the bow-to-stern axis of the *Volkov*, Prebin looked down to see the large launch waiting alongside as expected.

The helmsman had managed to attach four of the magnetic grapnels to the hull, using compressible rubber bumpers to keep the ship and the launch from rubbing together too violently in the sea state. The launch needed to be tightly bound to the *Volkov* now, and as stable as possible. The helmsman threw Pavel the ladder; he hooked it onto the lower lip of the cargo door, and then helped Prebin remove the tie-downs holding the fuel rod in place on the cradle.

When the rod was free, Prebin rotated the cradle 90 degrees so that the rod pointed out the cargo door, while Pavel climbed down the ladder into the large launch. Prebin reached down and lifted the end of the rod on the far end of the cradle. He could feel the residual heat through his gloves, estimating the temperature of the rod at about 150 degrees Celsius. Judging by that alone, this rod was probably removed from the reactor nearly a year ago, otherwise it would have been warmer. It was a pity the required equipment wasn't aboard the cargo ship for him to conduct the necessary assay of the fission by-products to be certain.

As Prebin lifted the fuel rod past the 45-degree point, he felt the weight shift, and called out to the men in the launch in English.

"Be ready!"

His concern was not justified. Both the helmsman and Pavel were prepared. Their hands caught the far end of the fuel rod as it began to slide forward into the launch, guiding it toward the front of the small boat's interior. Once it touched the fiberglass floor, Pavel and the helmsman maneuvered it toward the far right side and laid it flat, blocking it in place with five-pound sandbags from the small pile at the stern. One down.

Prebin turned and saw that his fellows had removed one more rod from the pool. Vasily and Arkady were pushing their cradle steadily across the deck toward the cargo door. Prebin pushed his now-empty cradle out of the way, and climbed down the boarding ladder into the launch. Once Vasily and Arkady were in position, Prebin and Pavel helped them load the second rod into the launch. After it was also shimmed in place with sandbags, Vasily and Arkady climbed down into the boat while Prebin and Pavel looked back in through the cargo door. Viktor and Leonid should have been pushing their rod in its cradle across the floor by now.

Prebin moved past his colleagues in the launch, careful not to disturb the fuel rods, and began to climb the ladder, calling out as he reached the top, "Viktor! Leonid! What's going on?"

As he was about to step back onto the *Volkov*'s deck, he heard the grinding roll of the cradle wheels on the steel deck coming closer, and caught sight of the two men rounding the corner of the shield wall.

Viktor called out, "We had a problem getting the grasper to release the rod once it was resting on the cradle."

"Nichevo," Prebin replied. "I'm glad it was nothing more. You left the door open, yes?"

"Da," replied Viktor. "As you directed, Professor."

While Prebin and the others helped Viktor and Leonid load the last rod into the launch, he wondered about the odd instructions from Captain Esteban and Ramirez. He would have thought they should have closed all the hatches and doors when they were done to conceal what they had accomplished from casual inspection. No matter. The boarding operation was their concern, not his. He had what he needed to prove himself to the scientific community now; that was all that mattered to him. His years of scientific exile would come to an end in a few short days.

With the fuel rods loaded and braced by the sandbags, and all the men back onboard the launch, Prebin looked at the helmsman and gestured away from the *Volkov*, back in the direction they had come. The helmsman looked at him briefly with seeming indifference before making a gesture toward the lines holding the launch tethered to the *Volkov*.

Prebin cursed himself for a fool. "Comrades," he addressed the men closest to the lines, "pull in the grapnels. It's time to return to the *Sea Titan*."

When they cleared the lines and removed the grapnels from the hull, the helmsman engaged the propeller. Once she was clear of the *Volkov*, the launch pulled smoothly away, heading not in the direction they had come, but south toward the open ocean.

Prebin shot a surprised look at the helmsman, having expected him to guide them back the way they came. He was about to protest when he saw the looming bulk of the *Sea Titan* appear through the steady rain, and the helmsman's smug expression as he looked back over his shoulder.

Now that he had proved to Prebin that he knew his job, the helmsman had another task to perform. The launch was approaching the davit lines along *Sea Titan*'s port side, so he turned the wheel sharply and killed the engine. *Sea Titan* was stopped nearly dead in the water, and the launch's forward momentum was enough to hold it in place alongside, while the nearest of Prebin's colleagues reattached the davit lines to the fore and aft anchor points on the topline of the launch.

When they were secure, the helmsman looked up and waved at the seaman watching from the rail, five stories up. Excess radio transmissions now, this close to completing the mission, might alert the nearby oil rigs. The davit lines took the strain of the launch's weight easily. A few minutes later, the launch was locked in place.

Captain Esteban looked down from the portside bridge wing and watched as Prebin and his men began to unload the fuel rods onto individual dollies and guide them below deck to the makeshift machine shop. Allah be praised. He surely had provided for them tonight. Only one last thing to do. He reached for his radio.

"Allahu Akbar," he said clearly.

Aboard the *Volkov*, Ramirez heard the words of praise and acted. He began to power up the two Azipod thrusters beneath the hull, and then activated the internal public address system.

"Anchor and Engine room details! Carry out your final orders and return to the boats now!"

Ramirez looked at his watch and waited. They had no more than five minutes. At the two-minute point, he could see the bright, steady flares from the bow and stern anchor points as the thermite that was wrapped around the thick anchor chains melted and burned its way through the steel links, cutting the *Volkov* free of her anchors.

When the time was up, Ramirez ran the throttles on the two Azipods to full power and locked them in position. He took one last look around the wheelhouse, smiling at the sight of the bodies, closed and locked the hatch behind him, and then headed back down the internal stairway to the first deck and forward to the bow.

He saw two of his men moving quickly toward the bow, their backpacks noticeably absent. Good. Ramirez reached the last hatch and ducked through it, then headed to the boarding ladder and clambered down into the launch. The other boats were already gone. The *Volkov* was moving, her Azipods finally overcoming her 21,000-ton inertia, and Ramirez had no desire to follow her to her next destination.

"Hurry," he admonished the men working on the magnetic grapnels. He checked his watch. Only three more minutes. The last grapnel came free and the helmsman gunned the launch's motor. They sped through the rain to the southeast in the wake of the other boats, heading for the *Sea Titan*. Ramirez looked back and watched as the launch cleared the *Volkov*'s line of advance. The *Volkov* was not moving at more than five knots, and her Azipods alone could move her at only about eight knots, but he felt better knowing that any possibility of a collision was removed.

Suddenly, Ramirez heard a brief rumble from the direction of the *Volkov*. He kept his eyes on her, trusting the helmsman to find the *Sea Titan* in the weather. They were 200 yards away from the *Volkov* now and that distance was growing. He had expected more when the charges had gone off, but he surmised they were too deep in the hull for that. There. He could see it now.

The *Volkov*'s bow had begun to pitch down, ever so slightly. He looked back toward the bow of the launch and saw the *Sea Titan* before them. She had moved east to clear a path for the doomed *Volkov*. The other launches were already being hauled aboard, even as the *Sea Titan* began to gather speed to clear the area.

Ramirez looked back to see that the *Volkov*'s bow was even deeper into the water now, the cold Pacific Ocean lapping at the edge of the forward deck. Thousands of gallons of water must have poured in through the gashes torn in the hull by the timed explosive charges. Between that, and the flooding caused by the jihadis opening all the sea cocks they could find, the *Volkov* had no chance of remaining afloat.

The bow was underwater now, the water beginning to rush in through the open forward hatch as the sea began to claim her latest ship. Ramirez could hear the hissing sound of escaping air as the water displaced the air inside the hull, causing it to rush out every opening. The stern had risen enough so that he could see the upper portion of the port side Azipod's blades churning through the water, driving the ship deeper into the ocean.

Suddenly, a great cracking sound echoed across the water as the power lines connecting the *Volkov* to the oil platforms snapped under the heavy strain. The lines, designed to break at specific connection points during rough weather, saved Ramirez and his men from having to sever them sooner, thus killing the power and alerting the platforms. The crew would have no doubt radioed the *Volkov*, or sent a team to investigate.

The *Volkov* was now one-third submerged, and the ocean was beginning to slide in over the lip of the open starboard side cargo door. The slow stream became an unstoppable flood as the ocean smothered the two KLT-40S reactors, mixed with the water from the cooling pool that had been partially emptied as the bow lanced deeper into the ocean.

Ramirez noticed that the *Volkov* was picking up speed, sinking faster now. The water had completely claimed the reactor room, and encroached on the generators. As it did, the main power panel was caressed by the cold ocean water and shorted out immediately. Every light on the *Volkov* went out, and with one last rush of air escaping the rear access hatch, the *Volkov*'s stern slid into the ocean. A few small, loose pieces of flotsam bobbed on the surface to mark the *Volkov*'s ocean grave, but they were only temporary, already drifting and tossed by the sea.

Ramirez turned back, surprised to see that the launch was already stowed at deck level on the *Sea Titan*, the other men in the launch also standing stock-still, watching the *Volkov*'s final death throes.

Addressing the men, he said, "All right. Let's get below decks, clean weapons, and get ready to repel boarders. Remember, we aren't safe for another two days."

The men rushed to obey, taking their gear and heading below decks for fresh ammunition, food, and hot coffee before they broke into three watches. The lucky ones would sleep, or at least try to while the adrenaline wore off. The unlucky ones would patrol the decks in the rain until they were sure the Russians were not pursuing them. As the men moved off, Ramirez looked up at the bridge wing and waved at the captain, who returned it jauntily.

Behind them, as the *Sea Titan* continued to slowly accelerate and move deeper into the Pacific Ocean, the *Volkov* was still sinking. Its 6-knot forward momentum had driven it far enough out to sea that it was diving toward the 6,000-meter-deep Kuril Trench. Once it was 100 feet down, a pressure switch near the top of the main mast released the emergency buoy.

The advanced electronics had already noted the failure of main power when the line that kept its lithium polymer batteries charged went dead. The external sensor at the top of its bubble-shaped fiberglass body was wet with salt water, and its internal pressure sensor told the minicomputer that it was 90 feet down and rising.

Once it breached the surface, the small whip antenna at the top of the bubble-shaped body began broadcasting the *Volkov*'s international identification number, a set of geo-coordinates obtained by the Russian Glonass GPS system, and the emergency code number for sinking.

Russian search planes would not reach the area for five more hours, and, finding no survivors and nothing but the constantly broadcasting beacon, could only circle until their fuel state dictated that they return home. It would take another ten hours before the first Russian naval vessel, the *Admiral Panteleyev*, an Udaloy I class anti-submarine vessel, arrived on the scene. By then, the *Sea Titan* was more than 260 miles away, and nothing could tie her to the *Volkov*'s fate.

CHAPTER 8

THIS WAS THE FIRST TIME they had all been together in nearly three months. Even after the attacks on the power infrastructure, they had refrained from meeting. Rahman thought it was good to finally have all his brothers in one place again, even if they were in the heart of the Great Satan.

They had entered the United States from Egypt on student visas nearly eight months ago, finding places to live in and around Frederick, Maryland. The visas had not been too difficult to acquire. A man in the Muslim Brotherhood in Egypt who lost his son to an Israeli helicopter strike on a rocket-assembly house in Gaza was happy to provide them with authentic Egyptian passports and verification of their undergraduate studies at the University of Cairo.

Once they had applied for the F-1 visa at the new U.S. Embassy in downtown Cairo, all they had to do was wait a few weeks and they could fly to Baltimore. They had even obtained approval from the U.S. Citizenship and Immigration Services to work in specialties related to their undergraduate studies to earn money. Rahman was proud of that. The Americans were kind enough to let him come to their country, get an education at one of their schools, and earn a living while he and his brothers planned to carry forward the jihad. That women were permitted in classes with men, and that most dressed like common whores, would be addressed after this idolatrous country was brought under Sharia law.

Rahman and his friends even gave some of the money they earned to the imam at the local mosque to help the less fortunate, in keeping with the requirement of Zakat. They had discussed with the imam the struggle of their Palestinian brothers and sisters to get a better sense of his perspective, but he was one of the weak ones. He admonished them to help Islam and those who shared it by practicing their faith peacefully and showing kindness within the community to all the Ahl al-Kitab. The foolish imam had even condemned the recent car bombings in San Antonio, and the many acts of martyrdom in Afghanistan, Iraq, and Israel against the occupiers. "It is not the true way of Islam," he had said.

Even worse, the other Muslim men Rahman spoke to before and after Friday prayers felt the same way. He would not approach the men actually born in this vile country, of course; there was too much risk in that. He did speak to several of the Pakistanis, some of the Indians, and even a few of the Egyptian men who had emigrated here to find a better life for themselves and their children; but none were interested or understood Islam enough to choose the proper path. All seemed remarkably enamored with the life they had found in this country, perhaps seduced by Satan himself. Some even had sons serving in the military of this unholy nation and claimed to be proud of their service, speaking of how their children had been accepted and respected by their fellow soldiers.

Rahman could not understand that. This country killed thousands in the name of either the "war against extremism" or the "war on terror," which in reality was a war against Islam. Why could they not see it as clearly as he could? Fortunately, he was wiser than they were, and he and his friends would fight back. In fact, their role in the newest action in the war against the Great Satan would start tonight.

Rahman had checked the e-mail account two days ago. The power outage would have made that problematic, but the small generator he bought from Home Depot after Abdul's warning several weeks ago was coming in handy. He even let a few of his neighbors recharge their cell phones and laptops from it, and nearly all of them had given him a few dollars to pay for more fuel to run it. The hugely inflated price of gas was more financially burdensome than he would have preferred, but he did not run the generator every night. He was not nearly as soft as the infidels around him, who used theirs constantly.

After deleting Abdul's e-mail, he went to the free e-mail provider Abdul always used, logged in to the account, and retrieved the scans of all the hand-drawn diagrams left in the draft e-mail box for him. The photos Abdul left for him on Google Earth and the diagrams of the targets would be very useful.

Rahman said a brief prayer to Allah for Abdul. He had never met the man, but he admired his courage to roam widely in this hostile country and gather information. In that, he was as much a part of the jihad as Rahman and his friends were.

Rahman had drawn all the blinds on the first floor of his tiny, wood-and-brick town house in Frederick. They shielded him and his two friends from the prying eyes of his American neighbors as they headed out to work in the early morning darkness, the little generator chugging away just outside the back door. They had only one light to work with, and Rahman's laptop for Internet research, but it would do.

Rahman looked over the hand-drawn diagrams again, before glancing back to his two fellow jihadis. They sipped orange juice as they studied the photographs and drawings.

"We have been given worthy targets, have we not, my brothers?" he asked in Arabic, the only language suitable for this conversation.

Both men nodded, smiling at their good fortune. Amari, his dark brown eyes and strong features reflecting his Pakistani heritage, spoke eagerly. "Yes, thanks be to Allah. These are targets worthy of our skill."

"We will need everyone for these," Nahas chimed in, motioning to one of the diagrams, his angular features and brown skin showing the near-perpetual five o'clock shadow of his Arabian ancestors. "This one is heavily defended."

Rahman agreed. "Yes, but the other two should be easy to destroy. If each group uses the less obvious routes we've looked at, the infidels will not know what hit them, and our force will be preserved for the last."

"Yes," Nahas replied, "I also like the idea of keeping your team in reserve in case we run into trouble."

"But what of Abdul?" Amari asked. "He thinks the primary target is this one, yet you propose we strike the other two first. If they are in flames, and the infidels are wary, that will make attacking the last, most heavily defended target more difficult."

Rahman shook his head. "No. The confusion caused by the nearby attacks will distract them, aiding us. That will make hitting the primary target much easier."

Amari was unconvinced. "I'm not sure, my brother. I think we must remain flexible, and alter our plan on-site if needed."

Rahman was always grateful for Amari's tactical insight. He had proven himself better at such things in the Yemeni training camps. "Yes. We'll need radios."

Nahas nodded. "We have them in the storage sheds at the place off Route 40. I'll lay out the equipment for each team tonight after work. One rifle, one pistol, and the explosives." Looking at Amari, he asked, "Can Sarraf meet me there tonight? He'll need to set up the charges."

"Yes. I'll speak to him after class this afternoon."

"Good," Nahas replied. "I'll give each team member a similar load-out. One G3 assault rifle and four spare twenty-round magazines, and one Glock 23 pistol and two spare magazines. That's one-hundred rounds for each assault rifle and thirty-nine rounds for each pistol."

"Excellent," admired Rahman, "that should be more than enough. Remind your men to fire in semiautomatic or three-round bursts only. Getting more ammunition from Windmere will be difficult now that the infidels are more alert. I'm still waiting on word from our contact to arrange a pickup for last week's delivery."

He checked his watch. "It's getting late. We don't want any mistakes now. Contact your people today. Tell them to be ready, but no specifics yet. Tonight and tomorrow night, we'll spend more time studying the pictures and Google Earth images and refine this plan a little more."

"THAT'S BETTER." THOMPSON WAS TALKING to herself while she fiddled with the camera controls, adjusting the clarity of the image in front of her. The RQ-4 Global Hawk was airborne again, this time en route from its home base—Beale Air Force Base in California—to Joint Base Andrews, just east of Washington, D.C. The launch-and-recovery pilots were probably sipping coffee now, feet up on their consoles and bullshitting, she thought.

Once the Hawk was airborne, the pilots relinquished command of the flight controls to the onboard computer, and the Hawk followed a programmed flight path to its destination. Right now, Thompson's console showed the UAV at 21,000 feet, climbing at a steady 280 knots. The Hawk was programmed to make a slow loop over San Francisco to the west, and then fly south to Los Angeles and San Diego before heading east for Joint Base Andrews, more than 2,000 miles away.

It was another chance to work with the onboard sensor suite and improve her familiarity with it. She had used the extra day off, as Cain had suggested, to get some more sleep. Jerry had been sweet enough to give her a massage that night after Jeff was asleep, wanting to make up for their argument the previous night. His hands had relaxed and excited her, and she made sure he knew all was forgiven. She had nodded off in his arms afterward, and did not even wake when he carried her from the couch to their bed and covered her with the blankets. The extra sleep had improved her mood and her outlook a little. And although the voice still accused her when she was not busy, she now had a new distraction to keep her occupied.

"How's it going?" asked Cain.

Thompson started out of her chair, surprised by his unexpected presence behind her.

Cain put his hand on her shoulder. "Sorry, I didn't mean to make you jump."

"It's all right, David. I just didn't know you were behind me."

Cain smiled as he nodded toward the screen. "Enjoying the new toy?"

"Oh, yes," she grinned like a child ready to play a prank on one of her friends in grade school. "The Hawk is incredible. The cameras and synthetic radar are fantastic. Look."

Cain leaned in over her shoulder and looked at the upper right display where the image from the Hawk's electro-optical video camera burned. Thompson zoomed in on the image to a strip of sand along a shore containing a long line of people. Studying the image, Cain could see that they were running along the beach in white shirts and dark pants.

As he watched, Thompson moved the mouse to slew the camera a little to the left, so that the crosshairs on the image centered themselves over the lead person in the group, then she left-clicked to steady the image.

"I'm locked onto him now. The camera will track him automatically, based on the size and shape of the object I locked."

"That's nice, but the image quality isn't any better than what we'd see from a Reaper," Cain opined.

"You think so?" Her sly grin firmly in place now that she had the target of her prank hooked, she zoomed in even more until the runner appeared to be about 20 feet away. He was a young man, clean shaven, hair shorn to stubble, wearing camouflage pants, combat boots, and a white T-shirt with the name LEGG written on it in black, block letters.

"Whoa!" said Cain, leaning back to consider the image.

"Nice, eh?" Thompson asked.

"It's fantastic. Look at the clarity. I can even see the sweat. What the hell are we watching, anyway?"

Emily was pleased with herself. "It's a beach near the Naval Amphibious Base in Coronado, California. Looks like the SEAL trainees are out for a run today."

"Nice." Then he had a horrible thought. "The recorders aren't running, are they?"

"No, sir. That would be illegal. I checked and then double-checked the recorders before I started. They don't have DVDs in them, and I inhibited the record function in the software."

Cain let out a long breath of relief. "Good. Keep working with it. I've got a few things to do."

Cain headed back to his desk and sat down to break the screen lock on his computer. He glanced over at Emily to see that she was still engrossed in the Global Hawk's sensor systems. She looked a lot better than she had the other day. Makeup, hair in place, no bags under her eyes, and enthusiastic about her work. Hopefully she had turned a corner and was past whatever was bothering her. Time would tell.

In the meantime, he needed to catch up on his usual day's reading. He had interrupted it to see if Emily was okay without trying to seem overbearing. In his early career as an intelligence analyst, Cain always felt it was important to stay informed and aware of various world events. Even though he had moved on to being a manager, some professional habits would never go away.

Bringing up INTELINK, he quickly went through the daily intelligence update pages: the CIA's Daily Intelligence WIRE, the DIA's Overnight Developments, and NSA's Windshield. Each page covered a wide variety of topics and global hotspots, often in great detail, with graphic products, all available imagery, and even hyperlinks to all the source material if he wanted a more in-depth look at the actual source reporting. Even the president did not have this kind of access, primarily because he never had the time to really dig into all of this and digest it. His national security team did that for him, as did the intelligence officers standing watch in the White House Situation Room.

Any events or subjects of specific interest to the president and his Cabinet officers were identified by the principals during their daily intelligence and national security briefings. Each item was then painstakingly researched by the CIA-led President's Daily Briefing staff, supported by the professionals in the agencies that specialized in those geographical areas or subjects of interest. Each topic's briefing was written and rewritten at least six times at six different levels within each agency before being approved by the senior leaders of the "Big 3" agencies for presentation. At that point, the presidential briefers took over. Up at 2 A.M. most days, the officers of the presidential briefing team met by 4 A.M. and were on the way to brief their "principals" no later than 5 A.M., with short vignettes loaded onto tablet computers and sometimes with one or two experts in tow from the various intelligence community agencies.

The briefers themselves were a select group of senior intelligence professionals, not political appointees, drawn from across the intelligence community. It was a special-duty assignment, and the briefers each dealt specifically with only one principal. The CIA's briefer nearly always briefed the president; the NSA's briefer usually dealt directly with the Secretary of Defense, but depending on the SECDEF's preference, the briefer could be a DIA officer. The rest of the briefers handled the Cabinet secretaries for each of their departments or agencies.

By nine in the morning, all the briefers and the support staff would gather in their common office in the Pentagon for the "hot wash." The larger group would cover what items the principals were interested in for the next day, what went well during that morning's brief, and what went poorly, although that was a rare occurrence.

Afterward, the staff would withdraw, and the principal briefers would have a private session to discuss anything their principal may have mentioned regarding disagreements between the cabinet secretaries, any direct and candid feedback from the principal, or opinions they may have shared. Such details were not for the junior staff members and were held in confidence by the senior professionals, while also being used to keep themselves informed and aware of the "tone and tenor" of the current crop of politicians in temporary custody of the U.S. government.

Cain had spent a year on the presidential briefing team, and as much of an invaluable experience as it was, he did not miss it. He was an analyst at heart, and he enjoyed having the time during his duty day to troll the available summary and other reporting from the agencies and dig in to any item of interest that caught his eye. As usual, he saved the DIA's J2 briefing for last.

The intelligence summary from the DIA's Joint Intelligence Staff, it was a short set of PowerPoint slides intended for rapid consumption by senior staff officers and the Joint Chiefs of Staff at the Pentagon. There was usually one slide for each major event or subject of interest, usually keyed to the current world situation. Each of the slides was classified TOP SECRET//SPECIAL INTELLIGENCE as a starting point, and most included intelligence information from three or four different security compartments. The three- and four-star flag officers sometimes read the briefing during the short ride in their official cars from Fort McNair to the Pentagon, or with the first cup of morning coffee at their desks before their first appointment.

The slides for today's briefing were predominately routine—military forces in various parts of the world conducting exercises, more outlandish statements by the North Korean regime, and continued Palestinian efforts to pretend Israel did not exist. At the end of the briefing were the usual "also happened" minor items, grouped in two and sometimes three per slide, because they were not important enough to have an entire slide dedicated to them.

One item did stick out this morning, captured entirely from OSINT, which the source said was a translation of a Russian news broadcast. The Russians were conducting a search and rescue operation in the North Pacific. A floating nuclear power station supplying power for three deep-ocean oil production platforms had apparently sunk. The Russians had aircraft and ships in the area, and the search was continuing. In the meantime, the crews of the oil platforms were being evacuated as a precaution.

Cain mentally tagged that as an item of interest, purely out of curiosity. The sinking of a floating nuclear power plant could have a serious environmental impact, and like any good analyst, he wanted to keep a weather eye on things that were out of the ordinary. You never knew when they might blow up in your face.

MATHEWS STIFLED A YAWN AS he stretched his arms and legs in the fresh air outside the hangar. It was another bright, sunny day on the East Coast. Still cold as hell, but sunny at least. So far, it had been another Sierra Square, Delta Square day. Up in the morning with his team at 6 A.M., eat a quick breakfast at the Joint Base Andrews dining hall, grab their weapons and armor, and pile into the Chevy Suburbans for the hour-long ride to Quantico. The FBI snipers were still losing to his sniper team, but by a lot less now. Those FBI guys had taken their losses seriously and put in long afternoons practicing to make up for it.

Afternoons back at the hangar on Joint Base Andrews were usually pretty tame. The men of Wraith Team Four told a lot of war stories from their time in the individual service's special operations schools while they cleaned weapons, loaded fresh magazines, and performed routine maintenance on some of the gear in the C-17.

Their massive C-17 Globemaster III cargo plane barely fit inside the hangar they were using as their informal operations center on the base. Its three-story-high tail stuck out of the hangar doors, preventing them from being fully closed. The rest of the aircraft fit very snugly inside, and the hangar provided plenty of cover from prying eyes. The only thing visually odd, beyond the massive tail sticking out, was the small VSAT antenna that sat on the concrete apron, just outside the doors. Pointed toward the southern horizon, it was boresighted on one of the latest generation of military communications satellites, and provided Mathews and Team Four with the encrypted voice and data links they needed. The VSAT terminal inside the hangar, connected to the antenna by an innocuous black cable, allowed them to stay in touch with the Wraith

Base in the southwestern U.S., and keep one of their high-performance laptops connected to INTELINK for intelligence updates.

Suddenly, the secure cell phone in Mathews' back pocket started to vibrate. He looked around quickly as he fished it out. While there was some activity on the far side of the parking apron, there was not a single human being closer than 200 yards from him.

The phone looked like the twelfth-generation iPhone, but it had been bought by the DoD under a special arrangement with Apple's government contracting division. The phones were bought in blocks of two to three hundred, each phone being picked at random out of the shipping cases after they entered the U.S. at an intermediate shipment point. This random selection guaranteed that the DoD ended up with a set of phones whose electronic identification numbers were never sequential and prevented any attempt by the manufacturer to implant phones used by the DoD with covert tracking or intercept technology. The phones were made in China, after all.

The phones were then sent to the NSA, where the wizards of secure communications examined them electronically to ensure that they really were unmodified, and then loaded a unique application onto them. The application provided a set of unique encryption variables that leveraged the existing encryption hardware already built into the phone. As long as the owner enabled the encryption with his or her personal identification number, and called, or were called by, an STE, or similarly set-up cell phone, the call was secured by a practically unbreakable chained set of AES 256-bit encryption keys.

Mathews looked at the flexible display on the phone and saw, "Incoming Secure Call" across the display. He swiped his finger across the display to unlock the phone and tapped in his eight-digit personal code. The display changed to "Going Secure," and he put the phone to his ear.

A few seconds later, he heard the application's sexy female voice say, "Line is secure. Top Secret Special Intelligence," and then the familiar side tone of a connected call.

"Lieutenant Mathews," he said into the phone.

"Simon here," was the reply.

"Yes, Colonel. How can I help you, sir?"

"How are things with you and your team, Mathews?"

"Good, sir. We're keeping qual'd up and the base's emergency generators run for a few hours every night so we can catch the news and a movie or two on the flatscreen TV in the visiting officer's quarters. We even get hot showers in the base gym." In truth, it was pretty austere, but as Mathews had reminded his men and the support team, it was better than what most of their fellow citizens in the Mid-Atlantic were able to enjoy. He had not heard a single complaint yet, and morale was pretty high.

"The biggest problem is keeping the cell phones charged. I've got a few people with family in New England and they want to call and check on them pretty regularly."

"I understand. I'm glad you and your people are keeping things in perspective. I've got orders for you."

"Ready to copy, sir."

"Take your team, comm gear, and the standard weapons load-out and head to the Calvert Cliffs Nuclear Power Station. The president has issued orders to assume federal control over some of the National Guard military police units and station them at major power plants to help secure the vital components of the power infrastructure."

What the hell? "Sir, we're a special operations team. What's our mission if the Guard is already on sentry duty?"

Colonel Simon heard the derision in the young man's voice, but at least he framed the question the right way: "Give me a mission sir . . ."

"These are guardsmen, Lieutenant. They are weekend warriors patriotic enough to serve their country, but they can be a little too 'civilian casual' about that duty. I want you to go there and instill some fear of the enemy in them, and challenge them to step up to your level. You've seen the intelligence briefings on terrorist tactics, and I think what you and your people have been doing out at Quantico shows that you have the right attitude for this job. There is no way they can reach your level of training and capability over a couple of days, but I want you to give it a shot and see how it works. Do you understand?"

Mathews considered the orders. It made sense. They wouldn't spend as much time in the Kill House doing live fire exercises, but they should be able to come up with some good drills in the environment. Hell, they might get called on to assault a nuclear power plant in some faraway land and secure it. With a wry smile, Mathews also realized that working with the on-site security folks and learning what not to shoot at in that kind of an environment would also be good.

"Yes, sir. I do. I think we can accomplish that mission, and leverage it for some good training as well."

"Good," replied Colonel Simon.

"Anything else, sir?"

"No, just keep sending in those daily reports. Get there as quickly as you can and get set up. A military police platoon from the Maryland 58th Troop Command is already on-site. Link up with a Lieutenant Allen Corvin when you arrive."

"Yes, sir."

"Out here."

The connection dropped out, and Mathews heard the woman's voice say, "Call Terminated."

Mathews headed back into the hangar and started issuing orders. An hour later, Wraith Team Four was loaded into five black Chevy Suburbans along with their weapons, armor, personal gear, and the spare VSAT terminal and a ruggedized laptop. The three heavy-duty vehicles headed out the Joint Base Andrews main gate and headed north toward Upper Marlboro. Forty minutes later, the convoy turned south on Route 4. The main gate of the Calvert Cliffs Nuclear Power Station was an hour away.

CHAPTER 9

SADDAM STRETCHED UNDER THE LIGHT sheet, the cool, dry air of Bani Hawat wafting through the open window, carrying with it the sounds of a quiet early morning. Saddam lay on the thin mattress of a small twin bed along the wall beneath the window. The room was spartan, with only a small wardrobe, a night table next to his bed, and a single lightbulb suspended from the ceiling.

The rest of the house was just as modest—a one-story brown sandstone with running water, and as clean as six single men would ever need or want it to be. The other five men had spread themselves throughout the house to sleep. There were only four bedrooms, and by unspoken agreement, the two youngest of the group were sleeping on the floor in the small common room. Having only one bathroom might prove difficult, but they would have to manage.

The increasing sound of powerful jet engines invaded his thoughts, and he looked toward the partially open window. He could just barely see the stark white fuselage of a four-engine aircraft climbing over the low rooftops through the curtains drifting in the cool breeze. He was surprised he had fallen asleep so quickly last night with the constant air traffic. He glanced over to the night table where only a few hours ago he had placed his wallet and his new Moroccan passport before stripping to his shorts and climbing, exhausted, into bed. Just after he had settled himself beneath the sheets, another aircraft had taken off from

El Rahaba Airport, the bright beams of its lights spearing the night sky as the sound of its engines thundered overhead. He had expected to be kept awake by the regular takeoffs, but he was obviously more tired than he thought.

Saddam propped himself up on one arm and reached for the passport, flipping it open to see his face on the photograph, in part to convince himself he was really here, ready to begin training for jihad. Even clean shaven, the face in the photograph was familiar, but the borrowed white shirt and tie were odd. It was the same shirt and tie that each of them had worn for their passport photographs, used to make them appear, at least on superficial inspection, well-groomed young men, but no one in immigration in Paris or Rome was interested in shirts and ties, only faces.

Saddam was surprised how easy it was to come to America. The imam's "reliable" travel agent had arranged everything in Paris. He had bought the plane tickets with what he had called a "clean" American Express card, thinking it was enormously funny that the travel arrangements for a group of new jihadis was paid for with it. The imam had checked their bags before driving them to Charles de Gaulle Airport, to be certain that security would not find anything of concern, and wished his new brothers well on their long trip.

Even entering this country was absurdly easy. Immigration and customs officers at the El Rahaba Airport seemed more interested in looking for alcohol and pornography than they did questioning newcomers to their country. Saddam wondered if some of them were sympathetic to the jihad, but there was no way of knowing.

Saddam tossed the passport back on the table and grabbed his wallet. There was nothing in it but the 200 euros that the imam had given him, "a gift from your friend Aziz," he had said, but it was more money than he had ever had in his life. Seeing it still in his wallet further confirmed that his new life was very real.

He rose and went to the small wardrobe. There were four pairs of colored T-shirts and tan cargo pants, along with underwear, socks, and boots. He gathered fresh clothes, and then peeked out the door of the small room. The hallway was empty, and the door to the small bathroom open. He crossed quickly to the bathroom door, shut it, then showered and dressed quickly. The others would be up soon, and he wanted to be ready for whatever happened next.

By the time he was finished, two of the other men were up, waiting for the bathroom. While they cleaned up, Saddam thought he would go outside to look at his new surroundings in the daylight. The house, set on a wide dirt path he could see tire tracks on, was in the midst of a small group of houses, all of similar construction. The bright sun was warm on his face and bare arms, chasing away the chill of the night, and the sounds of the surrounding buildings coming alive in the morning reached his ears. He could hear distant snatches of Arabic here and there among them, but nothing was intelligible.

He looked at the sun and ashamedly remembered he had not prayed last night before bed or this morning. He silently begged Allah's forgiveness and resolved to pray twice at the midday call and the evening prayer to make amends, should his training allow.

Behind him, he heard the others leave the house and turned around. The youngest, and most eager, a man named Omer, spoke to him.

"Shall we go now, Saddam?"

The others looked at Saddam expectantly. Apparently, he had been made de facto leader within their group. Perhaps because he alone spoke to Aziz?

"Na'am, my brothers." They all knew where they were to go, but it made sense for someone to lead the way.

Saddam headed north through the small maze of alleyways between the houses and then across a much wider, paved road that bisected Bani Hawat, into a group of houses that were much more dilapidated than any he had seen so far. They all were a uniform sandstone, but with shattered windows, missing doors, and damaged roofs. Saddam thought they were all abandoned, and with a quick peek into one or two as they walked along, his suspicions were confirmed.

At last, they came to an open space in the center of the cluster of houses that was supposed to have been an open-air park. There were barren areas that should have held grass for children's play areas, low sandstone walls surrounding them, split by bricked paths with wooden-and-concrete benches every 20 meters. Across from the park, in the middle of a row of houses facing them, a man sat on the steps of a low, two-story sandstone house that looked just as abandoned as the ones on either side of it.

Saddam led the group across the park toward the man. As they approached, he saw the man studying them with obvious distaste.

"As-salaam 'alaikum," Saddam greeted him. "We were sent by Imam Assaf to study the ways of Allah's fury." Saddam held the older man's gaze as he spoke the code phrase Abdel had shared with them. The man had skin darkened by the sun, close-cropped black hair, and dark eyes hidden under thick brows. He wore the same boots and cargo pants as the six of them and a black T-shirt. The man's upper body was lean but muscular, the flecks of silver at his temples lending him an air of long experience. Strangely, he was clean shaven. As he rose, Saddam fought the urge to take an involuntary step backward.

"I am Hazar. I see that Imam Assaf continues to send me children." His Arabic was simple and direct, not the artful and measured phrasing of a scholar or university-educated man. Hazar continued to study them, gratified that he was seeing uncertainty and even fear in at least two pairs of eyes.

Saddam watched Hazar as his eyes roved over them. "Sayyid—"

"Do not call me that!" Hazar bellowed, taking a step forward toward Saddam. This time Saddam did step back.

"I am your instructor in the ways of Allah's might and the techniques of jihad. You will obey me, or I will send you to Paradise myself. I serve those greater than I, as do you. You will call me Hazar and nothing else." Hazar paused and looked at each of them in turn, seeming to wait and almost hope for one of them to disagree with him. Saddam and his fellows wisely chose silence.

"In time, if you learn well, I will be pleased to call you 'brother' and walk into battle with you. For now, you have much to learn." Hazar walked toward them, and the six young men parted quickly to allow him a clear path. As he moved past them, Saddam saw the grip of a holstered pistol in the small of his back.

Hazar turned back to them and gestured to his left. "Do you see the small stakes in the ground with the white strips of cloth tied to them?" Each man nodded, not daring to speak.

"Your first lesson. The stakes form a path through the abandoned houses that surround the park. You will run this path until I tell you to stop. Run. Now!" With the last word, he moved toward them, and almost without thinking, Saddam began to run toward the first stake.

Twenty minutes and six complete circuits later, Hazar stood before them on the path, his hands raised for them to stop.

The younger men, strung out in a sweaty line, all stopped short of Hazar on the path, chests heaving and sweat streaming from every pore. Saddam's breath came in ragged gasps. He was not the first to reach the point where Hazar stopped them, but he was not the last, either.

"Do not sit down," Hazar admonished two of the men who had begun to drift toward the steps Hazar sat on when they first encountered him.

"Walk. And keep walking until your breathing is normal again." They all obeyed. In a few minutes, Saddam was breathing close to normal, feeling the sun's rays beat down on him even as the cool breeze evaporated his sweat.

Hazar surveyed them. "All right, into the house. It is time for your next lesson."

Hazar led the way into the house and climbed the central wooden staircase to the second floor. He entered the master bedroom and motioned them to sit.

Simple folding chairs sat in a semicircle around a metal folding table. On the table was a laptop computer. It was an old Toshiba, with a 17-inch color screen, and Hazar touched the power button to boot it up as the six young men collapsed into the chairs.

While the laptop booted, Hazar left the room and returned a few moments later carrying a white ice chest. Placing it on the floor, he opened it and gave each man a liter bottle of water and an apple, saying, "Breakfast."

Saddam accepted his water bottle and apple. "Shokran. Might we shower, Hazar?" He hated being dirty and sweaty. Hazar's glare made the answer clear before his words did.

"Sweat now, or you will sweat more when you face the infidels in combat."

Saddam grimaced but held his tongue, instead choosing to rub the ice-cold plastic bottle along his forehead and against the back of his neck before taking a long pull from it.

After closing the ice chest, Hazar adjusted the laptop to ensure that the screen faced them, and then addressed them as they ate and drank.

"You have chosen to aid us in the fight against Allah's enemies. You must know the nature of our enemies and the evil they purvey on this earth. Only then will you understand the infidels well enough to fight them. Watch and learn."

Saddam watched as Hazar tapped on the touch pad, and a video began to play. This one was worse than those Imam Abdel had shown him. He had never seen a documentary like this before, made by an anonymous Palestinian who called himself Allah's Servant. He detailed the numerous Israeli atrocities in the occupied territories. The bombings, the rocket attacks, the secret nighttime raids by Israeli commandos that killed women and children sleeping in their beds. The images from inside the homes after the raids clearly showed the bloodstains on the walls, and the after-images of the rocket attacks from Israeli helicopters were shown in gruesome detail.

Saddam found the video heart-wrenching and horrifying until he noticed something odd. The woman screaming, "My children, my children!" in the aftermath of a rocket attack looked very similar to the woman saying, "They came like assassin's in the night" during the early portion of the film with the bloodstained walls. He wanted to ask Hazar to reverse the film so he could see it again, but noticed Hazar watching it intently and could not summon the courage to ask.

The narrator went on to say that the Israelis had attempted to hide these attacks from the world, that they went so far as to blame the Palestinian and Arab peoples for rocket attacks on Israeli cities and settlements, rocket attacks they claimed killed women and children. At the end, as uplifting verses from the Holy Qur'an played in the background, Allah's Servant called upon all able-bodied young men to defend their Arab brothers and join the fight against the Zionists and their Crusader allies.

As the first film faded from the laptop's screen, Hazar asked, "Do you see? Do you now truly see the injustices they inflict upon our Arab brothers?"

"Na'am," the other men replied as one. Then Hazar looked at Saddam directly. "Do you see?"

"Na'am, Hazar, I saw it." Thinking he must have been mistaken about the woman, he added, "It is truly horrible what they have done."

"Na'am," Hazar replied. "Yet there is still more." Hazar reached into the ice chest again and withdrew a small pile of cereal bars and handed them around, then keyed the laptop again.

Saddam bit into the bar hungrily as the second video started. This one was made by an Iraqi and detailed the horrors inflicted on his people by the American occupiers during their false war there. The narrator did not identify himself in this one, but Saddam thought the images and music were stirring.

The narrator spoke of how the Americans raped the homes of innocent men, turning their families out into the streets and treating their women and children without respect, always claiming to be looking for "insurgents" and aided by traitors to Islam and the Iraqi people. The Iraqis fought back successfully with improvised explosive devices. There were many video clips displaying great columns of American armored vehicles traveling down the roads and then suddenly vanishing in a great cloud of smoke and fire as they passed near roadside bombs, the calls of "Allah Akbar" heard clearly from the jihadi videographers a few hundred yards away.

The next video was about Afghanistan, and how the CIA propped up the puppet government as it continued its war against Islam by providing the Afghani president with huge sums of cash to buy influence and spread corruption amongst the various tribal chiefs. How the terrorist forces of the United States, the so-called Special Operations Forces, moved around like ghosts, sneaking into villages at night to rape the women and kill the men and children. How their soulless machines, the drones, visited death on innocent families, killing hundreds at what the U.S. described as terrorist camps and meetings in villages, but what were in fact weddings and peaceful family gatherings to celebrate birthdays and Islamic Holy Days.

Saddam watched it all, amazed that he had never heard any of this on the more mainstream news media in Morocco or in France. That such things could be hidden from the world seemed impossible, but the proof was right there in front of his eyes. How could this be? How could he help stop it?

Hazar brought up one more video for them, and each man leaned forward, craning to get a closer look at the screen. A professor from Tehran University, an elegantly dressed and obviously well-educated and pious man, narrated this video. He spoke calmly and proudly of the many artistic, cultural, and scientific contributions made during the time of the Islamic Caliphate.

He talked about the preservation of texts from classical antiquity in the "House of Wisdom" in Baghdad, where thousands of manuscripts existed in the ninth century. He explained how the Islamic Caliphate and its people had given the world algebra and advanced medical knowledge, and provided the surgical guide used in European medical schools for 600 years. He went on to speak of how Islamic men laid the foundation for chemistry in Europe with the earliest works on alchemy and chemistry, and offered an understanding of the heavens that led to later advances in space science.

The professor then spoke of the great Pakistani scientist Ahmad Khan, who helped Iran develop its nuclear power research efforts, in spite of the Western world's false attempts to portray those efforts as intending to develop nuclear weapons. He laid out the lies spoken against Khan by the United States and other Western powers, and talked about the just verdict rendered by the Pakistani Supreme Court, absolving Khan of any wrongdoing and declaring him a free citizen of Pakistan, allowing him to come and go as he wished.

The video ended with a stirring montage of all the contributions Islamic scholars and scientists had made for mankind, and how the West sought to suppress this clearly superior scientific capability from being reborn within the Islamic world so that they could continue their domination of the Middle Eastern countries.

As the video ended, the laptop beeped and Hazar shut it down to change the battery. While he worked to pry out the battery and replace it, he spoke to the men.

"Do you now see the lies you have been told? Do you see how the Western occupiers and the Great Satan wish to destroy Islam, how they kill the innocent and suppress our rightful place in the world, all the while claiming to be 'helping' the nations of the Middle East?"

Saddam looked at his fellow trainees and saw them nod, eyes wide in sudden realization. He could not deny what he had seen. Except for the one lingering doubt during the first film, which must have been a mistake on his part, it was all detestable. How could he not want to fight back, not just for his mother and dead brother, but for all those innocents in Afghanistan, Iraq, and Palestine? He may not be able to do much, but he could learn and take the fight to the unbelievers.

Hazar finished snapping the fresh battery pack into the laptop, and gestured at the younger men.

"Bring your chairs closer. Now that you understand the infidels and their evils, I will begin teaching you how to fight them. You have each been chosen for a very special mission that will hurt the infidels very badly. Pay close attention to what I show you now. You will begin practicing this afternoon."

Saddam dragged his chair closer, being sure to have an unobstructed line of sight between his fellow trainees' heads and watched as Hazar rebooted the laptop. He activated the wireless connection and then logged in to a password-secured website. Saddam caught the name just before the login prompt obscured it: the "Al-Fajr Center for Action."

Once he was past the login prompt, Hazar navigated to a series of videos and selected one. As it played, he alternately watched the video and spoke to the young men. The video had no narration, only uplifting music praising Allah coming from the laptop's integrated speakers.

"Watch carefully. Note the patterns of movement. Each man moves with another. They approach a door, throw the grenade, and wait. After it detonates, they enter. One stays to the left, the other to the right of the door. Always working as a team. As you shall be."

THEY HAD DIMMED THE LIGHTS a little for the mid-shift, and that was just fine with Emily. It made the displays on the terminal for the Global Hawk that much easier to read. Right now they showed the RQ-4 orbiting over Norfolk, Virginia. Checking the displays, she could see the instrument overlay on the launch-and-recovery camera that the remote pilots used if the drone needed to be manually flown for a landing. The camera itself showed nothing but blue sky and broken clouds. The altitude tape superimposed on the view showed the drone to be at 45,000 feet. An hour ago, it was at 40,000. It was drifting upward as it burned off fuel, and should be nearing its programmed altitude limit.

Emily checked the time zone clocks up on the wall over the watch standers' central semicircle. A little more than an hour to go before shift change. Returning her attention to the console, she checked the altitude tape again, just under 45,000 feet this time. She picked up the communications headset laying on the desk and set it on her head.

Keying the microphone, she said, "Launch and recovery, this is sensors. The Hawk seems to be descending. I thought the off-station time wasn't until 0900 this morning?"

After a moment, she heard a click in her ear. "Sensors, this is launch and recovery. We've seen a low oil pressure warning light from the turbofan and we want to bring her down early. We've ordered the onboard computer to throttle back and begin a slow descent to recovery altitude."

"Copy that," she replied. "Will you being declaring an IFE?" An inflight emergency was serious, and she had some notifications to make if they did that.

"Negative. We've seen this before. The engineers who designed the Hawk tell us she can run for about an hour with no oil pressure at all before the turbofan tears itself apart, so we aren't overly worried. Besides, we can glide her about 30 miles with no engine power if we need to. Plenty of time and altitude to find a runway to land on."

"Roger that. Give me the word when I need to shut down the sensor links. I want to keep working with them as long as I can."

"Will do. You should have nearly two hours or so before we need to shut them down for landing. Have fun."

"Thanks. Out here."

Emily took the headset off and put it back on the desk, and then turned her attention back to the infrared systems. She could see the heat signatures from the stacks of the ships at Norfolk Naval Base, and zoomed in on a couple of them.

The hulls were only faint outlines on the ghost-gray image, but the white bloom of heat on the stacks of the two northernmost ships tied alongside the piers was distinctive. The main wharf was north of Norfolk, and the fourteen or so piers she could see ran roughly east to west, jutting out from the base itself. The northernmost piers had massive aircraft carriers tied up alongside them, with the slightly smaller Marine landing ships immediately to their south. Farther south were several cruisers and destroyers.

She zoomed in on the cruiser she had seen the heat bloom from and waited a moment for the image to steady. She could clearly see the outline of the forward 5-inch gun, and the vertical launch cells for the Tomahawk land attack missiles. She could even see the tiny white traces of the crew members on deck walking back and forth, most of them alongside the portside of the ship, nearest the pier. Maybe they were getting ready to head to sea.

She continued to watch the ship, switching back and forth from the infrared to the electro-optical cameras. The sun was not up yet, but the low-light mode on the electro-optical cameras let her see the ship clearly. There were no identifying marks or numbers topside; she would have to hope for a better angle at some point to catch the hull number. Once she had the hull number, she could look up the ship's name and know just who she had been watching in the early hours of the morning.

A tap on her shoulder startled her away from the screen.

"Good morning, Emily. Quiet night?" It was Technical Sergeant Thurston from the Bravo shift, a blond movie buff, and in Emily's opinion a pretty good operator. He and the rest of Bravo shift were on days while Emily and the rest of the Alpha shift were on mid-watch.

"Yeah," Thompson replied, "it's been really quiet. I've been spending most of the night working with the Hawk. The infrared camera is sweet. By the way, it's experiencing an oil pressure problem and the launch-and-recovery team are bringing her home early. You'll need to shut down the sensors in about an hour."

"Shit," Thurston said. He had been hoping to get in more time with the sensor suite before the Hawk went off-station. "Oh, well. Not much I can do about that. Anything else going on?"

Emily went through the usual litany of things while Sergeant Thurston read the watch log. Then he accepted responsibility for the position with the traditional, "You're relieved." Emily grabbed her black backpack and headed for the restroom, where she changed into a pair of running shorts and a tank top. Pulling on her top, she thought that she was very lucky to be able to do this job, even if things went wrong once in a while.

The plans are wrong!

Dammit! The relentless echo of the hostage rescue team leader's last words before the explosions still haunted her. Her failure. How her inattention had cost those men their lives, and made fresh widows and orphans of innocent people. The words, the explosions on the monitors... she could still see the image of one man's leg, or maybe his arm, flying through the air, out of the visual range of the camera.

Emily closed her eyes as the invisible fist crushed her heart again and the tears began to well. She wanted to wail and scream . . . no! She would not let this beat her. There were better ways to deal with the guilt. Focus on her son, work, and exercise to mitigate through the stress. Running helped. She could run until her legs gave out. The minor aches and pains from the muscles helped.

She grabbed her backpack and headed out of the ladies' room to the elevator core down the hall. The gym was in the basement of the building. As she waited for the car to arrive, her mind found a new way to torment her. *Are you running to cope with what you've done, or are you trying to run away from it?*

AZIZ ADJUSTED HIMSELF MORE COMFORTABLY on the leather couch in the spacious living room and returned to reading *Al Riyadh*, the local paper. The "Kingdom" section was just as bland as ever. Congratulations to the custodian of the Two Holy Mosques on the twelfth anniversary of his ascension to the throne, construction on local streets carried out with the "blessings of His Highness," and other such pandering news stories. Aziz suspected that if he bothered to check, the editor of *Al Riyadh* was probably some distant relation to the king.

One item did catch his attention as he scanned the second page in the section: "Apostate Beheaded for Committing Hiraba." What was this? The article was brief but disturbing. "Saudi authorities beheaded a national convicted of committing unlawful warfare, the Interior Ministry said. Sadig al-Faisal was found guilty of importing weapons; planning violent acts against other nationals; committing violent acts against Afghani Muslims, among them murder, rape, and false imprisonment; as well as extortion, theft, and entering the Kingdom illegally. The criminal was a former member of the Taliban government, and was attempting to foment unlawful warfare within the Kingdom when he was arrested, it said in a statement carried by SPA state news agency. He was executed in the city of Riyadh."

Aziz sat back a moment. One of the faithful, and a warrior, too, it seemed, executed by the king's government. One more reason to follow through with his plans. The man should have been held up as an example of the righteous warrior, risking everything for his faith and for Muslims everywhere. Instead, he was publicly butchered, no doubt to the great amusement of the supposedly pious onlookers who then returned to their comfortable homes with Internet connections giving them access to all the pornography they wished to view.

Well, nothing could be done for him now, Aziz thought. The man was foolish enough to get caught, but he was a warrior in the holy cause, and Aziz would ask Allah to carry him to Paradise swiftly in his meditations after evening prayer tonight.

Aziz breathed deeply to let out a chagrined sigh. He smelled the rich odor of roasting lamb. His host was being generous, even though he was late for their appointment. The man's eldest son had greeted him warmly at the door, and offered him water and fruit juice while he waited. Aziz was content to be treated with such respect. It was proper, after all. His host was a powerful man in Saudi Arabia, subject to others in authority, of course, but powerful nonetheless. That he recognized Aziz's power and influence, in addition to agreeing with Aziz's goals, was also useful. Aziz was less pleased with the man's regular requests for euros to continue the struggle, but such was the way of things.

The sound of the front door opening interrupted Aziz's thoughts, and he rose slowly. He was the more powerful man, but to show no respect to his host in his own home would be a great insult. He could hear the authority in the man's voice as he spoke to his son in the entryway, and when he rounded the corner and stepped into the living room, the voice of authority matched the man himself.

The general stood slightly less than 6 feet tall, his military bearing evident in the sharp creases in the uniform and the polish of his boots. Aziz knew, from the men he paid handsomely on the general's staff, that enlisted men kept his clothes pressed and his boots shined, but the effect was still the same. In spite of the superficial trappings of his office, the force of his authority shone from his eyes, and he approached Aziz on the basis of that authority.

"Welcome to my home. Please sit." The general smiled warmly, but Aziz detected a hint of the manner used by the general when addressing any competent professional under his command. Now was not the time to dissuade him of that attitude.

"Shokran, General. You are most generous. I am pleased you've made time to see me this evening."

The general waved a dismissive hand. "I am pleased to see you. Without you and your resources, what we plan would simply not be possible. I still think it is very audacious and likely to fail without additional resources and guarantees."

Not this again, Aziz thought. Keeping his voice pleasant, he said, "We have discussed this many times, General. I believe it can be done. It is simply a matter of timing."

"Yes, but I am still uncertain . . ." The general's voice trailed off, and he looked at Aziz expectantly.

Aziz thought briefly and then continued, "I appreciate your caution and your council. If I may bring up a delicate matter, we have not discussed your future thus far, only the plan. What is it that you would like to do once the situation has evolved?"

The general considered that briefly before replying, "The National Guard will need strong and competent leadership."

Ah, yes, thought Aziz. "Of course, General." The Saudi National Guard was the only standing army in the Kingdom. Command of the army would place the general in an even more powerful position of influence and authority. "Have you discussed that with our mutual friend?"

The general shook his head. "No. I could never approach him with such a matter."

Aziz smiled warmly. "I would be pleased to do so on your behalf. I'm sure it would receive serious consideration and approval, perhaps even that night."

"Shokran. I am grateful for your help. Then the only thing left to concern us is the exact timing and the additional resources needed."

"Na'am," Aziz responded. "When do you think would be the best time to do it?"

The general leaned a little closer and lowered his voice as he replied. Even in the safety of his own home, it was wise to be cautious. His explanation was brief, but Aziz found the reasoning sound and the venue ideal, particularly since their mutual friend would be there as well, and it would not arouse suspicion.

"Excellent," Aziz told him.

"What about the additional resources I need?" the general inquired.

Always interested in the money. Well, Aziz thought, a man of position and influence should be able to afford many wives. The general already had two, but that was not Aziz's concern.

"I shall place another 100,000 euros in the Arab National Bank account for you to draw from for all reasonable expenses. Whatever is left, you may keep, but I ask that you give some of it as a Zakat."

The general considered that, then responded, "I think that may be less than what will be needed for those who will help us, but I am pleased to offer a percentage of what remains as Zakat for those in need."

Aziz knew at that moment that if all went well, he would need to send the general to Paradise sooner than he would want to see it. Greed for wealth would not see the Caliphate returned, and the general's greediness would only grow with time.

Aziz put an understanding smile on his face and nodded. "I am willing to do what I must to ensure that those who help us are justly compensated for their risks and the risk to their families. I will place 300,000 euros in the account. See to it that it is used wisely."

"I will." The general rose, his goals for this meeting accomplished, and the thought of another 300,000 euros within reach making him feel very pleased with himself. The Zakat, if he actually gave it, would only be a few thousand. Once he was in charge of the army, he would find a way to supplement his salary with some of the operational funds.

Reaching out an arm, he beckoned Aziz toward the dining room. Aziz would have preferred to recline on comfortable cushions and eat like a civilized person, but the smell of the roasting lamb was overwhelming. He would tolerate eating at the general's table—for now.

As Aziz drew alongside the general, the general raised his hand and stopped him.

"What of the Americans? Are you certain they will not be able to intervene?"

Aziz nodded confidently. "Yes. They have their hands full right now, and I will restrain their ability to act against us in other ways. Besides, the initial steps will be over in a few hours, and then they will be powerless to act."

PREBIN PAUSED AND LOOKED AROUND the converted forward hold. He was sweating inside the lead-lined anti-radiation suit, sweat running along the edges of the air filter he wore. He was used to the discomfort from his long experience with nuclear materials in the lab and the field, but he would relish a cold shower when this shift was over.

The hold itself was the ideal place for what they were doing. Large and open, with steel bulkheads separating it from the other portions of the ship, it had been modified to his specifications to limit contamination and facilitate easy cleanup. Ramirez and his men had covered the walls, floor, and ceiling with thick tarpaulins, each faced with thick felt and held in place by hooks. Any particulate contamination would become trapped in the felt and be removed during the decontamination procedure.

The work area was surrounded on the deck by thin lead shields, similar to those used in a doctor's X-ray room. Prebin had even checked the thickness of the steel walls and decking. Given the relatively low level of radioactivity from the rods, the steel was thick enough to avoid inadvertently exposing the crew. No one should ever spend an extended period of time in this hold, but the captain told him that wouldn't be a problem, since the crew did not live in the holds.

After nearly two days' worth of work, Prebin was immensely satisfied. He and his colleagues had disassembled the first of the fuel rods, stripping away the inert cladding and carefully removing the cylindrical pellets of uranium fuel. Most of the U235 had been converted to other less useful elements and isotopes, but there would be enough left in all the rods for what they needed to do.

Moving the fuel pellets around in the makeshift hot zone of the hold required some careful choreography, but Prebin had known his colleagues were experienced, and their economy of movement and focus during the process had proven it. Prebin would remove each pellet, check it quickly for extreme damage, like pitting or severe cracks, and then put it in a makeshift holder. The holder was designed to handle only four pellets at a time, ensuring that the combined mass of the set in close proximity would not induce an unexpected nuclear reaction.

Arkady then carried the holder to one of the two small vats, and either Viktor or Leonid would remove the pellets with a set of long tongs and lay them gently in one of the vats of nitric acid. Pavel and Vasily monitored one vat each, occasionally stirring the mixture carefully, checking its chemical composition, and watching the pellets slowly dissolve. When the proper ratio of pellets to nitric acid volume in the vats was reached, they halted the process, and let nuclear chemistry do the rest.

When the bright green crystals began to form and fall to the bottom of the vat, Pavel and Vasily stirred a little less often, letting the compound clump together into larger and larger crystals. Then, using a special set of long-handled strainers, they carefully began to scoop out the crystals and lay them out on a long table to complete the crystallization process.

As they dried, the remaining fluid was drained into special stainless-steel casks brought aboard for the purpose, and fresh acid was poured into the vats. Then more fuel pellets, and the cycle began again. A day or two more, Prebin thought. The sickly green crystals would need to be dissolved in water, and that took time.

CHAPTER 10

"M'AN, YOU OR SAQR WILL remain with me at all times from now on," Aziz ordered.

"Yes, Sayyid," M'an replied. "Do you anticipate any particular threat?"

"No, my friend. Our war against the infidels reaches a dangerous stage now, and I do not know exactly who visited my home in Iran. It is wise to be more cautious now, I think."

M'an tilted his head left and slightly back toward Aziz in the rear seats of the Mercedes S500, and nodded once. "I understand, Sayyid. We will both accompany you from now on. Do you need anything?"

"No, shokran." Aziz sank deeper into the black leather of the rear bench seats of the Mercedes and considered his plan. M'an and Saqr were loyal beyond any question. He had seen that loyalty demonstrated more than once since he had sought them out two years ago.

Both were serving in the Hay'ah, Arabic for "commission" and the shortened form of the more formal name for the Commission for the Promotion of Virtue and Prevention of Vices in Saudi Arabia.

Known more informally as the Mutawwa', the religious police in the Kingdom, they enforced the strict standards of Sharia law throughout the nation. They ensured that shops closed during prayer times, prohibited unrelated men and women from socializing and any perceived homosexual behavior in public, and enforced a complete ban on any music, videos, or magazines depicting anything contrary to Islam and proper standards of modesty by confiscating any such material and arresting the offenders.

Aziz had interviewed both men shortly after they were fired for the flogging death of a man accused of trying to spread the Catholic faith on the streets of Riyadh. The man had been handing out leaflets advertising the location of a small house he had rented for a Mass later that week. Such things were not tolerated in the Islamic Kingdom. M'an and Saqr had taken him into custody and began questioning him in the local Mutawwa' field office.

The man, a devout Frenchman in his fifties, began to question their faith, calling Islam "the faith of the devil" and upbraiding them for not seeing "God's true path" in their lives. Enraged, M'an and Saqr chained him to the wall and began to flog him, as they would any apostate the Mutawwa' found, in order to force him to see the error of his choice and make him see the truth in the path of Islam. The man must have truly found the path in M'an and Saqr's flogging, since he fled to Paradise during it, unnoticed by either of them.

Rather than praising the two men for upholding the highest standards of Islam and the purity of the land of the Two Holy Mosques, the weak fools in the Saudi government had fined them both 40,000 riyals and terminated their employment, claiming that both men had violated the law, of all things!

Aziz had spoken to them about their faith and as he thought, both men knew the true nature of Islam and how the unbelievers in the world needed to be dealt with. Aziz sent them to a training facility in Yemen to improve their skills and ordered a special test.

After two weeks, the head instructor at the camp in northern Yemen mailed him the flash drive with the video. Watching it had taken nearly an hour, but it was worth it to know their true character.

Both men had taken their time to execute the six captured infidels, three men and three women from the local Red Cross contingent. The women and two of the men had wailed aloud and cried out for mercy as M'an and Saqr beheaded each one in front of the others. The last man had greater courage, and Aziz thought he was likely an American or British spy. The man neither cried out nor beseeched them to stop. He merely looked at them with undisguised hatred; fighting, even with his hands bound, to keep them from putting the hood over his head. In the end, they overpowered him, M'an swung his blade, and the man's head rolled free to their shouts of "Allahu Akbar!" M'an and Saqr, splattered with the blood of the infidels that would guarantee their entry into Paradise, had embraced as brothers, and were congratulated by the other Mujahedeen in the room as the video ended.

Aziz's thoughts returned to the present as Saqr turned right off Airport Road toward the private aviation terminal at King Khalid International Airport and drove toward the fence line on the north side, stopping before the automatic gate. Reserved for private jet owners, the vehicle entry gate slid open as soon as Saqr held the card up to the reader. Once past the gate, Saqr guided the heavy S500 smoothly up to the G550. As expected, Aziz could see Zaki in the left seat through the thick cockpit window, the red glow of the lights from the instruments giving his features a demonic cast.

M'an exited the car and briefly scanned the area through the orange glow of the impending sunset, then opened the rear door for Aziz. Aziz headed straight for the jet's stairs, flanked by M'an and Saqr, and clambered aboard. Instead of heading directly to the rear of the jet, he stuck his head in the cockpit. Zaki turned to give Aziz his full attention.

"Yes, Sayyid?"

"You have not found another pilot yet?"

Zaki swallowed quickly. "No, Sayyid. I have not yet found anyone fully qualified on this aircraft."

Aziz hardened his voice. "I must be in the Maldives tonight. Will that present a problem?"

Zaki looked stricken, but forced himself to answer. "No, Sayyid. I can fly you there myself. The aircraft is fueled and ready to go. I filed the flight plan via phone and we can be airborne in ten minutes."

"Excellent. Depart immediately."

"Yes, Sayyid." Zaki gestured to the empty copilot's seat. "Would you care to sit here for takeoff?"

Aziz looked at Zaki closely. The cockpit was for his qualified servants, not him. "No. How long will the flight be?"

"A little more than five hours, Sayyid."

"Very well. Let's hope it is a smooth flight." Satisfied to see Zaki's eyes widen at the implied threat, Aziz turned on his heel, heading back to the passenger compartment.

Zaki closed the cockpit door behind Aziz and locked it, whispering a brief prayer to Allah. He could never be sure about what had happened to Hamzah, but he had his suspicions and no wish to tempt fate. Zaki turned to face forward again and belted himself in before bringing up the engine start and taxi checklists on the flight computer between the pilot and copilot's seats.

"MORE COFFEE?" AKEEM HELD OUT the carafe to Johnson. Johnson sat in the leather chair before Akeem's steel-and-glass desk, eyes focused on the windows behind it, the orange glow of sunset lighting the sandstone exteriors of the buildings across the street from the Ministry of the Interior.

Akeem studied him while he held the carafe, and then rested a hand on his shoulder.

"Dave." Johnson's eyes left the window and focused on Akeem, his mind coming back to the present. "Coffee?"

Johnson looked at Akeem and had enough presence of mind to answer him in Arabic. "La, shokran." The gold-lipped china cup in his hand was still a third full.

Akeem rewarded him with a slight grin of understanding and returned to the Herman Miller mesh chair behind the desk. He paused to contemplate Johnson's distracted behavior before addressing him.

"You are still bothered by the execution of Sadig."

Johnson stopped looking out the window and put his attention on Akeem. "Yes. I've never seen anything like that before."

"I understand. If you are a decent man, it is a difficult thing to watch. You must remember that Sadig was a criminal and he was part of an organization that made war on your country, as well as abased himself before his god. You should not waste your time thinking about him. He did not give others that consideration in life."

Johnson considered that. "Yes, but to witness a life being ended is a hard thing."

"Yes," Akeem responded soberly, "it is, but I think you should place your thoughts on something more important. You will be a father in a few months, and you should remember that in helping to find and hold Sadig responsible for his crimes, you have made the world safer for your child and your wife."

Johnson nodded pensively. "That's why I wanted to be an FBI agent. I just don't think I expected to be so directly exposed to an execution in my career. I knew it might happen one day if I worked a capital case, but I always expected that I would have the option to see the sentence carried out. And that would have been a lethal injection, not a beheading."

"We do not believe in making harsh punishment clean and clinical," Akeem told him. "If the punishment is severe and known by all to be severe, then people are better encouraged to obey the law. Making things seem less than what they are by cloaking them in some other form for appearance's sake is an escape from the truth."

Johnson sipped at the last of the strong coffee in his cup and placed it on Akeem's desk. The images of the execution would fade in time, he supposed, and Akeem's advice was sound. His child would be better off growing up in a world with one less Sadig in it.

Turning his mind to matters at hand, he asked, "When do you think he'll call for us?"

Akeem shook his head. "I'm not sure. Minister Ali has many issues to deal with, but he was most insistent that he wanted to speak to you."

The phone on Akeem's desk gave an electronic double warble. Akeem reached for it, and try as Johnson might, his Arabic was not up to the task of catching Akeem's side of the conversation. Native speakers were just too fast for his ear. As Akeem spoke his eyes rested on Johnson and he knew the minister was ready for them. Johnson rose and buttoned his suit coat, then straightened his tie.

Akeem put the phone down. "Come, my friend. Let us see what Minister Ali has on his mind."

As Johnson followed him out of his office, he asked, "Do senior ministers always work this late?"

Akeem smiled and prepared himself to deliver another lesson in Saudi government culture. "Dave, this is a desert country. Most government business is conducted after 6 P.M. to avoid the heat of the day, and during Ramadan that helps ensure that people spend their focus during the daylight hours on fasting, praying, and giving generously to charities. Moreover, by conducting many official activities later in the day, we place ourselves in a better position to be available to speak with our counterparts in Europe and America, given the time differences."

By the time Akeem had finished his explanation, the two men had made their way to the central elevator core and up to the top floor, exiting into the marble-sheathed hallway and along the corridor to a 9-foot-high pair of heavy maple wood doors. Beyond them was an opulent outer office covered in thick cream carpets and dark wood furniture. A male assistant in a white thawb and a black-and-white checked keffiyeh looked up as they entered, peering over his reading glasses.

Akeem merely nodded to the man and proceeded to the inner door. Johnson nodded politely to the male assistant, who, after a moment's consideration, returned the gesture in a decidedly neutral fashion before rising from the desk and walking toward them. Akeem knocked once on the inner door, and without waiting, opened it. Johnson followed him through, hearing the soft click of the assistant closing the door behind them.

The Minister of the Interior, Ali ibn Haroun ibn Hashim al-Saud, rose to greet them. Johnson had not anticipated meeting him at all, and was not sure what to expect. The man was easily in his late fifties, tall, with intelligent eyes and a neatly trimmed full beard, solidly shot through with silver.

"Special Agent Johnson, welcome." His English was extremely fluent and carried a mild hint of a British accent. Johnson guessed he had spent many of his years of formal education in England.

"Thank you, Mr. Minister." Johnson was going to be having a long talk with SAIC French after this. The U.S. Ambassador should be here.

"Please sit." Minister Ali motioned toward the small conversation pit on one side of the huge office, and Johnson had a few seconds to study the room. The office was huge, easily taking up an entire corner of the building's floor. More cream-colored carpet covered the entire floor. The minister's desk and work area sat far back on the left against floor-to-ceiling windows. On the right, nestled up against the windows, was a small dining area with seating for six, and midway toward the entrance along the right was the small conversation pit of two thickly cushioned chairs and a short couch, all upholstered in black leather. The walls were bare except for a huge portrait of the Masjid al-Haram, the Grand Mosque in Mecca, that dominated the wall behind the conversation pit.

When they were all seated, the minister began. "Akeem and I were friends in school, and we studied for a time at Cambridge. He also tells me you are a man of good character." Ali paused, seeming to wait to see what Johnson would say in response.

"Mr. Minister, I am pleased to call Akeem my friend, and I appreciate his efforts to teach me about the Kingdom."

Ali nodded, "Then I will speak to you as a friend, and I ask that you to help me understand something."

This was what Johnson was afraid of. The minister was going to make another back-channel request through him. SAIC French had already chewed his ass once about this. He was far too junior to be dealing with officials in the Saudi government this high up.

The minister must have taken his silence as acquiescence, and before he could protest, Ali continued, "His Highness and I have spoken at length about the permission he gave to allow a U.S. Special Forces team to infiltrate Iran, a sovereign neighbor of the Kingdom, on a Saudi airliner. You know of this mission, do you not?"

Johnson could do nothing but answer truthfully. He had worked through Akeem to arrange permission for the Wraith Team under Mathews to enter the Kingdom, and watched them board the Saudi Airlines jet for the flight into Iran to attempt Aziz's capture. Naturally, Akeem had worked through his friend the minister to reach the king for approval.

"Yes, sir. I am aware of this mission."

Ali nodded. "Good. Then as one friend to another, I want you to share with me what the real reason was for that team to go into Iran."

Johnson was puzzled by Ali's request. "Excuse me, Mr. Minister, I don't understand. I know that the king spoke directly with the president. I'm sure the president told him exactly why we wanted the team to enter Iran."

The minister leaned toward him, looking directly into his eyes. Johnson knew that this was a crucial cultural behavior, and willed his eyes to stare back steadily. The next set of questions and answers would be very important to Ali.

"Yes, young man. Your president did tell the king why, and the king approved the use of our nation's airline for the infiltration, making the Kingdom complicit in your actions. We need to know what that team did in Iran. We were told it was to capture a man likely responsible for the recent attacks on your nation's power infrastructure, oil reserves, and people."

Johnson leaned forward to speak, and Ali held up his hand to stop him, then continued.

"We have heard nothing from the director of your CIA or defense secretary about the results of this mission, who this man is, and what you have learned from him. In fact, our sources in Iraq tell us that several bodies were given Islamic burial after being taken off one of your V-22 Osprey special operations aircraft, before that aircraft melted away into the night sky along with a mysteriously unmarked 747."

Johnson was surprised that the Saudis had not been told, and it must have shown on his face, along with the mild shock that they knew at least part of what had happened after the team returned to Iraq. Either way, it was not within his authority to explain either, certainly not at this level. He kept his eyes locked on the minister's and began in what he hoped was his best pseudo-diplomat voice.

"Mr. Minister, I understand and respect your concerns. If it were up to me alone, I would share with you what I know. I must ask you to be patient while I seek the permission of my government to discuss this with you." Johnson saw Ali break eye contact for a brief glance at Akeem, a combination of accusation and a request for help, and he hurried on.

"Sir, I can assure you as a friend that what you have described to me is what I understood to be the reason my government sought permission to covertly enter Iran from the Kingdom. If there was another purpose, I do not know of it. If you want or need additional details, however, I must contact my government for them." Now it was Johnson's turn to break eye contact for a quick look at Akeem for affirmation. "I am obligated under my oath as an FBI agent to keep my nation's secrets, and I am not senior enough to elect to break them, even if an ally and friend asks."

Ali looked away, disappointed, and leaned back in the black leather chair. Akeem took the opportunity to speak up. "Ali, we have known each other many years, and I have known Agent Johnson for only a few

AUTUMN FIRE | 165

days, yet I consider him as much a brother as I do you. I do not believe that he would try to deceive us, and your request places him in a difficult position."

Ali considered Akeem and Johnson in silence for nearly a minute before speaking again. Johnson wanted to say something, but instinctively, he remained quiet.

"I will give you the time you need, Agent Johnson. Speak to your superiors and let them know of our need for answers. I will give you two days, and then I will be forced to ask His Majesty to call your president directly."

COFFEE WAS A STAPLE OF watch centers everywhere, particularly on a mid-watch, and this shift was just getting started. Thompson took her first sip from her Starbucks cup and made a face. She forgot the sweetener. Pulling open the drawer in the drone console's desk where she hid her stash of Splenda, she took out four of the little packets and tore them open, lifting the cup's lid to pour in the white powdery contents. A quick stir from one of the spare plastic spoons she kept next to the Splenda box, followed by a test sip, and she reseated the plastic lid on the thick paper cup while nudging the desk drawer shut. Now her duty shift was officially under way.

The lights were dimmed as usual, and she studied the displays for a few minutes while she drank her coffee. She had mastered all of the sensor controls and needed to think of something to do tonight. The Global Hawk was airborne again, this time on a lazy orbit that took it over Baltimore and Washington, D.C., in an elongated racetrack aligned between the two cities.

Ideally, she would like to practice downlinking data to a ground team, but none of the Wraith units were active right now. Maybe she could make a deal with the Pentagon's watch center and practice streaming the data to them. The J2 or J3 watch desks in the Joint Operations Center might appreciate a break from the normal routine. She would have to get David's approval before calling the JOC watch officer first.

As she turned toward Cain's desk to ask, one of the three phones on her desk rang. Looking back, it was the outside line with the Secure Telephone

Equipment attached to it. The STE, when linked with another STE across the public telephone network, could encrypt a voice call so thoroughly that it could be used in Top Secret Sensitive Compartmented Information–level conversations. SCI calls on the public network were rare, given that she also had a grey phone on her desk, one of the intelligence community's telephones linked to switches owned and controlled solely by the DoD or the intelligence agencies themselves, and impossible to intercept or access, unless you were physically inside one of the buildings.

It was probably some phone solicitor, she concluded. Those calls came routinely as telemarketers often called phone numbers in sequential order, and the exchange prefixes for the public lines were publicly known, if you knew where to look. That fact mandated that she answer that phone in a specific way.

Turning to the room at large, she raised her voice. "Phone's up!" Everyone's conversations became more muted, and one nearby at the CIA desk ceased altogether to avoid allowing classified information from being heard over the open phone line. It was an accepted procedure that everyone working in classified environments knew and understood.

"2238."

"Hi, honey." It was Jerry. Personal calls were always allowed, she just had to keep it brief, especially since she had forced a classified conversation to stop by answering the outside line.

"Hi, babe. I need to be quick. Some people had to stop working when I answered."

"I understand. The little guy wanted to tell Mommy goodnight." Emily smiled. Her son hadn't learned to talk yet, but he was starting to make vocalizations when he wanted things.

"Okay. Quick though."

"All right, here he is." She heard him move the phone and then the wet sound of breathing. He probably had a finger or two in his mouth.

She could hear Jerry in the background, prompting Jeff, "Tell Mommy goodnight. Tell her."

She then heard his little voice cooing in her ear, smiled, and tried to encourage him.

"Good night, sweetie. Mommy loves you." She heard nothing, then the phone shift to Jerry again.

"I think that's as good as we get tonight," he said, "He just pulled away from the phone and put his head on my shoulder. He looks like he's ready to go out."

"That's okay. Did he hear me?"

"I think so, he looked at me and smiled before he pulled his head from the phone. I think he recognized your voice but isn't far enough along yet to understand how he heard it."

"Is he dressed warm enough?"

"Yes," he answered, mildly exasperated. He knew she was thinking that no man could properly care for his child better than the mother. "I put the blue snuggy suit on him. He's nice and toasty warm. He'll be fine. I notice you never ask if I'll be warm enough when you work a mid."

Always a little playful at these bedtime calls. She loved him for that. "You always keep me warm, remember?"

"Yes, I do, but that's because having you next to me makes my heart race."

That was her man—a little cheesy, but she knew what he meant. "Yeah?"

"Absolutely. I miss you when you aren't in bed next to me. In fact, I think we should start thinking about giving the little guy a playmate."

That was a surprise. "I don't know about that."

"I do. You are a wonderful mother . . . and you looked terrific when you were carrying Jeff."

That was definitely not convincing enough for Emily, especially not with where her head was now. "Thanks, but you didn't have to go to the bathroom every twenty seconds to pee, and you didn't have the backache from hell for the last two months."

"No, I didn't, but I know you want to, we've talked about it before . . ."

"Yes, but now's not the time. We can talk about it later."

"Okay, I recognize that tone. Do you want anything special for breakfast? I'm getting pretty good with the camping cook set."

"No. Whatever you want to make is fine."

"All right. I love you."

"Love you, too. Bye."

Emily hung up the phone. Another baby? How could she have another baby in the middle of this? An attack on her country, her failure and the deaths of all those men? She loved her husband, but having another baby . . .

"Emily, your call finished?"

She started out of her internal debate and realized the people at the CIA desk were looking at her expectantly.

"Sorry," then a louder, "Phone's down!"

Everyone went back to their discussions, and Emily turned back to the drone console. No one would bother her for saying a quick good night to her infant son and husband, but she couldn't keep getting pre-occupied like that. *Dammit. Time to get back to work.*

MATHEWS HAD HAD ENOUGH. "IF anybody did that on one of my teams, I'd bounce his ass out the door so fast, his head would spin."

Mathews and his team, the Calvert Cliffs Nuclear Power Station's Emergency Reaction Unit, and the men and women of the Military Police platoon from the Maryland National Guard's 58th Troop Command, were enjoying an impromptu movie night. Mathews and Team Four had arrived at the power station yesterday afternoon and identified themselves as special advisors from the DoD to Lieutenant Robert Corvin. Corvin, however, caught on quickly for a guardsman. "Yeah, right," he replied, cocking his head to one side. Mathews could not exactly blame the lieutenant for his disbelieving response—his team was obviously carrying some nonstandard-issue weapons and equipment, and their collective confidence and swagger could be seen from 100 yards away by any soldier with eyes.

Nonetheless, Corvin accepted the help gratefully, instructing his men to cooperate with the DoD SpecTeam, as he referred to them, but also made it clear his men were his responsibility, not Mathews'. Mathews took no issue with that. His orders were to assist and advise, not take over.

The next people Mathews met were the full-time contracted guard force for the power station. Most were ex-military or police and every one of them was cross-trained in basic life-support skills and group tactics. The most highly skilled on the team earned assignments to the power station's Emergency Reaction Unit. The ERU drilled to deal with anything from a severe vehicle accident outside the main gate to an attempted terrorist attack.

When Mathews had looked over their equipment this morning with their team leader, Kevin Sanders, he discovered that they were not well equipped and had to make some immediate recommendations to Colonel Simon. They had no long rifles at all, only 20-gauge shotguns with slug loads, good for short-range work, but not for situations that would need medium- to long-range firepower. Given where the power station was, that was a problem.

The windshield tour that Corvin and Sanders took him on the afternoon the Wraiths arrived illustrated their need for better weapons. The Calvert Cliffs Nuclear Power Station was a large facility, nearly a mile long and a mile wide. Designed to be as far away from people as practically possible, it was bordered by heavily wooded areas on three sides: northwest, southwest, and southeast. The Chesapeake Bay completed the encirclement to the northeast and provided cooling water for the reactors. Access roads meandered through the southwestern woods, and an internal perimeter fence wrapped around the main part of the facility, where the transformer bank connected it to the national power grid and where the two massive concrete containment domes and generator hall were located. With all of this wooded and open ground, they needed at least a few M-16s or M-4s, and probably a couple of M110 sniper rifles, along with the training to use them properly.

Mathews was pleased to be getting along well with both Corvin and Sanders. Sanders was an ex–Air Force Security Policeman, and he seemed to know his job, working with what he had and keeping his men and women well drilled. The three men had even agreed to Mathews' suggestion that a few of the Wraiths stand guard duty with the nighttime guard force as an exercise in unit cohesion.

The National Guard soldiers had appropriated the gym as their sleeping quarters, and the larger shower facilities were coming in handy for the twenty-five men and women of the platoon. The Wraiths and the eight-person ERU team were sharing the smaller yet spacious main guardhouse, which doubled as both an emergency command post and sleeping quarters. It even had power. The transformer damage kept the nuclear plant from being attached to the main grid, but it was still providing power to the compound's facilities. Sanders had kindly offered to share the attached sleeping quarters in the command post with Mathews and his team, and they had gratefully accepted.

The VSAT dish was set up outside, and an empty desk in the corner had been allocated for the use of the secure laptop. Mathews used the laptop to look at the latest daily intelligence summaries from the DIA and CTS, but didn't find anything to concern him. He then headed over to the power plant's small cafeteria for the evening meal, where he and his executive officer and senior NCOs worked out a game plan with Sanders and Corvin. Tomorrow would see the first full day of tactical training by the Wraiths.

During dinner, Sanders thoughtfully suggested tonight's entertainment as movie night, and both Mathews and Corvin had thought it was a good way to let the team members get to know one another better. Sanders invited the off-duty soldiers, reaction team, and Wraith Team members to join them for a DVD and popcorn contributed by his team. Everyone who was not out on patrol in the cold night air crammed around the widescreen LCD in the main guardhouse to watch *Navy SEALs*.

Charlie Sheen's character had just compromised his SEAL team's safety, getting one of his teammates killed on a retrieval mission, when Mathews had made his remark.

"You wouldn't just shoot him?" Sanders asked, passing across another can of Coke and the half-empty plastic bowl of popcorn.

"Can't. That's murder. He'd probably end up on charges of reckless endangerment, maybe manslaughter in the real world. He sure as hell would get his ass booted off the team. Contributing to the death of a teammate is a one-way ticket out of the SEAL community. Hollywood just overlooks that, though."

Sanders nodded in agreement. "Yep. They get to just make it up, and not really conform too closely to reality, don't they?"

"Mmm hmm," Mathews replied as he watched the funeral scene. He had not had to attend one of those yet for anyone on the teams or for one of his Wraiths. He hoped he would never have to, but he knew that one day it was going to happen. For now, his job was to keep them alive, because he never wanted to face anyone's family over a casket.

* * *

"ALL IS IN READINESS, MY brothers." Rahman looked into the rear-view mirror from the driver's seat, and saw the other two vehicles slide in behind him alongside of Trueman Road, then cut their lights. The men in the blue Chevy Econoline van looked anxious but seemed to be holding themselves in check. Rahman raised the radio to his lips. The frequency of the Motorola handheld was already set.

"Akdar, Azrak, this is Ahmar. Are you ready?" They had already decided that only Arabic would be spoken this night. They would need clear communications in the heat of what was to come.

"Akdar is ready."

"Azrak is ready."

Rahman keyed the microphone again. "Proceed, and may Allah travel with you."

Behind him, the lights on the two cars flipped on again, and they pulled out onto the road and headed south. For Rahman and his Team Ahmar, named for the red blood they would spill tonight, the waiting began.

A half mile down the road, Nahas turned Team Azrak's car sharply left into a driveway entrance, killing the lights again as he stopped in front of the horizontal steel pole guarding the parking lot beyond. The pole pivoted upward, with the far end chained to its support to secure the lot. There were only four of them in the car, but they had prepared well for this. The jihadi in the right rear seat exited the car quickly with a pair of bolt cutters. A few seconds later, the steel pole was free, and he swung it up to clear the path for Nahas to drive through. Once it passed through, the man lowered the pole again and hurried back to the car.

Nahas drove deeper into Calvert Cliffs State Park and angled right, following the looping road in a counterclockwise direction until his lights struck a five-slot parking area facing a small lake. He slid the car into a slot, hit the trunk release, and killed the lights and the engine.

Nahas and the three other jihadis of Team Azrak exited the car quickly and removed their equipment from the trunk. Each man would carry a heavy burden tonight, but they had all been exercising in their local gyms to be ready at any time for the demands of the jihad against the Great Satan.

They donned vests festooned with extra magazines, packs with the explosive charges they would need, and G3 assault rifles slung over their necks and shoulders, before dragging the large rubber mass from the trunk. Nahas grabbed the small creeper they had modified with rubber tires from a grocery cart and closed the trunk lid. Each man then grabbed one of the mass's carry handles and set it on the modified creeper.

Working together, the four men used ropes to pull the creeper along, with two men in front steering and two in the back braking when needed. They maneuvered their burden onto the hard-packed trail marked with the white blazes on the trees and started to walk quickly toward the lake, then past it, melting into the woods.

AMARI HAD DRIVEN TEAM AKDAR, named for the green of the woods they had to travel through, a mile farther south onto Cove Point Road, before turning left into Cove Point Park. Following the road deep into the park, past the tennis courts and the pool area, he turned right toward the baseball fields and took the first left toward the soccer field. When he came to the roundabout where the road ended, he let the car roll slowly to a stop and parked, turning off the ignition.

Amari and his three teammates exited the car quickly and headed immediately east toward the tree line. Each man already carried his G3 rifle, vest, and explosives-laden backpack. Five meters inside the tree line they saw it: a dirt service road heading north, resting a few meters lower than the wooded berm. Amari led his small team down the road for nearly 100 meters, where it ended at a crossing that was nothing more than a 20-meter-wide open strip of grass running east to west. Amari could see the slope of the land off to the east, and knew from his study of the overhead images that they were in the right place. He angled right and started to lope toward the far tree line, then deeper into the woods. The ground sloped up to his left, and he knew that if he kept his path level, neither climbing the slope nor descending it, he would reach his next sign post in about 400 meters.

NAHAS AND HIS MEN HAD made good time. They had just reached the strip of beach at the end of the trail Repin had stood on a few days ago. Their target lay bathed in the glow of floodlights nearly 1,800 meters away. It looked as if the power failures had affected them, too. He could see large gaps in the pools of light on the structure. The emergency generators likely were not up to the task of powering all the lights. Truly, Allah did provide.

Moving quickly, Nahas and his three jihadis lifted the mass from the creeper, unfolded it quickly, and moved it closer to the water. They removed the lightweight aluminum handles, paddle ends, and the cylinder of compressed air. Attaching the cylinder to the inflation port with a rubber hose, Nahas cracked the valve and the black rubber six-man raft began to inflate, while the men screwed together the aluminum handles and paddle ends.

Nahas keyed his radio as the men dragged the inflated raft closer to the water.

"Azrak to Ahmar. It floats."

Nahas did not expect an answer, and walked into the water a few feet before climbing in the rear of the raft with his paddle. As the team leader, he would guide them to their target.

RAHMAN AND HIS SEVEN MEN all heard the radio call from Nahas and Team Blue in the van. The men began to murmur in unison, "Allahu Akbar," repeating it again and again. Rahman also felt his pride swell in their mission and began to say it softly to himself.

THINGS SHOULD BE GETTING UNDERWAY soon, Repin thought. It was nearly ten o'clock. The local news had gone on about the dire situation on the East Coast, and the nighttime anchor signed off with a "Have a good night!" after the obligatory human-interest piece. Tonight's was about a woman in Maryland who was walking through her neighborhood each day, giving all the neighbors freshly laid eggs from her chicken coop to help alleviate some of the stress that came with the power outage and lack of heat in their homes. Repin knew it was a small gesture, all things considered, but in difficult times, even small things helped to keep a civil population resilient.

He had to admire the Americans. In spite of the inconveniences he had helped to impose on them, their willingness to help one another out to get through the current crisis was admirable. A more caring man would have felt pity, but Repin's experiences as a member of the Russian SVR had insulated his soul against such feelings, and besides, he was more interested in the money he was earning. It was why he took the job, after all. Well, not exactly why, he thought, glancing at the loose photo of his daughter on the coffee table before the couch.

The eight-year-old Tatiana in the photo was probably nothing like the seventeen-year-old she was now, and Repin longed to see her again one day. To gain the financial freedom to give her everything his wife would not allow him to provide meant that Aziz's plan would continue, and Rahman's people would move things another step forward tonight. Repin hoped that when he saw Tatiana again after her eighteenth birthday, she would understand why he had been away for so long and would allow him to make it up to her. Assuming her mother had not poisoned her too much against him.

Repin rubbed his eyes and rose from the couch, grabbing the remote and keying in a new channel for the satellite receiver. While the receiver switched from the local CBS station to Fox News, he walked over to the computer and sat down, breaking the screen lock.

A couple of mouse clicks later and the web browser was up, using secure HTTP to connect to a dozen news sites from around the world and to Google's search engine. Repin wanted to see how each of the news outlets reported the actions of Rahman's men.

He asked Google to find the web cameras near the targets, hoping to watch at least some of the strikes in real time. That would give him an independent perspective from what the news reports provided.

In seconds Google provided a list of possible links to the web-cam feeds. Repin chose one at random and clicked on it. The corresponding web page came up, but the video feed was blank. Repin frowned and backed up one page to select a second link. Another web page, another dark video feed. He tried four more that also returned nothing but blank feeds before he concluded that the web cams were likely damaged or nonfunctional due to the power outages.

He leaned back, disappointed. He had hoped that the web cameras were powered by sources other than the local grid on the East Coast. It was worth a try, anyway. For tonight's operations, he would have to rely on the East Coast's local news stations. Stealing a quick look at his black Casio G-Shock watch, he knew it would be another thirty minutes at least, and decided to reexamine his planning for the harvesting operation. A few more mouse clicks, and Google Earth was showing him the aerial imagery of the West Coast. Now where would be the best place for the handoff?

CHAPTER 11

NAHAS LOOKED AT HIS WATCH. It was just after midnight. The sky was clear, the breeze on the water cold, and the moon would not rise for another three hours. But the closer they paddled to the huge platform just off the western shore in the Chesapeake Bay, the closer they came to being spotted. The only hope they had was to slip in between one of the dark places where the light was not working.

They were only 300 meters away now, and Nahas could see the target clearly for the first time. It was more than 800 meters long, but the ends were only spindly ribbons of concrete supported by thick concrete legs, just mooring points really, compared to the center three sections. Placed equidistant from one another, the center sections were their targets for tonight. The outermost sections held and supported the four pipe derricks, huge unloading arms of white steel and stainless-steel piping. They literally "plugged in" to the cargo manifolds of one of the largest ships that ever roamed Earth's oceans.

Nahas knew that Liquefied Natural Gas tankers were comparable in size to the largest of oceangoing oil tankers, the Ultra Large Crude Carriers. At more than 700 meters long, one LNG tanker could carry more than 200,000 cubic meters of liquefied natural gas. Because one fully laden ship could supply enough natural gas for a city of 45,000 for a year, the platform was a very attractive target.

It was unfortunate that they could not find the shipping schedule online to determine when the next LNG tanker would dock, or they might have waited and attacked it instead. The explosion resulting from the uncontrolled ignition of the LNG aboard would be nearly as powerful as a nuclear weapon.

The center section had the most lights on it, and Nahas could see the huge column surrounded by the concrete support pilings. Inside the column was the off-load piping that led to the shore installation and LNG storage tanks. There was no way they could breach the column, but causing the legs to collapse, dropping as much of the platform as possible into the Bay, was something Rahman, Amari, and their friend Abdul felt could be done.

They were closer now. The pools of light from the platform illuminated the gray of the supporting concrete pilings and the white of the support buildings. Less brightly lit but still visible to Nahas were the large white painted bands wrapped around the support pilings. Nahas could hear the sound of machinery, generators and welding most likely, coming from the central section. Nahas maneuvered them slightly left of it, pointing the raft at two smaller-diameter support pilings that were holding up the narrower part of the platform between the center section and the northernmost section.

"Get the first charge ready, brothers," Nahas whispered. "It is time to strike. Watch the platform for infidels."

The two jihadis at the bow, Khayri and Oma, stopped paddling, laid the paddles to the side, and then readied their G3 rifles, sighting along them the platform. No one was in sight. Behind them, Batul had already set the timers on all their charges. He reached for the first charge and then grasped the gunlike device he would use to attach the charge to the concrete piling. The pilings were entirely smooth and so initially presented a problem for affixing the charges, but the solution was simple, if a little risky.

Nahas guided the rubber raft closer, paddling and steering, now that the other men were occupied with more important tasks. Their forward momentum and a few more strokes from Nahas carried them under the platform and alongside the first of the two legs. Nahas struggled a little, but sidled the raft up against the first piling, then back-paddled a few strokes to hold their position.

"Khayri, help me steady the boat for Batul," he whispered.

Khayri exchanged his G3 rifle for the paddle again and dug into the water. Batul waited until the two men had steadied the raft against the piling and then leaned forward, placing the charge's canvas bag against the piling with his left hand and setting the tip of the Ramset gun in his right hand just inside the cloth loop at the top of the canvas bag. He pulled the trigger.

The .22-caliber blank round in the gun fired, forcing the 3-inch drive pin mounted in the tip halfway into the piling. The sharp crack of the round firing was expected, and Nahas listened and looked up at the platform. He heard no voices or shouts of alarm, only the steady drone of the machinery on the central part of the platform, 60 meters away. They had hoped that both the distance and the usual noises on the platform would allow no one to hear the gun in use. Batul released the canvas bag holding the charge and hung it on the newly installed hook on the piling. Batul turned and smiled at Nahas, then motioned toward the next piling in the support pair a few meters farther under the platform.

Nahas began to paddle and Khayri helped. They were firmly under the narrow span of the platform that supported only the LNG transfer piping and a walkway for the engineers. Someone would actually have to swing from a rope beneath it to see them now. Batul reloaded the Ramset gun with a fresh .22-caliber round and another drive pin, then readied the second charge. Seconds after they reached the second piling, it too had an explosive charge hanging from it.

Staying within the shadow of the platform above them, Nahas guided the raft farther north with Khayri, arriving at the next two pairs of support pilings where Batul affixed four more charges. The last pair of pilings was 5 meters in front of them, and the machinery sounds from the central part of the platform had diminished somewhat.

"Hey, Charlie. It's Dave over in operations." Nahas could tell it was coming from a radio speaker, the volume obviously turned all the way up to overcome the machinery noises on the platform. As Khayri reached for his rifle again, Oma trained his rifle up to the platform in the direction of the sound. Nahas held his hand up and shook his head. Oma did not shoot but kept the rifle pointed, waiting for the order.

"Yeah, Dave. Go ahead." The infidel had raised his voice to be heard over the noise on the platform, and the sound carried over the water to Nahas' ears.

"How much longer will you be?"

"I'm almost finished here. Just a couple more things to check, and we can button it up for this shift."

"Is the purge complete?"

"Nah. It will take another couple hours to get the remaining LNG from the last off-load replaced with Cee-Oh-Two, then air so we can change out section twenty-three of the piping."

"Sounds good, Dave. That means the day shift will have to start it. I'll keep the coffee warm for you. Out."

"Thanks. Out here."

Nahas could not hear the infidel's footsteps, or see him, but Nahas suspected he was still up there. Batul looked at him expectantly. The man would be able to hear the shots from the Ramset gun and would almost certainly investigate, but they could not wait much longer. The timers were still counting down on all the charges, and two of them were still in the raft. Nahas thought quickly, then started whispering orders.

"Oma, Khayri, grab your paddles. Batul, you plant both charges as we get to the pilings, then pick up your rifle and cover us while we paddle back to shore. Oma, Khayri, right piling first, then the left. We'll be pointed toward shore after the second charge is attached. Ready?"

All three men nodded, and once Oma and Khayri had their paddles ready, Nahas helped them position the boat near the rightmost piling. Batul reached up, positioning the canvas bag and the Ramset gun, and looked at Nahas.

Nahas nodded and Batul pulled the trigger. The shot sounded incredibly loud this time, but that was probably because of the adrenaline racing through Nahas' veins. They paddled furiously now, uncaring of whatever noise they made, and reached the second piling. Another shot, and they were paddling again, this time out from under the platform.

Batul grabbed his rifle and pointed it behind them to the left of Nahas' head. Nahas had enough sense to get down, but that left him unable to paddle. No matter—Khayri and Oma could see the shore in the distance and were pulling hard for it. They needed distance now.

On the platform, Charlie Risdon, chief piping engineer on the night watch, thought he had imagined the first sharp sound, but then he heard it again, only a couple of minutes later. Looking around on the narrow expanse of the walkway next to the piping, nothing seemed amiss, but he reached for his big flashlight anyway, unclipped it from his bright yellow work coveralls, leaned over the left side, and looked down. His yellow hard hat nearly slipped off, but he held it in place with his free hand, as the offshore breeze blew past his face.

The platform's structure didn't show any cracks and there was no sign of fire. But as he shined his powerful work light down, he noticed that the water beneath the platform seemed disturbed. It was flattened in an arrowhead-shaped pattern and slightly churned, like in a boat's or canoe's wake.

Panning the light across the disturbance, he moved it toward the shore, intrigued as the churned-up water became more pronounced. His light struck a raft. *What the shit is this?* he thought. *Kids doing something stupid, I'll bet.*

Suddenly, he felt a hammer blow in his upper chest, just beneath his throat, and before his ears could register the loud bang, his whole body went numb from the neck down. Already leaning forward over the safety rail, the weight of his upper body, no longer under the command of his nervous system, dragged him over the edge for an 80-foot drop into the frigid Chesapeake Bay.

"Why did you fire?" Nahas demanded.

"I had no choice, his light found us. He would have told someone," Batul answered.

"We would have been discovered either way," Oma offered, looking over his shoulder as he continued to paddle. "At least now, time will be spent looking for him first."

"Yes," Nahas answered acidly. "As long as no one heard the shot."

Nahas reached for the Midland radio on his vest and keyed it. "Ahmar and Akhdar, this is Azrak, do not respond. Daylight will soon be upon us." The pre-agreed code phrase was to tell the others that they had been compromised.

Replacing the radio on his vest, Nahas addressed Batul, then the others. "Continue to cover us. Faster, my brothers." He reached for his own paddle and dug deeply into the waters of the bay, the resulting splash of icy water chilling his lower hand instantly. Looking up, he could see that they were still 100 meters from shore.

AMARI HEARD NAHAS' RADIO CALL and froze. Behind him, Dabir, Jamil, and Omar saw him halt and stopped, looking down the barrels of their G3 rifles and scanning the woods around them. Amari looked through the last 15 meters of the woods bordering their objective and saw nothing but the perimeter lights along the fence line. He listened closely but heard only the gentle breeze through the trees and the distant hum of a generator.

Amari moved forward, and his small team shadowed him to the edge of the tree line, forming a queue behind the last of the trees. He waved, and Dabir and Jamil took off their packs and removed a set of heavy wire cutters. When Amari saw that they were ready, he waved again, and the two jihadis moved toward the fence, shouldered their rifles, and started cutting through while Amari and Omar covered them.

After the hole was cut, Dabir motioned to Amari to signal his completion. Amari waved at Omar, who then raced to pick up Dabir's and Jamil's packs and followed Amari to the hole in the fence. Once all four jihadis were through, Omar redistributed the packs and the men moved to their tasks. Omar, the group's fastest runner, had the farthest to go; he ran east along the silvery mass of piping heading in that direction. He had shown the most courage during the planning, telling the others, "Allah will be my shield." Dabir and Jamil separated and headed deeper into the facility.

Amari took twenty seconds to survey the area for the best position to hold their entry point in the fence. The Krieger LNG storage tank facility did not occupy a large amount of land, only about six acres, but it held some impressive structures. The four LNG storage tanks were enormous and very substantial structurally. The tanks were arrayed in a square, surrounded by 3-foot-high dams of packed earth, backed by coarse white stone. If the tank's supercooled contents ever leaked, the dams would contain the volatile liquid as it boiled off in the warmer temperatures.

Beyond the tanks were three white cinder-block and concrete support buildings with black shingle roofs. The one closest to the tanks likely held the pumping equipment, Amari reasoned, given its proximity to the tanks and the mass of silvery stainless-steel piping leading from the tanks to the building. The two farther out were probably the facility control and monitoring center, and the guardhouse for the site security force. Both had vehicles parked near them marked SECURITY. Amari had not seen any evidence of an interior patrol yet, but he could see the well-lit vehicle checkpoint and the four guards on duty there nearly 300 meters away.

Choosing a spot in the shadow of the dam around the closest tank, Amari ran over and laid flat on the ground. It was in Allah's hands now.

Dabir was panting heavily by the time he reached the left tank, closest to the support buildings. He kept the tank between him and the buildings and raced up the coarse gravel outer layer of the earthen dam, then down the packed soil to the steel outer shell of the tank. He took off his black nylon pack, set it on the ground, and removed the first device. He checked the small black canvas bag that held it until he saw the white tape, and, making sure to face that part of the bag toward the tank, laid it on the ground up against the cool steel. Hanging from the black canvas was a simple cylindrical timing fuse, and he pulled it, making sure he did not dislodge the bag from its position against the tank.

The steel and the insulating "bottle" within the tank that allowed the liquefied natural gas to stay at −106 degrees Celsius was more than 2 feet thick combined. An ordinary explosive would have serious trouble penetrating it, which was why he carried two. Throwing the strap of the black nylon pack over his shoulder and gripping his rifle tightly, he ran back to the packed dirt of the dam. He looked around nervously and, seeing no one, dropped the pack and his rifle and began digging with both hands, looking around every few seconds as he worked. In a couple of minutes, he had a shallow, rectangular, inset shelf in the dirt that faced the tank, much like the medicine cabinet in his apartment.

Dabir's hands were caked with dirt and sweat dripped from his forehead, but he reached for the pack and withdrew the last item from it: an unmarked brown canvas pack. He fitted it into the dirt shelf, but the top would not fit squarely, so he scraped at the dirt with his hand and then wedged it in. Another pull of the cylindrical timing fuse on this pack, and he began to shift some of the dirt he'd removed to make the cabinet back up against the pack, trying to camouflage it as best he could. Looking around again, he could feel time slipping away. He could not tempt fate any longer. Donning the now-empty black nylon pack again, he hoisted his rifle, and ran back the way he came.

Where were they? Amari was growing more nervous by the moment. He checked the luminous dial of his watch. Nearly six minutes, and they were not back yet. Suddenly, he heard pounding footsteps and raised the G3. Racing in from the east was Omar. He saw Amari in the shadow of the tank and waved, heading directly toward the hole in the fence. Omar would run to the tree line and wait, covering them against the infidels if needed.

Amari glanced down at his watch again and heard more footsteps. Dabir rounded the tank and sped past him, saying, "It is done, brother." Jamil raced past seconds after. "Done, my brother."

Amari waited until they were through the fence and headed to the tree line, then he looked back toward the tanks and listened intently. No shouts, no demands to halt. Nothing. They had done it. Allah was truly with them this night.

Amari ran for the fence, ducked through, and climbed the slight rise to the tree line. All four men were waiting, breathing heavily, the sheen of sweat on their brows. Omar's pack was nowhere to be seen, and Dabir and Jamil's were on their backs but obviously empty. *Good.*

Conscious of their fatigue, Amari led the men deeper into the woods, back the way they came, giving them a chance to recover as they followed. They could not dawdle long, and so after they reached the open area where the dirt service road began again, they jogged down it. A few minutes later, they ascended the wooded slope, and then went down the other side to the parking lot. The car was undisturbed, and the park was still and quiet.

Amari reached for his radio. "Ahmar and Azrak, this is Akhdar. Do not respond. Packages delivered."

RAHMAN HEARD THE RADIO CALL from Team Green and gripped the steering wheel on the Chevy van. Nothing more from Team Blue yet. Nahas and his team must still be moving back to their car at Calvert Cliffs State Park. At least he hoped they were. Had the Coast Guard intercepted them before they got back to shore? They should have thought to bring radios to monitor the police and Coast Guard radio frequencies.

DAVID BUTLER WONDERED WHERE CHARLIE Risdon was. He had been monitoring the carbon dioxide purge on the northern off-load pipes, and he should have been back by now. Butler tried his radio again. "Charlie, this is Dave, what's going on? Report, please."

Nothing.

The off-load monitoring center was sparsely manned at this hour, but Butler had no choice. Like him, Charlie was in his midfifties and might have had a sudden medical problem, although it was more likely the battery had failed on his radio. Butler grabbed a spare battery pack for Charlie's radio, donned his foul weather coat and reflective vest, and headed out the door.

About halfway to the northern off-load point, he started calling, "Charlie!" But there was still no sign of him. As he got closer, Butler flicked the switch on his flashlight and started playing it around. *Where was Charlie?* After a quick circuit of the off-loading equipment, there was still no sign of him. Then he looked at the rail. *Oh, he couldn't have.* Butler leaned over the rail and played his light on the water. The light flashed on the reflective orange and yellow from Charlie Risdon's safety vest. Butler knew it was probably hopeless, but he called out anyway as he pulled out his radio.

"Charlie! Charlie, answer me!"

Keying the radio, he shouted, "Man overboard! Medical emergency! Notify the Coast Guard immediately! Get the storage facility to launch its boat, man overboard near support piling thirty-two."

He kept his light on the base of the piling and looked at Charlie's body, unsure whether his friend was dead or unconscious. He was face-down in the water, not moving at all. Butler was helpless. There was no rigging he could use to rappel down from the platform to pull Charlie up, and it wasn't safe to do that anyway. Instead, he looked around for clues that might explain what had happened. Could he have slipped on something? Then he saw the piping to his right, the blood covering it, and the gash the 7.62mm round tore through the pipe after it had exited Charlie's body.

Butler was a lifelong hunter and knew a high-velocity bullet hole when he saw one. He looked down at Charlie again. He could see what looked like a dark halo around his form, spreading and diluting in the water. He also knew now that his friend was probably dead. He reached for his radio again, his voice laced with panic and urgency.

"This is Butler! Contact the state police and the Coast Guard. I have evidence of a high-powered rifle shot and blood out here! I believe Charlie Risdon was shot, and then fell off the platform! We need help out here, now!"

"MARYLAND STATE POLICE, BARRACK U, this is Sergeant Tomlinson."

"Sergeant Tomlinson, this is Ensign Delisio, United States Coast Guard. We have reports of a shooting and a man overboard at the Lique-fied Natural Gas off-load platform near Calvert Cliffs. The Coast Guard is requesting state police assistance with the shore-based portion of the investigation. One victim reported, male, no other details. The Annapo-lis station is responding with a Defender-class rescue craft, but they are at least thirty minutes away."

Tomlinson was taking notes at his watch desk behind the bulletproof glass overlooking the Barrack U lobby. "Understood, Ensign Delisio, we'll dispatch two patrol cars to secure the area."

"Thank you, sir. Our time is zero one zero four. Out here."

Tomlinson was about to radio in the officers when he realized that the LNG platform was on Homeland Security's list of Priority One infra-structure items. Any criminal activity at a Priority One infrastructure item mandated more than a typical patrol response.

He looked at the car patrol plan on the wall and keyed the dispatch radio microphone. "Trooper 34, Trooper 29, Trooper 16, and Trooper 18, respond to the Krieger LNG platform, shooting reported by U.S. Coast Guard. Respond Code 10-39. Code India, repeat Code India."

Now that the four officers were headed to the platform, Tomlin-son reached for the Homeland Security Manual and turned to the tab marked "Krieger LNG." He had some phone calls to make. The first was to the FBI.

"MR. CAIN." ANOTHER MID-SHIFT in CTS, and for the third time tonight, somebody was interrupting his reading on INTELINK. Cain shifted his upper body to the right, so he could look past his computer's monitor and see down into the watch officer's area on the lower level. Fred Simpson was on duty again at the FBI liaison desk, and he had broken into Cain's reading about ongoing Malaysian counterterror efforts.

"What is it, Fred?"

"The FBI watch center just relayed a report of a shooting on the Krieger LNG platform in the Chesapeake. The Maryland State Police and U.S. Coast Guard are responding, but since it's designated a Priority One item of homeland infrastructure, the FBI is sending a two-man investigation team out."

"Okay. Any assistance request from the Bureau?"

"No, sir. Informational only."

"Thanks, Fred. Let me know if anything else comes in."

Cain leaned back, thinking. This was a problem for the locals and the FBI, but if they asked for any help, Wraith Team Four was just up the road at the Calvert Cliffs Nuclear Power Station. Then another thought struck him. "Emily!"

"Yes, David?"

"Where's the Global Hawk?"

She consulted her console. "Forty-two thousand feet, on an extended orbit over Joint Base Andrews." As an afterthought, she added, "Four hours of on-station time left."

"Okay. Did you catch what Fred told me?"

"Yes, sir."

"Swing the cameras over toward the LNG platform in Chesapeake Bay and just keep a weather eye on things, all right?"

"Sure. On it." Thompson switched screens to the Internet connection and did a quick query for the Krieger LNG platform's geo-coordinates. Once she had them, she switched back to the drone control screen and selected the electro-optical camera controls. She typed in the coordinates, and the camera slewed itself over and locked on them. After a few seconds, the autofocus system sharpened the image and she could see the platform. She zoomed in until it was a bit clearer, and then switched over to the infrared camera.

The previously dim, very dark image now turned a ghostly white from the heat. The platform itself was uniformly dark, with bright spots in the center where equipment was operating. She could also see a group of men clustered near the halfway point between the center of the platform and the northern end. She leaned in to look at the image. That must be where the shooting happened.

"FIFTEEN FOR TWO." MATHEWS SMILED as he moved the peg to the next hole on the cribbage board. Sanders was losing his third game. Movie night had gone really well, but even after the second film, Mathews was not ready to nod off, so he offered Sanders a game or two of cribbage. The ERU leader had accepted and was now regretting it. Lieutenant Corvin watched, having never played the game. Mathews would deal him in on the next hand.

"Damn navy," Sanders smiled to take the sting out of the comment and laid down another card. "Twenty-two."

The rest of the teams were sitting in small clusters, talking, swapping stories from their military or civilian careers, and generally winding down before everybody packed it in for the night. A few of them had already headed into the sleeping area and had started to get settled in.

Mathews was about to lay another card down for two more points when the police scanner in the corner locked on to the Maryland State Trooper broadcast frequency for Calvert County. "Trooper 34, Trooper 29, Trooper 16, and Trooper 18, respond to the Krieger LNG platform, shooting reported by U.S. Coast Guard. Respond Code 10-39. Code India, repeat Code India."

Sanders looked up from the game and locked eyes with Mathews. "Code India is a Homeland Security priority code. There's been an incident at a piece of vital national infrastructure."

Corvin looked at Sanders. "Do you have any actions to take?"

"Not normally," Sanders replied, "but with everything that's been happening lately, particularly with the power infrastructure, I'd feel better if we stood to."

"Agreed," said Mathews. Corvin nodded.

"Let's get everybody kicked loose and geared up," Sanders said as he rose. Responsibility for security at the site was his; Corvin and Mathews were only there in a support capacity.

"I'll reach out to our support people and see what we can learn about the situation," Mathews said, pulling out his iPhone and tapping the secure application to activate it.

A few minutes later, the automated woman's voice said, "Line is secure. Top Secret Special Intelligence." Followed by Colonel Simon's voice, "You're up past your bedtime, Mathews."

"Yes, sir. The local security force has monitored a report of a shooting at the nearby Liquefied Natural Gas platform. Mr. Sanders, the local emergency reaction team leader, described the platform as a Priority One national infrastructure asset, so we're getting everybody up and ready as a precaution."

"Understood. Lend any assistance the local authorities require. Remember that they are in the lead. I'll give the CTS folks a call and make sure they stand by to support you, and remember, the usual rule applies." Mathews, like any other officer in the United States military, knew that rule by heart: Take all measures consistent with the safety of your command.

LIGHTS FLASHING AND SIRENS BLARING, four Maryland State Police cruisers sped south on Route 4, turned left onto Cove Point Road, and then left again into the access road to the Krieger LNG storage facility. The officers driving two of the cruisers immediately put them into position to block entry or exit from the site and began coordinating with the guard force. One officer followed the site's deputy security chief's vehicle for the short ride to the end of the pier, where the insulated silver piping from the offshore platform first came ashore. There, the two men boarded a service boat for the ten-minute ride out to the platform. The last officer drove to the facility's security post to provide on-site coordination with the on-site security chief.

＊ ＊ ＊

"DAVID!" EMILY SHOUTED.

"What is it?" Cain answered as he walked over, donning his headset and clipping the encrypted transmitter and receiver to his belt. He had just gotten off the phone with Colonel Simon. Wraith Team Four was prepping to support local law enforcement, and Cain was beginning to think tonight was not going to be the quiet shift he had been expecting.

When he reached the drone control console, he plugged into the spare jack for the internal comm and asked, "What do you have?"

Thompson pointed at the screen. "I've got what looks like four men moving through the woods here. I put the map overlay up and they're in Calvert Cliffs State Park. I've been there with my family; it's usually closed after dark."

"Kids, maybe?" Cain opined.

"I don't think so. Look." She scrolled up with the mouse wheel, and the Global Hawk's infrared camera zoomed in, locked on the small group of men. Cain could clearly see the outline of the rifles all four men carried.

"Holy shit," Cain breathed. After a few seconds to think, his training kicked in. He raised his voice and addressed the entire floor.

"Ladies and gentlemen, we are in lockdown as of now! The Global Hawk is tracking four men carrying rifles in the middle of a state park, shortly after a man was apparently shot on a Priority One national infrastructure resource. We will provide support to local law enforcement as needed."

Looking over toward Fred Simpson at the FBI LNO desk, he said, "Fred, get either the FBI command post or the Maryland troopers online now. Feed them this as a voice tactical report. Do not refer to how we know. The Hawk's abilities are still classified."

Fred nodded once as he donned his headset. "Got it, 'National Technical Means' it is."

"David," Emily said, "there's more."

Cain turned his attention back to the screen. "Show me, but first, tag those four as Uniform 1 and track them. Also, get the feed up on the main displays."

Emily carried out his instructions, and in seconds, the four men were tagged in the Global Hawk's memory as Unknown 1, known as "Uniform 1" to the team. From now until Emily commanded the drone otherwise, the onboard systems would track that group of four. Next, she linked her display to the leftmost large projection monitor so the entire team could see what she saw. Then she pulled the camera back so that a larger area around Uniform 1 could be seen, and pointed at the screen in front of her.

"Look here, David. See this? These four guys are in the woods, just west of what the map says is the Krieger LNG storage site. That platform was the LNG offloading platform, right? Something weird is going on here."

Cain looked at the display. He could see what looked like another group of four men moving briskly down a dirt road in the woods. After a few seconds, they took a hard right turn into a thin strip of woods. Beyond the woods was a lone car in a parking lot.

"My God." Cain was incredulous. "Zoom in on them now."

Thompson did as she was told. The rifles stood out with this group of four, too.

"Tag them as Uniform Two." Turning to Fred, he said, "Fred, you up with the FBI or the State Troopers yet?"

Simpson looked at him, exasperated. "I'm up with the FBI watch center, but they haven't reached the state police yet."

"Okay. Let me try something." Cain reached down on the transmitter and flicked a switch.

"Whiskey Four Six, Charlie One, how copy?"

Nothing. He repeated the call twice more before he heard, "Charlie One, Whiskey Four Six. Have you five by five. Go ahead." Mathews and his Wraith Team at the Calvert Cliffs Plant were online.

"Whiskey Four Six, Charlie One. We're tracking two groups of men, armed with rifles, a few miles south of you. One group appears to be moving through Calvert Cliffs State Park, and the other entering Cove Point State Park now. Does the site security team there have communications with the state police?"

"Checking Charlie One, wait one." Thirty seconds later, "Affirmative, Charlie One. The leader of the reaction team here is talking to the local barrack now."

"Roger. We can assist with tracking via National Technical Means if they wish. Understood?"

"Roger that, Charlie One. I'll pass that along."

"WELL, DO THEY WANT OUR help or not?" Mathews asked Sanders. Sanders had the phone glued to his ear listening to the state police lieutenant in command at Barrack U. Mathews had his helmet in his hand, the radio earpiece in his right ear, listening for any calls from CTS.

"Yes. Sure. They can tell you exactly where they are." He looked at Mathews for confirmation, who nodded vigorously. All the men from Team Four and all of Sanders' ERU team were clustered around the guardhouse desk where the two men stood, body armor in place, weapons slung and helmets in their hands.

"Relaying this via phone and radio may take too much time. We can have two of them meet you at the entrance to the park," Sanders was saying, looking again at Mathews who nodded in the affirmative.

Sanders confirmed, "They'll be there in five minutes," and hung up.

"Shane," Sanders said, "have two of your people go to Calvert Cliffs State Park. Go south on Route 4 for 3 miles and turn left. Look for the brown signs; you can't miss it."

Mathews turned to his people. "XO, take three of the team and get moving. Use one of the site security cars outside. Meet the State Troopers and follow their lead. You are there to support them. Got it?"

Mathews' Executive Officer, Army Lieutenant Mike Cochrane, replied, "Got it, boss," picked three of the Wraiths nearest him, and headed for the door.

Once they were gone, Sanders turned to Mathews. "I said two, not four."

"I want the troopers to have all the help they might need out there, and my operators always work in pairs."

IN CTS, THOMPSON CALLED OUT, "David, look. The group in Cove Point Park is in the car, heading out."

"I see it. Relay that to Wraith Four Six."

* * *

MATHEWS HEARD THE NICE FEMALE voice from CTS speaking to him again. "Wraith Four Six, this is Charlie Five. Uniform 2 is heading toward the entrance of Cove Point Park now. Request you relay to the troopers."

Mathews spoke into his helmet, "Charlie Five, Wraith Four Six copies. Thanks."

He immediately turned to Sanders with the order. "Call the troopers again. The second group in Cove Point Park is heading toward the park exit now." Sanders quickly punched the speed-dial button for the barrack while Mathews addressed his team.

"Wraiths, I don't know exactly what's going on here yet, but I think it's time we readied up. Master Sergeant Simms, take as many of the team as you can cram into one of our Suburbans and set up a blocking position behind the vehicle control point on the main access road. You're in charge there until I arrive. Leave one of the team here and have him keep the other Suburban's engine running."

Simms had everyone moving in short order for the door. Mathews looked at Corvin and Sanders. "Guys, I think we do it this way. Kevin, your people know the site and are on point, Rob's people and mine will back you up. We've got heavier weapons and if needed, we can be a very visible threat that should discourage any casual troublemakers. Rob, you've got more people than I do; I suggest you augment the ERU, and I'll use my team, divided into two elements, as a mobile rapid-reaction force. I'll also advise you both via radio based on what the National Technical Means cue us to. How does that sound?"

Corvin looked grim, but nodded. "I like it. I'll get my people in position if you're good with it, Kevin—it's your site." Sanders looked at both men, grateful to have their help. They didn't really know if what was going on was any threat to the power plant, but two groups of armed men nearby in the middle of the night was not giving anyone a warm and fuzzy feeling.

"Sounds good, guys." Sanders reached behind him and pulled two radios from their recharging receptacles. "Here, take these. We'll need to be able to talk to one another for this to work. Shane, I don't know how you are going to do it wearing that helmet."

Mathews smiled at him. "I'll manage. The radio headsets are detachable."

Mathews led the way as the three leaders headed outside to join their men. In less than five minutes, each leader had his people deployed and ready for whatever might come.

CHAPTER 12

. . . .

"THERE THEY ARE." MIKE COCHRANE'S comment was unnecessary. Chief Petty Officer Darren Klein, driving the Calvert Cliffs Nuclear Power Station patrol car with Cochrane and the three other Wraiths, could see the four olive-and-black Maryland State Police cruisers clearly, their red and blue lights flashing. Klein slowed the patrol car down as he approached, prepared to turn left into the park entrance.

The four State Troopers were already out of their vehicles, watching the approaching patrol car. Three of them remained near their cars—one just inside his open driver's-side door, the other two behind that vehicle's right side near the trunk. One of the troopers, a corporal, was walking out to Route 4, hand up, ordering them to halt. Cochrane noticed the other officers putting their hands on the butts of their service weapons, and seeing that they were also in good cover positions, assessed their level of caution instantly.

"Hands in the open, Wraiths. Chief, get the interior lights on. We aren't having any friendly-fire incidents tonight." Each of the three passengers left their advanced M8 rifles leaning against the seats, muzzles pointed at the floor, and brought their hands up above the level of the windows, resting them on the windowsills, seat backs, or dashboard. Chief Klein touched the window control to roll down the window on his side and turned on the cabin lights before returning his left hand to the wheel and sliding both hands to the top so they were visible.

The corporal approached the car carefully, staying near the front wheel, allowing his fellow officers to cover him from the roadside, and then stopped dead when he saw the camouflage and body armor the four men were wearing. He placed his hand on his holstered service pistol's grip.

"Identify yourselves!" he challenged.

Cochrane leaned a little to his left and shouted past Chief Klein to be sure the corporal would hear him. "I'm Lieutenant Mike Cochrane, United States Army. With me are Chief Darren Klein, U.S. Navy; Staff Sergeant Tom Kegan, U.S. Army; and Technical Sergeant Sam Wainwright, U.S. Air Force. You should be expecting us."

The corporal visibly relaxed a little, the military haircuts and bearing reassuring him, and came closer to the driver's-side window, looking carefully inside the vehicle, eyes widening as he saw the assault rifles.

"I'm Corporal Hicks, Maryland State Police. I was expecting advisors, not an assault team."

"Sir," Cochrane responded, "we are here to assist you in whatever way we can. The men in the woods appear to be armed with assault rifles and our commanding officer was not sending us out here without the ability to defend ourselves."

The corporal considered that silently and then turned to his fellow officers and said, "Code Four." The other officers took their hands off their weapons.

Turning back to the car, Hicks said, "I'm not sure how you think you can help. This is a law enforcement matter, and you have no jurisdiction here."

"I understand, sir," Cochrane replied. "This is a heavily wooded area, and four armed men, possibly involved in a shooting, will be coming out of it soon. If they rabbit on you, we have the means to track them and help facilitate their arrests."

"Really?" asked Hicks. If Cochrane had failed to miss the skepticism in his voice, he could definitely see it in his face. He knew he could remedy the trooper's doubts.

"Absolutely, sir, I'll be happy to prove it to you," Cochrane said. He tugged his earpiece and integrated microphone free of his ear, then turned the volume way up.

"Charlie Five, this is Wraith Four Five, give me the present position of Uniform 1."

From the earpiece, Thompson said clearly, "Wraith Four Five, Charlie Five, Uniform 1 is still within the Calvert Cliffs State Park, roughly 1,000 meters from the small pond immediately east of the parking lot. It appears that they are staying on the trail and moving west at a good pace."

Corporal Hicks' eyes widened.

Cochrane responded, "Wraith Four Five copies. Still just the four men?"

"Affirmative, Wraith Four Five. We've also taken a closer look at the weapons. They look like G3 assault rifles. Advise the troopers to be ready for hard contact in ten minutes or so."

"Copy Charlie Five. Thanks." Cochrane, turned the earpiece sound down before returning it to his ear. He looked at Hicks. "Still think we can't help?"

After a few minutes of discussion, the troopers and the Wraiths agreed on a plan. The suspects had a vehicle parked in the small lot just west of the tiny pond near the trailhead. The parking lot was shaped like a short, crooked finger, and the troopers moved their cruisers to side-by-side blocking positions at either end of the lot—two cruisers to the north, and the other two to the west—all oriented toward the suspect vehicle at no more than 20 meters away. The cruisers' positions would inhibit a vehicle escape. Each of the Wraiths teamed up with one of the troopers, who were in charge. The Wraiths would back them up and make sure each trooper knew exactly where the suspects were, whether they fled or chose not to exit the woods.

Corporal Hicks had placed an urgent call for additional backup, but with the other four cruisers in the immediate area already deployed to the Krieger LNG storage facility, additional help was more than twenty minutes away.

Each trooper stood behind the open driver's-side door of his vehicle, with a Wraith opposite him behind the passenger door. This gave the small force a wall of armed personnel and police vehicles facing both the suspect vehicle and the trailhead exit leading into the woods. All lights were extinguished, and the Wraiths had donned their helmets, activating their low-light gear. CTS was now providing regular updates on the progress of Uniform 1.

"Wraith Four Five, 300 meters. Passing you tracking data now." Good, Cochrane thought, they had finally gotten the rest of the Global Hawk's communication suite activated. In seconds, through the night vision mode of his helmet that turned the darkness of the woods into a spectral pale and dark green, four yellow diamonds appeared on the high-impact–resistant glass of his helmet's visor. The sophisticated electronics in the helmet and attached computer rig created an augmented-reality view of the world invaluable to a soldier in combat, and years ahead of what any military or law enforcement unit would have. Cochrane made a mental note to tell Colonel Simon to get some nondisclosure forms to the troopers to sign—the technology was still highly classified.

Cochrane and all the Wraith Team members watched the helmet's projected symbols as the group of four armed men moved down the trail toward the blockade point.

"Hicks," Cochrane whispered. "We can see them now." He quickly glanced at the range scale on the mini-map in the upper left-hand corner of the screen. "Two-hundred meters away. They're approaching the far side of the pond."

Hicks, kneeling behind his car door, looked across and through the front passenger section of the cruiser at Cochrane, kneeling behind the passenger side door. "How the hell are you guys able to do that?" he whispered.

"Sorry, Corporal. That is classified information. Just call it 'National Technical Means,' and believe me when I tell you it's utterly reliable. I'll let you know when I have them visually." He could hear the other three Wraiths advising their new law enforcement partners, too.

Minutes passed by, and then: "Hicks, I've got them. About halfway around the pond. Approaching 50 meters. Hang on a second."

Cochrane concentrated on what his low-light system was showing him: four men, all with G3 rifles and vests with extra magazines. Pistols in holsters, too. He missed the backpack straps in his rush to assess them. "Wraiths, relay to your trooper partners. Hicks, definitely four men, can't tell the ages, but they are not out hunting deer. G3 assault rifles and vests with extra magazines, pistols, too."

Hicks thought a second and then said, "I'll let them get off the trail but not to the car. I don't want them to have it as cover."

"Copy," Cochrane replied. Then he said, "Wraiths, remember, this is the troopers' responsibility; cover them as needed. Weapons free." With their helmets, the Wraiths could see the Hawk's feed from CTS and the men, with the yellow diamonds superimposed on them, marching inexorably closer. Cochrane used his right thumb to move the safety selector on his M8 from "safe" to "three-round burst." They had about two minutes until contact.

NAHAS AND HIS MEN WERE keyed up and ready as they reached the trailhead. They had done what they could to deny the raft to any future investigators, opening the air valve and using pocketknives to puncture the hull in a dozen places before pushing it farther out into the water for the tide to take. Knowing the man Batul had shot had likely been missed by now, they had moved steadily and quietly down the trail, trying to make good time.

Once they had reached the small pond he knew they were close to the car. Hopefully, they could make their rendezvous with Rahman and his team soon and proceed with the rest of the mission. He looked back quickly at his men. In the dim light, with his eyes fully accustomed to the darkness, he could see that they were anxious but determined. Nahas knew the infidels would be focusing their attention on the platform now, trying to rescue the man. That would take time. There was practically no chance that the police would figure out what had happened until he and his men were long gone.

Almost to the end of the pond now. One more bend in the trail to go, and he could just see the outline of their car about 25 meters away. The woods were thinning out a little, too.

"DAVID," THOMPSON CALLED OVER HER shoulder. "The car that left Cove Point Park just pulled a U-turn off Route 4, and pulled over behind another vehicle."

Cain looked at her and away from the big display, currently showing the movement of Uniform 1 toward the state police officers and the Wraith sub-team led by Cochrane.

"Any personnel transfer between the vehicles?"

"No, sir. I've now designated the car Uniform 2 and the van they're parked behind as Uniform 3."

"Why?"

"I can see the van's engine running on infrared. They were waiting for them."

Cain felt a tingle go up his back. "Where are they parked, exactly?"

Emily put the map overlay up again. "At the corner of Route 4 and Saw Mill Road." She zoomed out a little.

Oh, shit.

She turned and looked at Cain. "Saw Mill Road is the main road that leads to the Calvert Cliffs Nuclear Power Plant."

Cain's eyes widened. "Those bastards. Broadcast that to all the Wraiths now!" Cain touched the control that allowed him to broadcast on the Wraith tactical frequency.

"Wraith Six, this is Charlie Six. We have two unidentified vehicles parked on the access road to your location, just off Route 4. One of the vehicles is carrying the members of Uniform 2. We believe the vehicles and occupants may be working in concert or related. Recommend you approach with caution and in force."

MATHEWS HEARD THE CALL FROM Cain and relayed the information to Sanders.

"We'll check it out," Sanders told him.

Mathews didn't think that was a wise idea. "Get some additional backup from the state police or the Guard guys. Let Rob and his people back you."

"No. My people and I can handle it. We're trained for these kinds of 'stop-and-frisk' actions, you guys aren't. Besides, we need you guys here at the control point."

Mathews didn't like it, but it was Sanders' call. Sanders and his reaction unit of eight men and women were already running toward their patrol cars when Mathews shouted, "Good luck!" at his retreating back.

Sanders waved in acknowledgment once he crossed to the passenger side of his Chevy Impala patrol car, then he jumped in. In seconds, the engines roared to life, and the patrol cars sped out through the control point, blue lights flashing, heading for the two unknown cars.

RAHMAN LOOKED IN THE REARVIEW mirror as the car pulled in behind them carrying Amari and his team. Nahas and his men were a little late, but he knew from the radio call that they were on their way. He would give them another ten minutes and then proceed with the last piece of the mission, with or without them.

Suddenly, there was a flash of white light farther up Saw Mill Road. Two Chevy Impalas came speeding toward them, blue police lights flashing. Rahman nearly cursed aloud. He could see the white, blue, and red markings of the Calvert Cliffs security force on the hoods. They had discussed this contingency. Looking over his shoulder from the driver's seat, he nodded once.

Farua, the jihadi closest to the Econoline van's right sliding cargo door, pulled the handle and slid it open forcefully. He immediately jumped out, followed closely by the seven men behind him in the van. He laid flat on the ground; others knelt, and some, trusting in Allah's protection, stood. All clicked off their safeties and opened fire on the two cars from a range of 40 meters.

The 7.62mm rounds exited the barrels of the assault rifles at more than 2,000 feet per second, slamming into the unarmored bodies of the Chevy Impalas.

Sanders barely had time to scream out "Gun!" as he saw the men carrying rifles rush out of the Econoline van before the bullets started to scream through the Impala's bodywork. The first three rounds ripped through the center of the dash, and then the fire shifted right and immediately killed the driver. The car began to swerve left, but the hail of bullets did not slacken. Four rounds hit Sanders in the chest, tearing through his standard-issue body armor and turning his heart into shredded muscle.

Without a driver, the car veered left and ran off the road at full speed into the concrete barrier lining alongside the roadway. More high-velocity rounds followed, chewing into the right-hand passenger doors. Sanders was beyond harm now, but the two ERU members in the back seat were only unconscious from the concussion of the impact with the barrier. Then two rounds passed through the man on the passenger side and through the woman on the driver's side, before embedding themselves in the left rear passenger door.

They might have lived if the next five rounds had not hit the rear of the car. The first two ruptured the gas tank, spilling fuel over the pavement. The next three ricocheted off the rear axle, causing sparks that ignited the gas. The car exploded, sending flames and smoke into the air and turning the interior into a crematorium.

The last few men out of the van concentrated their fire on the second police Impala while the other four reloaded. They had taken their time to aim with more deliberation, and their rounds all uniformly blasted through the windshield and windows, sending the car out of control, the ERU members' upper bodies broken and bleeding from the impact of forty-eight rounds ripping through the passenger compartment.

Farua and one of the other jihadis ran over to the second Impala as it slammed into the concrete barrier on the right side of the road. They reached the car in seconds, its engine still screaming at full throttle, the dead driver's foot mashed on the accelerator, and looked inside. The three men and one woman were obviously dead. None were moving, and the bodies were bullet-ridden and bloody. Farua, his zeal overtaking him, fired at the heads one by one to be sure.

Rahman stepped out of the van and shouted, motioning them all back inside the van. "Hurry! We must move now!"

MATHEWS HEARD THE AUTOMATIC WEAPONS fire and instinctively took cover with everyone else. Using the radio Sanders had given him, he screamed, "Kevin! Kevin! Respond now!" Then he heard the small explosion and saw the smoke.

IN CTS, THOMPSON HAD HER eyes closed. She could not look at the infrared display from the Global Hawk, the fire from the first car flaring that small piece of the display out. Not again. Every member of the watch team watched the two cars full of security personnel taking fire from the gunmen. At her desk, Emily's fists were clenched in anger and disbelief. It had happened again. Those animals just stepped out the van and opened fire without any warning at all. Cain saw the fire and ignored it. He could think about them later. Instead, he scanned the watch center. Almost all of the team members wore looks of hardened resolve and resignation. Most of them had witnessed this kind of thing before—it was part of the profession. Usually they were the ones initiating the lethal force, but oftentimes they had to watch helplessly as the military operations they supported resulted in injuries or deaths of U.S. troops.

The younger, less experienced people were the ones he worried about the most. He looked at Emily. Her head hung, and she had her eyes closed at her station. Seeing this so soon after what had happened in Chicago . . . He went over to her and put a hand on her shoulder.

"Emily, stay in the fight. We aren't done here yet. We have to remember them later. The Wraiths need our help now."

Emily looked up at him and took a deep breath. She had chosen this profession, and the anger inside her at the cold-blooded murder of U.S. citizens was pushing the guilt aside for now. "Yes, sir. They do." She looked at the Global Hawk's camera feed. The van and the car were moving, heading east on the road toward the power plant's vehicle control point. She double-checked that the system was still tracking them, pulled the switch on her microphone, and made one slight adjustment to the data feed as she spoke. Her voice started out a little rocky but firmed up as she continued, anger creeping in as she finished.

"Wraith Four Six, this is Charlie Five. The ERU vehicles are gone. No apparent survivors. Uniforms 2 and 3 are now confirmed hostile. Now designated Tangos 1 and 2. Engage and eliminate."

According to a technical reading of law and procedure, only Cain could give that last order, either when the Wraiths were on an overseas mission, or when providing direct support to law enforcement. Seeing the anger and resolve on her face, however, he said nothing. Besides, he agreed. He would log the order officially during the after-action review to keep Emily from any undue scrutiny by the lawyers or Congress later. They were watching an apparent terrorist act happen right in front of their eyes, on U.S. soil, and there could only be one response to that by the Department of Defense. Too late, he remembered the Wraiths assisting the state police with Uniform 1 and grabbed his microphone.

NAHAS WALKED PAST THE TRAILHEAD with his men, only feet from their car, when he heard the distant sound of automatic gunfire. Before he could react, the blinding white light from all four patrol cars' high intensity headlamps and the red and blue strobes from their light bars assaulted his eyes. Then he heard the blaring yelp from one of the sirens. He instinctively raised a hand to cover his eyes and backed away as a man's voice boomed out.

"Stay where you are!" ordered Corporal Hicks over his cruiser's loudspeaker. "This is the Maryland State Police. Lay down your weapons now! You are under arrest."

Nahas tried to think, but suddenness of their appearance shocked him into indecision. The lights did not blind Batul, who was standing directly behind Nahas, and he could barely make out the shape of the two police cars blocking the lot on his left and right through the haloed glare created by Nahas' body.

"Run!" Batul shouted, and he turned around and sprinted down the path. Oma did not hesitate and ran after him. Khayri was just as surprised, and chose to raise his weapon to open fire into the blinding pool of light. As soon as his weapon came up, the combined team of State Troopers and commandos opened fire repeatedly at the two clear targets, their Glock 22 pistols chambered for .40 S&W making distinctive heavy reports.

Corporal Hicks scored first, two of his rounds hitting Khayri in the upper right chest at 1,325 feet per second, shattering his clavicle and ricocheting off the backside of his shoulder blade to corkscrew down into his right lung. Lieutenant Cochrane's rounds were more precisely aimed and instantly lethal. He let the iron sights of his Heckler & Koch M8 assault rifle rest over Khayri's head and squeezed the trigger once. Three 5.56mm NATO rounds from the M8 left the barrel at 2,675 feet per second and entered Khayri's right nasal cavity before slamming through the back of his head like a freight train. As Khayri's body began to fall,

Trooper First Class Monahan's three shots traced a line up the left side of the body, perforating his stomach and left lung.

Simultaneously, Nahas raised his weapon in the confusion to defend himself, but he was a half-second too late. Trooper First Class Zimmerman already had lined up on him—and as soon as she saw the rifle muzzle move toward her and her team members, she fired two quick shots. Both hit Nahas' center mass, tearing into his aorta and left ventricle. The three rounds from Technical Sergeant Wainwright's M8 followed close behind and finished the job, shredding the right ventricle and upper left lung. No surgeon on the planet could save him as he fell backward onto the pavement.

Staff Sergeant Kegan also fired a three-round burst at Nahas, but his body was already falling. The three rounds destined for his upper right chest zipped past his falling form and raced down the trail behind him. The first of the three hit Oma squarely in the neck, shattering the first cervical vertebrae and driving bone splinters and bullet fragments into the base of his brain, killing him instantly. The next two rounds ripped through the initial impact point, severing his spinal cord completely and tearing through his throat. A second later, his body dropped on the trail face-first. His brain never even had time to register how he died.

Trooper First Class Zimmerman could see the last of the four suspects fleeing down the path, and immediately left the cover of her cruiser to give chase. Cochrane saw her race off, and before he could order it, Technical Sergeant Wainwright was running to back her up, only a few steps behind. The trooper was part of their team now, and no team member worked alone.

Hicks started shouting orders. "Troopers, secure the bodies and weapons. Call in shots fired and get us ambulances! Lieutenant, follow me!"

Cochrane was furious. "No! You follow me. I've got the gear to track them, and I'll know where they and the Tango are." Over his helmet-mounted radio, he called to the Wraiths. "Wraiths, Wraith Four Five. Stay on-site here and help the troopers, stay sharp. Wraith Eight, SITREP, now!"

WAINWRIGHT HAD CAUGHT UP TO Trooper Zimmerman and put a hand on her shoulder to stop her. "Wait," he said. "I can track him for you. You'll never find him in the dark and he just might try to ambush you."

Zimmerman was angry at being stopped, but the soldier's words made sense and she belatedly realized that she should not have pursued the suspect in the dark without backup. These suspects were clearly heavily armed and dangerous.

"Okay, soldier, just where is he?"

"I'm not a soldier," he replied. "I'm an Air Force Pararescueman."

"What's that?"

"A cross between a paramedic and a commando. We go behind enemy lines to rescue downed aircrew members. Hang on a second." Wainwright scanned the surrounding forest, the low-light gear built into his helmet imaging systems letting him see as if it were daylight. He couldn't see the Tango, but the yellow diamond superimposed on his display and the marker on the mini-map showed him exactly where he was.

"Got him. One-hundred twenty meters down the trail. He must be running, the distance is opening quickly. You in shape?"

She smiled at the challenge. "You just better be sure we don't lose him, Mr. Paramedic-slash-Commando."

With such a brilliant smile, she was cute as hell for a cop—but now was not the time for romance, Wainwright thought. "No problem. I'll get you within 50 meters of him and then you can make the arrest. Let's hope what we did to his friends makes him more willing to surrender."

Wainwright led off at a jog, and Zimmerman kept pace. As they started off, he heard the XO call for the SITREP.

"I'm with Trooper Zimmerman, sir," Wainwright reported. "We're tracking the Tango deeper into the forest. Zimmerman has point if we close on him."

"Negative. Continue to track but do not close without Corporal Hicks and myself. We're on your six, about 60 meters back."

"Copy that, sir."

At that point, Cain chimed in from CTS. "Wraith Four Five, this is Charlie Six. Be advised, we have a firefight at the Calvert Cliffs Nuclear Power Plant. An unknown number of Tangos just engaged and eliminated the site emergency response team. Two vehicles headed for the plant now, Wraith Six has the word."

Shit, Cochrane thought. Mathews had the bulk of the team with him, and he and his people were too involved in this to help, anyway. He did the only thing he could.

"Wraith Four Five copies all, Charlie Six. Keep me advised."

"Will do, Wraith Four Five, we have eyes on you and the fleeing Tango. Data feeds will continue, we can support both actions. Call in if you need our help."

"Will do, Charlie Six. Thanks."

A FEW MINUTES LATER, WAINWRIGHT could see the distance marker scrolling down. They were closing on the Tango. The mini-map showed him stationary. Wainwright was starting to breathe harder from the jog, but he knew he could go another 2 miles in this gear before he started to feel fatigued at all, especially with the temperature-control garment working to keep his core temperature regulated.

In his peripheral vision he could see Zimmerman staying right with him. Granted, she was not carrying as much kit, but she was also not showing any signs of fading. At 100 meters from the Tango, he slowed to a stop and knelt by a thick tree at the side of the trail for cover. Zimmerman took his cue, and knelt next to him.

"Are we close?" she whispered.

Wainwright kept his eyes front, looking around the tree's trunk in the direction of the yellow diamond painted on the helmet's display by his onboard computer. As he watched, the symbology changed from a yellow diamond to a red square. CTS had just "officially" changed the Tango's status to hostile. The range indicator was steady. "One hundred and four meters," Wainwright said quietly to Zimmerman. "He's either beat from the run, or he wants to lay an ambush for any pursuit."

"Okay. We need some backup to do this right."

"Yep," Wainwright agreed. "Should be here in a minute."

Trooper Zimmerman was about to ask him why he thought so when she heard the footsteps behind them and turned, bringing her service weapon up. Corporal Hicks, led by Lieutenant Cochrane, jogged down the path toward them and knelt behind the same tree. How did Soldier-slash-Medic know they were coming? she wondered. Must be that motorcycle helmet he was wearing. The thing was unnerving. Flat black with the dark glass front, the helmet made the military men look like featureless machines, and very intimidating. Especially in the dark.

"Running after the suspect like that was courageous but incredibly stupid, Trooper Zimmerman," Hicks chided her as he knelt down.

Zimmerman agreed, but was self-aware enough to understand her actions. "I didn't want the suspect to get away, Corporal. I know it wasn't what procedure calls for, but I was too keyed up from the shooting."

"We'll talk about that later. Lieutenant, are you still tracking him?"

"Yes. How do you want to proceed?"

"We wait, and you keep an eye on him. We will call in more troopers and our SWAT team. We'll blanket the area and give him a chance to come out peacefully. We want to question him, and I'm pretty sure the FBI will, too."

"Oh, shit," said Wainwright. "The Tango is coming this way. Looks like he's decided not to hole up."

Cochrane and Wainwright could see the red square growing larger in their HUDs and the distance measurement was scrolling down fast. Cochrane thought quickly.

"We need to set up to defend ourselves."

"Agreed," said Hicks. "Zimmerman, Wainwright, get on the left side of the path by those trees and take cover. We'll move forward a little so we have him in a crossfire."

Zimmerman moved first and headed across the path, Wainwright hot on her heels, when he noticed the range display scroll past 10 meters and looked to his right. The Tango was racing down the path toward them both, screaming something.

Already having chosen to see Paradise this night, Batul screamed, "Allahu Akbar!" as he ran directly toward the infidels he knew were pursuing him. Batul saw the four figures on the path in front of him in the darkness, arbitrarily chose the one on the right, and squeezed the trigger.

Wainwright saw the Tango aim at Trooper Zimmerman and knew he couldn't bring his weapon around in time. He used his forward momentum and longer legs to leap at her from behind, shoving her forward as hard as he could. She stumbled and fell flat on her face, as Wainwright's momentum carried him into the Tango's line of fire.

The selector on Batul's G3 was set on semiautomatic. In the confusion after shooting the man on the LNG platform, he had not safed it or put it on full auto after the ambush back at the car. He intended the sweep of the muzzle to mow down the infidels, but only one round fired, crossing the distance between Batul and Wainwright faster than a human brain could form a thought. The round slammed into Wainwright's right side.

Inside the advanced body armor Wainwright wore, the controlling microprocessor sensed the initial stages of the high-speed penetration, and sent a micro-electric signal to the megnetorheological fluid within the vest in less than a microsecond, causing the already semirigid fluid to harden to something closer to solid steel in another microsecond. The metal molecules suspended inside the unique liquid aligned to become even denser, particularly at the point of impact, catching the bullet and distributing the shock load across the remainder of the semirigid fluid within the vest. The vest saved his life, but the kinetic energy from the shot still slammed Wainwright into the ground with enough force to rattle his teeth.

On the other side of the trail, Cochrane and Corporal Hicks wasted no words of warning after the Tango loosed the single round, and opened fire. The three-round burst from Cochrane's M8 and the four shots from Hick's Glock 22 slammed into the middle of Batul's chest, shattering ribs and shredding his heart and lungs. The close-range shots from the M8, with their higher velocity, created a horrendous, softball-sized exit wound in Batul's back, traveling on for more than half a mile before embedding themselves 2 feet deep in the beach sand at the end of the trail. Batul dropped to the packed earth without even a cry of surprise as death claimed him.

RAHMAN HAD HIS RIGHT FOOT planted firmly on the floor, and the Econoline van was barreling down Saw Mill Road. Amari and his team were right behind them. The police from the power plant coming out to investigate them had changed the timetable. He could only hope Allah would guide Nahas and his team to safety. Surely they would hear the gunfire and withdraw.

With the police alerted, Rahman and his men began to carry out the second option for their attack. They were nearly halfway down Saw Mill Road when Rahman saw ahead of him the overhead power lines leading away from the plant. The vehicle checkpoint was about a half-mile away. After what they had done, it would be locked down now, with armed security guards watching the road. Looking to the right, Rahman could see that the concrete barriers on the side of the road had vanished. Perfect. They had counted on the infidel Americans being fools, and this security breach proved them correct. The security here was really only skin-deep. Once he was directly under the power lines, he shouted to the jihadis in the back of the van, "Hold on!" and turned the wheel hard right.

"CHARLIE FIVE TO WRAITH FOUR SIX. Tangos 1 and 2 have turned right, off the road. Repeat, they have turned right, off the road. Now traveling overland through what looks like an open field."

Mathews was watching the two red squares designating the two targets superimposed on his helmet's visor and checked the mini-map. The Tangos were not heading down the road toward the barricaded vehicle control point any more—they were going to bypass the checkpoint and come overland at the facility.

"Wraith Team, this is Four Six. Relocate to the intersection 400 meters west of here now. Set up a blocking position now."

His second call was to Corvin. "Rob, the hostiles are coming in overland. It looks like they are trying to bypass the checkpoint."

"Copy all, Shane. I'll send some of my people to back you."

"Negative. Hold what you have, but be aware of any threats on your left flank. They have two vehicles and they may split up on us. We'll handle the left flank and fall back to you if needed."

"Copy that. Good hunting."

Mathews and the Wraiths quickly reboarded their Suburbans and raced west down Calvert Cliffs Parkway to meet the incoming threat.

RAHMAN KNEW THIS WOULD BE a rough drive, but he did not

expect it to be this bad. On the imagery they reviewed, it looked like a smooth, open field beneath the three sets of catenary towers supporting the heavy, steel-and-aluminum stranded electrical transmission lines. In reality, the ground was rutted and pitted, and the van bounced and dipped as he guided it across. The men in the back were being thrown about without warning, sliding along the floor because the seats had been removed to allow them to move freely in the interior.

Just as Rahman saw the gap in the trees that heralded their exit from the field to the paved road for their main target, one of the jihadis accidently fired his weapon. Unlike professional soldiers, who always kept the business end of a gun pointed only at things they intended to shoot at, the jihadis had been holding their weapons slung, muzzles pointed forward toward each other and the front end of the van.

Farua fired ten rounds on full automatic before he took his finger off the G3's trigger, and all the bullets went wild. Three of the rounds exited the passenger side of the front windshield, three went through the roof, and the last four lanced through the empty passenger seat and front right firewall, and glanced off various parts of the right suspension before burying themselves in the dirt of the field. The last four rounds passed through Sabir's upper back, killing him instantly.

Rahman looked in the rearview mirror and yelled, "In Allah's name, be careful!" He turned hard left after they passed the trees onto what the maps said was Nursery Road. Farua wasted no time mourning the newest martyr to the cause, and rolled his body out of the way to the left side of the van. They needed to keep the path to the right-side cargo door clear now.

Rahman barreled down the road, remembering that he needed to bear left to reach the target when he saw the large concrete domes. Two black Chevy Suburbans were parked nose to nose in an arrowhead shape at the junction. Ahead, he could see what he thought were armed men behind them and made his first tactical mistake of the night, slamming on his brakes and shouting, "Infidels before us, brothers. Clear them from our path!"

Hamid was closest to the side door and yanked it open, allowing the remaining six jihadis in the rear of the van to spill out. Rahman opened his door and reached back for his G2 rifle, staying behind the door for cover. Behind him, he heard the screech of tires on asphalt as Amari and his men stopped behind them.

IN CTS, EMILY SAW THE vehicles stop. The Tangos began spilling from the cars, and she slammed her fist against the console in frustration. The Global Hawk was not designed for combat. It was a long-duration reconnaissance platform. If she had just one Hellfire missile, they could reduce the odds in about five seconds and give the Wraiths a better chance at succeeding. Without missiles, there was only one thing she could do. She grabbed her mouse and zoomed in tight enough on the scene to be sure to see each of the Tangos. She clicked on their images on her display as fast as she could and the computer put little red boxes around every human shape. Half a second later, the Wraiths knew exactly who they needed to shoot at, and, more important, exactly where they were.

MATHEWS SAW THE MEN EXIT the van and the car behind it through the glare of the headlights pointed his way. He knew his team was outnumbered. He also didn't care. Sudden hard contact was something he and his people trained for regularly. They would have preferred to do a little more "operational preparation of the environment" before contact, as the military textbooks called it, but that was not in the cards this time. The Wraiths did have enough time to get a couple of surprises ready, though.

Mathews and three of his people were crouched behind the two Suburbans, one man each behind the front and rear of the vehicles. The Tangos had opened up full auto, and the Wraiths stayed behind the armored bodies of the Suburbans to avoid the fire, their advanced systems showing them the multiple red squares of their adversaries. Mathews let them have the first few shots. He could feel the body of the Suburban rocking slightly from the hits, as its Kevlar and steel-plate armor absorbed the hits. Now it was their turn.

"Wraiths, this is Four Six. Smoke!" He took the canister from his belt, pulled the pin, and lobbed the smoke grenade over the roof of the Suburban. The other three team members did the same thing, and from four discrete points, huge clouds of smoke billowed and roiled halfway between the Suburbans and the van.

Mathews used his helmet's optics to look through the vehicle and see the positions of the Tangos. Some were lying in the grass, others knelt, and a couple were smart enough to use the vehicles as cover. He took a quick peek around the body of the Suburban, and saw the wispy outline of the smoke on his display. The four smoke clouds effectively hid the Suburbans from the Tangos' vision but clouded his night vision display, too. The team could shoot using just the visual cues from the data feed, but that was not good enough.

Mathews slid his finger along the side of his helmet until he felt the recessed button and then pressed it. The helmet's vision systems switched from night to thermal, and now he could see through the smoke as the world was rendered in a black-and-white monochrome. He saw the black outlines of the van and the car behind it, and also the human shapes of the Tangos: white where their hands and heads were, with shades of lighter and darker black for their limbs and torsos that were covered with clothes, which reduced the heat signature.

"Wraiths, Wraith Four Six. Engage and eliminate," Mathews ordered.

BEHIND THE COVER OF THE Econoline van's driver's-side door, Rahman ejected the empty clip from his G3 rifle and slammed home another as the smoke grenades sailed over the roofs of the black Chevys and landed between the two sets of vehicles. As white clouds blossomed on the road between them, he raised the G3's muzzle over the door hinges and started looking for infidels to shoot. These unbelievers were better prepared than he'd expected. He had emptied one magazine at the vehicles and had yet to see one man to shoot at, then the smoke grenades landed in the road before them—and still nothing. The fools must be thinking of attacking them through the smoke.

Suddenly he heard gunfire in front of him and ducked reflexively. Two of the men from Amari's team, Jamal and Omar, who had been kneeling in the grass to his left, were both now on their sides in the dirt, obviously dead. Rahman stayed down behind the door and looked to the right. He could just see Farua standing bravely, firing into the smoke, when his head suddenly exploded like a ripe fruit, his body dropping instantly to the pavement. Rahman looked back toward the smoke again, expecting to see men advancing through it toward them. But he saw nothing.

In Allah's name! The guards must have advanced visual systems. They were shooting at them through the smoke, not advancing through it! How did Abdul not know about this? In that instant, he knew they would all be martyred and see Paradise that very night. Rahman stayed as low as he could and climbed back into the driver's seat, throwing his rifle onto the floor of the passenger seat; he would not need it any more. He reached out and grabbed the driver's door handle, feeling something hot burn his left forearm, but ignored it as he slammed the door shut, rammed the gear-shift into drive, and flattened the accelerator to the floor.

MATHEWS LEANED OUT AGAIN, CHOOSING a man-shaped outline through the smoke with a red box on his chest. This one was standing just to the left of the dark outline of the van, and Mathews could see the shape of the assault rifle in his hands as the man fired on full automatic, the rounds going high and wide, missing by 4 feet the rear end of the Suburban Mathews was crouched behind.

Mathews brought his M8 up to his shoulder, thumbed the selector to three-round burst, centered the iron sights on the man's head, a bright white blob, and squeezed the trigger twice to be sure. The impact of the six rounds literally blew the white blob into dozens of flying white specks, and the body fell. He shifted his sight picture left, intending to engage one of the five remaining Tangos, and saw two of them fall. The two Wraiths he put on the left flank, in the cover of the small stand of trees, were clearing their sector of the battlefield quickly. The third Tango drew Mathews' attention, suddenly standing and running toward the smoke, firing his weapon continuously. Mathews wasted no time with an attempted head shot at a running target; he aimed center mass and again squeezed twice. The silhouette fell and did not move.

"Seven, jam! Reloading," Mathews heard on the link. It was Mellinger, the other Air Force Pararescueman, on the left flank with Tate, one of the other SEALs on the team. The pair was temporarily one gun short. Mathews widened his sight picture and saw the last two men.

"Lead, engaging on the right," he said, trusting the other SEAL to understand the short message.

"Eight has him on the left," Tate responded.

Mathews heard an engine roar as he fired twice more, seeing his target drop, and in his peripheral vision, Tate's target fell. The left flank was clear, and Mathews turned right, just in time to see the outline of the van as it began accelerating toward the front end of the Chevy he was hiding behind.

Mathews immediately rolled to his left and heard a loud crash as the accelerating Econoline clipped the front end of the nearly three-ton Suburban before racing down the road toward the nuclear plant. *Oh, God,* he thought, rising to a kneeling position and bringing the M8 to his shoulder again. As the sights lined up on the target, he flicked the selector to full-auto and held down the trigger. Across from him, Simms, just recovering from his dive away from the oncoming van, did the same.

RAHMAN CRINGED LOWER IN THE seat as the rear windows blew out. He felt the hot stab of searing pain from his left calf as the first of Simms' hastily fired shots tore through the muscle and shattered his shinbone. Mathews' first rounds tore up more of the van's interior, as stuffing from the passenger seat exploded like popcorn. Then two of Mathews' subsequent shots lanced through Rahman's lower abdomen on an angle, spraying blood everywhere as they exited his body. Three of Simms next rounds also hit him. One tore into Rahman's left buttock, boring its way into his left hamstring. The second punctured his left lung, and the last ripped through his left triceps, missing the bone and exiting through the front windshield.

Rahman's left arm suddenly dangled uselessly, and the new pain in his belly and left leg doubled him over further in the seat. He knew that pain and shock would claim him soon, but he was almost there. Martyrdom was within reach, but Allah was testing him and his desire to see Paradise. Rahman gritted his teeth and held the wheel steady with his body, reaching down between the seats with his right hand for what he needed. He could see the power lines stretching toward the sky from the huge transformer station. Almost there.

* * *

THE M8 RIFLE IN MATHEWS' hands locked open on an empty chamber. The van was nearly 200 yards down the road and still accelerating.
He ejected the empty magazine and slammed home a fresh one as he ran
for the Suburban driver's-side door on the left of the blockade. Corvin
and his guardsmen were still at the checkpoint. Between the two forces,
this last Tango had no chance. Jumping in the driver's seat, he gunned the
engine and picked up the handheld radio set to the Guard's frequency.

"Corvin, Mathews! One of them got past us. Dark blue van heading
your way. Stop him. We are in pursuit, check your targets!"

Dropping the radio on the passenger seat, he felt the Suburban gain
weight. In the rearview mirror, he saw Mellinger and Tate piling in the
back through the lift gate.

"We're with ya, boss!" Mellinger shouted.

Mathews threw the big Chevy into gear and tore after the van. He
could already hear the gunfire in the distance.

CORVIN AND THE GUARDSMEN AT the vehicle checkpoint had
wasted no time. Corvin had reoriented part of his team of military
police to watch the rear while the Wraiths engaged the hostiles. A few
seconds after Mathews' radio call, they saw the blue van hurtling down
the Calvert Cliffs Parkway toward them.

"Stand by, people!" Corvin shouted. He wanted the van well within
the kill zone. The Parkway swerved left and would carry the van right
into the kill box he had envisioned.

RAHMAN WAS IN PAIN, BUT knew that he would know bliss soon. He
could see the transformer station through the sparse tree line to his right,
and the bright glare of the vehicle control point to the left. He could also
see the HMMVs and the armed soldiers. How they came to be there were
not his concern now. It did not matter. Using his right hand to drag the
largest and last of the explosive charges assembled for tonight closer to his
seat, he released it briefly to grip the wheel and turn slightly right.

* * *

AS CORVIN WATCHED, THE VAN angled right, away from the ambush he had set, to race over the clear ground away from the road and along the tree line, passing the transformer station. "Oh, my God," he breathed, realizing the driver's true target now.

"Open fire!" Corvin screamed at his people.

THE MORE POWERFUL ENGINE IN the Suburban was helping Mathews and the two Wraiths close on the van, but they were not in a position to engage yet, still 200 yards back. In front of him, he saw the van angle right.

"He's heading for the transformer pad!" exclaimed Tate.

Agreeing, Mathews tried to press the accelerator through the floor-board, even as he saw the flashes from the M-16 fire start off to his left. He put his eyes back on the van and then noticed it moving past the transformer station toward what was looming in the distance.

"He's going to car bomb one of the reactor containment vessels!" Mathews yelled with sudden realization. "Shoot that son of a bitch now!" he screamed at the two Wraiths.

Mellinger and Tate looked at each other, impotent in the knowledge that they were in an armored car whose windows did not roll down. Mathews quickly realized this and again tried to push the gas pedal through the floor. They would never close the gap in time.

"Charlie Six, this is Wraith Four Six, is there anything you can do?" Mathews implored CTS.

Cain's voice came back instantly. "Negative, Wraith Four Six. We have no national assets available."

RAHMAN WAS NEARLY THERE. THE grassy area he had driven over led him past the vehicle checkpoint and the Parkway curved back to the right to meet him. He could see the three-story-tall cylindrical Containment Building in front of him. This deep in the complex, there was nothing more than a wire fence between him and Paradise. He coughed once, spitting up blood from the ruptured left lung.

The pain was growing worse now, but he kept his foot on the gas, and the van barreled forward. With the last of his strength, he gripped the steering wheel hard as the van blasted through the chain link fence, the bumper tearing away a 14-foot section and dragging it along.

Sixty meters. The containment-building tower loomed large before him, nothing between him and the impact point. He had volunteered for this during the planning. The others had tried to dissuade him, saying that he was a valued leader in the jihad, but he had insisted. He was ready to look into the face of Allah, and his martyrdom would do incalculable harm to the infidels and the Great Satan.

Thirty meters. Rahman reached down, felt the cylinder of the timing fuse and pulled it. Nothing would stop him now. He tried to cry out to exclaim the greatness of Allah, but only coughed up more blood.

Impact. The front of the van hitting the concrete wall of Containment Building 1 caused the van's crumple zones to deform and the airbags to burst open. Under normal circumstances, Rahman would have been seriously injured but likely to survive after a lengthy hospital stay. In this case, however, the large nylon duffle bag next to his seat finished the work the bullet wounds started.

The twenty pounds of C-4 detonated a half-second after the impact, as the five-second timer Rahman triggered reached zero. The explosive wave front obliterated Rahman's body and the van. The van burst into thousands of pieces of metal shrapnel, and Rahman's body split into hundreds of charred fragments, blasted and burned by the compression and heat waves moving too fast for the human brain to track. The sturdier engine block survived, laying at the bottom of an 8-foot-deep crater next to the tower.

Debris flew into the air. Sensors embedded deep in the rebar-lined concrete surrounding Reactor Unit 1 as a precaution against earthquakes registered the vibrations from the high-explosive pressure wave and triggered immediate reactor shutdowns of both Unit 1 and Unit 2. As the small fires at the impact point burned, there was a foreboding silence for nearly two full seconds, and then alarms began to blare all over the site.

CAIN AND THE TEAM IN CTS watched the van hit the containment building and detonate, bound by their own helplessness. Cain crossed the watch floor to the desk area, picked up the grey phone, and punched a four-digit number from memory.

"2988, McKenzie, Team 3 SOO." The Senior Operations Officer in the National Security Operations Center, Don McKenzie, was DIRNSA's personal representative after hours, with the authority to issue operational orders.

"Don, David Cain."

"Hey, David. Working mids again, eh?"

"Yeah. We have a problem. I need you to call DIRNSA."

McKenzie's voice lost its friendly tone. "What about?"

Cain glanced back to the main display panel, watching the Global Hawk's live feed of the area. Emily had pulled the image back a little so that the surrounding area was now visible, the smoke cloud from the explosion drifting east.

"There has been an apparent terrorist attack on a nuclear power plant in Calvert Cliffs, Maryland," he finally said.

The immediate silence on the other end of the line was telling.

Suddenly a brief flash on the screen caught Cain's eye, interrupting his conversation with McKenzie.

"Emily!" he shouted. "What was that?"

"I don't know," she replied. "I can run the tapes back—" she started to say, but then a much larger explosion lit up the screen.

AT THE LNG OFF-LOAD PLATFORM, the four charges planted by Nahas' team detonated within milliseconds of one another, creating the flash that Cain and Thompson noticed. The explosions cratered the pilings supporting the section between the main pumping station and the northern off-load pipes. Three of the supports collapsed immediately, and the fourth buckled.

Seconds later, the two charges planted next to the LNG storage tanks detonated, the shaped charges hammering into the tanks and cutting through the outer skin, insulating bottle, and interior tank skin. The liquefied natural gas poured from the shattered tanks, the supercooled liquid pooling in the surrounding dams and boiling off instantly into its gaseous state in the warmer temperature. Sixty seconds later, just as Cain was about to tell McKenzie what had happened at Calvert Cliffs, the two incendiary charges that were buried in the dam walls around the tank ignited.

The resulting fuel-air explosion created a column of fire fifteen stories high, rising into the night in a red-and-black roiling spire that morphed into a mushroom cloud. The blast wave fanned out in all directions, smashing the pumping, security, and control buildings flat, instantly killing everyone inside. The vehicle windows in all the parking lots blew out and the cars were thrown into the air, tumbling away like rolled dice. The security guards standing in the open at the main gate were flung down the access road across State Route 497, their bodies hammered to pulp against the neighborhood houses and trees.

Within a mile of the blast's center across Route 497, the overpressure wave blew out all the windows of houses, and while the sound of the detonation was heard 20 miles away in Mechanicsville, the wall of fire racing outward from the center of the blast bore down on the unprotected homes, ready to turn them into individual torchlights dotting the landscape.

CHAPTER 13

. . . .

MATHEWS SAW THE VAN DISINTEGRATE and the fireball blossom at the base of the containment building. Instead of stopping the Suburban, he continued to drive toward Containment Building 1. He grabbed the radio on the passenger seat.

"Corvin, Mathews. Myself and two of my team are in the Chevy headed for the containment building for a visual assessment of the damage. Hold your fire."

"Roger that, Shane," Corvin replied before ordering his people to regard the black Suburban as a friendly. He then reached for his cell phone. He had to call his CO.

Mathews guided the Suburban around the small chunks of burning wreckage from the van and drove as close as he could to the containment building. He stopped near the blast site, examining it. The concrete of the containment building was scorched and blackened, with a ragged, foot-deep gouge scooped out of the rock-hard cylindrical wall. Mathews could see the rebar lattice, buried more than a foot into the concrete, bent inward and torn, the green corrosion-resistant paint on the rebar blackened in some places. He couldn't see through the concrete wall into the containment building, though. Satisfied, he drove back toward the vehicle control point, picking up his men en route. On the way, he noticed Corvin's military police unit dispersing around the area, wearing gas masks and establishing an inner perimeter 100 yards from the blast site.

Suddenly, the ground shook and the deep bass sound of the explosions at the LNG storage site rumbled by.

"Charlie Six, Wraith Four Six, we heard and felt one or more explosions. What the hell is going on now?"

It took a minute, but Cain's voice spoke into his ear. "Four Six, this is Charlie Six. We just saw a large set of explosions to your south at the LNG storage tanks. We've got a massive fire at the site. County fire and rescue appears to be responding now. Looks like every fire truck and ambulance in the county is headed that direction."

"Copy that," Mathews responded.

In the next hour, Mathews recovered his team and huddled with Corvin. They both decided that the best thing they could do was secure the site and wait for the experts. It didn't take long before the yellow-suited nuclear engineers and pink-suited nuclear safety experts streamed from the main complex of buildings and began setting up decontamination stations, running radiation-exposure checks of all the people outside and examining the containment building.

Mathews admired their efficiency. In less than a half hour, they had checked all the military personnel and declared them clean. After Cochrane drove his sub-team back from the park, escorted by State Trooper Zimmerman, the on-site medical team even checked out Wainwright after being shot by the Tango. Mathews noticed that the State Trooper kept a close eye on Wainwright, as the bruise on his right side was still a livid red. Based on what Cochrane told him during their quick debrief on the park's events, he was pretty sure Wainwright and Trooper Zimmerman were going to be staying in touch.

REPIN THOUGHT THAT THE SPEED of the Western news media was something to admire. The first reports of the explosions in the Calvert Cliffs area came from the night desk commentator on Fox News, who, as usual, gave the breaking news in a broken and disjointed fashion. Repin suspected it was tough for veteran newscasters to report breaking news, but more so for the talking heads who were far better at providing political commentary than they were dealing with a fast-breaking current event.

Soon enough, Fox had managed to call in some more qualified yet more bleary-eyed prime-time anchors who stepped on set just as the first news helicopters arrived on the scene. The video from the news choppers showed the vast LNG tank farm fully ablaze, and the enterprising pilot, working for the Fox 45 affiliate in D.C., caught sight of the smoke from the nuclear power station, too, focusing the long-range lens of his onboard camera systems on the impact point at the reactor containment building.

Repin rose from the computer and moved closer to the TV for a better view of the footage, even replaying it a few times with his DVR to be sure he saw everything. He could see the yellow- and pink-suited figures near the containment building, and the yellow-taped perimeter they had erected, but he could also see a large number of other people milling about outside the perimeter.

Repin crossed his arms and cocked his head, watching the replay one last time. It was not likely that so many people would stay that close to a breached reactor. The danger and fear of radiation exposure would have caused them to move as far away as possible. Rahman and his men must have failed in their primary mission. There was no way Repin could determine why from looking at just the video footage, and in any event, it did not truly matter. Aziz would realize the benefit of additional police and National Guard forces being deployed to cover the nuclear reactors anyway, adding to the perceived—if not the actual—chaos in America, because even the threat of possible nuclear contamination mandated prudence and public attention.

On the other hand, Repin thought as the helicopter camera swung back to the raging fire, the explosion and uncontrolled burning of the LNG storage tanks also lent itself to the overall objective. Natural gas just became much scarcer in the Delaware, Maryland, and Virginia areas, and although he had not seen any footage of it yet, the damage to the LNG off-load platform was probably significant.

Repin stepped away from the television and walked over to the refrigerator for another can of Sprite, popping the top before heading back to the computer and settling in. Another two or three hours of monitoring the news and he could get some sleep.

JOHNSON COULD SEE SAIC FRENCH shaking his head on the video monitor. He was in a small conference room in the U.S. Embassy in Riyadh, safe from the early afternoon heat, and the secure VTC had just begun. The state-of-the-art fiber-optic connection resulted in a crystal-clear picture, enabling Johnson to see French's displeasure in stunning high definition.

"Explain that again, Agent Johnson," French demanded. What made the situation worse was that French wasn't alone—there were at least two other senior agents on camera. Judging by their gray hair and stern expressions, they were equally unimpressed with the young agent speaking to the Saudi Foreign Minister.

"Yes, sir," Johnson intoned. "I was asked by the minister's special assistant, Akeem, to meet with Foreign Minister Ali last night. The minister asked me what our real purpose was in gaining Saudi assistance to send the military mission into Iran."

"And you told him?" French inquired acidly.

"I told him that I was a junior agent, and needed to speak to my government superiors before giving him more information than he already knew."

French leaned in toward the camera, wondering if Johnson might be playing semantic games. "And what does he already know?"

Johnson read between the lines and responded, "He described a Special Forces mission to capture a man in Iran using the Saudi airline as a covert insertion platform. I told him that was all I knew as well, sir, and that I presumed the president had told the king the same thing."

"Why do the Saudis think we were running a hidden agenda on this?" French asked.

Johnson spread his arms open in a work-with-me-here gesture. "They know from their sources in Iraq that several men were given Islamic burial after their bodies were taken off of an Osprey, sir. We went in to get one man, told the Saudis that, and then we came back with four dead bodies instead, and it's making them wonder if they were played."

French leaned back in his seat. "And they approached you with this because?"

"Because I'm personal friends with the minister's special assistant, who is personal friends with the minister. They went to school together.

It's culturally important to them that they ask through an informal channel first. I also don't think they want to damage or ruin diplomatic relations with a formal request and have it ignored."

French shook his head again. The INHERITOR investigation was giving him more headaches than he expected. The money trail had gone cold, virtually guaranteeing that they would not be able to track Aziz through his financial transactions, and now he was the conduit for back-channel diplomatic conversations between the U.S. and Saudi governments. At least Johnson had the good sense to call home this time. That lesson seemed to have sunk in.

Johnson ploughed on, "Sir, I'd like to recommend that the AUTUMN FIRE reports be passed along to the Saudis. I think they would do quite a bit to reassure them that they were not duped or used in any way."

French paused, considering. "It's not a bad idea, and one I'll pass along, but those reports are classified material and both SECDEF and the president will need to sign off on them being shared, even with a friendly government. Is that clear?"

"Yes, sir," Johnson replied. "I had no intention of passing them along without orders to do so. I just think it would be expedient."

"Good. By the way, you'll probably be hearing some reports in the press soon about an attack against a nuclear reactor and a natural gas storage facility in Maryland."

"Sir? What happened?" Johnson asked, worried. His wife was in Virginia.

"Initial reports are that a small group of terrorists planted explosives at the storage tank farm and conducted an armed assault on the nuclear plant. Both facilities are along the western shore of Maryland deep in Calvert County. The fires will probably burn for days at the tank farm, and there was no radiation leak from the power plant, just a lot of dead terrorists and citizens." Johnson could see the weariness in French's face stemming from what he probably considered a professional failure. One of the FBI's jobs was to stop domestic terrorism, and so far, the Bureau wasn't doing too well of late.

"All right," French continued. "I'll up chain this to the director, and I'm sure he'll call the president and the SECDEF. Once I have an answer, I'll get back to you. It might be a day or two."

"I understand, sir, but Minister Ali said he expects to hear from me in two days. Otherwise, he will recommend that the king call the president directly. That deadline hits tomorrow night, Riyadh time."

French hung his head, exasperated, and then looked up at the camera again. "Great. I'll be back to you when I have instructions. Keep your cell phone handy."

Johnson was about to reply as he saw French reach for the touch pad in front of him, disconnecting the video link and cutting the secure connection. He stared at the blank screen and thought he would head up to the Legal Attaché's office. The attaché was still in the States, but his staff would probably know more about the recent attacks than the news networks would. After he spoke to them and learned what he could, he would call his wife.

SLEEP, RUN, EAT, AND WORK. Saddam thought that this is what military training was like. Every night at sunset when he returned to the small house, he would go straight to his tiny room and collapse on the bed, sleeping until morning. Hazar had only been training them for three days, but it seemed much longer.

On the second day, he ate breakfast before leaving the house, and vomited halfway through the morning run. After that incident, he started to bring his food and leave it on the steps of the training house, using it as his reward for finishing the run as quickly as possible.

This morning, with his breakfast still waiting on the steps, Hazar stood before them, just as imposing as ever.

"Put these on," Hazar instructed, gesturing to the low wall with his left hand, where a set of padded jackets, goggles, and baseball hats sat. His right hand firmly grasped a large, green nylon gym bag.

Saddam was sweating as much as the other men from the run but didn't even think of objecting to the order. The heavy cloth of the jacket was uncomfortable, and the bare skin of his arms, still slick with sweat, itched. As he donned the clear goggles and ball cap, he took a deep breath and let it out, feeling the increased sweat in the small of his back and armpits as the padded jacket trapped his body's heat, preventing it from escaping into the cool morning air.

Saddam tensed as Hazar unzipped the green gym bag and reached inside. Hazar withdrew a long black shape and held it out to the closest of the trainees.

"This is a training weapon. It fires colored balls with compressed air. A gift from the witless infidels to aid us in our jihad."

Saddam took the proffered paintball gun and looked it over. It seemed easy enough to use, and he had to admire the ingenuity. Real rifles would make a great deal of noise and attract the attention of the Yemeni police and military forces. These were virtually silent and could be explained away as young men playing a young man's game if they were questioned during practice.

"Now that you are all ready," Hazar continued, "assault the training house as I have shown you."

The other men gathered around Saddam, again confirming his place as de facto leader of their small group. Saddam stole a quick glance at Hazar, seeing the stern watchfulness of disapproval. He must expect them to fail. They would prove him wrong today.

"My brothers, divide into pairs and remember what we have learned. Work together and clear the ground floor first. Let's go!"

Saddam made eye contact with Jabir, the man closest to him, and nodded, cementing an unspoken agreement to be partners for this exercise. Saddam headed for the front door of the house Hazar had pointed toward with Jabir hot on his heels and the other four men not far behind. Saddam brought his paintball gun up in ready position and approached the front door, staying on the hinged side, Jabir at his left shoulder.

Saddam looked back over his shoulder, past Jabir, and saw the other three pairs of men laying back and covering them from the street, just as the videos had shown. Hazar was nowhere to be seen. He must be watching them from somewhere else, Saddam mused.

Glancing at Jabir to warn him and then back to the door, he stepped out in front of it and kicked once. The door was a flimsy piece of plywood, obviously hung by Hazar for the training exercise, and it burst inward easily. Saddam headed through the door, angling left, as Jabir followed in behind him, angling right. They took two steps into the dilapidated house and knelt immediately, trusting the others to do their part, and keeping their paintball guns up and sweeping back and forth, looking for anything that might be a target. The first-floor room was largely open, with an empty living area to the left in Saddam's field of view, and a small kitchen to the right, just behind the stairwell to the second floor, in Jabir's area of responsibility. The walls were damaged, with wiring and insulation exposed and hanging, and carpets, fixtures, and appliances were gone.

Suddenly, Jabir's paintball gun whuffed twice as the compressed carbon dioxide cartridge propelled two blue paintballs across the room to smack wetly into the paper target hung on the far wall. As he fired, the first of the two pairs in the street came through the front door, angling right through the door and moving to secure the stairwell to the second floor, kneeling at the base and training their weapons up the bare wooden stairs.

In the rush of adrenaline, Saddam wanted to rise and ascend the stairs, but he held his place. He and Jabir had to secure the first floor in case of any surprises.

The last pair of men came in, identified the second team's position and the stairwell, and moved toward them. Climbing the stairs quickly, they vanished from view. Almost immediately, the second team of two followed them. Too soon, Saddam thought. The third team needed to reach the second floor first and secure the landing.

The four men had been gone only momentarily when the sound of repeated paintball firing began. Then there was an unholy scream, and Saddam's eyes widened. He could feel the hair on the back of his neck stiffen as the scream grew closer. What had gone wrong?

A man came down the stairs from the second floor and turned toward him. Saddam held his fire and paid for it when he felt the sharp sting of two paintballs splatter his padded coat, pressing his upper body back with the impact.

Incredulously, he looked down to see the red splotches of paint begin to drip before looking up just in time to see Jabir's face vanish behind a cloud of red paint.

"It's over!" Hazar screamed. "You are all dead. Killed by an unbeliever."

Saddam rose to his feet as Jabir removed his goggles, now thoroughly saturated, along with most of his face, with red paint from Hazar's paintball gun. The other four were coming down the steps slowly, their torsos, like Saddam's, bearing bright red splotches of failure.

Hazar motioned them to him. "You are fools. If this had been real you would all be dead." He looked at Sabih, the leader of the second team. "What went wrong?"

Sabih looked bewildered. "I do not know, Hazar. We followed the third team up, to go left at the top of the stairs . . ."

Hazar cut him off. "And discovered what?"

"You."

"Yes, but more than that. You stopped. You should have shot me instantly, but you hesitated, why?"

Sabih was silent, realizing the answer and not wanting to speak it, shame coloring his face.

Hazar spoke for him. "I will tell you all, and there is no shame in this. You were startled."

Saddam noted that Hazar did not say scared, which is what Sabih surely was at the sight of a screaming form appearing unexpectedly. Saying he was scared would have shamed Sabih deeply. They had all expected paper targets, not someone who would shoot back.

Hazar crossed to Sabih and clapped his hand on his shoulder. "Even I was startled in my first training exercise. This is why you cannot just watch videos of jihadi training, you must do it for yourself. You must expect the unexpected."

Hazar took a few seconds to look them over before speaking. "You all hesitated, and you are all dead. Now you will practice this again until you no longer hesitate. We cannot begin the special training for your mission until you are proficient in the basic skills all jihadis must know."

Hazar looked at Jabir. "Go get bottles of water from the cooler and come back. Rinse your goggles outside, then share the water with your brothers. You will need it."

Saddam's stomach growled in protest, knowing that Hazar would not allow them to eat until they had shown at least some improvement. He wiped the sweat off his face, watching Hazar. The man had skills and obvious experience conducting jihad. Hazar would not have allowed his brother to die, Saddam thought.

The thought of his brother caused him to wonder about his mother. She was probably worried about him, but he had faith that Imam Abdel would see to it that the other Muslim women in the community looked after her. He missed her, but hardened his thoughts. He was here to learn how to fight against the people who took his brother's life.

Jabir returned with the water bottles and gave each man one. Saddam took a long pull on his, placing his thoughts on the task ahead. No hesitation this time.

"All right, we have wasted enough time," Hazar told them. "Get outside and organize yourselves. This time I will walk behind you and I will show you your mistakes as you make them."

Saddam wiped the sweat from his face again, his body now thoroughly drenched beneath the warm padded coat, and walked toward the open front door, placing the half-empty water bottle just inside the door in a small sliver of shade. He expected that he would come back through that door many times today. No hesitation.

THE *SEA TITAN* WAS DRIFTING slowly forward on her course again. Captain Esteban had ordered all stop on the engines an hour ago, and as usual, his expertise at handling the large vessel had placed them right on the mark at only a few knots of headway.

Darkness had fallen three hours ago, and Esteban was on the portside bridge wing, scanning the horizon out of habit more than any real need. The radar was operating continuously now, and it showed only the one ship they expected. Esteban could see her marker lights in the distance. Both vessels were just north of Sand Island, about 300 miles from Midway. A quick call on his INMARSAT phone to the other ship's captain had verified each vessel's identity, and the launch was already heading toward them, a single light in the darkness.

Esteban let the binoculars drop onto his chest and hang from the strap. Then he unclipped the radio from his belt. "Transfer party to the portside docking hatch. Launch coming alongside."

At nearly the *Sea Titan*'s waterline, a small rounded-edge rectangle of light appeared, then grew to a bright beacon reflecting across the water. The pilot of the incoming launch adjusted his course to head straight for it, reducing his throttle to idle 40 yards away and allowing momentum to carry the bright orange-and-white launch the rest of the way.

As soon as the launch was positioned underneath the portside hatch, hydraulically lowered to now serve as a platform, four of the Abu Sayyaf jihadis dropped the free ends of already secured ropes to the rear well deck of the launch from the portside platform. When the ropes smacked the fiberglass deck of the launch, the four men wasted no time and immediately slid down the ropes to the launch, followed by all the remaining Abu Sayyaf men brought aboard for the assault on the *Volkov*.

In less than a minute, only Ramirez and two other seamen were left on the portside platform, and they began dragging the ropes back up, hand over hand. Ramirez heard the launch's motor wind up and suddenly it squirted forward, gathering speed and taking the group of courageous jihadis over to the other ship. In a few days they would be back in the Philippines, continuing the jihad against the unbeliever-led government in those lands. Ramirez silently wished them well as he watched the launch fade deeper into the night, its white foam trail quickly vanishing behind them.

Looking around briefly, he checked that they had gathered all the ropes, and stepped back into the compartment and off the loading door before motioning to one of the seamen, who touched the switch to close the door. As the three-ton steel hatch lifted up into position, Ramirez raised the radio to his lips.

"Transfer complete, securing the hatch now."

On the bridge, Captain Esteban heard the radio call and ordered, "All ahead standard." Moving to the computerized navigation display in the center of the bridge, he looked at the pre-plotted course. Four more days to San Francisco. Prebin and his fellow scientists should be finished with their tasks in two.

"SAYYID, WE ARE APPROACHING OUR anchorage for the night."

"Thank you, Captain," Aziz replied.

Sunset was still an hour away, and the Indian Ocean swells glittered like jewels in the dancing sunlight. The flight to the Maldives from Riyadh had allowed Aziz to sleep for a few hours, and the sail from Feydhoo Yacht Basin to their destination on board his personal yacht, the M/Y *Saladin*, had taken another day.

Fortunately, the *Saladin* was a yacht designed according to Aziz's personal tastes, and his comfort and privacy was assured. The *Saladin* was four stories tall, 70 meters long, nearly 20 meters abeam, and outfitted with all manner of modern luxuries. The hull and superstructure were a combination of aluminum and steel painted a deep charcoal gray, with a sheath of layered Kevlar installed around vital areas like the engine room, bridge, and Aziz's personal stateroom.

Viewed from the dock or the ocean, she was smooth and sleek, with a knifelike bow. Her large, manta ray–like swept wings grew from the center of her superstructure, then drew up and back to wrap around the upper bridge and mid-deck levels at the stern, hiding both from view from anywhere aft of the yacht, but leaving ample open-air deck space. Her four passenger decks topped the combined engine room and crew quarters level, consisting of various staterooms and offices, a gym, a media center, and Aziz's opulent personal stateroom. Although it appeared from the outside that the upper two decks were wrapped in smoked glass, many of these were false windows that merely covered steel bulkheads.

The bridge was a master mariner's fantasyland of the latest generation of marine navigation equipment, automated controls, and global positioning devices, along with all manner of radio communications and Internet connectivity that serviced the entire vessel. Astride the short main mast were two smoky gray, R2-D2–shaped radomes 1 meter tall each, housing multimillion-dollar Raytheon-built ocean surveillance and weather radars.

At the stern, Aziz had even seen to it that the built-in pool conformed to Islamic standards of modesty while still allowing guests access to plenty of sun and fresh air. The pool sat 2 feet lower than the main deck level and was surrounded with 6-foot walls of ocean-wave–etched privacy glass blocks that had not received ultraviolet light treatment. The sheets of privacy glass forming the roof were supported by a lightweight aluminum frame etched with a pleasing pattern of ocean waves. At the very rear of the pool's glass privacy box, extending 10 feet over the water and supported by thick, black steel legs, was the helicopter landing pad and access stairs.

The engine room contained two gas-turbine engines linked to a pair of generators and three Azipod thrusters—two at the stern and one amidships on the centerline. Together, they could drive the *Saladin* at nearly 25 knots in the open ocean and allow the yacht to turn within its own length.

Aziz had been enormously proud of the ship when he had first seen it as it neared completion, deciding then and there in the shipyard to call it "*Saladin*" after the famed Salāh al-Dīn Yusuf ibn Ayyūb. Salāh al-Dīn, the descriptive epithet of the great leader known to the world as *Saladin*, meant "Righteousness of the Faith" and seemed appropriate for the vessel that he would use to sail the seas around the nations of the restored Caliphate.

The bridge interior was a pleasing mix of dark wood walls and a carbon fiber–wrapped main control console that spanned the length of the bridge, holding video displays of engine systems, navigation instruments, and the helm controls.

Only Aziz and the captain, a former officer of the Iranian navy who felt that captaining this floating palace was far better than the ill-equipped patrol craft that was his last command, stood on the bridge. Aside from himself, the ship's cook, and two engine specialists—all men he knew personally as faithful men of Islam—there was no one else on board except the eight men from his newest organizational acquisition, Abu Sayyaf.

Aziz could see the protected harbor before them beyond the pointed bow of the yacht, and motioned toward it, addressing the captain, "Ensure that we anchor bow on to the harbor. I do not want anyone to observe the rear deck from the anchorage."

"Yes, Sayyid. It will take us about twenty minutes to set the anchors properly so we do not drift. I would tell the navigation systems to hold our position with the Azipods, but that would prove a great danger to your men."

Aziz considered his suggestion and agreed. "Take your time, Captain. We cannot conduct our operations until well after midnight."

Aziz took up a pair of binoculars sitting on top of the bridge console and scanned the anchorage. Only three of the ships were present. He checked again to be sure he did not miss the last ship, and still saw only three.

"Show me the radar display of the harbor," Aziz commanded the captain.

The captain saw the anger in Aziz's eyes and hurried to obey, moving to one of the consoles on the right and pointing to the symbols clustered together.

"Here, Sayyid. This display shows all the ships in the harbor and those beyond for a range of nearly 25 miles."

Aziz studied it and shouted, "This tells me nothing! Where are those three ships on the display?" he demanded, motioning to the three largest vessels visible in the distance.

The captain studied the display and then made a small adjustment. "Sayyid, I have decreased the range so that you may see them more clearly." The captain pointed to the three symbols now much larger on the display than they were before and added, "The three ships are less than 2 miles away, as you requested, Sayyid."

"Yes," Aziz countered, "but there should be four ships, not three. Can you see where the fourth ship like those is?"

The captain looked worried and bent to the radar display, changing the range again and looking for a vessel with a similar-sized radar return. He searched as quickly as he could. He had worked for many men like Aziz in the Iranian navy, and knew how quickly anger could become lethal violence.

"Sayyid," the captain said, motioning again to the display. "I've found a similar ship, but it is nearly 3 miles away from our anchor point." Making a quick adjustment and asking Allah to bless the engineer who built the capability into this version of the radar's software, he continued.

"Sayyid, look. The radar return is near what the topographic overlay shows as the main dock. I suspect the ship has moved from its normal anchorage in the bay to the dock either for maintenance or perhaps to on-load or off-load equipment or supplies."

Aziz frowned at the display and then resigned himself to wait. The plan called for strict adherence to the expected time line, but he had learned from Repin in the early days of his planning to build in extra time to account for unforeseen circumstances.

"We will need to wait, then. Once the ship returns to the anchorage, we will strike and the infidels will suffer." He only wished he could be here to witness the labors of the men from Abu Sayyaf.

CHAPTER 14

"IS THAT ALL, LIEUTENANT?" THE charge on Mathews' iPhone was down to 30 percent, but the encrypted line was still crisp enough to hear the weariness in Colonel Simon's voice. The weariness was not surprising. Sunrise was still a few hours away at Calvert Cliffs, and Simon was three time zones behind him. The normal tiredness of a late shift combined with the frustration at another successful domestic terror attack was wearing on both of them.

"Yes, sir. The State Troopers tell us the fires are raging to the south and we can see the fireball from here. That tank farm really took a hit, sir."

"I know it," Simon responded. "Cain and the CTS guys are sending us a live video feed from a UAV over the area. The entire facility is on fire. Looks like fourteen or fifteen fire trucks around the perimeter now, and I can see a couple of Coast Guard vessels near the shore. How's your team?"

Mathews inhaled the cold morning air, thinking about how close it had been. "Tech Sergeant Wainwright was shot once by a Tango before my XO and one of the troopers managed to take the Tango out. Wainwright's body armor took most of the hit, and the paramedics say he's fit for duty, sir. Just a bruise. The high-tech armor really works."

"Yes, it does. I was impressed with the tests before we decided to issue it. I'll send the manufacturer a nice note. Pass my best to your sergeant."

"I'll do that, sir, but I'll be writing him up for a decoration when I get the chance."

"Why?"

"My XO tells me Wainwright saved the life of a State Trooper. The fire from the Tango probably would have killed her."

"Sounds good to me. I'll see to it that General Crane signs off on it," Simon assured him.

"Thank you, sir. Any word on reinforcements for this site?"

"Affirm. The Maryland Guard commander is sending two more platoons for site security."

"Good. We heard from the power plant folks that a Site Team from the Nuclear Regulatory Agency is assembling in King of Prussia, Pennsylvania, for deployment. Until they get here and survey the damage, the plant is permanently off-line."

"Damn," Simon observed. "Looks like the bastards achieved the objective anyway, at least in the short term."

"Yes, sir." Both men knew that even though the plant was not physically damaged in any significant way, the mere fact that it was attacked resulted in the inevitable procedural actions that would delay its return to operation. Every minute the plant was inoperable contributed to the perception, if not the reality, that the Tangos had won this round.

"All right, Wraith Six," Simon said, shifting to orders mode, "once the two additional platoons of guardsmen arrive, I want your unit to return to Joint Base Andrews."

"Will, do sir, but we really didn't get enough time to work with the guardsmen here."

"I know, but I need you back in Andrews. General Crane has been talking to SECDEF about you and your team, and he wants you closer to transport. We'll reach out to the Marine Security Battalion at Quantico and ask them to spare some of their combat veterans to help out the Maryland Guard."

"Understood, sir." Mathews did not like leaving Corvin and his people hanging, but the Marines would certainly help him out.

"I also sent you some upgraded PICTURE WINDOW sensors," Simon continued. "The specifications and operational guidelines are already in your secure e-mail. The equipment should arrive by midday at your hangar."

"Roger that, sir. Anything else?"

"Negative. Out here."

Mathews deactivated the secure app, slid his iPhone into the right rear pocket of his camouflage pants, and walked over to his XO. The Wraiths were standing in a loose perimeter around their two Chevy Suburbans, once again backing the Guard soldiers securing the vehicle checkpoint.

"Let's get everybody loaded up. We're heading back to Andrews after some Guard reinforcements arrive, but we have something to do first."

As his team piled into the two heavy-duty vehicles, Mathews approached the driver's side of the lead Suburban and pulled out the radio set to the Guard frequency. "Corvin, Mathews. Can you and a small team from your unit follow us out to the main road? There's something we need to do."

Corvin's reply was immediate. "Copy. Do we have a situation?"

"Negative. Just one last duty to perform for a friend."

Corvin understood immediately. "Copy that. We're right with you."

Mathews slid behind the wheel and fired up the engine, driving through the main gate and down the access road toward the site where Sanders and his emergency reaction unit had been ambushed.

Mathews saw that the fire was out now. Both vehicles were right where they had stopped. Maryland State Police cruisers barricaded the turn off from the main road, lights flashing. Someone had covered the remains in each car in white sheets, the bodies in the second vehicle having stained them red with blood in irregular splotches. Crime-scene tape ringed the area, and two State Troopers watched the yellow-taped perimeter.

Mathews pulled the Suburban to within 20 feet of the encircling yellow tape and got out, his team following him and automatically spreading out, forming a loose tactical formation. The trooper's eyes widened as they saw the camouflaged uniforms, the armor, and the assault weapons.

Mathews approached the tape, and the trooper closest to him said, "Sir, I'm sorry, this is a crime scene."

Mathews just looked at him. "My friend died in one of those cars, and the people who killed him and his colleagues are dead. You won't be bringing anyone to trial on this one."

The trooper took a long look at Mathews and the armed men behind him. It was probably true, he thought, and when he was responding to this scene, he had heard some of the radio chatter about a military unit on-scene involved in a firefight with a large group of armed suspects. He took a breath to politely but firmly tell the soldier he still could not enter, when he smelled the spent gunpowder on Mathews' uniform.

"Only a minute, and don't approach the vehicles," Trooper Collins said instead.

Mathews nodded his thanks. He could already see what he wanted and it was nowhere near the cars. He motioned his team to stay put, and ducked under the tape. He walked about 20 feet into the scene, toward the right side of the road, and bent down to retrieve one of the AR-15 rifles Sanders and his people used. It must have been thrown from Sanders' car at some point before the car struck the roadside barrier.

Mathews thumbed the magazine release and neatly pocketed it, then pulled the charging handle back to clear the unspent round, pocketing that too, visually ensuring that the chamber was clear. He could not see a helmet, and he could not use his special one, but he had a pair of boots. He knelt, placing the rifle on the ground, then unlaced and removed both of his boots.

Standing again, he took the rifle and pointed its muzzle toward the ground, then swung it up in the air and down again, stabbing it deeply into the frozen earth. Once it was started in the hole, he used his body weight to lean on the butt, burying it another inch or two down. Then he placed his boots on either side of it, doing his best to be sure the makeshift memorial would not fall.

Satisfied with his work, Mathews returned to the perimeter and ducked under the tape again. He could feel the cold pavement against his feet through his socks, and ignored it. He turned back toward the memorial to Sanders and his brave team and bowed his head.

Behind him, the remaining Wraiths and Corvin and his small group moved in closer, bowing their heads and standing in silence. Trooper Collins, moved by the soldiers' gesture of respect, removed his tan felt Stetson hat, and bowed his head as well.

"EMILY," CAIN ASKED, "HOW MUCH LONGER?"

Emily made a quick call to the pilots. "Less than an hour. They've already ordered the Hawk to begin a descent toward the pre-planned insertion point for a landing at Joint Base Andrews."

"Copy that," Cain replied. "When do you think we'll lose usable video?"

"Call it thirty minutes. Maybe a little more. The look angle is already approaching the point where the camera can't gimble higher and the decreased altitude will eventually mean the explosion site is beyond visual range, even with the cameras this thing has."

"Okay. Keep the feeds going as long as you can."

Cain knew DIRNSA and the senior staff of each intelligence agency was riveted to the live feeds coming from the Global Hawk's cameras. Homeland Security had even cross-decked the feed to the Department of Energy, whose experts were already assessing the damage at the LNG tank farm. FEMA had set up a command post just west of the blast site, and the Maryland governor had declared the entire site a disaster area.

Cain noticed that the Bravo team was starting to drift in for the start of their day shift. A lot of them had actually shown up early. Some were using the showers in the gym to get a break from sponge baths at home, and others had heard about the explosions on the radio and had hoped CTS might have more information than the newsies.

"That's it, David. Just lost the look angle. All we can see now is the massive pillar of smoke."

Cain looked at the main screens and decided enough was enough. CTS had done all it could tonight. Simon had told him the Wraiths were heading back to Andrews for a potential overseas deployment, location TBD, and with the Hawk off-station, there was nothing left to do but prep for the shift change briefing and then go home to the last of the dehydrated breakfast food. He and his wife had been using their stock of backpacking food as a convenient way to have hot meals, but after more than a week, they were starting to become monotonous. Maybe he could stop by the cafeteria over in the Ops 1 building on the way out. They were still serving cooked-to-order breakfasts because the NSA's backup generators were more than able to keep the power on. He could grab a couple of takeaway breakfasts and they could reheat them on the propane stove at home.

First things first. He could call his wife and tell her about his breakfast surprise after he took care of his people. "Emily. Go ahead and shut down and give your pass on brief, then go home. Don't wait for the formal stand up. You haven't had a break in hours."

Emily wanted to stay for the formal handover, but after she shut down the video feeds from the Hawk, she noticed her bladder had been calling to her. "Thanks, David. See you tomorrow."

She waved once to him, and found her relief. After a quick run-through of the night's events, she practically ran to the ladies' room.

Once the urgent call of nature was dealt with, she grabbed her backpack and headed to the elevator core. About halfway to the lobby, the fatigue started to hit her, and her mind began replaying the night's events. The car exploding at Calvert Cliffs. More people dead. The ambush and explosions in Chicago. All those lives lost.

Then she remembered designating those animals as Tangos and ordering the Wraiths to "engage and eliminate." Cain might talk to her about that tomorrow. Legally, she was not empowered to issue that order, but he didn't countermand it, either. Damn, it felt good to help the Wraiths track those bastards through the woods and the smoke and kill them. She left the building and headed out toward the parking lot to her usual parking spot near the perimeter fence line. Suddenly, it came to her.

She was sad and felt for the people who died at the power plant and LNG storage facility last night, but she was glad the Wraiths and State Troopers killed the people who were responsible. She had watched it all on the Hawk's video feed. The ghostly black-and-white images of the Wraiths. The hot white streaks of the bullets striking the Tangos, and their bodies falling. They deserved death for what they had done. They had attacked her nation, killed her fellow citizens, and now they were dead.

She knew why the voice in her head from the nightmare in Chicago would not stop torturing her. She needed to help the Wraiths find whoever killed the hostage rescue team and those Chicago cops. Then she would no longer be helpless in the face of her failure. She would atone for it and be able to look at her baby boy with the confidence that she was a good mother and NCO, the defender of her nation she had trained to be.

She reached her car and clambered in, slamming the door behind her, and started the engine, her mind focused on the *how*, oblivious to the chilled air inside the car. She could contribute in CTS, and what she did was important on the watch, but there might be another way. A better way to help get them. She would need to talk to David about it.

The drive home was short, but she smiled for the entire ride.

THE UNIFORMED GUARDS AROUND THE house left nothing to chance. Men stood with slung MP-5 submachine guns every 30 feet around the 8-foot-high outer wall of the upscale but not opulent home on the outskirts of Riyadh. A senior captain with a reserve force of twenty similarly armed men stood in a loose group in the large circular driveway before the house, within the outer wall. The black steel gates were closed and would remain so until the meeting was over. The general insisted on tight security for this meeting with his senior officers, and personally discussed the security arrangements with the captain before permitting him to execute the plan.

Tonight was the ideal night for this meeting. The general's wife and younger children were at his father's house on the other side of the city, with instructions to spend the night. His oldest sons were enjoying a night on the town with their friends, no doubt talking about politics, football, and what they each wanted in a prospective wife. The general was holding his meeting in a small conference room adjacent to his study, and his chief of staff, Major Najjar, had seen to it that pitchers of ice water and bowls of fresh fruit were on the glass conference table.

The general looked over his assembled colonels before continuing. The six men had listened intently during the presentation, and he could see that they were in agreement thus far. "So you see, my friends, the new organizational construct will streamline our structure and consolidate our forces. Some of you will assume new responsibilities, but all of you will now command elements of the same size and material composition. This will give us maximum flexibility and allow me to assign each of you any mission in defense of the House of Saud. Any questions?"

One of the more senior men, Colonel Habib, spoke up first. "Sir, which units will be assigned to Jeddah and Mecca? You seem to have left the two Holy Cities without nearby military protection."

The general nodded, smiling. He had expected Habib to notice the omission. "Protection of the two Holy Cities will now be accomplished with regular rotations of a company of men from each of the six battalions. Each of you will have the opportunity to reward deserving companies of men within your battalion by choosing one to enjoy the privilege and responsibility of guarding the Holy Cities. Each company you select will divide itself between the two cities. This will promote interoperability among our younger leaders and give them a chance to patrol the streets of the Holy Cities with pride, and I will select from deserving candidates a lieutenant colonel to be in overall command. We will continue the standard rotation of full battalions for the increased security needs of the Hajj. Any more thoughts?"

The colonels around the table looked at each other in silence for a few moments, and then the general continued.

"The last item on the agenda for this evening is the future vision for the Kingdom. I have spoken to His Highness about this repeatedly, and I believe now is the time to take you, as senior leaders, into my confidence."

The general paused to look them over and gauge their reactions to his words. Two of the younger officers in the group leaned forward in their chairs, grateful to be so trusted and eager to hear what their King saw for their future. The rest sat expectantly with their eyes glued to the general.

"In addition to modernizing our portion of the military, the King wishes to improve the professionalism of the military services as we continue forward in the twenty-first century. The Kingdom we defend is a leading nation here within the Middle East, and His Majesty believes that we should take a more direct stance in defending Islam in regards to our relations with some of our non-Muslim neighbors."

"He means Israel, doesn't he, General?" interrupted Colonel Habib, his eyes narrowed in suspicion.

"Yes," the general replied. "His Majesty also recognizes that he is no longer a young man, and that his future health may not permit him to see this policy through with the vigor that he would prefer. In a few days' time, he will be calling a meeting of the Allegiance Council to begin the transfer of power to someone more prepared to carry the heavy burden."

Colonel Habib spoke up again. "General, are you saying we are to prepare for war with Israel under the leadership of a new king in the coming days?"

The general nodded sagely. "It is very possible. Insha'Allah, it will not be so, but we have our oaths and we will do all we can to support the new Majesty's efforts to contain Israel and give our Palestinian brothers the homeland they deserve. To facilitate this, each of you will be promoted to General and placed in command positions throughout the—"

"General, this is madness," Habib cut him off. "If we provoke a war with Israel, they will attack us in return, and the Israeli military is very capable. More important, we will alienate a regional partner, Egypt, whose peace treaty with Israel still stands, and worst of all, we shall anger the Americans beyond belief. The American military is not to be trifled with." Isa had served as a young lieutenant alongside the Americans at the Battle of 73 Easting as a liaison officer, seeing firsthand the lethality they brought to the battlefield.

The general looked at Habib with a mixture of indulgence and growing impatience. "The Israeli military is not capable of harming our forces. We outnumber them nearly three to one, and the Americans are not the superpower they once were. I can guarantee that they will not be able to interfere."

Habib opened his mouth to protest anew, and the general raised his hand, silencing him. "Colonel, the decision has been made. I respect your personal views, but I am in command here." Habib lapsed into a sullen silence, and the general could see his eyes flitting back and forth as his mind worked. Habib was always smart, the general mused. Too bad for him.

The general spent a few more minutes discussing the impending promotions for each of the colonels, and which units within the Saudi National Guard each man would prefer to command, and then dismissed them, save for Colonel Habib.

"Habib, come join me in my study. We will speak of your concerns." As he led the way out of the small conference room, he glanced at Major Najjar and nodded. The major looked at Colonel Habib and followed the two men into the study. The general liked his comforts, but his study was relatively spartan, with only a large glass desk for a work area and computer stand, a couch covered in tan fabric, and two chairs.

Major Najjar held out a chair before the general's desk for Colonel Habib and bade him to sit, then returned to the conference room. Once inside, he gathered one of the pitchers of water, two fresh glasses, and a small bowl of fruit from the table and brought them into the study before withdrawing, closing the communicating door behind him.

"So, my old friend," the general began, "tell me of your problems with this new course of action."

Habib was exasperated. "Aren't they obvious? A war with Israel! Putting aside the massive political and moral issues for now, just look at the logistics. Do we strike through Jordan or Egypt? Which of those nations is willing to be our partner and ally in this?"

Habib continued as the general poured a glass of ice water. This conversation was going to take awhile.

NEARLY AN HOUR LATER, MAJOR Najjar knocked on the door and barged in. Colonel Habib was in the middle of making his third heated argument against the attack, this time on political grounds, and turned to upbraid the major for interrupting, but Najjar spoke first.

"Excuse me, General, but your wife is on the phone. She says it is urgent."

The general rolled his eyes and looked at his watch before addressing Habib. "It's probably nothing that urgent. I suspect the children want to speak to me before bed, and she is indulging them as any good mother would."

Habib nodded, and leaned back into his chair, a knowing smile on his face. "I understand, General. My children are long past that age now, but I remember wishing them a good night on many occasions. I would be pleased to wait."

The general shook his head. "No, my friend. This always takes longer than I expect. Come to my office at noon tomorrow and we will continue this conversation. I want you to share your thoughts with me. You have made some good points regarding the strategic and operational concerns, and I would have all your concerns fully aired."

Mollified and appreciative of the general's openness, Colonel Habib stood and saluted. "Thank you for taking the time to listen to them,

General. I will come better prepared for our meeting tomorrow with some documentation. I believe it is important that His Highness see the facts before him so that he may reconsider his decision."

"As do I," the general replied, returning the salute. Habib's own chief of staff, a young captain, was waiting in the hallway to escort him out to the circular drive where the colonel's staff car, a blindingly white Mercedes S55, waited. The young captain held the rear door for his colonel before getting behind the wheel himself, starting the powerful motor, and smoothly driving away.

The general and Major Najjar watched from the windows.

"How long?" the general inquired.

"About ten minutes, sir. Long enough for him to be halfway home."

"SO, DID YOU SPEAK TO your government?" Akeem was lounging on one of the cushions in his living room, his youngest child's plastic toys arrayed around him. Johnson had his back up against the rear wall, sleepy from the good food and his body's unfinished adjustment to the time zone. The television on the far wall was set to the Al-Jazeera English language channel out of deference to Johnson's burgeoning command of Arabic, the volume set low out of deference to the sleeping children.

Johnson could hear Akeem's wife in the kitchen, chatting away on her cell phone. As usual, he had not spoken to her beyond being welcomed to their home and thanking her for the delicious meal of lamb. They had eaten very late, and it was nearly midnight.

"Yes." Johnson yawned and covered his mouth with his hand. "I spoke to SAIC French via VTC at the Embassy. I still haven't heard anything back yet. They are probably still discussing the request at various levels in D.C."

Akeem rose up off the cushion a little, concerned. "This was an informal request, Dave."

Johnson looked at him resignedly. "Yes, Akeem. I know. In your culture, it is an informal request, but in my culture such things cannot be treated informally. You know that from your time in the UK. The president won't be calling the king. I think."

Akeem was not satisfied. "Dave. If he does . . ."

"Look. I can't release or discuss classified information with members of a friendly government without approval. I just can't. I would go to jail. My wife wouldn't like that."

Akeem looked at him and smiled. "No, she wouldn't. I do understand, Dave, but if the president does call the king, the minister will consider it a personal betrayal—on both our parts."

"I know. We must wait, and hope that Insha'Allah, it will work out as we expect."

Akeem laughed aloud. "Yes, we must. You are becoming a very good Arab, you know."

Johnson smiled. "Thanks. I'm trying to learn as much as I can. I regret that my presence inconveniences your wife. I'm sure she would prefer to spend some time with you now that the children are asleep."

"No," Akeem replied. "It is no inconvenience. She would rather catch up with her sister on the phone than spend time with me." Akeem smiled, one man to another. "She has already told me that we have spent too much 'time' together. Four children is enough."

Johnson smiled again, and was about to put his head back against the wall and close his eyes when he saw the burning car on the television screen. He motioned toward the flat panel, "Turn the sound up a little, would you?"

"Fire officials have since extinguished the blaze and we can now confirm the death of Colonel Habib ibn Karim ibn Mahir al-Tuma, a battalion commander of the Royal Saudi Guard. Investigators from the Department of Public Safety have not commented on the cause of the horrible vehicle accident that has taken the life of one the Royal Saudi Guard's most senior colonels, except to say that General Mahir ibn Salib ibn-Hasna al-Issa, commander of the Royal Saudi Guard, has claimed jurisdiction over the investigation."

"Poor guy," Johnson observed, looking over to find Akeem's head bowed, his mouth quietly moving, obviously uttering a brief prayer for the man's soul.

CHAPTER 15

"HOLD IT STILL, VASILY." PREBIN held out the long-handled silver ladle and waited for Vasily to steady the aluminum bottle on the table. A spill now would only contaminate the area further. Their daily radiation checks were showing the expected increase in background radiation, and the men had all followed strict shielding protocols. They had been careful so far, and no one had violated the safety protocols they had devised. The heavy black radiation suits, gloves, boots, and integrated gas masks they wore were rated to protect them against high-energy beta particles and gamma rays up to 130 Kev, as well as toxic chemicals, more than enough to shield them in this relatively low-level radiation environment.

Prebin angled the ladle and began pouring the luminescent green liquid into the spun aluminum bottle. This was the last of the liquid uranyl nitrate, and Prebin watched carefully as he slowly poured. The ladle emptied before the bottle was completely full, and Prebin placed the ladle back into the large stainless-steel bowl they used to hold the supply of uranyl nitrate they had distilled from the fuel rods.

Vasily put the plastic cap on the bottle and made certain to tighten the rubber seal securely, then took it over to the plastic bin filled with water. He swirled the bottle a few times through the water, careful to check for air bubbles that might signify any leaks. Seeing none, he removed the aluminum bottle and dried it on the last of the heavy towels next to the bin. When it was dry, he walked over to the cardboard packing case at the rear of the compartment and placed the bottle into the last slot formed by the tic-tac-toe-board–shaped insert in the packing case. The other eleven aluminum bottles were already in the case.

Prebin carried the bowl and ladle over to the line of three large stainless-steel cases on the right side of the compartment. "Pavel, ready to seal it?" Prebin inquired.

"Da, tovarisch Academician." Pavel had already placed the other contaminated tools they had used to make the uranyl nitrate into one of the steel containers, to join all the remaining radioactive components from the disassembly of the fuel rods. The long zirconium tubes, Zircaloy cladding, bolts, and other parts were now useless pieces of radioactive metal and needed to be disposed of properly. The stainless-steel casks were already sealed in one of the three cases.

Once Prebin placed the bowl and ladle into the case, he and Pavel closed the heavy lid and used the heavy locks to seal it as the others began carefully rolling up or folding the felt-lined tarps and depositing them into the third of the large stainless-steel cases to join the collapsible worktables. Then they sealed that case as well.

The large, lead-lined cases each weighed close to 400 kilograms now. Pavel ran the portable Geiger counter over the sealed cases twice, eyes glued to the electronic readout. Satisfied with the zero reading, Pavel stood, giving Prebin a thumbs-up.

"All right, everyone," Prebin said, "let's get the decontamination procedure started. Vasily, once you are decontaminated, take the packing case outside." Prebin and Pavel walked toward the center of the compartment, and Vasily joined them.

Arkady and Viktor already had the fire hoses ready, but they waited until Leonid opened the drains in the floor at the front of the compartment to move toward the center to stand with the others.

"Hands up, tovarischi," Arkady said, opening the valve on the hose. Viktor followed suit.

Prebin and the rest of the group stood with their backs to them, raising their hands to shoulder level as Arkady and Viktor directed the streams of water over their heads, backs, and legs. After several minutes, Viktor ordered them to turn around while both men continued to wash them down.

Viktor motioned them forward. "Head directly out of the compartment, tovarischi." Prebin led them out, and the men followed in a single file toward the heavy door of the compartment. Vasily bent down near the door and retrieved the cardboard box with the aluminum bottles, while Pavel opened the hatch.

Once the men were clear, Arkady and Viktor began methodically washing the compartment, starting with the lead shields, the stainless-steel cases, and then the ceiling, walls, and floor, always working together and being sure to cover every inch of the room while pushing the runoff water toward the drains near the front of the room. After the room was thoroughly decontaminated, they spent several minutes washing one another down for twice as long as they had washed the others.

PREBIN STRIPPED OFF THE RADIATION suit in the outer compartment. It was fitted out as a makeshift dressing room, with thick white towels on tables, two portable showers, and hooks for street clothes. Portable radiation alarms hung on the walls. Prebin was tired and sweaty, but elated. They had done it. Soon the world would know he was right. He smiled at his friends.

"Tovarischi, I cannot thank you enough for your help and the risks you have taken."

Before any of them could respond, the dressing compartment door opened and Ramirez, the first mate walked in.

"Professor, is it finished?"

Prebin looked at him, mildly annoyed that he had interrupted his moment of celebration with his friends and colleagues. "We are finished. The uranyl nitrate is in the bottles and ready for the press conference. We have enough independent samples to allow for confirmation from every major lab in the United States. No one will be able to argue with what we can now prove."

Ramirez smiled broadly, and crossed the compartment to shake Prebin's hand. "That is wonderful news, Professor. Congratulations. Soon the whole world will know of the dangers of these floating reactors. The Russian government will be forced to shut them all down."

Prebin shook Ramirez's hand, mildly surprised that he was concerned about nuclear safety. "Thank you. Without your help, none of this would be possible."

"Professor, the captain and I are very pleased to help you. When we were told about your concerns, we could not help but share them."

"Spasiba."

"Not at all, Professor. After all your hard work, the captain would like to offer you a chance to dine with him. Knowing you were close to finishing, he has had a few Russian dishes prepared for you tonight. After you and your men have had a chance to shower, he would be very pleased if you were to join him."

Prebin thought some good food to celebrate achieving their milestone was an excellent idea. The ship's cook probably would not be able to prepare the Russian dishes properly, but he appreciated the thought.

"Certainly. Please tell the captain we would be pleased to dine with him. Can we meet him in an hour?"

Ramirez smiled broadly again. "Of course, Professor. I'll let him know."

PREBIN WAS STARVING. IT WAS nearly 7 P.M. local time, and he had not eaten since this morning's shift began. As he approached the captain's mess on the second deck, the smell of the food reached him and he started to salivate. The door was open and he could already hear the voices of his fellows drifting into the corridor. This deck was one of the three crew decks in the stern superstructure, and its white tile floors and carpeted walls made for a pleasant living environment on long voyages.

Prebin turned the corner and entered the captain's mess to see his friends already seated at the long table, set with white linen, fine china, and glassware. Ramirez stood near the head of the table.

"Tovarisch Akademician Prebin!" Vasily exclaimed, rising from his chair. "So good of you to join us. Ramirez insisted on waiting for you to arrive."

"Oh? Why is that?" Prebin asked, puzzled.

Ramirez spoke up from the head of the table. "I had hoped the captain would be here by now. He has been looking forward to congratulating you on your hard work. Unfortunately, he is still dealing with a call from a shipper on the West Coast of the United States. I suggest you start your meal, and I will remind him that you are waiting."

Prebin's stomach growled in agreement. "I think that is an excellent idea, Mr. Ramirez. I'll look forward to the captain's company."

"Excellent, I'll ask the stewards to begin serving you. The menu is printed on the cards before you. We hope it is to your liking."

"Spasiba, Mr. Ramirez." Prebin smiled and sat at the empty place at the end of the table nearest the door, picking up the menu. The first course was listed as traditional *shchi*, cabbage soup. The main course was a choice of minced lamb or beef stuffed in thin dough, called *pelmeni*, accompanied by pickled vegetables. Prebin would need to express his thanks to the chef. These traditional Russian dishes were easy enough to make, and they would no doubt be very savory.

Prebin looked up as three stewards came in, one using hot mitts to carry a large tureen of steaming shchi, and two others holding two bottles each, which they placed around the table.

"*Kvass*, compliments of the captain," one said, as he withdrew. Prebin took one of the bottles and gave its open top a quick sniff as he felt the chilled glass cool the skin of his hand. He smelled the light, fruity, earthy aroma and smiled. Kvass was a fermented beverage made from black or rye bread, and was only mildly alcoholic. It was a perfect way to start the celebratory meal. Prebin poured a generous amount into Vasily's glass on his right and then Pavel's on his left, before filling his own and putting the half-empty bottle back on the table.

Seeing that the others had filled their glasses as well, he raised his glass, and his voice. "My tovarischi. This would not have been possible without your friendship, and your trust in the science, and in me. I am deeply grateful to you all. Spasiba."

Prebin raised his glass in salute, and his friends did likewise, toasting him in return and drinking deeply. Prebin swallowed the cool kvass and was pleasantly surprised to taste strawberries along with the rye. He took another sip as Pavel ladled some of the shchi into his soup bowl.

The shchi smelled wonderful, and he nodded his thanks to Pavel as he tasted it. It was excellent. He began to eat as quickly as manners allowed, and was thinking about asking Vasily to pass the black bread down the table to him when he noticed something disturbing. Viktor had suddenly stopped eating, his face appearing very pale. He began to rise from his chair but fell back into it heavily, struggling to remain erect as he clutched his chest.

"Viktor!" Prebin called out. He began to stand up when he felt a stabbing pain in the center of his chest. Suddenly, his strength left him, and he, too, clutched his chest as a second pain stabbed into his heart. His vision began to cloud; something was very wrong. He could not feel his heart beating beneath his hand, he was having trouble breathing, and was sweating profusely.

Prebin's eyes passed over the table. All of his friends were holding their chests, slouched in their chairs. Viktor was slumped over to the left in his chair, beginning to fall toward the floor. Prebin's vision was growing darker, and an overwhelming sense of panic gripped him. He needed to get help for his friends, but he could not move.

He shifted his eyes right, toward the door the stewards came through, praying someone would come in and help them. Just before death clouded his vision permanently, Prebin saw Ramirez walk through the doorway, smiling inexplicably.

Ramirez looked at each of the infidels in turn, watching as the poisoned kvass finished its work. When the last man was dead, Ramirez looked back over his shoulder and issued orders.

"Take the bodies of these fools and wrap them in chains. I want them overboard before sunrise, along with the large steel boxes in the forward hold where they worked."

"Yes," answered the steward in his native Tagalog. He was one of the last of the Abu Sayyaf men on board. "How shall we get them down to the weather deck?"

Ramirez grinned, sharklike. "Drag the bodies to the hatch on the forward facing side of this deck, and throw them over the rail. They won't mind."

SADDAM HAD LOST TRACK OF the number of times they had assaulted the training house. He and the others were waiting outside in the morning sun before what would surely be another attempt. Hazar would no doubt harangue them again for missing something beforehand, though.

Saddam heard the heavy steps of Hazar's movement through the dilapidated house toward the front doorway and braced himself.

Hazar walked through the open door and motioned the trainees to come closer. "I am pleased. You have done well. In fact, the corrections I gave you earlier were minor. I believe you have earned the right to advance in your training. Follow me."

Saddam was surprised. Hazar's instruction over the last few days had been just as tough as the first. He had even begun timing their practice assaults and reducing the time by five seconds every few attempts.

Saddam followed Hazar, with the other trainees falling in line behind him as usual, over to the main building where they watched the training videos on the first day, and then up the stairs to their second-floor classroom. It had been rearranged. Now there were individual desks and chairs for each of them.

Hazar ushered them into the room. "Take off the safety glasses and padded jackets, and put them in a pile in the corner. Then take a seat."

Saddam went to the cooler by the door, pulled out a bottle of water, and walked over to a random desk, landing heavily in the chair. Taking a long pull of the cold water, he wondered what was next. Hazar was a stern taskmaster, and whatever they were training for would not be easy. The next tasks must be even more difficult than the urban assault basics they had been learning.

Saddam heard Hazar's footsteps again, and the large man came through the door carrying a gray, heavy-duty plastic crate. Saddam leaned forward, wondering what he would take out of the box. Hazar lifted the lid and withdrew a small stack of thin silver cases that Saddam recognized instantly as laptop computers. Hazar handed each man one of the devices.

Saddam placed the laptop on his desk and opened it. It was an older Dell, but it was very light and thin. The case showed some minor scratches, and the lettering on some of the keys on the keyboard were faded, but the laptop was otherwise in good repair. Condition aside, though, how was a used laptop going to help him gain revenge for his brother's death?

"Pay attention!" Hazar demanded. Saddam and the other men fixed their eyes on Hazar immediately.

"You may not think it, but these are also tools of the jihad. They can be very effective tools if you learn how to use them properly." Hazar paused to look them over. "You will learn, because you have been chosen for a very special mission. If you succeed, you will harm the infidels who wage war against Islam in a way that they will never recover from. You will also be guaranteed to see the face of Allah."

Saddam leaned in toward Hazar, curious how they would do that, and noticed some of the other men sitting up straighter in their seats.

Hazar continued, "You have all used laptop computers before? Perhaps in school or at home?"

He had never owned his own personal laptop, but Saddam nodded, having used them in school in Morocco. The others also nodded their heads affirmatively.

"Good. Now I will teach you how to connect your laptop to a network and run a program from a small memory stick. Once you can do it quickly enough, I will show you what to do next."

"I THINK IT'S A GREAT idea!" Emily said forcefully. Why was Jerry being a pain in the ass about this? They were talking in the kitchen, Jeff playing with his toys on the floor, while a gas lamp hissed on the table, throwing bright white light everywhere and casting stark shadows in odd places.

"Sweetheart, why do you want to go on a TDY in the middle of all this?" Jerry asked, the exasperation creeping into his voice. A temporary duty assignment meant lonely nights without her, and those would be worse now without power and only Jeff to talk to.

Emily fixed him with an intense stare. "Because it's my job and I think it's important, especially with everything that's going on."

"Where are you going to go? How long will you be gone?" Jerry asked.

"You know I can't tell you that. In this office, everything we do is classified, even where we go if we go TDY. We went over that when I took the job."

"I know," Jerry replied, exasperated, "and you know I want you to do things that will let you advance your career." He walked over to her and held her by her shoulders. "I just wish you could tell me more about what you do and where you would be."

She started to protest but he quickly interrupted her. "I know, you aren't allowed to tell me. But can you at least let me know if you'll be in danger?"

She looked at the floor, thinking. She didn't think she would be, but if she had the chance to shoot some terrorists . . . "No," she said, looking back up at him, seeing the concern in his eyes. "I shouldn't be in danger. I'll be working with people who are capable of taking care of both themselves and me." That was as close as she could come to giving him an idea of who she would be working with, and she could see from his softened expression that he must have understood she would be with some sort of armed military unit.

He looked deep into her eyes. "I want you to be careful, and I want you to come home to us."

Her heart swelled as she acknowledged that all of his questioning was borne only out of his genuine love for her. "I will," she promised.

Now she just had to convince Cain to let her go. He had to let her go. She needed to get more directly involved in this fight.

MATHEWS TAPPED THE SECURE APPLICATION on his iPhone and waited for the call to go secure. He and his team were about forty minutes away from Joint Base Andrews on Route 4, about 10 miles south of Dunkirk, Maryland. The sun had set an hour ago, and there was only the barest hint of pink left in the western sky.

"Simon," said the voice in his ear after the call went secure.

"Mathews, sir. I just wanted to give you a quick update."

"Go ahead."

"The reinforcing Guard unit is in place at Calvert Cliffs. The initial reports from the NRC team on-site is that there is only minor structural damage to the containment building, and the plant will be able to power up again by tomorrow morning."

"Copy that. We've just seen a directive from Homeland Security to further increase security at all nuclear plants and other power plants on the East Coast. Additional National Guard units should be geared up and deployed in the next few hours. By sunup, every site will have two companies of troops as well as state police to provide local law enforcement authority."

"Sounds like a plan to me, Colonel," Mathews responded.

"Anything else, Lieutenant?"

Mathews hesitated. "Yes, sir. I've been thinking about what's being going on, sir. These attacks have been pretty costly to the nation's energy infrastructure, but something else has occurred to me."

"What?"

"They're keeping us pretty busy, aren't they?"

"I'm not following you, Lieutenant." Simon's tone was flat, communicating the "explain yourself" order without actually saying it.

"Yes, sir. What I mean is that I'm wondering what the intent is behind these attacks. Sure, they are crippling and inconvenient as hell, but I'm wondering what the underlying goal or motivation is."

Simon paused to consider his theory. Mathews thought he might need to add more, when the colonel responded. "I see where you're heading, Lieutenant, but we're not in a position to figure that out, unless you have seen some intel reporting I haven't yet."

"No, sir. I haven't seen anything pointing to why yet. I'm just wondering what the goal is."

"Maybe that bastard Aziz just likes killing Americans, if he's behind it."

"That's possible, sir, but with all these incidents, the police and National Guard are working overtime, and the people in D.C. must be putting in a lot of late nights. It sure is keeping us busy here at home, if nothing else."

MILES FROM MATHEWS AND COMPLETELY unaware of the lieutenant's theory, Cain had reached the same conclusion as he stared into the fire in his living room. His wife was asleep in their bedroom, but Cain was still coming off the last mid-shift cycle and his sleep pattern had not returned to normal yet. This gave him time, however, to replay all of the recent events in his head. The people attacking his country had focused predominantly on the energy infrastructure, not conducting mass killings of civilians. People had died, to be sure, but mostly during an attack on an energy infrastructure site. The rush-hour shootings were the only anomaly, which gave Cain pause.

The shootings seemed to be motivated by pure terror. Random violence, initially at bus stops. Cain thought those were related to the larger attacks, but he couldn't figure out how or why. The other shootings of the repair crews at the transformer stations were probably related directly to the strikes on the power infrastructure, which left everyone in the mid-Atlantic and northeastern states without electricity.

Cain's mind kept coming back to the question of "Why?" One of his instructors in intelligence training once told him about what he called, "the enveloping arms of the angry bear." It was a military planning option that the American defense planners had learned from studying Soviet tactics in the 1960s. Use multiple forces on a battlefield and bring them in from different directions to overwhelm the target, potentially confusing the commanders by giving them too many targets to deal with. Was that what was happening now? The attacks on the power infrastructure had occurred at multiple sites and were certainly damaging, but they were only one threat vector.

For the angry bear analogy to be valid, these other attacks needed to support the main objective, whatever that was. That missing piece— the main objective—brought Cain's thought processes up short. Well, it was a *potential* missing piece. What was it? Was there one? Maybe the objective was the deaths of Americans and forcing others in the U.S. to live primitively. The letter the FBI recovered claimed as much. Cain supposed that the real question was, if there were other attacks coming, what might they be?

Cain considered that carefully. He had been doing his usual daily reading of all the intelligence summaries, but he hadn't been able to spend a lot of time looking deeper at some of the raw reporting for other attack indicators. If those indicators were out there, they might be subtle or seemingly so minor that anyone would overlook them. Moreover, he still didn't know what the main objective might be. If he knew that, he would have a better idea of what to look for.

Starting next shift, Cain would begin a more thorough search of the existing intelligence reporting, determined to find the answers.

CHAPTER 16

REPIN WALKED THROUGH THE APARTMENT one last time, checking to ensure that he'd left no papers out anywhere. It was a routine and ingrained precaution; he did his best to commit nothing to paper that did not end up destroyed shortly after. Passing the computer desk, he touched the mouse and the monitor flared into life, showing the splash screen of a locked desktop. Even if the machine fell into hostile hands, all the drives were encrypted and could not be read without the security keys generated for his logon ID.

If someone tried to guess the password, the special utility he loaded on the machine would activate after two consecutive entries in the security log, recording failed password attempts. The utility would wipe the encrypted hard drive, filling every empty space on the low-capacity flash drive with zeros and overwriting all the data on the drive. Then, for good measure, the utility would trigger a complete reload of a virgin copy of the operating system, leaving a computer forensic expert with nothing to work with.

Satisfied, Repin grasped his brown leather travel bag and hefted it. Unbolting and unlocking the door, he slipped out of the apartment, and knelt down to put the telltales on the door. Once they were in place, he headed down the stairs and out the main door.

The cold wind from the northwest brushed past his face, and he turned east to walk two blocks. Rounding the first corner he continued south until he reached the drive and checked his watch. He had less than five minutes.

He headed up the drive and walked through the automatic glass doors into the large, atrium-like lobby of the Comfort Suites Hotel and sat down in one of the chairs facing the doors. Two minutes later, he saw the green-and-white cab pull into the drive. He rose and headed back out the doors to the cab.

"Hi," Repin said in his best Midwestern-accented English, leaning down to look in through the open passenger-side window. "You here for Corbin? One to the airport?"

"Yeah, buddy," replied the cabbie. "The fare is about twelve bucks, one way. That okay?"

"Sure," Repin answered him.

"Any bags?"

Repin held up his leather bag. "Just this. I'll keep it with me."

The cabbie remotely unlocked the rear door on the passenger side and Repin climbed in. Ten minutes later, he was standing at the electronic kiosk, getting his boarding pass. Another ten and he was through security and standing at the boarding gate. The flight to Oakland was scheduled to last about two hours. He had time for a quick call. After he dialed, he heard three distinct clicks and an increased level of noise on the line. Knowing where he was calling, he assumed the clicks were the telephone system switching him through the INMARSAT relay.

"This is *Sea Titan*, Captain Esteban speaking."

"Captain, this Mr. Green. I was calling to see if the shipment will still be on time."

"Oh, Mr. Green. So good to hear from you. The shipment will be on time. The manufacturers have been paid as we discussed, and we are approaching port now."

"Excellent, Captain. I shall be available to take delivery tomorrow. Who shall I meet with?"

"My first officer, Mr. Ramirez, will meet you. Please call him tomorrow to make the final arrangements," he said, providing Ramirez's phone number.

Repin was about to reply when the gate agent made an announcement, drowning him out. "Thanks for waiting, Southwest Airlines is now boarding Flight 324 to Oakland, with continuing service to Anchorage. Passengers with a Group A boarding pass, welcome aboard."

"I will call Mr. Ramirez tomorrow morning. When must you sail again?"

"We are spending two days in port on-loading supplies and cargo for delivery to Malaysia."

"Good. Thank you, Captain."

The line went dead, and Repin turned off the phone and pocketed it. Time to pick a seat on the airplane.

THE EIGHT MEN AZIZ HAD chosen for this mission busied themselves with equipment checks on the rear deck of the *Saladin* while he watched. The fourth vessel was in position, now anchored close to the other three as was usual. It was nearly 3 A.M. local time and the night was dark, the waning crescent moon having set two hours ago. The captain had been certain to display the standard "ship at anchor" lights on the superstructure, and activated only the stern deck running lights, leaving the brighter, more powerful floodlights mounted above the stern deck on the roofline dark. With the bow facing the anchorage nearly 2 miles away, blocking direct sight of the stern from the harbor and the small amount of light given off by the deck lights, even the most expensive night vision equipment would see nothing if trained on the *Saladin*.

"My brothers." Aziz addressed the Abu Sayyaf men in a clear but muted voice as he stood among them. They all stopped and turned their attention toward him.

"I have prayed to Allah twice this evening for your success. Your actions tonight will be the first direct attack that will lead to the reformation of the Caliphate." Aziz ran his eyes over them, seeing some stand a little straighter under the heavy dive gear.

"Allah will travel with you this night and guide you to the warships of the infidels. Be swift. Be sure and precise in your work, and return. Allahu Akbar!"

"Allahu Akbar!" the eight men responded, keeping the volume of the rejoinder quieter than usual, and repeating it quietly as they headed toward the opening in the stern deck's safety rail. Then, two-by-two, they donned their face masks, put the mouthpieces of the regulators between their teeth, and put one hand over both to hold them in place before taking a long step forward to drop into the Indian Ocean.

Each pair submerged to a depth of 10 feet and swam left a few yards to the line of four orange buoys floating alongside the *Saladin*'s starboard side. Tethered to each buoy by the crew prior to the dive were four Cuda Fury 1500 diver propulsion vehicles. The black, cylindrical vehicles consisted of a tubular battery pack and motor connected to a shrouded propeller. Operated with one hand, with the power to pull two men through the water for eight hours, they were perfect for the night's mission.

Each dive pair approached a Fury 1500 and using hand signals, prepared to move out. The lead diver in each pair gripped the DPV controller with one hand, unclipped it from the buoyed tether with the other, and waited to feel the second diver wrap an arm around his lower leg. When the lead diver felt an additional tap on the leg, he engaged the DPV and set off at 3.5 knots, descending to 20 feet, and using the sharp bow of the *Saladin* to point him toward the targets. The other three pairs of men followed in their wake.

Thirty minutes later, the lead pair saw the first of the massive hulls looming before them and slowed to a crawl, letting the other three dive pairs catch up. They had already studied the radar returns on the bridge of the *Saladin*, but to be certain of their positioning, the lead diver of the first pair motioned the others to wait and angled the DPV toward the surface, turning it off to drift the last 2 feet. As soon as his head broke the surface, he looked around quickly and descended again. Only standard anchorage and deck lights illuminated the four huge ships, and they had come upon the third ship in the column.

Once the lead pair had returned to the others, the lead diver motioned the pairs toward their targets, and then pointed his DPV directly at the ship before him. He guided the DPV back to a depth of 20 feet, and in minutes they were at the stern of the vessel. He could see the massive bronze single screw and rudder, and guided his DPV toward the point where the propeller shaft met the red anti-fouling paint–covered hull. When he was within 5 meters of the ship, he stopped the DPV and looked back at his dive buddy, motioning him forward.

The second man released the lead diver's leg and quickly swam directly toward the shaft entry point. When he could touch the hull, he unclipped the nearly 2-foot-diameter limpet mine from the front portion of his harness. The mine was unwieldy in the water and trailed a long red ribbon attached to a pin, but with two strong kicks, he nestled it close to the spot he had selected, 4 feet from the point where the shaft entered the vessel. The large magnet encircling the outer edge of the mine clamped it to the hull almost as firmly as welding it in place. The second man grasped the end of the red ribbon closest to the pin and pulled it free, allowing the ribbon to sink slowly into the depths of the Indian Ocean, before returning to his partner. A few seconds later, his arm wrapped securely around his dive buddy's leg, the DPV pulled them away from the ship and back toward the *Saladin*.

AZIZ WAS BEYOND PLEASED. HE stood on the stern of the *Saladin*, looking out over the ship's white, frothy wake pointing toward the four large ships, slowly shrinking in the distance. The sun had turned the sky pink, then white. Another few minutes would see it light the hulls of the ships in orange fire, and Aziz did not wish to miss it.

The recovery of the four dive teams had gone well. The men were below, no doubt conducting the morning prayer before enjoying their breakfast and a few hours of well-earned rest. Aziz would retreat to his private quarters to pray shortly. He would have to beg Allah's forgiveness for delaying his morning prayer until after sunrise, certain in Allah's forgiveness because of his duty to the jihad.

Aziz knew it would happen, but he was surprised nonetheless when the sun climbed quickly above the horizon, casting the bright light of a new day on this part of the world. It painted the distant hulls of the four ships in fiery orange and red, in deep contrast to the deep blue-green of the ocean and the crisp, clear blue of the sky. It was a magnificent sight, sure to leave any person in awe of the beauty of nature and with the human drive to sail across seemingly infinite stretches of ocean.

Instead of beauty, Aziz saw in his imagination the fire and death that would open the door to the completion of the first step in restoring the Caliphate under his rule. He smiled. It was time to go to his private quarters and pray.

* * *

CAIN STOOD AT HIS DESK and looked around the CTS watch floor. He had just activated the program that slowly dimmed the overhead lights for the approaching mid-shift and was enjoying the effect. The computer-controlled LED lighting was not only energy efficient, but the program gently shifted the light spectrum from bright daylight to a soft reddish-orange, before assuming a soft twilight glow. The effect was akin to a sunset, which was what the designers had intended, and the behavioral psychologists felt was beneficial in the window-less environs of the CTS. Either way, Cain liked to pause and enjoy it when he worked swing shifts. He felt it was calming somehow, which was probably what the psychologists wanted, he thought with a smirk.

His people, now halfway through the swing shift, were sipping their caffeinated beverages, discussing the latest intelligence reports and opining about one agency's conclusions to one another as they went about their duties.

"Mr. Cain?" Emily Thompson was heading over from her UAV desk, more bright and cheerful looking than he had seen her in the past few days. Cain was pleased to see the change in her, but his instincts warned him that he probably needed to know why.

"Hi, Emily," he responded. "How are you?"

"Good, sir."

"'Sir'?" Cain looked at her quizzically. "What are you up to?"

Emily smiled sheepishly. "Sorry, David. I wanted to ask for permission to do something."

Cain became even more wary. *She's decided to leave CTS. Damn.* "Ask away. What do you want to do?"

"I'd like permission to join a Wraith Team in the field to gain a better appreciation for their operational capabilities and procedures."

Cain was pleasantly surprised, but needed a minute to digest the request. "You rehearsed that, didn't you?"

Emily looked at the floor, her hand figuratively caught in the cookie jar. "A little."

"That's all right. I certainly didn't expect your request, but I'm not opposed to it, either. Tell me why you want to go," he said, adding gently, "Being with a team in the field is going to be very different from watching it through the eyes of a UAV."

Emily looked a little chagrined, but not put off. "I know that. I think that's part of the problem. I want to be closer to the action, and I need to learn firsthand the Wraith Team capabilities. The best way to do that is to be in the field with them."

"Is your deployment readiness up to date?" Like every military member assigned to CTS, Emily was required to keep current on her medical readiness—things like inoculations, recent dental and medical checkups, and minimum physical-fitness standards. She also needed to remain proficient in small arms, maintaining qualifications with the M9 Berretta pistol and the AR-15 assault rifle.

"Yes, sir. I closed out the last of the inoculations and the weapons training just before I reported for duty."

Cain mulled her request over for a few seconds longer. Since the murders of the HRT and SWAT units in Chicago, Emily had seemed distracted and begun showing up late for work. Obviously, the work in CTS had taken its toll, but now she seemed enthusiastic and motivated again. There was no way he would want to dampen that motivation and cause her to backslide in any way. Prior to the attacks, Emily had shown herself to be capable and more than competent, and Cain wanted her to stay on his team for a good long time.

"Okay, Emily. Hang on a second."

Cain leaned down and grabbed the handset for his grey phone, punching in the number from memory.

"Simon."

"Aaron, David."

"Hi, David, what's up?" Simon was immediately on edge. Cain calling him probably meant that shit was going to hit the fan.

"Got a request for you."

Simon relaxed a little. A request was better than notification of another attack.

"Shoot."

"I'd like to deploy one of my people to one of your Wraith Teams for some firsthand experience with Wraith operations and give your people an opportunity to learn about CTS from one of my people."

Simon wasn't so sure that was a good idea. "I don't think now is the best time. We're all up to our eyeballs right now. Most of my teams are overseas anyway, pre-positioned to give us a better rapid-reaction capability."

Cain appreciated his concern, but was not going to be put off. Besides, if it didn't work out, he wanted Emily to hear him try so that she knew he was on her side. "True, but I think having one of my trained people working directly with your folks could be advantageous." Thinking quickly, he added, "Particularly if they are a team we've worked with recently or a new team you have getting qual'd up."

Come on, Aaron, get the hint, Cain thought. It would be good for her to work with the people who were there when the SWAT and HRT units had died.

Simon had worked with Cain for a few years now, and he knew the man well enough to read between the lines. If he was getting the message clearly, there was only one reasonable affirmative answer.

"As it happens," Simon responded wryly, "Team Four is back at Joint Base Andrews now. Your man could work with them if you like."

"That would be ideal. She's got her deployment items in order, and she can be there in six hours or so."

She, eh? thought Simon. Well, that was never a problem. Cain would not send someone who was not capable and qualified. "That works. What's her name?"

"Technical Sergeant Emily Thompson."

"I'll let them know she's coming. Make sure she brings a couple of weeks' worth of personal gear along with her uniforms. If the team deploys, she'll be going along. You know the drill."

"Yes, I do." Once Emily signed out from the CTS, she would be on temporary duty orders to an undisclosed location. Only Cain, Simon, and Emily would know where she was outside of the Wraith Team. Cain would call the commanding officer of her local military unit and let him know she was on a classified deployment with the 152nd, but that was it. As long as she brought along her personal items like clothes and toiletries, she was set. Everything else she would get from the team's set of deployment gear.

"Who should she report to?" Cain inquired.

"Have her go to Hangar 802 at Andrews and ask for Lieutenant

Mathews when she reaches the security perimeter. Are you sending her down in a government vehicle?"

The question surprised Cain. "I hadn't thought about that yet, but yeah, probably. Why?"

"Have her sign out a small van or truck from the NSA motor pool. I need her to take a package to Team Four."

SADDAM'S HANDS WERE A LITTLE sweaty from the morning run, and he wiped them on his pants before letting them hover again over the keyboard and touch pad of the laptop computer Hazar issued to him. There were only two other objects on the rickety desk: his water bottle in the corner and a slim, black, innocuous piece of plastic—a 2 GB flash drive. The bottle's cold exterior was only slightly slick from the low humidity. Saddam wanted to have a drink, but he could not. Hazar was timing them again.

"Go!" Hazar ordered.

He touched the mouse pad and tapped once on the wireless icon in the lower right corner. The wireless network window spawned and Saddam saw the icon for the available wireless network right where he expected it to be. He tapped on it once, and the laptop displayed "connecting." A few seconds later, it was connected. Working quickly, Saddam picked up the compact flash drive and slid it into one of the laptop's ports.

"One minute and forty-five seconds," announced Hazar from behind him. Saddam nearly jumped out of his chair. He had been concentrating so hard on the laptop he had not noticed where Hazar was as he walked around the room watching the trainees.

Using the touch pad, Saddam double-tapped the file icon and opened the file manager, then waited. The laptop still was not showing him the icon for the removable drive. Saddam looked at the display in panic and then remembered that the laptop was still loading the driver for the flash drive. He watched the laptop's display, concentrating on the open file window and waiting. Hazar had told them the driver had been specially configured to choose a random delay time within a certain range to keep the exercise unpredictable.

"Two minutes and fifteen seconds," intoned Hazar, still pacing behind the students. Saddam did not start this time and kept his eyes locked on the laptop's screen.

There it was. The icon for the removable drive appeared and Saddam wasted no time, moving the cursor over the drive and quickly double-tapping it to see the contents. There was only one file, an executable named tictactoe.exe. Without hesitation, Saddam moved the cursor onto it and double-tapped.

The laptop read the software from the drive, loaded it into memory, and ran it in seconds. As soon as Saddam saw the multipart display come up, he raised his hand and turned to face Hazar, now standing near the front of the room.

"Done, Hazar."

Hazar turned toward him, looking at his watch. "Excellent. Only three minutes." He turned to the others. "What about the rest of you?" he asked.

Over the next minute, the other five men slowly raised their hands and nodded. When the last one had done so, Hazar checked his watch again.

"Just over four minutes. Well done." Hazar looked them over, the satisfaction showing on his face. Saddam took advantage of the pause to take a long pull from the water bottle.

"Now it is time for you to learn how we will attack the Great Satan itself."

Saddam nearly choked on his water. They would attack America directly? He could feel the ripple of surprised delight move among the other trainees. Carrying the battle directly to the Americans was more than he had hoped for, but how? Saddam put his eyes on Hazar, waiting for an explanation. Hazar did not make them wait.

"Take a look at the displays on your laptop. We'll start with the large center window. The window has only three gauges on it: one large one in the upper center, and two smaller below it, side by side. Look at the smaller one on the right. It is called an airspeed indicator."

JOHNSON WAS IN THE SHOWER in his hotel room when his phone rang. Shutting off the water and hastily wrapping a towel around himself, he slid the shower curtain aside and stepped out of the tub, snatching a hand towel as well. The ringing continued as he crossed the small suite, dripping water everywhere. He snatched the phone off the desk.

"Johnson."

"Special Agent Johnson, this is SAIC French."

Johnson should have known. French always seemed to call at inconvenient times. Johnson tried to towel off most of the water with one hand as he spoke. "Yes, sir. What can I do for you?"

"I just got off the phone with the director. As a sign of good faith with the Saudis, the president is willing to make your friend Shane and his colleagues available to Akeem and his boss. You'll no doubt remember making some travel plans for them a week or so back."

Johnson had to think to translate French's oblique references. They were willing to send Mathews and his entire team to the Kingdom to explain the mission into Iran to Akeem and the minister.

"All right, sir. When should I expect Shane and his friends to drop by?"

"Not just yet. We want you to talk to Akeem and his boss first and see if it would be okay. Your friend Shane's superiors have also approved the trip, so everything is ready on our end, if your hosts are willing. We can also send along some confidential information, if Akeem's boss would like to read it."

"I understand. I'm seeing Akeem in his office later this morning. He's having a package of Sadig's trial and interview transcripts prepared. I'm supposed to pick them up and formally sign for them today. I'll ask him and call you as soon as I know the answer. I think making Shane available and sending along the confidential information will be very convincing."

"That sounds like a good idea. I hope your hosts appreciate that we are asking informally first," French offered wryly. "If the meeting goes well between you, Shane, and Akeem, we'll arrange for someone more senior to come out for a ministerial-level meeting."

"I think that the informal request will be welcomed, and probably accepted after some back-channel discussion," Johnson responded.

"Good. Call me back when you have an answer."

The line went dead, and Johnson checked the time displayed on his phone. He had enough time to finish cleaning up and get a leisurely brunch in the hotel restaurant before heading for his appointment with Akeem at noon.

CHAPTER 17

THE LATE PART OF THE mid-watch aboard the M/V TSgt *John A. Chapman* was always a quiet one, especially resting at anchor in the center of the Indian Ocean at her homeport of Diego Garcia. Jerry Sondheim always found the mid-watch as peaceful as the other members of the twenty-one-man contracted crew did. Unless sailing the *Chapman* out on one of her regular deployment cruises, the ship usually sat anchored in her normal location just offshore of the Diego Garcia base, her nearly 700-foot-long black hull, white superstructure, and dark red container off-loading cranes contrasting sharply with the deep blue of the Indian Ocean.

Sondheim had served aboard her under his current contract for nearly a year. His duties as a lead engineer kept him below decks when she was underway, or when she was undergoing an annual overhaul of all of her engine and power systems. He took pride in his duties, understanding not only the mission of the ship, which was to provide munitions and spare parts for U.S. and Allied Air Force aircraft in the event of war anywhere in the Middle East, but also learning about the man the ship was named after.

Assigned to the 24th Special Tactics Squadron, and fighting against the Taliban during Operation Anaconda in Afghanistan, Technical Sergeant John A. Chapman died a hero back in 2012.

Chapman and his team were in a helicopter, and as they prepared to land, the helicopter came under heavy machine-gun fire and took a hit from a rocket-propelled grenade. The RPG explosion caused a SEAL team member to fall from the helicopter, and the severely damaged aircraft made an emergency landing 7 kilometers away from where the SEAL fell. Chapman called in an AC-130 gunship to provide close-air support and cover for the stranded team before directing the gunship to search for the missing team member.

Chapman then called for, coordinated, and controlled an evacuation helicopter for the team, limiting their exposure to enemy fire. Once they were evacuated, Chapman selflessly volunteered to go with the rescue team to recover the missing SEAL commando. At the rescue location, he engaged and killed two hostiles and continued advancing toward the SEAL's position until he encountered and engaged a dug-in machine-gun nest. The rescue team came under enemy fire from three directions, and Chapman continued to exchange fire at close range with the Taliban forces until he succumbed to multiple wounds.

For his heroism and courage, the Air Force posthumously awarded him with the Air Force Cross, the nation's second-highest award for valor, and the Department of Defense ordered the ship renamed in his honor.

In Sondheim's opinion, the very least he could do was everything possible to keep the ship ready for her mission to honor the young man's memory and courage.

In keeping with his usual custom on a mid-watch, Sondheim had come up on the weather deck and worked his way along the starboard side toward the bow, waiting for the sun to come up. Most of the rest of the contractor crew was sleeping. Only he and two others kept watch when the ship was anchored in Diego Garcia. The long-established British port in the Indian Ocean was nearly 1,000 miles from any trouble spot in the Middle East or the Far East, but close enough to be no more than four or five days' sail from either area.

Sondheim took a few deep breaths of the salty ocean air and leaned on the rail, looking east. The sky was only just starting to lighten, the stars closest to the horizon just beginning to disappear into the sky, while the others twinkled serenely.

* * *

AZIZ LOOKED DOWN AT THE dock, satisfied to see M'an and Saqr waiting for him on shore next to the silver Land Rover. The deckhands were securing the lines, and the captain was slowly but expertly maneuvering the *Saladin* into its reserved berth, the bright lights along the dockside eliminating all shadows at the Feydhoo yacht basin in the Maldives. The cruise from the dive location had taken all day and most of the night, and dawn was nearly two hours away, but Aziz knew it would be a slightly brighter dawn for him than for others.

As fate would have it, Aziz looked down at his gold Rolex Oyster perpetual watch just as the minute hand touched the top of the hour. Four A.M. "Allahu Akbar," he said quietly, bowing his head and wishing he could see the explosions for himself as the infidel vessels were consumed by the depths. "Insha'Allah."

Aziz raised his head and turned away from the dock, walking toward the interior stairwell. He needed to get ashore and head back to Riyadh. He would trust in Allah's magnificence to ensure his success.

BELOW THE WATER LINE, AT the stern of the ship, nearly 700 feet from where Sondheim was enjoying the salt air and peace and quiet, the timer embedded in the limpet mine attached to the hull of the M/V TSgt *John A. Chapman* reached zero. The hammer blow from the thirty pounds of shaped high explosive in the limpet mine worked as it was designed to, punching through the hull plating, tearing the propeller shaft from its mountings and snapping it in half. Pieces of steel and debris were accelerated upward into the steering gear compartment, shredding control equipment and dozens of electrical and hydraulic cables.

The ocean instantly rushed through the 15-foot gash in the hull, immediately flooding the shaft alley and sending a cascade of water toward the unmanned engine room.

Sondheim heard the deep rumble of the explosion coming from the direction of the stern and turned to look aft. Then he felt the hull shudder as the shock rippled through the ship's two-football-field length.

Knowing instantly that something was wrong, he raced aft, pulling his radio from the clip on his belt. "Sam, Jerry. Did you hear that?"

Sam Horvan was standing watch on the bridge, monitoring the radios and radar, his feet up on the forward console while he turned the pages of an old Vince Flynn novel on his e-reader, a hot cup of coffee resting on the console next to him. The book was one of his favorites in the Mitch Rapp series, and he always thought it a shame that Vince had passed away at so young an age.

"Jerry, Sam. I heard it. I . . ." Horvan trailed off as electronic alert tones started wailing from the damage-control computer in the central section of the bridge. He put his e-reader down next to his coffee and headed aft. He took one look at the console and reached for one of the handsets nearby, punching the large yellow button next to it, ignoring the increasingly strident calls from Sondheim on the radio.

The handset he held to his face put him on the ship-wide public address system; the yellow button activated the attention-getting alert tone. The PA system reached every interior space of the ship and broadcast over speakers spaced evenly along the weather deck. As soon as he heard the alert tone stop, he took a deep breath to calm himself, and spoke.

"Attention, all hands. Flooding in the engine room, flooding in shaft alley. I repeat, flooding in the engine room, flooding in shaft alley. This is no drill. All hands lay to the damage-control locker at Frame G2, Engineering level. Repeating, all hands lay to the damage-control locker at Frame G2, Engineering level. Watertight doors will not activate."

Horvan tried to place the receiver back in the form-fitting cradle, but his hand was shaking so much he had to use both hands to steady it enough to set it in place. He noticed the marine radio set to the harbor frequency was squawking, with multiple voices calling out, sometimes talking over one another.

"This is the *Carter*, we've had an explosion aft, we have flooding in the engine spaces . . ."

"We are now down by 5 feet at the stern, *Button* requesting immediate assistance . . ."

"This is the *Lopez*, requesting emergency assistance! Most of our crew is dead. They were in the aft spaces conducting a generator overhaul. We have flooding . . ."

Horvan stared at the radio in shock for a few seconds, and then raced toward the aft windows of the bridge. He could only see the massive bow, forward superstructure, and the huge yellow cranes on the weather deck of the USNS SGT *William R. Button* behind them. The bulk of the 100-foot-wide combination container and Roll-on/Roll-off ship blocked the view of the other ships, all anchored in a line one behind another.

The *Button* looked peaceful, but as Horvan watched, he could see the bow slowly rising out of the water, a thin wedge of her red anti-fouling paint standing out in the early morning darkness. *What the hell happened?*

IT TOOK NEARLY TWO HOURS of heroic damage-control efforts on the part of the surviving contracted crew members and the British naval experts at the Diego Garcia base to keep the ships afloat, and another three hours to recover all the bodies of the crew who died aboard the USNS 1st LT *Baldomero Lopez*. Once the ships were no longer in immediate danger of sinking and the naval architects had finished their damage assessments, Captain Timothy P. Calloway, Commander of Maritime Pre-positioning Ships Squadron Two, sent a message that he knew presaged what was likely the end of his naval career.

SECRET
PRECEDENCE: FLASH
DTG: 1408Z 18 NOV 18
FM: COMPSRON TWO
SUBJ: DEEP BLUE: MPS SQUADRON TWO SHIPS DISABLED BY
      MINES/EXPLOSIVES
TO: JCS//CHAIRMAN/J2/J3
    JICPAC//J2I
    JSOC//J2/J3
    SECDEF
    USCENTCOM//Commander
    USPACOM//Commander
    WHITE HOUSE//SIT ROOM

1. Four MPSRON TWO vessels have been damaged by high explosives, likely attached to the submerged area of the stern portion of the hulls. The damaged vessels are the USNS SGT *William R.*

Button, M/V SSG *Edward A. Carter Jr.*, the M/V TSgt *John A. Chapman*, and the USNS 1st LT *Baldomero Lopez*.

2. Each vessel has suffered serious damage to its single propeller shaft and steering gear, propulsion plant, other engineering systems. Complete damage assessments and repair needs will be provided via SEPCOR within two hours. Initial damage estimates by naval architects from the Diego Garcia Naval Base indicate that all four vessels will need to be dry-docked for two to three weeks of repairs, once spare parts arrive.

3. In addition, fourteen AMCIT contractor personnel died aboard the USNS 1st LT *Baldomero Lopez*. A British and American skeleton crew is currently manning the *Lopez*.

4. COMPSRON TWO, in concert with the Commander of Diego Garcia Naval Base, are deploying 24/7 armed small boat surface combatant vessels to provide perimeter security around all COMPSRON TWO vessels.

5. These COMPSRON TWO vessels represent the complete afloat equipment, logistics, and munitions set designated to support rapid-reaction forces deployed to the Middle East and Far East for crisis, contingency, and wartime operations. COMPSRON TWO recommends that SECDEF, USCENTCOM, and USCPACOM alter all CONPLANS and OPLANS accordingly.

S E C R E T
//EOT//

CAIN SAT BACK IN HIS chair, shocked. He had started trolling the various intelligence agency websites on INTELINK during this swing shift, and one of the first things he came across was the message from COMPSRON TWO on the Joint Intelligence Center Pacific's website.

"Mike," Cain called out to his deputy, Mike Goodman, "did you see this report on the JICPAC website?"

"The one from COMPSRON TWO?"

"Yeah."

"I caught it this morning in my on-shift reading. What do you think?"

Cain considered his reply for a second or two before answering. "I think somebody just crippled our ability to deploy forces in the Mid and Far East."

"No doubt," Mike agreed. He and Cain shared a similar base of experience in the intelligence community. When both of them agreed on something, their analysis was generally spot-on. "I'd like to know how the hell they got close enough to plant the explosives."

"Fair question," Cain agreed. "If the II MEF has to deploy, they're screwed." The II Marine Expeditionary Force was the nation's on-call military unit ready for immediate, long-term deployment, and they specialized in the Middle East.

"Oh, yeah," Goodman agreed. "Those Marines would be seriously stuck without the supplies and equipment on those ships."

The problem was that the Marines of the II MEF would board aircraft with their personal weapons and gear, and then fly to either Qatar or Kuwait to secure the deepwater ports in those countries. The Marines would then wait for the COMPSRON TWO ships to arrive carrying the armored vehicles, bullets, fuel, food, water, and spare parts for thirty days of combat operations.

If the logistics and planning experts had done their jobs properly, the COMPSRON TWO ships would arrive at nearly the same time the at-sea Expeditionary Strike Group moved into the area offshore to secure the sea lanes and reinforce the II MEF Marines already on the ground. The ESG was a very powerful formation, centered on an America-class amphibious assault ship and her supporting Landing Ship Docks, all carrying more than 2,000 Marines of a Marine Expeditionary Unit, along with the attack and transport helicopters, F-35B fighters, and MV-22B Osprey troop transports they needed to fight effectively. The ESG also had supporting guided missile cruisers, destroyers, and submarines as part of the formation for at-sea protection. Although the ESG was an important component of the mission, only the Marines could take and hold territory ashore.

That raised a question in Cain's mind. "Mike, what if our buddy Aziz is somehow behind the hit on the COMPSRON TWO ships?"

Goodman looked over at him in surprise. "Whoa. That's an ugly thought. Did you see any indicators of that?"

"Not so far, and the FBI and NSA analysis of the hard drives the Wraiths recovered from his house hasn't yielded much of use. The little SOB didn't seem to store much on his computer. No hinky financial records, no odd e-mails, and no encrypted files, either. They're still dumping the web-browser logs and checking all of the sites, but most of what they've seen so far is nothing more than news websites, both Western and Eastern."

Goodman was surprised. "I haven't read those reports yet. No social media, no jihadist websites?" he asked quizzically.

"Not a one," Cain replied. "He's either not what we think he is, or he's the great puppeteer, leading the believers but not actually participating."

"I'll vote for the latter," Goodman offered.

"Same here," Cain agreed. "Let's start keeping a sharper eye out for other events or indicators. I'll give DIRNSA a call and tell him what we think about the attacks on the ships. He can reach out and talk to USCENTCOM and USPACOM directly at his level, but I'm sure they are already starting to ask themselves the same questions."

Goodman was about to turn back to his computer when Cain expressed another thought. "Mike, have our team start pinging their agencies for any information they have that might be related to the attacks on the COMPSRON TWO ships. Let's see what we can find."

"ID, PLEASE." THE "PLEASE" WAS ordinary politeness, but there was no air of request in Chief Petty Officer Tate's voice or manner. Emily noticed that both of his hands were on the strange-looking rifle, its muzzle pointed at the ground, and his eyes were alert and watchful. When she had pulled up to the vehicle gate near Hangar 802, she stopped right under the blazing white light of the twin floodlights illuminating the gate, and the glare was making it hard for her to look directly at Tate.

She grabbed the white Air Force ID card off the center console of the blue government-issued Ford Econoline van and showed it to the man in the all-black combat uniform. Had he pointed the rifle's muzzle more in her direction when she had been turned away?

"I'm Technical Sergeant Thompson," she said, "here to see Lieutenant Mathews. He should be expecting me."

Tate kept the rifle pointed toward the van's nose and came one step closer to take the proffered ID, his eyes never leaving hers. She rested her right hand on the wheel and her left hanging out the window while she waited, keeping her eyes mostly focused out the windshield to avoid the glare from the floodlights. Tate glanced at her ID, matching the face with the photograph and the name.

"Whiskey Five, this is Ten. Is Six expecting company?"

The answer came back quickly in his ear. "Copy that, Five. I'll send her along."

"Here's your ID," Tate told her, leaning forward to look into the van's cargo area. "Anyone else with you?"

"No," she replied, "just me." She saw him look in the back and before he could ask the question, she told him, "Colonel Simon asked me to deliver these from BWI."

Tate looked at her anew. In addition to being expected by the ell-tee, she seemed to know the right names. "Drive straight through and park alongside the hangar, with the other vehicles near the front. Please don't park in front of the hangar."

"Thanks, Chief," she smiled, putting the van back in gear and driving off.

Across the entry road, Tate heard a voice from the shadows call out, "She's hot." It belonged to Tim Mellinger, Tate's backup who was concealed in a set of thick bushes inside the perimeter fence.

Tate smiled wryly. "Cool it, man. Wedding ring."

"Damn," Mellinger called back, "all the hot ones are married."

EMILY SAW THE LINE OF black Chevy Suburbans and slid her van in beside them. By the time she had gathered her ID and the keys and stepped out, two men were bearing down on her. Both wore the same black combat uniform as the man at the vehicle gate, but they carried only sidearms in gunslinger holsters. One was tall and dark, the other, medium height with sandy hair and blue eyes. Neither wore any rank insignia, and both were pretty attractive. She thought this TDY was off to a good start so far.

The blue-eyed man spoke first. "I'm Lieutenant Mathews"—he motioned to the taller man—"and this is Master Sergeant Simms, my

NCOIC. He's Air Force, so he'll be your supervisor while you're with us."

"Hello, sir. I'm Tech Sergeant Thompson." She reached out to shake hands with both men, and she saw a question on Mathews' face.

"Something wrong, sir?"

He shook his head, a slight smile on his face replacing the confused expression. "No. I recognize your voice, that's all. You're Charlie Five."

Thompson smiled broadly, "Yes, sir, and you're Whiskey Four Six."

"That's right. Simms will get you settled in. If you're going to work with us, you'll need a few things. There are a few other women on the support team that's out here with us. We've segregated a place in the hangar as a sleeping/changing area, and the hangar already has separate men's and women's washrooms and showers. It's not an apartment, but we're making do."

Thompson nodded. "I'm sure that isn't a problem, sir. I'm looking forward to working with you. And the team," she added hastily. To cover her inadvertent slip, she hurried on. "In fact, Colonel Simon asked me to pick up a couple of packages for you. They're in the van."

She turned to open the side door, and Mathews found himself involuntarily looking at her butt. She was as attractive as her voice on the radio link had suggested. But when she slid the van's side panel open with her left hand, he saw the gold glint and the flash of the diamonds from her wedding ring, killing the romantic notions that had started to creep into his head. Figures, he thought.

"Here they are," Thompson announced, motioning like Vanna White.

"Good," Mathews said, nodding. "Colonel Simon called me about these earlier in the day. They're an upgraded version of some gear we already have. We'll head over to Quantico and practice with them in the morning. That will also give us a chance to let you get familiar with our weapons and equipment."

Mathews turned to Simms. "Terry, take our new guest inside and show her around. I'll grab a couple of the guys and we'll get these out of the van and check out the new toys."

REPIN CHECKED HIS WATCH AGAIN. It was just after 9 p.m., and Esteban should be calling any minute. Repin sat in the large blue Ford

Transit van in the nearly empty parking ramp of Highland Hospital, waiting. He was only fifteen minutes away from the pickup location he had agreed on with Esteban this morning, and if he was burned before then, the parking ramp would be a good place to leave the van. He had finished the prep work a few minutes ago, making sure to secure the set of small black Pelican model 1150 hard-shell cases behind the passenger seat. Slid in next to them along the van's wall was a thick stack of collapsed cardboard boxes. He would need both the cases and boxes to complete tonight's mission.

Repin drummed his fingers against the van's steering wheel impatiently. His old KGB training officers discouraged smoking for health reasons as well as it being a bad habit that also left physical evidence behind that might betray an agent. Nonetheless, sometimes he wished he could think of some time-consuming activity that would take his mind off the waiting without leaving any evidence.

Suddenly, the burn phone began to vibrate. Repin picked it up with his gloved hands, flipped it open, and pressed the green talk button. "Yes."

"All set. I'll be there in about twenty minutes."

"Good. Any trouble?"

"No," Esteban replied. "There was a line at the customs station. See you there." The line went dead. Repin did not hear any nervousness in Esteban's voice, but he would be cautious nonetheless.

Repin started the van and headed down two levels of the concrete parking ramp and out onto 14th Avenue, turning north toward the MacArthur Freeway. Several miles later, he turned into the parking garage at the Public Health Institute. Given what he was about to take delivery of, the irony of Esteban's choice of transfer points did not escape him.

On the third level, he slowed down and looked carefully for the cameras. Repin was pleased to see that they were mounted only in the immediate areas near the elevator cores and stairwells, and although they could see the entire length of the parking area, he could work under that restriction.

Selecting two spots farthest from the camera mounted near the third-level core, he backed the van into the slot, with the driver's side farthest from the camera. The van was nearly 8 feet tall, and the height would hide him from view. Shutting down the engine and setting the parking brake, he grabbed the burn phone and redialed Esteban's number on his caller ID.

"Yes?" Repin could hear the suspicion in his voice.

"It's me. Slight change of plans. Same place. Third floor now, instead of fifth. The tall blue van. Park on the driver's side of the van, away from the central core, and back in."

Esteban was wary. "Why the change?"

"Because the van's height will conceal us from the cameras in the parking ramp. Be here in five minutes." Without waiting for an answer, Repin cut the connection and walked toward the rear of the van, stepping past the black hard cases stacked behind the passenger seat to open the right rear cargo door first, then the left, before stepping out onto the concrete floor. The only weapon Repin had was the tire iron lying on the floor at the rear. If this went sour and Esteban had a firearm, Repin was likely a dead man. Nonetheless, he stood in the open, to the left of the open rear cargo doors, hands empty.

Repin expected that Esteban was nearby, probably in the parking ramp and waiting a level or more higher, when he called Repin and told him he was ready. The approaching engine noise in the nearly empty parking ramp proved Repin only partially correct. The engine noise was coming from below him. His contact was close enough to make the five-minute window he had imposed, but he was not waiting on the ramp.

The sound of the engine grew slightly louder and Repin tensed. He saw the flash of the headlights against the concrete wall to his left, and a green Dodge Ram pickup turned left as it came up from the second level. The headlights washed over Repin and he stood still, trying to glimpse the driver. The pickup continued past the van and then stopped, the bright white backup lights activating as Esteban put the truck in reverse. In one neat motion, he backed the truck smoothly into the slot next to the driver's side of Repin's van and killed the engine. So far, so good, Repin thought. Only one man and he could see the heavy cardboard packing case in the truck's bed.

Esteban opened the driver's-side door and exited the pickup. "Hello, my friend." Repin guessed he was in his mid- to late twenties, and from somewhere in Asia, but he had not caught an accent in any of the phone calls or in his greeting. If he had to go hand-to-hand with him, he would need to be quick and not miss. The younger man's age would give him an advantage.

"Good evening." Repin used his best Midwestern accent. "Do you have the package?"

Esteban smiled. "Yes. Our mutual friend would be very upset with my captain and me if we did not deliver it to you. Especially since those who made its contents can no longer make more."

Repin knew that the Russians would be silenced after they had done their part. He did not need to know how, and judging by what he had seen so far, he expected Esteban enjoyed doing it. Esteban was likely one of the members of Abu Sayyaf Aziz had authority over, and for him, killing a small group of non-Muslim Russians was probably of less concern than swatting flies.

"Let's get it in my van," Repin suggested, never taking his eyes off Esteban. He had never worked with this man before, and from what he had seen so far, allowing him an opportunity to take advantage would likely be a lethal mistake.

"Certainly," Esteban replied, watching Repin as closely as Repin was watching him. Esteban lowered the tailgate and was about to reach in and drag out the packing case himself, when he thought better of it. "Why don't you give me a hand with this?" he offered.

Repin looked the case over quickly, and not seeing anything untoward, agreed with a nod. Both men grasped a side of the case and slid it out from the truck's bed, their faces a mere 2 feet away from one another, still watching for any sign of treachery. Walking slowly, they moved toward the rear of Repin's van and laid the case on the floor inside. Esteban saw the tire iron and smiled.

"Expecting a flat?" he asked, not bothering to hide his amusement.

"Hoping I don't have one," Repin countered in what he hoped was a friendly way, his eyes locked on Esteban's, looking for any sign of imminent hostility.

Esteban held the knowing grin on his face as he backed steadily away from Repin toward the Dodge. Reaching the left rear corner, he raised the truck's lift gate with one hand, slamming it closed, still watching Repin with a hint of amusement.

"Relax, my friend. My instructions were to deliver the case." Esteban's grin broadened into a cold smile as he waved in the general direction of the world beyond the parking ramp. "The infidels deserve to suffer for the atrocities they have committed against Muslims around the world." Repin said nothing; he was not coordinating these operations out of any sort of religious fervor, only the money that would allow him to provide for his daughter.

Wary of Repin's lack of response, Esteban kept his eyes on him while he walked back toward the open driver's door and reentered the truck. Once inside, Esteban started the motor and drove down the ramp at a steady but rapid pace.

Repin watched him leave, then wasted no time stepping into the cargo area of the van and closing the cargo doors one at a time from the inside, checking to ensure that they were locked. He needed to work quickly. He tore open the cardboard carton and looked inside. The tops of the twelve spun aluminum bottles were easy to spot in the darkness, resting snugly in the black Styrofoam separator.

The research he had done told him the radiation level was relatively low, but he also knew time was a factor. It would not do to dawdle now. Repin moved to the pile of nearly 1-foot-square Pelican cases, removing the cargo-net tie-downs and taking one case from the pile.

Repin opened the Pelican case, withdrew one bottle from the cardboard container, and fitted it into the slot in the foam he had cut earlier. The cases were watertight and crushproof, serving as an added layer of protection for the next leg of the bottles' journey to their intended destination. Repin could not afford to allow the bottles to suffer damage en route. Any unintended spill of the uranyl nitrate within would compromise the operation.

Once each bottle was safely nestled in its own Pelican hard case, Repin reached for the collapsed boxes and began assembling them, placing one Pelican case inside each box prior to sealing it. The prepaid shipping labels were already attached.

In less than ten minutes, he sealed each case in its shipping box, and then opened the rear doors to slide the empty original cardboard carton that had contained the bottles out onto the parking ramp's concrete floor. He closed the rear doors and settled himself in the driver's seat once more, turning the engine over.

Repin drove the van down to the first level and exited the ramp, turning left on Milvia Street and then making a series of rapid turns over three blocks for the next few minutes, following a serpentine course through the cityscape and watching the rearview mirror closely.

Satisfied that he saw no signs of a tail, Repin worked his way back toward Martin Luther King Jr. Way before turning left onto 45th Street and pulling into the McDonald's, slipping into the drive-thru lane behind two sedans.

Luck was with him. Both cars were filled with teenagers undoubtedly out for a good time, and they would not be in a hurry placing their orders. Repin pulled the burn phone from his pocket and began to disassemble it. By the time the first sedan moved forward, he had the battery out. The kid in the second sedan was still giving his order when Repin pried the SIM card from its slot.

Now it was his turn to order. "An unsweetened iced tea, please," he answered in his Midwestern accent, tossing the phone body and battery into the trashcan next to the speaker. He paid the pimply faced boy at the first window with two singles, and then tossed his change into the Ronald McDonald charity box. Once he had his drink, he rolled forward only far enough to reach the second trashcan at the end of the drive-thru lane and toss the SIM card in.

When he got back on the street, Repin drove directly to the UPS Store on Piedmont Avenue and 41st Street, backing the van into the slot near the door, waving at the clerk inside as he slammed the driver's door behind him.

As Repin finished opening the rear doors of the van, the redheaded college-age clerk came out with the wheeled cart, just as she promised.

"Hello again, Debby," Repin greeted her, his fake accent back in place.

"Hello, Mr. Robins. Looks like you just made it back before closing."

Repin checked his watch. Ten minutes to 10 P.M. "Yes, just," he agreed. "Thanks for your help." Repin started stacking the UPS shipping boxes two at a time on the wheeled cart.

Debby smiled, "Oh, it's no trouble. I'll take these into the back. We're loading the van now. Zack is helping the driver load up."

"Ah, good," Repin responded as he stacked the last of the boxes on the cart. "So these samples will make it to the stores by tomorrow?"

"Oh, yes," Debby assured him. "The van will head straight to the sorting facility from here. Since you paid for one-day service, delivery is guaranteed by 5 P.M. tomorrow. You can use the tracking numbers to confirm the deliveries."

"That's great. Thanks again for all your help tonight," Repin said, reaching out to shake Debby's hand.

"It's really no trouble, Mr. Robins," Debby answered, returning his handshake. "Have a good night."

"You, too," Repin answered, waving as Debby pulled the cart back into the store. He climbed back into the van and watched through the rearview mirror until Debby and the cart were out of sight behind the counter. His total exposure was not quite an hour, but he still wanted to get back to his hotel and take a long shower, just in case. But first he needed to return the rental van.

CHAPTER 18

. . . .

"GOOD MORNING, SIR. THIS IS Max Robin from Outdoor Supplies. I'm just calling to let you know that we've shipped your order. It will arrive by the end of business today. Please be certain to provide your feedback to us as quickly as possible. Have a good day."

Repin punched the button to terminate the call, and turned toward the glass windows near Gate 6 in Oakland International Airport's Terminal 2. That was the last call. Repin began disassembling the phone in the bright morning sun. The sun's rays warmed him, and he arched his back, feeling his chest expand and the muscles in his back ease.

He had planned to make the calls from Denver, but the Best Buy kiosks in the gate areas were too convenient. One swipe of his credit card, and the entry of the false name and address that went with it, and his latest burn phone dropped into the slot. Five minutes later, he had unwrapped it, activated it, and dialed the first call to one of his "buyers" in various parts of the country. Twelve calls and twenty minutes later, and he was done. Time to head for Gate 12. His flight was boarding.

THE NOSE OF THE AMERICAN Airlines Boeing 737-800 pitched up, and a few seconds later, the 737 reached velocity two and began to climb away from Runway 29 into the mid-morning sky, leaving Oakland International behind. Repin heard the landing gear moving beneath the plane and leaned forward to look out his window.

The plane rolled slightly right for a few seconds, and then leveled out again. Repin looked down at San Francisco Bay to see a large ship making its way toward the Dwight D. Eisenhower Highway, the silver stream of its wake trailing behind it, stretching across the pale blue waters of the bay. It was a beautiful sight, and Repin let it soak into his memory until the cloud deck obscured it from sight. Repin turned away from the window, leaned back in his first-class seat, and closed his eyes.

ESTEBAN WATCHED AS THE JET disappeared into the high clouds, then turned his attention to the water in front of the *Sea Titan*. "The weather for the first few days looks good, Captain."

"Yes," Ramirez replied. "We should make Jakarta on schedule easily. The load of farm machinery barely took up two-thirds of the cargo decks. We'll get an extra couple of knots out of the engines on this trip." Ramirez looked off to the starboard side for a few seconds, watching the shorelines of Yerba Buena and Treasure Island as the ship passed under the highway, then looked forward to see Alcatraz in the distance. "It's a pity we won't be here to watch."

"Yes," Esteban agreed. "We'll have to keep an eye on the Star Network news once we are at sea. They should have never-ending video of the infidels running around terrified."

Ramirez smiled. The Western news services could always be counted on to help spread the fear and panic.

"SO HOW DID THE NEW gear test out?"

Mathews heard the concern in Simon's voice and wondered what was behind it. The call came through just as they were getting off the D.C. Beltway, about ten minutes from the main gate at Joint Base Andrews. The team was looking forward to some hot showers and an evening meal after the day's training at Quantico.

"Just fine, Colonel. No trouble at all. It's like magic."

"Really? No glitches, no problems?"

"No, sir. We used it all day in four different scenarios. The biggest problem we had was the batteries running out after about four hours. The addition of the more powerful UHF radios to relay the signal really gobbles up the power. It took us about an hour to figure out how to replace them with the spares in the equipment cases."

"An hour is way too much time if you're in the field."

Mathews was ready for that. "Yes, it is. So we spent another hour drilling the replacement process so that we got it down to ten minutes for the entire set."

"Sounds good. How's your guest doing?"

Mathews glanced back into the interior of the Suburban, where Emily was discussing her view of the mission in Iran with Lieutenant Cochrane and Master Sergeant Simms.

"Fine. We spent some time this morning kitting her out and letting her accompany one of the assault teams through a couple of scenarios in the Kill House."

"How'd she do?"

Mathews lowered his voice to answer. "She's smart and engaged, but she'd need a couple of months to get her shooting dialed in."

"That's all right. She's not going to be an assaulter, she's only on loan from CTS for familiarization. Speaking of which, she's going to get a little more than she might have hoped for."

"Oh? How so?"

"We have orders for you, and they come from the president and the SECDEF."

Whoa, thought Mathews. *Now what?* "Yes, sir. Ready to copy."

"Go ahead, sir." For a second, Mathews thought Simon was talking to him. There was no reason for Simon to call him sir.

"Lieutenant Mathews, this is General Crane."

Oh, shit, thought Mathews. "Yes, sir. Go ahead."

"Lieutenant, we've received a request from the Saudis for you and your team to return to the Kingdom. Colonel Simon and I are on the line because you need to know that two senior officers are aware of the orders I'm about to give you. Is that clear?"

What the hell was this? "I understand, sir, ready to copy."

"Lieutenant, you and your team will return to Saudi Arabia tonight. When you arrive, you will be met by Special Agent Johnson and his friend Akeem. Akeem will escort you to a meeting with the Saudi Minister of the Interior. You will brief him on the mission into Tehran and what happened from the time you parachuted out of the Saudi airliner, to the time you were picked up by the Osprey. Clear?"

"Yes, sir. May I ask why?"

Crane's voice reflected his appreciation of the young officer's savvy. "Yes, you may. Our Saudi friends believe we scammed them. They think we did something else in Iran because we left with four dead bodies instead of one live one, and they aren't too pleased with the United States right now. You are going out there to speak face-to-face to them to convince them otherwise."

Mathews considered Crane's explanation. How the Saudis knew what happened was not really his concern. What bothered him was that he would be revealing classified details of a Wraith operation to foreign nationals. The basic notion went against everything he had been taught, but the first duty was to obey orders.

"Understood, sir." His next question was obvious. "What do I do if they don't believe me?"

"We're going to help you out with that," Crane told him. "An AUTUMN FIRE summary report has been prepared for the Saudis. The president and the SECDEF have approved the release of the report to them. We've already sent it to your account on INTELINK. It's written in Arabic and English. Download it just before you break down the gear and load the C-17."

"That will help, sir. When do we leave?"

"As soon as you can get the plane loaded. The flight crew already received their orders and the diplomatic clearances are in place from the Saudis."

"Does that include the departure, too?" Mathews asked wryly.

"Actually, it does," Colonel Simon chimed in. "Your departure on the diplomatic clearance is open-ended. In effect, the Saudis will let you remain as long as you like, and leave whenever you wish."

"Really?" Mathews asked incredulously.

"Yes," Simon answered. "But bear in mind that it's only a paper promise. They can revoke or change it at any time. My evaluation is that it's a sign of good faith on their part."

Mathews focused his attention back on the road. "We're coming up on the main gate now. We should have the C-17 loaded in two hours or less and airborne no later than 2000 hours."

"That's fine, Lieutenant," General Crane informed him. "Don't try and break any speed records. Johnson isn't expecting you before 1500 Saudi time tomorrow. As long as you're airborne by 2100 local, you'll arrive on time, even with a refueling stop in Spain."

"Fair enough, sir, I expect we'll all be able to sleep on the flight across the Atlantic. The base at Rota is a good seven or eight hours away. Any other orders?"

Mathews and the rest of the team in the Suburban showed their military IDs to the gate guards and were waved through, as Mathews heard Crane's tone shift, taking on the firm and steady cadence of long experience.

"Read the prepared summary we've sent, and answer their questions candidly and directly based on what's in that summary and your experience on the ground in Iran. Defer any questions beyond that to the more senior-level delegation we will send to meet with the king."

"Understood, sir. I'll handle it."

"I'm sure you'll do your best, son, but I'd prefer to have someone much more senior to you at this meeting to give you some top cover and deflect any questions that might lead to political issues that are not in our purview. Unfortunately, a friendly nation has asked to speak to the officer who led the raid from their territory, and I can't get someone more senior there fast enough to work with you."

"Why not, sir?"

"Because the U.S. ambassador is not cleared for Wraith operations, and we don't have a military attaché in the Kingdom right now. Moreover, I'm appearing before a closed-door session of the Military Affairs committee in two days, and that means Colonel Simon needs to remain here at the base since he'll be in command in my absence."

Mathews let out a breath. "I understand, sir. I'll think carefully before I open my mouth in front of the Saudis."

"Good. You remember that and you'll be fine, son. You showed good judgment under combat conditions in Iran, and I'm sure you'll do fine."

Mathews was surprised at the general's words. After the dressing-down he gave him aboard the command 747 after Team Four's return from the mission into Iran, he didn't think the general trusted his judgment, in spite of Colonel Simon's assurances.

"Thank you, sir." Mathews answered, confidence creeping back into his voice. "I'll handle it."

"We know you will, Lieutenant. Safe trip. Be sure to contact Colonel Simon via secure SATCOM after landing. Out here."

"Copy that, sir."

NIGHTTIME IN BANI HAWAT WAS remarkably quiet, Saddam thought, at least compared to Paris. In Paris, outside his window at night, there were always cars in the street passing by, sometimes honking their horns, or people walking by talking until 2 or 3 A.M. After that, it became so quiet you could hear a five-franc coin hitting the pavement from three blocks away.

In this part of Sana'a, it was deathly quiet after sundown. Men would sometimes sit outside and talk for an hour or so afterward in the cooling air of the evening, but after that it was still except for the occasional cry of an infant in the night or the sound of dogs snarling at one another over scraps. The planes still took off, of course, but as the night wore on, the takeoffs became more and more intermittent until they stopped entirely after midnight.

Saddam leaned farther out of the window in his room and breathed in the night air deeply. It was dry and cool. Saddam guessed that it was about 10 degrees Celsius outside, and while his room held the warmth of the day well, with the window open it was cooling quickly.

He had fallen asleep for a few hours, awakened by a dream he could no longer remember. After a few minutes of tossing and turning, he had taken the thin blanket off the bed and wrapped himself in it before opening the window. Since he had woke, his mind kept turning back to what Hazar had been showing them.

It was certainly the path to martyrdom, there was no doubt of that. That they could kill so many with an unobtrusive device as a laptop computer was still surprising to him. It would only take minutes from the time he and his brothers booted the machines, and then a thousand or more infidels would die. He had never killed before. Now, he would be able to kill hundreds with a single tap on the mouse pad built into a laptop. They would die over several minutes, screaming, knowing that death was coming to them, and that they could do nothing about it.

He and each of the other men he had trained with would share in the fate of the infidels and so gain immediate entrance for themselves and all their family members into Jannah. He would enter Jannah through the bab al-jihad door, reserved for those who took part in the jihad to defend Islam. He would see Karim and his father again, for surely Karim and his father were already enjoying the pleasures of Paradise, and perhaps even the seventy-two Houri spoken of in the Hadith.

A chill breeze blew across him, and Saddam shivered. What if he were wrong? He had always considered his mother and father devout Muslims, and they had never spoke of harming others. They worked to provide for Karim and himself; his father in business, and his mother in the home. They had even prayed with the boys and read the Holy Qur'an to them in the evenings when they were young. His parents had not sought martyrdom, and even Father had once told him that "true Jihad" is the struggle within yourself to obey Allah's teachings and share that knowledge and truth with others. Saddam frowned at that thought, his eyes fixed on but not seeing the nightscape of Bani Hawat, his mind lost in his internal struggle.

The infidels had kept him from finding the means to support his mother and Karim after his father's death. They had killed Karim with their guns. How could he not want to avenge that? His parents were good people and had followed the tenants of Islam, passed them on to their sons. Instead of living a peaceful, if modest, life and having the opportunity to live it through to its natural conclusion, worshipping Allah as the Holy Qur'an and the Hadith taught them, the unbelievers had interfered.

They restricted his opportunities to find work, while provid-ing abundant opportunities to their own, unbelieving people. They trained guns on Karim and himself during a peaceful protest, killing his brother, while using the same guns and bombs and other weapons of destruction to oppress and kill Muslims in Palestine with the help of the Israelis, and in Afghanistan and Iraq during their so-called wars of liberation. They claimed to bring the rule of law to the world's people, yet Sharia law was not even acknowledged as anything other than medieval in most nations.

How else could they fight back? How else could he strike at those who killed his brother and left his mother in tears? Imam Abdel was right. There were no mighty Islamic armies to defend the faithful across all the Muslim nations, wiping the scourge of the Great Satan from this world and answering only to Allah's commandments. That would come one day.

For now, there were only the brave and capable men like himself to fight for the faithful. Most were men who would fight in small battles directly against the hated Israelis and other occupiers. A special few would serve in greater battles and bring to the faithful greater victories in Allah's service. In these battles, Imam Abdel had told him that martyrdom was sometimes commanded by Allah to achieve the greatest victories. His victory would no doubt cause other men to rally to the defense of Islam and the faithful, cheering his name and remembering him, much as the thirteen-year-old Hossein Fahmideh was remembered in modern times for blowing up an Iraqi tank during the Iran-Iraq war.

Breathing deeply once again of the chilly night air, Saddam knew it would be a hard thing, to leave the world Allah had gifted them with. He would not know the loving embrace of a wife, or the sounds of his children calling for him to help or play with them. He would make this sacrifice willingly, so that others like Karim might be spared the bullets and bombs of the infidels, and he would trust in Allah to lead him to a peaceful rest with his brother and father in Jannah.

With that decision made, Saddam settled himself more comfortably on the bed, leaning against the window, his head cradled in his arms. Dawn would come soon, and he wanted to watch it unfold before him, and remember it, knowing that it was a gift from Allah. A gift he would soon be able to thank Him for in person.

AZIZ WAS PLEASED TO BE back in Riyadh. The return flight from the Maldives was very smooth, and he had taken the time to stop by the flight deck and compliment Zaki on it. So far at least, Zaki had shown himself much more competent than Hamzah, and the new copilot, Ali, seemed to be doing well. Zaki had spoken to him about Ali's skills and experience flying for Qatar Airlines after they had arrived in the Maldives, before he had boarded the *Saladin* for the voyage to Diego Garcia. Once Saqr had completed a background check on him, Aziz felt completely satisfied and ordered Zaki to hire the man. Given the princely sum he paid even the copilot of his private plane, Aziz was not surprised that Ali managed to quit his job with Qatar Airlines and get to the Maldives before the *Saladin* returned to port.

Aziz looked at the face of his gold Rolex. "Saqr, the meeting is at 10 A.M., but take all necessary precautions to ensure that we are not followed."

Glancing in the rearview mirror of the black Range Rover at Aziz, he nodded once. "Yes, Sayyid."

Saqr expertly threaded the Range Rover through the mid-morning traffic heading south on Airport Road, watching the mirrors for any car that might seem suspicious. Taking the exit ramp smoothly, but at the last possible second, he continued south on Northern Ring Road.

A few minutes later, he executed the same maneuver and headed east on King Fahd Branch Road, expertly darting around the slower cars and keeping up his scan of the mirrors, always being sure to think ahead and keep the changes in direction as smooth as possible. He knew far too well his employer's distaste for bumpy travel.

As they continued down the road he glanced at M'an. "Clear?"

M'an held his eyes on the passenger-side mirror for a quick evaluation of what he saw before agreeing with his partner. "Clear."

Saqr, seeing an opening before him, smoothly accelerated and raced down the last 2 miles at more than 120 kilometers an hour before coming to a smooth stop at the red light straddling King Abdullah Branch Road. He glanced at M'an again, who nodded in unspoken agreement. Still no sign of any tails.

Once the light shifted to green, he turned left and then quickly right into the covered entrance parking lot of the Sheraton Riyadh, parking directly in front of the glass entryway. The seven-story main hotel was shaped like a "Y" with the base leg extending into the tower area that held the luxury villas. The covered parking area sat between the upper arms of the "Y," sheltering guests' vehicles from the equatorial sun.

Almost before the black Range Rover slid to a stop, Saqr could see the manager, Asad, wearing a dark and very expensive Western business suit, walk through the sliding doors of the hotel and approach the Range Rover.

Aziz knew that Asad was well educated in business and the hotel industry, born in Islamabad, with a wife and six children. They had met at the King Fahd School of Business Management many years ago, and Aziz had cultivated his friendship and Asad's understanding of Aziz's need for privacy. At this hotel, Aziz never checked in, and neither did his guests. He touched the control to lower the window, noticing as the window slid down that M'an's hand had slipped into his open jacket as easily as the dry warmth of the desert air moved into the SUV.

Aziz looked out the open window and smiled broadly. "Hello, my friend."

"Hello, my friend," Asad replied. No names were ever used between them during business hours, and it bothered Asad not at all. Aziz paid lavishly to protect his privacy.

Asad reached the car and extended his right hand through the window. M'an nearly drew his gun, but relaxed when he saw only the gold-rimmed white plastic of two electronic key cards in his hand.

"Your villa is prepared. I have personally deactivated the security cameras on that floor and in the VIP area of the parking garage. Would you like me to send up any food?"

Aziz reached forward from his seat in the Range Rover and shook Asad's hand, taking the two key cards from him as he did so. "Not yet. In an hour and a half, send up a selection of dishes from the Al Bustan restaurant buffet."

Asad did not even think to remind him that the buffet did not open until seven that evening. One did not offend wealthy friends. "I will be pleased to tell the chef of your needs. To provide you with the best service, he may need a little more time. Can I send up some fresh juices and fruit initially, with the buffet selections after?"

"Of course." It was better after all that they serve him properly. "The rooms are properly stocked, of course?"

Asad smiled, thankful that he had checked the villa himself and corrected that oversight. "Naturally. The chilled water and the cheese plate is in the kitchenette refrigerator. The fruit and juices will be up immediately."

"Shokran, my friend." Aziz raised his hand to Asad in farewell, and raised the window. Before the window was seated in its frame, Saqr had the Range Rover through the covered lot and into the underground garage. Aziz leaned forward and placed the key cards into M'an's out-stretched hand as the dark garage swallowed them.

Saqr drove down two levels, up to the gate marked VIP PARKING, and took one of the key cards M'an had dropped into his hand. Stopping at the electronically controlled barrier, Saqr swiped the card once, and the gate swung up out of the way.

The parking area beyond held only ten slots, one each for the villas on the top three floors, and an elevator core for the three elevators that serviced only the villas. Saqr and M'an exited the Range Rover first, scanning the area for the telltale green lights on the security cameras. If cameras were operating after Asad reported them disabled, Asad would receive a very stern phone call from Aziz.

Once Saqr was certain the cameras were off, he nodded to M'an and opened the rear door for Aziz while M'an walked over and called the elevator closest to the Range Rover by inserting his key card into the slot. This elevator served only the villa on the top floor, the most opulent of all the villas in the structure. M'an knew of the rumors that one of the younger princes often brought Western women here without his family's knowledge, but he had never been able to get any direct confirmation of that.

The elevator whisked them up to the ninth floor in seconds. Aziz looked at his watch again. "My guest will be here shortly. Saqr, please escort him up."

"Yes, Sayyid." Saqr responded, pressing the button in the car for the garage and disappearing from view. M'an and Aziz crossed the small entry foyer and M'an swiped the key card again, opening the door and stepping into the villa first, visually scanning for threats.

Seeing nothing alarming, M'an stood aside, allowing Aziz to enter. The villa was nicely appointed and very comfortable, with thick, cream-colored carpets and polished oak furniture throughout.

Aziz made his way to the master bathroom to refresh himself, and

M'an busied himself with visually checking the rest of the villa. They knew their guest would likely arrive late, and it was best to put the time to good use.

THIRTY MINUTES LATER, SAQR WAS back, and General Mahir, commander of the Royal Saudi Guard, strode confidently into the villa's living room. Wearing only keffiyeh and thawb, the senior officer could have easily passed as any normal middle-aged Saudi gentleman on the street.

"Welcome, General." Aziz came forward to greet him with the traditional three kisses. "It is kind of you to join me here."

"I am pleased to do so. Your bodyguard explained to me the steps taken to ensure our privacy. I am grateful for your efforts."

"It is nothing, please sit," Aziz responded, gesturing to one of the thick almond-colored leather chairs. The fresh fruit, juices, water, and cheese tray were arranged on the low table between them.

Saqr withdrew to take his post near the front door. M'an had already settled himself at the dining room table, far enough to give Aziz and the general the presumption of privacy, but with an unobstructed line of sight to the living room seating area and the general's hands and upper body. If the general made any motion M'an thought dangerous to Aziz, the general would find two .40 S&W bullets from M'an's silenced H&K P2000 SK pistol in his chest.

The general settled himself comfortably and politely declined Aziz's offer of juice or water. He got to business.

"When is the meeting scheduled for?" Aziz asked.

"Two days from now," answered the general with a satisfied expression. "They will all be there."

"Two days?" Aziz asked incredulously. That was sooner than he expected.

"Is that a problem?" the general asked.

Aziz collected himself. "No. I will need to put some things in motion sooner than I expected, but it does not pose a problem. Will *he* be there?"

The general smiled. "Oh, yes. *He* has to be. He's part of the Allegiance Council."

"Good, and the rest?"

"Them as well. They must all come as witnesses to the council's decisions."

"Good. You are certain the site will be secure?"

"Of course," the general smiled wickedly. "My men always control such venues. The perimeter guards will not know what is going on, but the small group inside the room will all be my men."

Aziz nodded. "Then we should proceed."

"Insha'Allah."

Reaching inside his own thawb, Aziz withdrew the special phone and dialed a number. It took a few seconds, but the distant end rang only twice before it connected.

"Yes." Repin's voice was sleepy and anxious.

"Sorry to disturb you so early in the morning, but it's important. How is your harvesting effort coming along?"

"Well. I expect the planters to send me the results in three days."

"That is no longer acceptable. The planters will need to send you the results in twenty-four hours."

Repin was not impressed with the sudden change in plans. "That will be difficult . . ." he began.

Aziz cut him off. "No, it won't. It is what must be done, and what I pay your considerable salary for."

Repin was silent for a full ten seconds. The adrenaline brought on by the ringing of the special phone he used only to contact Aziz was helping him process the sudden shift in timelines, but there were so many reasons that rushing things was not wise. The only thing he could think of was to counter with the truth.

"Contacting the planters again is risky. Moreover, if they rush their efforts, they may be subject to . . . penalties by the local authorities."

Aziz would not be put off, and he kept his tone flat and authoritative. "I understand your concerns, but it is very important to me that they move more quickly. Twenty-four hours."

Repin thought of a hard-learned lesson in the SVR: When a superior will not face objective facts, give an ambiguous reply to protect yourself when the operation invariably develops problems or fails.

"I'll do everything I can."

"Twenty-four hours." Aziz repeated, breaking the connection.

"Is there a problem?" the general asked.

Aziz looked steadily at the general. "No. Merely a subordinate who needs to find a way to carry out his orders." Aziz turned his attention to the phone again, hitting the keys to speed-dial a second number.

"As-salam alaikum." Imam Abdel's voice was not as sleepy as Repin's; the imam was probably up early for morning Salāt.

"Alaikum As Salaam."

"How may I serve you?"

"Do you recall the five young men whose schooling I'm paying for?" Even on this phone, he could not be sure the Americans or British were not listening in.

"Of course. I heard from their instructor the other day. They are doing well."

"I need them to be sent to their destinations within twenty-four hours."

Imam Abdel was surprised. "That is sooner than expected. I will check with the schoolmaster and ask if they are prepared."

"Prepared or not, they and the others must go to their destinations within twenty-four hours."

"I understand. I shall inform their schoolmaster and let you know exactly when they will leave."

"Good."

"Do you require anything else?" Abdel asked.

"No, my friend. May Allah grant you peace."

"And you."

Aziz broke the connection and looked at the general. "It is done. The last of the preparations will be complete in one day."

A light tapping came from the front door. Saqr looked quickly through the peephole, and then looked at Aziz. "The lunch buffet has arrived."

Aziz smiled and looked at the general. "Shall we finalize the details over lunch?"

CHAPTER 19

. . . .

SADDAM DRAINED THE LAST OF the water from the bottle and rose from his seat in the classroom to get another from the chest. Again, Hazar had dispensed with the assault training, and they had spent all morning working with the software, entering numbers and values, and then executing the commands. They had even done three complete timed runs. Every man could execute the whole sequence in well under five minutes.

The room had warmed as the morning went on, the sun baking inside to what he thought was a comfortable 80 degrees. He could barely hear Hazar in the next room talking on the cell phone. He had been gone for only a few minutes. While Saddam was standing at the ice chest, he heard what he thought was urgency in Hazar's tone. Suddenly, Hazar stopped talking, and Saddam hurried back to his chair.

Hazar barreled back into the room, sliding the cell phone into his rear pocket. He spread his arms wide and addressed them in a friendlier manner than he ever had.

"My brothers, I cannot tell you how pleased I am with the progress you have made."

Saddam wondered at the change. What was going on?

"I am pleased to tell you that you have completed your training. As of this moment, you are the newest members of the jihad. You will defend the faith against the Crusader armies and crush the infidels."

Saddam looked around as the other men began chanting. "Allah be praised" and congratulating one another. Had not Hazar said just this morning that they had made progress but were not yet ready? Saddam looked at him to ask what had changed, but found Hazar's eyes on him already, glaring steadily, and the question died on his lips.

Worse, Hazar walked over to him, placed his hands on Saddam's desk, and leaned down, towering over him. "You are wondering why I welcome you as brothers now, after what I said this morning about your preparedness."

Saddam tried to stop himself from leaning away from Hazar but he could not. "Yes, Hazar," was all he could think to say. The others had stopped talking when Hazar had moved, and now they were all listening to the exchange.

Hazar smiled with his lips, but not with his eyes. "You have always been the most observant among this group. I say such things to all trainees until they meet the high standards that all who carry the burden of this fight must meet."

Hazar stood erect again, and addressed the entire group again. "I am hard on you because I must be. The enemies of Islam, the Crusader armies, and the Zionists who support and motivate them have greater resources than the armies of Allah. Therefore, the righteous must train harder and fight longer if we are to achieve victory and see the Islamic Caliphate restored to its rightful place in the world."

Hazar paused and looked them over, his eyes lingering on Saddam. Saddam held his gaze, but knew there was more coming. Hazar's explanation made a certain sense, but the suddenness was still unnerving.

"Now it is time to put your training to use and light the way for others. Are you prepared?"

"Na'am!" the group shouted, Saddam joining them to be sure he did not draw Hazar's attention again.

"Good. Follow me," Hazar ordered.

He led the small group across the upper floor into the master bedroom, and they followed him inside. Saddam looked around briefly, his eyes examining everything.

The room was, in some ways, as dilapidated as the rest of the house, but in others it was not. The floor had been repaired, or at least patched, as had one-third of the rear wall, which was painted a bright white. Against the freshly painted section of wall a plain blue square of cloth was tacked, and about 3 meters in front of it a video camera stood mounted on a tripod, a small klieg light next to it. Both the camera and the light were plugged into a thick, black, eight-plug battery backup unit whose cable snaked along the wall and then up and through a crude hole punched in the left wall. Saddam guessed that it ran to a small generator, which would explain how Hazar managed to keep the batteries charged on the laptops they worked with.

The corner across from the camera setup had been turned into a workshop, with a small, raw wood worktable on four legs, and a peg-board on the wall behind it holding many tools. The worktable held a soldering iron, various electronic circuit boards, and other components and parts Saddam did not recognize. He thought that the small clay-colored bricks stacked neatly in one corner of the table might have been plastic explosives, but surely only a crazy man would leave such danger-ous materials just laying out in the open.

The last thing Saddam saw was the pile of boxes across from the workshop area and directly across from the door. They were arranged in a four-by-four square that towered nearly to the height of the 8-foot ceiling. Saddam tilted his head a little to read the lettering in Arabic, but the company name TOSHIBA emblazoned across each box was unmistak-able. From the Arabic, Saddam read that each box held a Toshiba Portege class Ultrabook computer. Hazar crossed to the pile of boxes and began handing each student one of the boxes.

"Take the box back into the other room, open it, boot the machine, and follow the prompts to complete the basic configuration," he ordered, adding, "Remember what I told you about security during all jihad activ-ities. When the machine asks you to name it, do not use anything from the Holy Qur'an or related to our faith. Also, be sure to set the language to Arabic, and the time zone to Paris time."

Saddam took the box holding his new computer and headed back to the classroom. Breaking the seal, he opened it and removed the thin Ultrabook from the packing material, leaving the manual and other printed material in the box.

Saddam booted the Ultrabook quickly, and the computer immedi-ately began its initial setup procedure. In a few minutes, Saddam had set the language and the time, and then the prompt came up for the name of the machine. He decided that if this machine was to be the instrument of his revenge, the only name it could be was "KARIM."

Hazar came back into the room. "When the machine asks to connect to a wireless network, decline the option. You will connect it later, remember?"

Saddam looked up and nodded, skipping that option when it came up and then ignoring the warning about not being able to get the latest operating system updates. A few minutes later, he was staring at a fresh desktop. He moved the cursor around with the mouse pad, and then opened and closed a few directories in the file structure, and played the pre-installed sample video. Everything seemed to be working fine.

To be certain, he right-clicked on the "Computer" line in the Start menu and selected "Properties" to compare what the machine reported to the information on the box's label. A second-generation I9 series microprocessor and 24 GB of memory. Everything seemed normal.

"Now what do we do, Hazar?" Saddam asked.

"Is the machine set up and working properly?"

"Na'am."

"Good. Check the battery level and be sure you have at least 50 percent of capacity. You can charge it later during your trip."

Saddam right-clicked on the icon. It read full.

"It is full, Hazar."

"Good." He turned his attention to addressing the whole group. "Once you have checked the battery level, power down the machine. From this moment forward, no one is to touch the machine but you. Do not endanger a brother warrior by allowing the infidel security services to take his fingerprints from your computer. Is that understood?"

"Na'am," Saddam and the others answered, nodding.

"Excellent, my brothers. Now, each of you will return to your quarters and gather all your belongings. Return here quickly and we shall speed you on your way to your targets and Paradise."

Saddam was surprised how quickly time flew after that. He returned to his small room and gathered his clothes and other things, then slipped into the bathroom for a brief shower and fresh clothes.

When they returned, Hazar was waiting for them, encouraging each man to sit in front of the video camera and speak of why they hoped for martyrdom and how they would risk all to bring death to those who warred on Islam. Saddam's stay in front of the camera was brief.

"You have taken the life of my brother and oppressed me as you have thousands of the faithful. I will do all I can to stop you, and if Allah wishes that I join him in Paradise, I will submit to His will. There is no god but Allah, and Mohammed his only true Prophet, may Allah's peace and blessings be upon him."

After each of the five men had recorded their messages, Hazar had them empty their bags on the classroom floor. Two had small pocket-knives, which he confiscated. Only one lacked a small bag for the laptop, and Hazar gave him a brand-new bag still in its plastic wrap.

Hazar then brought the men before him and checked that each had the passports and credit cards Abdel had procured for them. Using a lap-top Saddam had never seen before, tethered to one of the new iPhones with satellite communications capability, Hazar used the men's credit cards to buy their plane tickets out of Sana'a to their final destinations in the U.S.

By 2 P.M., they were back at their boardinghouse and ready to travel, Hazar's words of praise and encouragement still echoing in their ears. Shortly thereafter, the local imam who met them at the airport when they arrived drove up in his small Toyota van to take them on the first leg of their journey. This was the imam's second airport shuttle run of the day, and his second group of passengers, but he did not mind at all, treating his new passengers to the same prayers to Allah he offered for his first group.

THE GIANT C-17 GLOBEMASTER III flared out and settled onto Run-way 33 Left at King Abdul Aziz military airfield in the afternoon sun. Once its main wheels kissed the tarmac, the pilot brought the nose down gently and reversed the thrust to bring the aircraft to a speed more fit for driving a nearly 200-foot-long plane around an airfield. The C-17 then taxied south and turned left to cross the active runway before turning north toward its parking place.

As before, the Saudis had cordoned off the largest hangar on the base, its doors already yawning wide open. Expecting this, thanks to the directions from the control tower, the pilot skillfully maneuvered the C-17 into a right turn that centered the nose on the hangar's centerline and began to creep forward at a steady and sedate 2 miles per hour.

Keying the onboard intercom the crew shared, the major said, "Loadmaster, pilot. Give me the word on tail clearance."

"Copy that," came the reply from the Air Force Master Sergeant, standing on the edge of the lowered rear cargo ramp and looking up. The C-17 would never fit completely in the hangar, but they wanted to get as much of the aircraft as possible out of sight to keep the presence of an American military aircraft "off the radar."

"Stop, stop, stop," the loadmaster called over the interco.n.

The pilot applied the brakes, and the aircraft stopped with 3 feet of clearance between the hangar's forward roofline and the angled upward sweep of its huge T-shaped rudder and tail.

Mathews and Cochrane walked down the C-17's lowered cargo ramp and onto Saudi soil, followed closely by Thompson, who was stretching to get the kinks out of her muscles from the long flight.

"Nice to see you again, Lieutenant."

Mathews turned and saw Johnson grinning at him, holding up a six pack of water bottles and standing next to a Saudi man, dressed in thawb and keffiyeh, he had never seen before.

"You again." Mathews grinned in return and headed over to shake Johnson's hand.

"You remember my XO, Lieutenant Cochrane."

"Sure, and this is . . . ?" Johnson asked, gesturing at Thompson, who was hanging back a little, hoping not to be noticed, especially since there was a Saudi man nearby. She knew how touchy they could be about women.

"This is Technical Sergeant Thompson. She's along on this trip as an observer."

Johnson figured there was more of an explanation than just observer, but he would let the matter rest with Akeem alone.

"This is Akeem, a friend of mine from the Ministry of the Interior. He has arranged your visit here to the Kingdom."

"As-salaam 'alaikum."

Mathews and Cochrane said hello and shook Akeem's hand.

When the round of greetings reached Emily, Akeem looked at her and said nothing, a pleasant smile on his face.

Emily thought, *we aren't having any of that "ignore the woman" crap with me.* She extended her hand and said, "Wa alaikum s-salaam."

Akeem's smile widened and he stepped close enough only to shake her hand gently, and then backed half a step away, toward the men, being sure to put his eyes on them.

"I am pleased to meet you all," Akeem said in his perfect English.

Johnson chimed in, "Akeem was educated in England before he began to work here in the Ministry of the Interior. He's been kind enough to show me around and help me try to learn Arabic."

"When is our meeting with the minister?" Mathews asked.

"Tomorrow night," Akeem told him. "I will escort you and Agent Johnson to meet with him. I should warn you, his questions will be pointed and he expects candor."

Mathews fixed Akeem with a steady gaze. "I have orders from our president to answer any questions about the mission that your government supported. I also have an intelligence summary with me that I have been directed to share with the king."

"Excellent, I think . . ."

Thompson interrupted Akeem. "Excuse me, Lieutenant. Would it be possible for me to tag along? As long as I'm under your command, those orders would apply to me, and I did support the team during that mission."

Mathews was about to chime in with a resounding veto, but Akeem beat him to it.

"That is not possible. The minister is a prince of the House of Saud. It would not be proper for him to meet with a woman . . ."

"What?" Emily objected, her face a mask of frustration.

"Please," Akeem said, raising his hand imploringly. "Let me finish."

"Sergeant!" Mathews berated her in an unmistakably tone of warning.

The sharp tone drew Thompson's attention to Mathews. She saw the stern warning in his eyes and subsided.

"Thank you," Akeem told Mathews, before turning to face Emily again.

"It would not be proper for him to meet with a woman who was not a high-level representative of your government." Akeem placed his hand over his heart, and bowed slightly toward her, an Arabic gesture to show he spoke from the heart. "My nation has, as you obviously well know, a cultural and religiously based viewpoint toward women and their place in society that is an anathema to most Western cultures."

Akeem paused for any further comment. When there was none, he continued. "As an educated person, I recognize that there are some practices in our culture that may warrant change over time, but our culture, and my faith and its teachings, tell me that change will not be something I will see in my lifetime, or even my grandchildren's lifetime. This is Saudi Arabia, and here, our tribal cultural roots and Islam and its teachings are as much a part of our lives as your Constitution and sense of equality 'for all men' . . ." Akeem let these last words sink in, and smiled before continuing, " . . . is part of yours. I must respect your culture and beliefs, and I must insist that you respect ours while you are here. I am sure Sergeant Thompson is a capable soldier, but here, she would make what is sure to be a tense meeting more so by adding an unneeded 'cultural dimension' with her presence."

Mathews considered Akeem's words. He intended to deny Thompson's request for other reasons, starting with the fact that he did not have permission to expose the kind of support the CTS provided to the Wraith Teams, but Akeem's reasoning also made sense.

Mathews turned to Thompson. "Sergeant Thompson. You'll be staying here with the team, as an observer."

The look on her face showed that Emily was less than pleased with her latest orders.

"ARE WE READY YET?" CAIN ASKED.

"The equipment is coming up now." Mike Goodman was as exasperated as Cain was. The switchover from one backup generator to another was supposed to be seamless. When they took the primary generator down for some much-needed maintenance, the second generator was not fully up to speed. The brownout caused most of the non-mission-critical systems to fail, which included the VTC system, just ten minutes before the scheduled start time.

The DIRNSA, General Terry Holland, sat next to Cain in the CTS conference room, sipping from a cold can of Mountain Dew. Holland knew better than to interject himself into the situation. Cain's people were on it, and if Dr. Owens, the president's national security advisor, registered a complaint, Holland would take the heat for it.

"Here we go," Goodman said, seeing the VTC monitors light up and the power on self-test cycle and complete. After a few seconds, the CTS logo appeared. Cain always liked the logo, consisting of a black circular background with a full-color representation of the world overlaid on it. Over the world was a full color bald eagle, clutching a UAV in one talon and a set of ten lightning bolts in the other. Each of the jagged bolts symbolized one of the weapons systems at CTS's command. The first of those were the armed drones they could fly practically anywhere in the world. The other nine were closely guarded secrets, each classified in its own security compartment outside of CAPTIVE DRAGON. Cain mused that CTS had yet to use all the lightning bolts the eagle was holding, yet it was nice to know they were available.

"Looks like we're up," General Holland observed. The CTS logo had vanished and the VTC had automatically connected to the multi-point conference.

"CTS, you with us?" Dr. Jessica Owens' voice—and her exasperation—were unmistakable.

"This is Holland. Mr. Cain, CTS director, is here as well."

"We were scheduled for a 10 A.M. start, CTS, why are you late?" Dr. Owens inquired acidly. Owens sat in her usual spot at the head of the White House Situation Room conference table, wearing her usual well-tailored business suit, this time in power red. Her silver-frosted black hair made her stand out among the other presidential aides and advisors clustered around the conference table. Owens had a sharp mind, and of late, little regard for the U.S. intelligence community based on her perception of their utter failure in preventing the recent spate of attacks. She held her favorite sterling-silver pen at the ready amid a neat stack of briefing notes and two tablet computers before her.

Holland was not about to get into a lengthy explanation with her. "We had an unexpected brownout, Dr. Owens. Our systems are back up now."

"Good. Let's hope it doesn't happen again, General," Owens replied with an implied threat. Cain glanced at Holland to see him looking at the VTC screens calmly. Holland was a four-star general, and only the president could remove him or take his stars.

Without taking another breath, Owens added, "Let's get back to the status of the power grid. You were saying, Mr. Secretary?"

Eduard Munoz, a fifty-year-old former New Mexico long linesman turned physics professor–cum–Energy Secretary, elected to restart his presentation. "As you can see from the first slide, more than 85 percent of the mid-Atlantic and New England power grids infrastructure remains down. Repair crews, now under National Guard and police escort, are working to repair the damage at the transformer substations throughout the area. Repairs are being limited to the daylight hours at the insistence of the police and Guard units due to the threat of sniper attack. This limits the repair crews to about seven hours a day, rather than the around-the-clock schedule we would prefer, which will naturally draw out the restoration time. On a positive note, reserve equipment and high-voltage transformer gear manufactured in the Midwest is being trucked to the repair sites as soon as the equipment is built and testing is complete. I'm told by the operations officers of the major utilities that overall, repair-crew morale remains high, especially with the increased police and Guard presence. Any questions?"

Owens waited a couple of beats for anyone to chime in, then spoke up. "What about the situation at Calvert Cliffs?"

Secretary Munoz's relief was visible. "Fortunately, we did not suffer a reactor containment breach at Unit 1, in spite of the containment building being hit at high speed with what Homeland Security tells me was a vehicle-borne improvised explosive device. The reactor remains shut down while an emergency repair to the concrete structure is effected."

The Secretary of Homeland Security, Shawn Miller, chimed in, "DHS has recommended that all nuclear plants in the country increase site security until further notice. Each plant operator is cooperating and has expressed appreciation for the deployment of companies of local National Guard troops to augment their security."

"I'll pass that along to the president," Owens commented, taking a note. "What about the Liquefied Natural Gas storage site explosion?"

Both the secretaries of energy and HHS started talking at once, and then realizing they were stepping on one another, stopped. Owens held up a hand and said, "Secretary Miller, you first."

Miller, a former army ranger who had lost his left arm to an IED in Afghanistan, adjusted his prosthetic's position on the conference table and began. "Thanks, Doctor. I'll limit what I have to say to the investigation and ask the FBI to jump in if needed." Cain saw the FBI director nod in agreement.

Secretary Miller continued, "The fires were finally contained last night, and they'll take another two days to knock down completely. The area itself is too hot for investigators to access the tank farm, but from an in-depth review of the video footage provided by CTS, our estimate is that one team of unknown men likely entered the LNG storage facility and planted explosive devices."

Miller paused and Secretary Munoz slipped in a comment. "I've conferred with our experts and made them available to DHS and the FBI. Their consensus opinion is that the design of the tanks would not permit such a catastrophic explosion without malicious intervention. Each tank is basically a double-walled thermos bottle. The only way to breach them is cut through both walls with torches—which would be instant suicide once you breached the inner wall—or with explosives."

The FBI director added, "The FBI concurs with that assessment. We've seen the video footage as well. The suspects seen fleeing from the local park adjacent to the storage facility were likely involved in the explosion."

"Agreed," added Secretary Miller, "especially since the footage also shows another group of men who were also apparently involved in the attack on the LNG off-loading platform in the Bay. The explosives attached to the support pilings did not collapse the platform, but there are a number of severe structural weaknesses. The platform was evacuated and a group of marine architects are examining the structure and developing a repair plan. The Coast Guard has also cordoned off the area around the platform."

"Where did these two groups of men flee?" Dr. Owens inquired.

Cain took that one. "One group left the park near the LNG storage facility and headed north to meet another group of men in cars near the

Calvert Cliffs Nuclear Power Plant. The group who placed the explosives on the support legs of the LNG off-load platform returned to shore and after hiking through the woods toward their car, was confronted by the Maryland State Police and a small group from Wraith Team Four."

Owens, who had been taking notes, lifted her head when Cain mentioned Team Four. "What was anyone from that unit doing working with the state police?"

Cain expected that one. "Team Four had been ordered to the Calvert Cliffs plant to advise and assist a National Guard unit already on-site with security preparations. As you may remember, the members of each Wraith unit have all seen combat, and it was decided that having some seasoned professionals assist the Guard unit in an advisory capacity made sense."

"Who decided that, Mr. Cain? You?" The corrosive tone was back in Owens' voice.

"I did, Dr. Owens." The secretary of defense's voice was firm, and almost dismissive of her concern. "Mr. Cain is only reporting on actions I ordered in coordination with the commanding officer of the 152nd Joint Special Missions Unit, General Crane."

"I see," Owens replied. "I'll pass that on to the president." Her tone suggested disapproval, and virtually guaranteed that she would spin the SECDEF's instructions in a negative light, thinking that U.S. military forces were not supposed to operate on U.S. soil without presidential approval.

"Please do," SECDEF invited politely. "As you are well aware, U.S. military forces are permitted under the law to provide technical and other assistance to U.S. law enforcement and other Title 32 National Guard forces whenever I direct them, or whenever they are requested."

Owens had forgotten that. It looked like she would not win her ongoing feud with him for influence with the president today. "Yes, Mr. Secretary. I'll pass that along, too."

"Thank you, Dr. Owens." SECDEF smiled slightly as he added, "You can also tell him that Team Four was responsible for stopping most of the attackers at the nuclear plant, while also apparently saving the life of a Maryland State Police officer."

"I'll do that," she added, then sensing an opportunity, continued,

"I'm sure they did their best to stop the car bomb, too."

SECDEF looked up and began to retort, but Owens spoke first. "I need to meet with the president in ten minutes to update him. What can you tell me about the resupply ships in the Indian Ocean?"

SECDEF swallowed what he was going to say about the car bomb. This forum was not the venue for two senior advisors to the president to argue. Besides, he would make a private call to the president as soon as the meeting ended to ensure that the national security advisor didn't misrepresent Team Four's efforts or courage. He could dial a phone faster than she could walk to the Oval Office.

"Four of the Maritime Prepositioning Squadron II's ships have been disabled," he replied. "Each ship managed to avoid sinking due to the heroic efforts of their crews, predominately made up of contractors, along with the assistance of the men and women of the British naval depot at Diego Garcia."

"How were they disabled, Mr. Secretary?" Owens asked.

"The investigators from PACOM are still en route, but the initial reports from the British experts on-scene point to explosive charges placed on the hull beneath the water line."

"A deliberate attack?" Owens mused aloud.

"Yes. The damage was not caused by the cargo on board any of the vessels, and each one of them carries various forms of munitions."

The director of DIA, Admiral Haines, interrupted, "That puts a huge dent in our ability to deploy forces to the Middle East."

"Explain, please, Admiral," Owens requested.

"As you may know, ma'am, I was PACOM commander for two years. Those MPS ships carry thirty days of food, fuel, ammunition, and spare parts for any military force we need to deploy to any Middle East hot spot. Without those ships and the cargo they carry, we can't risk putting boots on the ground anywhere from the eastern Med to the Persian Gulf. Without the initial supply line those ships represent, any military force we landed would be crippled in terms of their ability to fight."

Cain agreed with the admiral's assessment. "Dr. Owens, CTS has been having some informal conversations with some of the experts at the CIA, DIA, and out at PACOM. We are all well aware of the recent events here at home. The result of those attacks has obviously had a serious impact on our civil population, resulting in an increased security posture here at home, as well as making our police and National Guard units operate at a higher tempo. Primarily, though, these events have been keeping our focus here, managing the ongoing internal problems of looking after our citizens. Now we have what appears to be a strike against the ships we use to resupply forces in the Middle East."

Cain paused to let his line of thinking sink in. When no one objected or disagreed, he plowed on. "I did some checking on INTELINK this morning. The Expeditionary Strike Group centered on the amphibious assault ship USS *America* just crossed through the straits of Gibraltar into the Atlantic for her homeport of Norfolk. Her replacement, USS *Tripoli*, and her amphibious group aren't due to leave Norfolk until tomorrow. When those 2,500 Marines get to the Med in a week or two, they won't have the supplies they need close by in the event of a crisis."

Cain paused again and took a deep breath to accompany the analytic leap he was about to make. It felt right, but he really wished he could have told General Holland first to get some backup and support. "We suspect this man Aziz is behind the infrastructure attacks here at home. If he's also behind the attacks on those ships in the Indian Ocean—and that's a big 'if'—then I would suspect he's up to a lot more than just attacking us."

Cain stopped and held his breath. He would either get outright ignored or laughed at later—or worse.

"Mr. Cain, is there any direct evidence to support your conclusion?" SECDEF was giving him a chance, at least.

Cain had to shake his head. "No, sir, there isn't. At least, not from the intelligence reporting I can see or the evidence recovered by the FBI at the incident scenes. All we have is a lot of dead bodies here at home with no identification and very few viable clues. Now we have an attack on some critical resupply ships in the Indian Ocean. Somebody is calling the tune we are dancing to, and for now, the only suspect I have to offer you is Aziz. Beyond the letter sent to the *New York Times* and other news outlets, there have been no claims of responsibility by any person or organization."

"I see," answered SECDEF, looking pensive. "Admiral Haines, I suggest you take the lead and put together a more formal working group at DIA to look at this situation in total. Make sure you invite representatives from DHS and the FBI," SECDEF ordered.

"Will do, Mr. Secretary," Haines responded.

"In the meantime, I'll pass orders to Atlantic Command for the *Tripoli* and her Expeditionary Strike Group to put to sea ASAP for the eastern Med. I'll also order USS *Enterprise* and her strike group to sail for the Med as well, once they've concluded the joint exercise Winter Palm with the Brits in the Caribbean."

Cain knew that the Ford class aircraft carrier and her strike group were a very powerful formation of ships, carrying more than a hundred aircraft and land-attack missiles, but the Marines in the *Tripoli*'s ESG would not be able to sustain themselves ashore for long without supplies.

Owens was already gathering her notes and rising from the conference table in the Situation Room. "Thank you, all. I'll pass this information on to the president. He's already mentioned convening a cabinet meeting via VTC in the next day or two. If he moves that up, I'll pass that along." With that, Owens walked off-camera.

General Holland reached for the touch-screen control and tapped the virtual buttons to mute the microphones and turn the VTC sound down.

"Well, David, it seems like you triggered the formation of a working group."

"I'm sorry, sir. I should have discussed my thinking with you before the VTC started, but with the power outage, I got a little sidetracked."

Holland clapped him on the shoulder. "No sweat. I think your reasoning is dead-on. I just wish we had more facts to back it up. Be sure to have the CTS watch teams keep a close eye on the Middle East reporting. Pass along to my XO anything that looks interesting. Does the CIA or FBI have any idea where this Aziz bastard is?"

Cain shook his head. "No. The information from Saudi intelligence was passed to the CIA, DHS, and FBI. Customs and border security have an alert out for the man, so if he tries to enter the U.S., Canada, or the UK he'll be detained. The CIA Chief of Station in Riyadh has good relations with the Saudi intelligence services, but they don't have anything more than what they've already provided. The FBI sent their man Johnson back to Riyadh and he's liaising with the Ministry of the Interior for the Team Four visit. If something breaks there, we'll know."

"So in the meantime," Holland observed, "we wait for new information."

"Or another attack," Cain said grimly.

THE MAN SWUNG THE BLACK Pelican hard case into the trunk of the car with ease, setting it next to the bolt cutters and small video camera before slamming the trunk shut and walking to the driver's side of the old blue Ford Focus. The old hybrid engine coughed once and caught, and he put the car in gear and drove off.

Noor was in his late twenties. He spent most of his time working in the local Kentucky Fried Chicken as the day-shift manager and taking online classes in engineering with the University of Chicago from his small trailer home in Hubert, North Carolina.

Today, Noor would get to work after the lunch rush once his errand was completed. He turned right out of the old trailer park onto Riggs Road. Fifteen minutes later, he was following Sneads Ferry Road as the road curved to head west toward Marine Corps Base Camp Lejeune. Huge stretches of thick trees bordered both sides of the state road. The whole area was an ideal site for the Marines to train. Close to the ocean and a protected bay, they could practice amphibious landings and assaults without disturbing any of the nearby communities.

Noor knew that Camp Lejeune was home to the II Marine Expeditionary Force, the primary response force for Middle East contingencies. It was one reason the man he knew as Abdul had sent him to live in the little town of Hubert after his training was complete in Yemen. The other was that Noor already held a U.S. F-1 visa, allowing him to travel to the U.S. on his Egyptian passport to study at an American university. Noor knew that after he had delivered this package, he could look forward to his next task, assuming he did not get caught.

Noor saw the green 3-mile marker along the road and slowed. The dirt road was exactly where the Google Earth imagery showed it. He turned left onto the dirt access road and drove deeper into the wooded plain for another mile before he saw it on his left. A small cleared area with a fenced perimeter, no more than 100 square feet.

Noor stopped the car just past the entrance in the fence line and then backed up, putting his trunk right next to the entrance. He expected that the site was wired with an alarm, so he would hurry.

Exiting the car, he opened the trunk and took out the video camera. Opening the small foldout LCD screen, he powered on the camera. He took a few seconds to pan over the scene, being sure to take in the white metal signs affixed to the fence, and focusing on one of them for twenty seconds to record the lettering: warning: u.s. military installation − camp lejeune − potable water test point 35A. entry forbidden to unauthorized personnel, by order of the installation commander.

Once he had the signs recorded, he took the video camera and balanced it on the rear bumper of the Focus, then zoomed in on the metal pipe sticking up a foot out of the ground. The black pipe was almost 2 feet in diameter with a large, dark blue plastic cap hinged on one side and secured with a padlock on the other. Ensuring that the video camera's focus was set to automatic, he stood and reached into the trunk, put on a pair of leather gloves, and picked up heavy bolt cutters.

Working quickly, he cut through the hasp of the padlock on the fence, and then moved to the pipe and snipped off the padlock holding the dark blue cap in place. He did not see any wires on the fence or the pipe's blue cover, but he could not trust that he had not set off an alarm.

Walking back to the Ford, he tossed the bolt cutters back into the trunk. They would find their way into the large Dumpster at work later today. He was also having new tires installed on the car right after he left. By taking both of these precautions, the Americans and their forensic scientists would not be able to use his tread wear pattern of the tires to place his car at the site or the bite pattern of the bolt cutters on the padlock's hasp.

He carefully popped the latches on the black Pelican case and removed the spun aluminum water bottle. He checked the video camera once more to see the field of view, assuring himself he knew where to place his hands and the bottle, and then returned to the pipe, flipping the blue cover open.

Next, he unscrewed the bottle cap and carefully poured the luminescent green liquid into the pipe, making sure to keep his face as far away as possible and his hands toward the bottom of the bottle. He could hear the sounds of rushing water below and thought he could almost make out the splash of the deadly uranyl nitrate hitting the water and mingling with it.

Once the bottle was empty, he replaced the cap and returned to the car, placing the bottle back in the Pelican case and latching it securely. He removed the gloves and tossed them into a small brown paper bag—yet another thing destined for the Dumpster at work.

Gathering up the video camera, Noor shut it off and got back in the car, tossing the camera on the passenger seat and then starting the engine. Pulling out quickly, he swung right, back up the dirt road, and right again onto Sneads Ferry Road, heading back to Hubert. After 3 miles of not being followed, he decided the Marines were not going to catch him today. He glanced at his watch and thought that he would just make his appointment at Pep Boys for his tire change. He smiled when he realized that Marines at Camp Lejeune would be drinking radioactively poisoned water while he waited at the shop, editing the video in the camera. Wasn't modern technology wonderful?

LATER THAT AFTERNOON AND INTO the early night, two men each visited the reservoirs feeding public water supplies in Baltimore, Philadelphia, Richmond, Washington, D.C., and Manhattan. The reservoirs were on public land and most closed after dark, but the men paid no heed to the posted signs and chains drawn across the parking lot entrances. In each pair, one man emptied the bright green contents of an aluminum bottle into the reservoir while the other recorded it.

Hours later, the memory cards from the video recorders were in small white FedEx envelopes destined for a FedEx location in the Midwest, all addressed to a man named Robins.

SADDAM SAT IN THE DEPARTURE lounge of Charles de Gaulle Airport's Terminal 1 and blew out a breath as he looked around. It was just after ten in the morning and the sounds and bustle of the terminal were things he had never really observed before. Now that he had time before his flight to America, he sat and wondered at them all. There were so many people. Coming and going, buying things from duty-free shops and food vendors.

Many wore Western dress, but he saw many in sari, thawb, abaya, and even a few in kimonos. Most dragged wheeled carry-on bags behind them. There were children everywhere—the older ones managed themselves, but the younger ones were in a constant struggle with their parents to be corralled, no matter the nationality. The infants seemed the easiest. They slept, unless they were hungry or had soiled their diapers, and then they wailed until a mother or father gave them a bottle or went to a restroom to change them.

The flight out of Sana'a essentially backtracked his trip to Yemen. First the hop from Sana'a to Cairo, then a two-hour layover before the overnight flight to Paris. Because he was not officially entering France, the customs check had been perfunctory, and thanks to Hazar's check of his luggage, uneventful. Immigration did not exist at the airport, and so he followed the signs directly to the international departure gates on level four. Twenty minutes ago they had called his flight and he followed the announcement's instructions, walking to the "L" hub off the main terminal. Saddam chose a seat near Gate 24, one of the three gates to the plane.

Taking out his boarding pass for the fourth time since landing in Paris, he scanned it again. He was on United Flight 933, a Boeing 777, due to depart in thirty minutes. Saddam looked at the arrival time at Washington Dulles International and calculated a flight time of nearly nine hours. He hoped to sleep for at least half of it if he could, but he knew he was probably too nervous to sleep.

He put the boarding pass away and looked around at the people arriving in the gate area for the long flight to America. Mostly men, but many women and a few children. One obviously American couple with yellow Remember the Troops ribbons on their carry-on bags was doing their best to keep their three children amused during the wait, the mother playing games with the youngest boy, and the father standing at the windows and pointing out planes and trucks to the older boy and girl, who were no more than eight. Their English was distinct, even from where he was sitting.

Saddam wondered where his brothers were at that moment, knowing that they too were on their way to America, ready to carry out their mission. He knew that a few of them were in the terminal somewhere, but they had all been placed on separate flights, so he did not expect to see any of them.

Unexpectedly, the gate agent's announcement broke into his thoughts. "Good morning, ladies and gentlemen. United Airlines would like to announce that Flight 933, nonstop service to Washington Dulles, is ready for boarding."

Saddam closed his eyes and bowed his head, asking Allah to accompany him as he began what would be his last journey by plane. His plea to Allah for safety accomplished, Saddam lifted his carry-on bag holding a change of clothes and his Ultrabook and made his way to the end of the line forming to board the jet.

CHAPTER 20

"WELCOME, LIEUTENANT." MINISTER ALI SHOOK Mathews' hand firmly, leaning toward him a little, and looking intently into his eyes. Mathews returned his handshake and willed himself not to lean away. Johnson had warned him about the cultural significance of looking or backing away. The last thing he needed now was to appear to be evasive or hiding something as the minister leaned into his personal space. It was even more difficult because he was forced to squint in the glare of the morning sun streaming in through the windows as he faced the minister. Regardless, he managed to hold still.

After a second or two to complete his assessment of the younger man, Minister Ali released his hand and gestured toward the conversation area for his guests to sit. Akeem motioned for Johnson and Mathews to precede him, and both men stood near the couch, allowing Akeem to choose one of the leather chairs before they all respectfully waited for their host to sit first. Mathews felt distinctly out of place, wearing only tan cargo pants and a long-sleeved shirt hastily bought in the local men's clothing store last night. He snuck a quick look at Johnson, envying the dark suit he wore, thinking ruefully that he had been right when he said Mathews' broader shoulders would not have fit in one of his jackets.

The minister offered them all refreshments from the tray laid on the conversation area's central table, and in keeping with the hospitality, the men availed themselves of glasses of fresh juice from the assorted carafes in the crystal bowl full of ice. Mathews took a healthy sip of his apple juice before placing the gold-lipped glass carefully on the matching glass coaster, expecting that he would be doing most of the talking.

"It is kind of you to travel so far to meet with me," the minister offered.

Akeem looked at Mathews expectantly.

"It is no trouble at all, Mr. Minister. I am pleased to meet with you, although I must apologize for my appearance. I brought only duty uniforms with me, and I felt arriving in your office in battle dress would have caused a stir."

The minister smiled understandingly. "Think nothing of it, Lieutenant. Akeem called me last night and explained that you were taken from your current duties and ordered here."

"Thank you, sir."

"It is important that His Majesty have a clear understanding of what exactly you and your team did in Iran. Would you please tell me?"

Mathews nodded affirmatively. "I would be pleased to, sir. In short, thanks to the cooperation of His Majesty, my team and I were able to covertly enter Iran and reach a house outside of Tehran. We believed that this house belonged to a man named Aziz Abdul Muhammad al-Zahiri. Our intelligence led us to believe that this man was involved in, or aware of, the recent attacks on my country's energy infrastructure. Are you familiar with them?"

The minister nodded, an intense look on his face as he watched Mathews closely. Mathews could not tell if the intensity was driven by interest in the attacks on America or the covert insertion into Iran that the Saudis helped with.

"Once we were on the ground," Mathews continued, "we approached the house on foot, and eliminated the guards."

"You killed them?" the minister inquired hotly.

Mathews nodded, chagrined. "I would have preferred not to, sir. We had brought along nonlethal weapons in order to simply subdue what we expected was a small unarmed or lightly armed one- or two-man guard force. Instead, there were six men armed with AK-74 rifles with attached grenade launchers."

The minister considered that before answering. "And you left their bodies where they fell?"

Mathews suspected the question was a probe to see if he would lie, since General Crane had told him earlier that the Saudis knew Mathews and his team left Iran with the bodies.

"No, Mr. Minister." Mathews broke eye contact and looked at the rug beneath his feet, tinted golden yellow by the sun's rays, before looking back up. No sense in hiding it. "I ordered the bodies of the men taken aboard our extraction aircraft, to remove as much evidence as possible of our presence."

The minister leaned back in his chair, and looked away from Mathews toward the bare wall.

"Did you throw the bodies into the sea as you did with Bin Laden?" he asked acidly.

Mathews, thinking about Johnson's talk about the importance of eye contact, slid closer to the edge of the couch, and leaned toward the minister. "Sir."

When the minister did not take his eyes off the wall, Mathews repeated himself. "Sir."

Reluctantly, the minister brought his eyes back to Mathews' and held them.

"No, sir. We gave the bodies to a Muslim military chaplain so that they could be buried with respect, in accordance with Islamic burial practices." The minister continued to look at him, and Mathews thought he saw a hint of change in his face. A slight lessening of his hostility? He plowed on, his eyes locked on the minister's.

"Mr. Minister. Those men died as members of an opposing force in battle. To my mind, they stood their ground in the face of a military force and died doing their duty. I had orders to leave them and I chose to disobey them for what initially were practical military and operational concerns. Once my men and I were back across the border and safe, we needed to decide what to do with them, and in my mind, a professional soldier does not treat the wounded or the dead with disrespect."

The minister held his gaze and then nodded. "Forgive me my directness. Many of the actions your government and your soldiers have taken since the attacks on New York are an anathema to many people in the Middle East. I was afraid that your actions with the bodies were not respectful and that another case of abhorrent behavior by American troops was before me. May I offer you more to drink or eat?" The minister waved his hand expansively at the table. "I can order some pastries brought in if you have not yet had a morning meal."

Mathews bowed his head briefly in the minister's direction. "No, sir. Not for myself, thank you." As an act of contrition, Mathews thought, as he watched Johnson and Akeem decline as well, it was not too shabby.

"Agent Johnson," the minister inquired, "did you have any role in Lieutenant Mathews' journey to Iran?"

"No, Mr. Minister," Johnson answered. "I did, however, work with Akeem to gain approval for the lieutenant and his team to enter the Kingdom, and relayed the information that the Kingdom's intelligence services were able to develop about Aziz."

"I see." The minister considered Johnson. "We shall come back to that. Lieutenant, please continue. After you were forced to kill the guards, then what happened?"

"We entered the house and searched every room," Mathews answered, hedging a little, but knowing the next question was inevitable.

"Did you find this Aziz?"

Mathews shook his head again. "No, sir. We did not. In fact, the house was empty."

The minister cocked his head to the side. "Empty?"

"Yes, sir. Aziz was not there. We also found no evidence of anyone else. Just furniture and other typical things."

The venom of disbelief began to creep back into the minister's voice. "So you enlisted our aid to capture and spirit out of Iran a man you claim might be behind the attacks on your country and he wasn't there?"

Mathews nodded, resigned to the truth. "That's correct, Minister."

The venom in the minister's voice was unmistakable now. "This is unconscionable. Your government has perhaps wittingly made my nation culpable in the attempted kidnapping of an Iranian national from his home country. What intelligence does your nation possess that makes you believe this man might be responsible and that he was in Iran?"

Mathews was afraid the minister would get to this issue. This might get very ugly in a minute. "I'm sorry, Mr. Minister. My orders do not allow me to share that information . . ."

"What!" the minister cut him off, nearly rising from his seat.

"My friend," Akeem interjected in Arabic. "These men are guests in our house, and following the orders men more senior to them have given."

The minister looked at Akeem and took a deep breath, clearly exasperated. After a few more breaths to calm himself, the minister settled back in his chair and nodded toward Akeem. "My friend reminds me that you are guests in my country. He also reminds me that you are following the orders you were given. Lieutenant, please finish what you were saying."

Mathews looked at Johnson, unsure exactly what the minister's reaction might be to what he was going to say, then put his eyes on the minister once again. "My orders do not allow me to share that information with anyone except the king, sir. Those orders have been relayed to me by my commanding officer, who tells me that they come directly from my president." Mathews licked his lips, then continued, "As far as the knowledge of Aziz's presence in Iran, sir, it was provided to us by your nation's intelligence services."

The minister was surprised by that last fact. "Intelligence matters are not within the purview of my ministry," Ali conceded, still annoyed that the young man would not tell him why the American government suspected this man Aziz. "I understand that as a military man you must follow the orders you have been given." Ali looked back and forth between Johnson and Mathews, considering what he had just heard.

"Please excuse me," the minister said at last, rising from the leather-bound chair.

"We can wait outside if you wish," Akeem offered, rising with him.

"La, intadhir daqīqa wahida," the minister instructed, motioning downward with his hand, lost in thought and heading across the room toward his desk.

Johnson looked at Mathews, translating "He wants us to wait here."

"Thanks, I got the gist of it," Mathews said with a smile as Akeem reseated himself.

"Shokran," Johnson said to Akeem. "I thought he was going to throw us out of the office."

Akeem smiled. "It is the least I can do for a friend. The minister is not a bad man, but I have known him for too many years to not know he has a quick temper."

Mathews watched the minister, now on the phone at his desk, deep in conversation with someone. "I should thank you as well. I have no interest in starting a diplomatic incident." Mathews shook his head. "This is something someone much senior to me should be handling."

"I agree," Akeem told him, "but having the actual commander of the unit here to speak with us says a great deal. If your government was trying to hide something from us, it would be easier to do with someone at a higher level. Making you available eases some concerns."

Johnson's eyes were on the minister. The phone conversation was over and he was walking back toward them. "Having you here to vouch for us makes this easier," Johnson said. "Shokran."

Akeem bowed his head in acceptance, and then they all rose as the minister returned.

"Lieutenant, your orders are to only share the intelligence information with His Majesty?"

Oh, shit, thought Mathews. *He called security and we are going to be thrown out of the country.* "Yes, sir. Those are my orders."

"Good. Then tomorrow night, you will meet with the king, share with him this information, and answer his questions as well."

SADDAM MOVED THE WINDOW SHADE up a little and bright sunlight streamed into the economy section of the huge Boeing 777. It was beautiful from this high up. Surprisingly, the seats next to him on Flight 933 were empty, but he was near the rear of the jet. Seat 35A gave him just the view he had hoped for, but for now, he pulled the window shade back down, and looked around.

It was dim in the rear of the jet. Most of the passengers had complied with the cabin attendant's request and lowered the shades to improve the visibility of the video displays mounted in the back of the seats.

Many people had fallen asleep after the light meal and their first movie, and a few were watching their second in-flight movie via the on-demand entertainment system. Saddam smirked. No doubt, they were watching movies with far too many women of loose morals and too much violence, their shame hidden from all but Allah in the artificial darkness of the cabin.

Saddam checked the clock on the large screen mounted to the cabin-dividing wall. The flight was more than six hours in. It was time. Saddam reached under the seat and pulled out his carry-on bag, then unzipped it. Pulling out the Ultrabook, he kicked his still-open bag back under the seat and twisted the latch to release the tray table. Once the tray settled into place, he sat the laptop on it carefully and opened the lid, pressing the power button and waiting for the boot sequence to complete. Once KARIM was up, he entered the password at the login prompt and then dug in his pants pocket for the USB memory stick.

The desktop appeared before him with the usual musical chime. He silently cursed himself as a fool for not turning the sound down, but then reconsidered as he remembered that no one would know what he was doing. After all, he was just booting up a portable computer. Everyone did that on a plane these days, just to stave off boredom with a movie or game if they did not have business to work on.

Saddam slid his finger across the touch pad to put the cursor over the wireless icon, and clicked once. The list of available wireless networks appeared and he double-clicked on the network labeled "InFlight." A few seconds later, the machine reported "Connected to InFlight network. No Internet Access." To connect to the Internet, he would have to open a web browser and use a credit card to pay for access, but that was not where his interest lay.

Saddam uncapped the USB stick and slid it into the connector on the side of the laptop. The file explorer window automatically spawned, showing him the one executable file named "tictactoe.exe" on the USB stick. He moved his finger on the touchpad to let the cursor hover over it before tapping twice to execute it.

In less than two seconds, the 25 MB program copied itself to the Ultrabook's memory and began to run. First, the program reached out through the Ultrabook's wireless connection to the network router at the front of the plane, and quickly scanned for open ports and cataloged them. Saddam saw the little "Catalog Complete" message pop up in the lower right portion of the screen, and slowly fade away.

When Hazar had trained them, Saddam had asked about how the software worked.

"I am not our exulted engineer, but I will tell you what I do understand," Hazar replied. He went on to explain that the ports were like many doors on a building. Each router, thought of as a building, might have only one Internet Protocol address, but for each IP address, there usually were many different doorways one could send a message through when it reached the building. Each door or port on the router was designed to allow only certain types of messages through, but with careful design, and a jihad's superior knowledge of technology, messages could enter one door, and then exit through a back door to go somewhere forbidden.

The software looked through the list of open ports it discovered on the plane, and found what it was programmed to look for. Port 45687 was available. The software sent a small test message, what Hazar had called a "ping," to the router, addressing it specifically to that port, and waited for the response. In less than 300 milliseconds, the software heard the reply and compared the originating IP address on the "ping" to the one it had already stored for the 777's onboard router. They were different. This difference triggered another message Saddam saw appear in the lower right-hand corner of the display, "FC Available," along with the startup of the software's processing and graphics display subroutines.

Three seconds later, the computer had sent and received more than 100 packets through the router and received a steady stream of return messages from the Boeing's flight control computer. Two seconds after that, and the Ultrabook was showing the multi-element display he was expecting, now populated with the real-time feed of information from the flight control computer.

The display took up all of his screen, and he looked it over carefully. Divided into three main sections, the left one showed an overhead map, with the plane's flight route superimposed over a crude map of the world. The map also displayed the navigational checkpoints and timings drawn from the flight computer's knowledge of the route and the plane's current position.

Saddam could also see the position and flight path of the other aircraft around them. Hazar had explained during training that the position of the other aircraft was provided by the collision avoidance systems all modern jet airliners carried, and that the engineer was working on software to use against Allah's enemies as well.

Saddam read the display carefully and saw that they were heading toward checkpoint DOTTY, just east of the northern peninsula of the island of Newfoundland, about 250 miles away. He had about twenty minutes before they made landfall. Plenty of time.

Saddam ignored the center of the display and looked carefully at the right-hand portion, what Hazar had described as the flight director updater. This subscreen's upper section showed the autopilot and throttle settings. Saddam scanned the numbers quickly, seeing what he expected. They were cruising at an altitude of 35,000 feet, at an indicated airspeed of Mach 0.82, which was nearly 550 miles per hour. The vertical speed setting was at zero, which was normal for level flight.

Reaching for the touch pad, he moved the cursor toward the lower half of the right window, where there was a duplicate subscreen, its similar readings for altitude and airspeed displayed by the laptop as empty boxes, waiting for input.

Positioning the cursor over the altitude field, he clicked and then entered the value of −1, 0, 0, 0. Moving to the airspeed slot, he entered 2, 9, 0. Lastly, he moved to the vertical speed setting, and entered −6000.

Saddam suddenly felt his palms sweating and he looked around the cabin as casually as he could, certain someone was watching him. Seeing no one, and after scratching his forehead in what he hoped was a convincing matter, he put his attention back on the screen. The center section showed the large ball of the horizontal situation indicator, still showing level flight, and electronic versions of the airspeed and altitude gauges. The gauges showed altitude and speed numbers that matched the ones programmed into the flight director, commonly called the autopilot, in the upper right portion of the display.

Saddam checked the entries he made in the flight director updater, and touched the mouse pad, sliding his finger down and right, leaving the cursor hovering over the button labeled "Commit."

Once he pressed it, the software would communicate one last time with the flight control computer, ordering it to execute three actions sequentially: overwrite all flight performance limitations to allow the flight director to operate the plane beyond its acceptable altitude and speed envelope; immediately delete altitude and airspeed values in main memory, and load the new ones Saddam had just entered for execution; and lock out the flight control inputs from the flight deck, and any future updates manually entered into the flight director.

Last, the software would use Saddam's entered altitude, airspeed, and vertical speed rate as new active flight parameters, descending at 6,000 feet per minute at 290 knots to an altitude of 1,000 feet below sea level. With the usual flight safeties removed, the descent from 35,000 feet would take only eight minutes, and there would be no chance to pull up from the dive. His finger still hovering over the touch pad, Saddam looked around the cabin one last time. His act would terrorize the Americans, and would ensure that he, his brother, and all his family would see Paradise, since the entire family of a martyr was admitted by Allah's servants without question.

Saddam's eyes settled on a mother and her child on the right side of the plane. The woman wore a long dress and covered her hair with the hijab, as was proper. Her son sat on her left and she was reading to him from the Holy Qur'an. He regretted the fear they would soon know, but she, her son, and all the other Muslims aboard would certainly be admitted to Paradise while the unbelievers on the plane suffered in eternal torment.

"Excuse me," said a voice behind him. Saddam nearly leapt out of his skin, and his finger strayed away from the mouse touch pad. The man leaning over his seat was in his late thirties, with pale skin, blue eyes, and a short shock of prematurely silver hair. He had been watching Saddam's Ultrabook screen through the small crack between the seats in front of him. His family was sleeping in the seats next to him.

He smiled, looking at Saddam's Ultrabook. "I'm a bit of an aviation buff myself. I like flying the simulators, too. I've never seen a flight tracker like that before, where did you get it?"

Saddam looked at the man, the surprise and shock at discovery evident on his face. The man shifted his eyes back and forth from the Ultrabook's screen to Saddam's face, momentarily confused by Saddam's startled expression. Then he looked at the screen a little closer and saw the same altitude and airspeed he had seen on his own built-in video monitor's tracking of the flight across the Atlantic.

In a half second, the silver-haired man made the connection and his soul screamed danger. "Stop! I need help over here!" he yelled, reaching over the chair and grabbing Saddam's hands.

Saddam struggled with him, but the man was fit and held on, desperate to save his family and the other people's lives on board. Around them, passengers were waking up to the commotion of the two men struggling.

The man yelled out again, "I'm an Air Force major! This man is trying to crash the plane! Somebody help me!" That got people moving. Two men in front of Saddam's row of seats stood up and turned around to survey the situation.

"Grab the laptop and help me with him! Don't touch the keys! He's trying to crash the plane!" the major shouted again. Both men reacted with alarm, and one slid into his seat on his knees to reach over and grab the laptop, while the other moved around their row of seats and helped pin Saddam's arms to his side.

Another man made his way across the jet and held up his air marshal credentials as two male cabin attendants a few feet behind him ordered people to stay in their seats and fasten their seatbelts. "I'm Air Marshal Taylor, what is going on here?" he demanded.

"I'm Air Force Major Jack Dyson. I think this young man was trying to crash the plane with that laptop."

"You a pilot?" the marshal demanded, taking a quick glance at the Ultrabook.

"Yes, I'm IFR-certified in light planes."

Marshal Taylor pulled the handcuffs from the pouch at his waist and looked around Major Dyson to address Saddam. "Sir, you are under arrest on suspicion of interfering with an aircraft in flight." Looking at Dyson and the other man, he said, "Bring him out into the aisle."

A few minutes later, Saddam was cuffed, searched, and sitting in a different seat. As Marshal Taylor read him his rights, Major Dyson showed the copilot the laptop, careful not to touch the keys or the mouse touch pad.

The copilot took the laptop to the cockpit and locked the door behind him. After two minutes' worth of conversation with the pilot, they agreed on a course of action.

The copilot reached for the transponder controls, setting the code to 7700, as the pilot keyed the radio.

"Gander Center, United 933 Heavy, we are declaring an emergency.

We have reason to believe our flight control computer has been remotely compromised by a passenger on board. Request immediate clearance to the nearest available field for landing."

"United 933 Heavy, Gander Center. Radar contact, descend at your discretion to 10,000 feet, expect radar vectors to Bangor International. Do you need fighter escort?"

"Gander Center, United 933 Heavy. Expediting descent to 10,000 feet. Affirmative on the fighter escort. Also request you have law enforcement standing by."

"933 Heavy, Gander Center. Copy all. Good luck."

The copilot looked across the cockpit. "Think we'll need the fighters?"

"I hope not," replied the pilot, leaning forward to disable the flight director before pushing the yoke forward, slowly nosing the aircraft into a steeper than normal 25-degree descent before using his right hand to pull the throttle levers back to idle. "If nothing else, they can mark our crash location if something goes wrong."

"MR. CAIN!" ARNIE MCMILLAN SHOUTED across the CTS Ops floor, his black STE phone to his ear. Cain, who was reading the latest Daily Intelligence Summary from the Joint Intelligence Center-Pacific on his computer screen, looked over at McMillan, the Department of Homeland Security liaison.

"The FAA is reporting the attempted hijacking of a United 777 from Europe."

Shit, Cain thought, rising from his chair.

McMillan stayed on the phone a few seconds longer, covering the mouthpiece to talk to Cain as he listened. "FAA also has lost tracking on eight other aircraft, all coming from Europe to airports in the U.S." McMillan's eyes widened in shock and surprise as he relayed the rest. "The aircraft in front and behind them are reporting hearing panicked radio calls about frozen controls and uncontrolled descents. FAA looked at the tracking data from the eight planes' onboard systems. They show massive losses in altitude before all data stopped."

Multiple aircraft just dropping into the ocean? Cain thought. That was not mechanical failure or accidental. The odds of that were just too high, especially with the report of an attempted hijacking. Oh, God.

"Attention in CTS!" Cain bellowed. "We're in lockdown! Everyone to your workstations." The CTS team scrambled to their workstations, donning headsets and activating the direct lines to their agencies. Cain returned to his desk briefly and put on his headset, plugging it into his desk for now.

"Master Sergeant Carmody?" Cain had arranged with his commanding officer at Beale to borrow Carmody to replace Thompson while she was TDY with the Wraiths. It had taken a little doing, but getting him CAPTIVE DRAGON cleared had only taken a couple of days, and his skills as a drone weapons officer were good, since he was already fully qualified with the MQ-9 Reaper and the Global Hawk.

"Yes, sir." Carmody's voice came back on the link as he turned to look at Cain from the drone desk.

"Is the Hawk airborne?"

"Yes, sir. Currently orbiting east of Baltimore. I've been watching the car carriers head toward Baltimore Harbor."

"How much time on-station does she still have?"

"She launched with a full on-load, so she'll be up there until this time tomorrow unless we have a mechanical problem."

McMillan chimed in on the link. "Everyone, DHS is relaying data about the missing flights from the FAA, posting to the main screen."

In seconds, the listing came up on the right-hand screen display.

Airline	Flight#	FROM	TO	PAX
American	121	CDG	JFK	243
American	41	LHR	MDW	269
American	6150	FCO	MIA	400
Delta	593	LHR	MDW	224
United	135	CDG	EWR	228
United	63	BER	ATL	395
US Airways	755	CDG	IAD	335
US Airways	45	FCO	MIA	325

"My God," Cain breathed, scanning the passenger count and doing some quick math. More than 2,000 people were on those planes. Then he noticed the common theme.

"They are all American-flagged carriers," McMillan said, voicing Cain's thought.

"Arnie, get last known coordinates for all the planes from the FAA," Cain ordered, thinking fast. "Carmody, what's your first name?"

"Dan, sir."

"Dan, once we get those coordinates, I want you to identify orbit points in the Atlantic that are close enough for the Hawk's cameras to begin a search. A major search and rescue operation is going to begin and we will help all we can. Got it?"

Carmody looked at Cain and hesitated just long enough for Cain to turn to look at him.

"Yes, sir," Carmody responded, the look on his face broadcasting more than his words.

Cain unplugged quickly and walked over to the drone desk. "What is it?"

Carmody unplugged his headset as well, keeping the conversation between the two of them. "I have no problem with your orders, sir, but you know the odds are pretty long here. If the flight data the FAA reported proves out, those planes may have hit the ocean at 200 miles an hour or more, and at this time of year, in that water temperature, survival is measured in minutes. If they are too far out to sea . . ." Carmody might not be a flier, but he had worked with enough of them in his nearly twenty-year career in the Air Force to know enough about crash survival to be pretty sure every one of those people was dead.

Cain nodded, a resigned look on his face. "Yeah. I know. We have to try, though." He looked at the passenger count on the screen again. "With more than 2,000 victims, a few might beat the odds."

It was a forlorn and unfounded hope, but they had to try.

REPIN COMPLETED HIS USUAL VISUAL checks after entering the apartment. Nothing seemed out of place, and he had been careful to double back a few times on the way back from the FedEx office. He dropped the dozen next-day envelopes on his kitchen counter and doffed his coat. The midday sun was shining through the kitchen window and he wanted to stand in its rays to let his cheeks warm from the chilly air. Repin thought that the mile-high altitude made things a degree or two cooler than normal, but it was nothing compared to the winters in Moscow he had endured as a younger man.

Pulling out the kitchen scissors in the wooden knife block, Repin snipped the tops of each of the twelve envelopes open, then dropped their contents on the counter. In a couple of minutes, he had a small jumbled stack of clear plastic cases, each containing the small, black plastic square of a flash memory card.

He dropped the empty envelopes into the kitchen sink, scooping up the twelve plastic cases before heading over to his computer and stacking them on the desk.

Twenty minutes later, all the flash memory cards had been through the same process: out of the clear case, into the slot on Repin's computer designed for them, the single video file copied to the machine's encrypted hard drive, and the flash memory card erased and overwritten with zeros by a special utility before being put back into its case in a stack on the opposite side of the desk.

Once the individual files were on his computer, he brought up the operating system's built-in Movie Maker software. He watched each video, editing some of them, and checking each to see that there was enough "establishing" video so that each of the uranyl nitrate dumpsites was visually identifiable.

When the videos were ready, he inserted an unused memory stick into one of the computer's USB slots and copied all twelve video clips to it. Then he shut down the video-editing software, logged off the computer, and pulled the memory stick out of the USB slot.

After a quick trip to the bathroom, he gathered his coat and put it on, then checked his watch. The library would close in an hour. He made a mental note to burn the shipping envelopes after he returned. Resetting his telltales and visually checking the apartment one last time, he locked the door, looking forward to the half-mile walk to the library in the sun and chilly air. He had previously checked the computers in use in the library. The USB ports were not electronically disabled, and the building had no video surveillance.

* * *

"DAN, WHERE ARE WE AT?"

Carmody checked his displays in response to Cain's question. "About twenty minutes to the first orbit box. The first leg of the orbit will bring us within visual range of the last known positions for American Flights 121 and 6150 along the North Atlantic Track called 'Victor.' Then the Hawk will turn south to let us look at the 'Whiskey' track and the three last known points along it."

"Copy," Cain said, his voice tense, but still clinging to a small glimmer of hope. It had been nearly an hour since the first reports, and the Coast Guard HC-144 Ocean Sentry patrol aircraft were moving into the area, but they were almost thirty minutes behind the Global Hawk and her long-range cameras. Coast Guard cutters were also steaming at full speed toward the last reported positions, but they would not reach them for several hours.

"Easy, David, the Hawk can only fly so fast," Mike Goodman said at his elbow. Goodman was also on the internal comm system, standing next to Cain and ready to support him as needed. He'd initially handled the warning calls to the Senior Operations Officers at the CIA, DIA, and NSA before stepping down to join Cain as he stared at the screen.

"I know," Cain responded sotto voce, with a chagrined look on his face. "I just wish flight physics weren't such a limiting factor." Goodman was a great deputy and had a similar depth of experience, something Cain always relied on to keep him balanced and calm in a crisis. When Goodman was promoted to take over the Delta shift in the next few months, Cain would miss having him on his Alpha shift.

A few minutes later, Carmody started moving the mouse on his desktop. "The cameras have locked on to the first set of crash coordinates. What kind of plane was Flight 121?"

McMillan handled that. "A Boeing 777-300ER."

"Copy," Carmody replied. A 777 was a big plane, 242 feet long with a 212-foot wingspan, and had a maximum takeoff weight of more than 600,000 pounds. If the jet or parts of it were in the water, they should be easy to spot.

Carmody make a quick adjustment, and the camera zoomed in as far as it could, electronically locked to the coordinates. One more mouse click and he transferred the image to the big screen on the left.

Cain saw nothing but endless ocean, reflecting the bright sunlight. "You see anything?" he asked Carmody.

"No, but we're still at the edge of the area. Give it a few minutes."

Cain and everyone in CTS kept their eyes glued to the display. Then they saw it.

"Damn," Cain said. He could not judge the size of the pieces of flotsam, but they were suddenly everywhere on the ocean, appearing at the top of the image, and then moving down as Carmody took manual control of the camera and began to pan it along the path.

"I'm not seeing any of the rescue slides or anything," Carmody said. He clicked the mouse again, executing a display command. "Arnie, see the set of geo-coordinates at the bottom of the image?"

McMillan nodded, looking at Carmody.

Catching the nod in his peripheral vision, Carmody continued, "Those coordinates are the point on the ground the camera is looking at dead center. Copy down a set and have the DHS relay them to the Coast Guard's Rescue Coordination Center in Norfolk. They can vector the HC-144's and cutters right to them."

"Rog," McMillan replied, grabbing a pen.

Cain liked that. At least now the search and rescue planes would know exactly where to go to get to each crash site. If CTS could use the Hawk to pinpoint all the crash sites for the rescue teams, lives might be saved.

"Leave the image up and we'll scan the debris for any sign of survivors. Get the second camera focused on the last reported position for Flight 6150. When you see it, put it up on the right monitor."

"Will do," replied Carmody, moving the mouse and giving the Hawk's remote sensors commands.

Arnie chimed in quickly. "Coast Guard RCC in Norfolk has the word. The cutter *Seneca* is closest, heading to the area at flank speed. They want to know how we were able to find the crash site so quickly."

Cain looked at him. "And you said?"

"The usual—National Technical Means," McMillan replied. The usual euphemism, which most interpreted to mean a spy satellite, was good enough for the Coasties.

Forty minutes and three more impact sites later, Cain's slim shred of hope was nearly gone. So far, the CTS team had seen nothing but debris fields and the oily sheen of what was probably aviation fuel. The largest piece of wreckage they'd identified was the tail assembly from United Flight 63, a massive Airbus A380. The rest of what was left of the jet and the nearly 400 people on board was represented by scattered, ragged chunks of metal bobbing in the cold north Atlantic.

Carmody was reprogramming the cameras for the next three last known positions when Arnie's black STE phone rang again.

"David. I've got DHS on the line again," Cain heard in his ear on the internal link. "They were tipped off by a D.C. television station about a set of a dozen videos up on YouTube. Each video shows two men pouring an unidentified liquid into various reservoirs and other public water sources in locations up and down the East Coast."

"What?" Cain was incredulous.

"It's confirmed. DHS is watching one of the videos now. The comments posted with it say that the video was shot near Camp Lejeune, and that the substance is uranyl nitrate."

"What the hell is that?" Cain turned to Goodman. "Mike, take over our support to the SAR effort." Goodman nodded once and moved a few steps left, closer to Carmody and the drone station, so he could talk to the man directly without using the link if Cain needed it for anything.

Looking back at Arnie he ordered, "Spell it," as he walked up the short steps toward his desk. He broke the screen lock on his Internet terminal, and as McMillan spelled, he typed uranyl nitrate into the Google+ search engine.

In seconds, he had the search results back, and clicked on the link to the Wikipedia page. Scanning the entry quickly, he read the important parts aloud over the internal comm for his team.

"Uranyl nitrate is a water-soluble uranium salt. It's a highly toxic compound that should not be ingested. Causes renal insufficiency and acute tubular necrosis. Target organs include the kidneys, liver, lungs, and brain."

McMillan spoke up again, "DHS also says the FAA is ordering an immediate precautionary grounding of all civil jet aircraft, particularly the Boeing 777, 767, 757, and Airbus A380s and A330s. They are also advising the European Aviation Safety Agency to issue the same orders."

Cain looked up as the enormity of what was happening began to sink in. The water supply for the II MEF at Camp Lejeune and God knows where else in the U.S. had apparently been poisoned with radioactive material. American-flagged airliners were crashing for unexplained reasons into the Atlantic and the FAA was ordering a precautionary grounding of the major airframes used for transoceanic flight.

Cain sat down heavily in his chair, his eyes unfocused while his mind sorted through what he knew. His nation was suffering a major attack again. The car bombs in San Antonio, the shootings during the rush hour, then the cyber-attack on the power infrastructure and the simultaneous attacks on the fuel oil storage tanks in the Northeast were only the first stage.

Now, more recently, the Calvert Cliffs and LNG storage attacks. Next, eight American-flagged airliners crashing in the Atlantic, likely killing more than 2,000 people. Right after that, public water supplies appearing to be poisoned.

Cain sat back in his chair, and an anomaly stuck in his mind. His eyes were still focused on a middle distance as he spoke into the link. "Arnie, what else do we know about the poisoning of the water supplies?"

Arnie conferred with the DHS watch stander on the other end of the encrypted STE link for a few minutes.

"Based on what DHS has seen so far, several public reservoirs and water treatment plants along the Mid-Atlantic and Northeast."

Cain leaned to the right in his chair, his eyes refocusing to look past his computer to McMillan. "You said DHS was watching a video of Camp Lejeune's water supply being poisoned too, right? That's not a public supply, is it? Was that the only military base in the videos?"

Arnie nodded. "I'll check." A quick conversation. "Yes. Camp Lejeune was the only military base cited in the set of twelve videos. All the others were public water supplies for major population centers."

"Holy shit," Cain said. The pieces were starting to fall into place in his head. "If you were going to start a war in the Middle East, and you wanted to keep us from interfering, what would you do?" Cain only asked it aloud to see how it sounded, as his mind kept sifting what he knew, checking and rechecking the facts, as sketchy as they might seem, the outline of a report starting to form in his mind.

Arnie looked at him quizzically, and then put his attention back on the phone. "David, DHS wants to know if we'll be handling the report on the water supply poisoning."

Cain shook his head. "No. Tell DHS to issue the TOXIC SNAKE report. We need to draft another AUTUMN FIRE message right now. It looks like that son of a bitch Aziz has been playing a bigger game all along."

CHAPTER 21

· ·

"MATHEWS?" AS USUAL, COLONEL SIMON'S voice was coming through crystal clear on the encrypted iPhone. Mathews and Mike Cochrane were discussing how they might approach the base officials for permission to let the team members run within the base perimeter when Colonel Simon's call came in.

The midday sun was streaming into the hangar on King Abdul Aziz airfield, giving the Wraiths plenty of light for routine weapons maintenance while they swapped war stories. Thompson was right in the thick of it, Mathews noticed, cleaning one of the support team's AR-15s within a small knot of the other women. She was fitting in well, spending every hour she could talking to the C-17 flight crew, the drone support team, and as many of the Wraith commandos she could buttonhole for knowledge.

"Yes, sir."

"You all set for your meeting tonight?"

"Yes, sir. We'll be meeting with him at 1900. Special Agent Johnson and his friend Akeem will accompany us."

"Good. I've got our friend Charlie Six on the line. He needs to update you on a few things, and none of it is good news. I've spoken to General Crane, and you are authorized to share what you are about to hear with your host tonight. We'll be sending you a hard copy in a few minutes. If you have any questions, save them for me. Charlie Six needs to be on a VTC with the White House in about five minutes. Copy?"

"Copy all, sir. Charlie Six, send it."

"Wraith Four Six, Charlie Six. Have you been watching the news?"

Mathews knew that question probably meant something very bad had happened back home. "No, sir. We've been camping out with our transport in the hangar, and our INTELINK connection is toast. The INMARSAT terminal's power supply blew out last night. Our maintenance troops are replacing it now. Our Saudi friends don't have cable service hooked up in the hangars, either." Mathews shared a grin with Cochrane, who was standing there, eavesdropping on Mathews' end of the conversation.

"Copy that, Four Six. I'll give it to you fast. Eight civilian airliners were deliberately crashed into the Atlantic last night. Initial investigation by the FBI and FAA indicates that a computer program was used on board the aircraft by a set of suicide hijackers to remotely hack the flight control systems through the onboard wireless network the passengers use for Internet access."

Mathews' smile quickly faded. "How many dead?" he asked.

"North of 2,000. We don't have a final figure yet. They hit American air carriers only."

"Aziz?" Mathews inquired.

"Probably, but we have no proof. We don't even know the bugger's current whereabouts. Ever since he vanished from Iran, we've had no luck finding the man. Only the Saudis had a solid lead on him from their Iranian source, and you already know how well that worked out."

"Copy that," Mathews responded, his tone flat and angry. "I'll be sure to mention that in passing to our host tonight."

"You will not antagonize the king, Four Six, is that clear?" demanded Simon. "You know how this works. Sometimes the intel isn't as good as we hope, and until boots are on the ground, you never know for sure."

Mathews blew out a breath, still pissed, more at the loss of life they were unable to prevent by catching Aziz than at the people who were probably risking their lives to get information out of Iran. "Yes, sir. I know. I just wish we could have captured the bastard."

"Look, I'm running out of time," Cain interrupted. "There are a couple of other pieces to this. One, the public water supplies in eleven cities from Florida to Maine appear to have been radioactively poisoned."

What the fuck! Mathews thought, holding his tongue.

"More important, the water supply for the Marines at Camp Lejeune was also poisoned. To make things worse, the pre-positioned supply ships at Diego Garcia were practically sunk by mines a few days back, and the nearest Expeditionary Strike Group centered on the USS *America* is halfway across the Atlantic heading away from the Mediterranean. In fact, the *America* and her escorts are using their planes and ships to aid in the search and recovery efforts for the downed airliners."

Mathews could not believe what he was hearing. His nation was not just being hit with a strike here and a strike there, but full-body blows and couple of good shots to the face. "We need to stop this man."

"Agreed, Four Six, but the real killer is that we aren't even sure he's behind it all. He's just the best suspect we have right now. What's really worrying me is that our ability to respond to a sudden crisis in the Mideast is seriously hampered right now."

Cain took a breath to continue, and Mathews could hear the exasperation building in his voice as he spoke. Mathews guessed the man had probably been working since before those planes crashed.

"The FAA is concerned about the airworthiness of the major civil airliners we call up as part of the Civil Reserve Air Fleet to move troops around the world. Military airlift just doesn't have the capacity by itself. America and her ESG is too far out of position, and worse, even if the troops and ships were there, without the resupply ships, any land-based force we try to put on the ground anywhere out there is crippled from the word 'go.' Without ammunition, fuel, spare parts, food, and water, an army or air force is nothing but expensive toys and a lot of men and women in good physical shape with nice haircuts."

Mathews considered Cain's reasoning. They really were crippled. "So, if it is Aziz, what do you think his next play is?"

Cain's voice came back almost immediately, talking very quickly. Mathews figured his rushed explanation indicated that his time on the phone was about up. "Nobody knows for sure. We're participating in a crisis working group with the CIA and DIA immediately after we get off the link with the president. I think he's going to try to take over a country in the Mideast. Yemen's government is looking pretty shaky of late; their latest dictator is losing support. Egypt and Iran are off the table, I think; their governments are too strongly backed by the military. Somalia might be a candidate, too. The place always seems to be in perpetual meltdown. Look, I've got to run. We need to put our heads together back here with the experts in the other agencies and see what we can come up with. Charlie Six out."

"Copy. Colonel, do you have orders for us? Should we reposition to another country?"

"Negative. You have a meeting tonight. Once the folks in D.C. get their heads wrapped around this, I'll let you know. For now, defensive measures locally. Make sure your people stay in uniform and armed. Keep it low key and stay close to the plane and the phone."

"Yes, sir. We'll leave the Apaches on the C-17 for now. My people are going to be worried about their friends and family on the East Coast or potentially on those planes. Can we route calls through the base to avoid compromising our deployment?"

Simon thought the reference to taking the Apache helicopters off the C-17 was a pretty good attempt at grim humor given the news from CTS, but he didn't let the smile creep into his voice, lest the young lieutenant get the wrong idea, and he liked how Mathews was thinking about his people's welfare.

"Do that. I'll let our comm center people know it's okay. Have them use your INMARSAT phone once it's fixed and they'll relay. I'll call you as soon as we have something for you. Out here."

The phone went dead in his hand, and Mathews touched the button to lock it.

"Wraiths! Support team! Rally up!" he shouted into the hangar to get everyone's attention. The commandos and their support unit of drone operators, helicopter and C-17 pilots, and the maintenance team all stopped what they were doing and headed over to form a rough circle around him. Mathews would make this simple, filling them in on the loss of the civil airliners and the poisoning of the water supplies as succinctly as possible before he got to the meat of the immediate danger. Then he would cover the details with his XO and senior NCOs immediately afterward.

"We've received word that a potential coup is in the offing some-where in the Middle East. There are no specific indications as to which country. From now on, no member of this deployed unit goes any-where without another team member. If you have to hit the head, you take somebody with you. Also, carry sidearms at all times. All team members are restricted to the immediate confines of this hangar and the base gym. We'll make arrangements for regular food deliveries with the Saudis, but for now, stick to the MREs and bottled water in our supplies."

Mathews looked over their faces. Everyone seemed calm, but he needed to be sure they kept their minds on their jobs. "I'm sure you are all concerned about your family and friends. I know that most of you have cell phones. Please do not use them to call home. As you know, you could compromise our location that way. As soon as the INMAR-SAT is fixed, I'll see to it that each of you who wants to gets a chance to call out. Questions?"

No one spoke up. "All right, everyone except for the officers and the senior NCOs are dismissed. Thompson, you stay, too."

The smaller group clustered closer around him, knowing they were about to get more of the details. Emily managed to get a place up front. Having a qualified drone operator on-site was going to be an advantage.

"Sergeant Thompson," Mathews addressed her, "I don't think our Saudi hosts would allow us to put up the Avenger for site surveil-lance—it's too big and noticeable. But what about the Outlaw?"

The MQM-170A Outlaw was a small, torpedo-shaped UAV with a 13-foot wingspan, weighing only 120 pounds. It was portable enough for emergency use, but with a cruise speed of 60 miles an hour and an endurance of little more than an hour, it was best used for short-range tactical applications.

Emily answered eagerly. "We can prep it, sir. I've been talking to the drone control team and I know I can help with the monitoring and command and control to support the team."

Mathews nodded. "I'm sure. But I also need to know if our Saudi friends can track it, shoot it down, et cetera."

She frowned, thinking. "I don't recall anything in what I've seen that indicates they could do that, but they buy a lot of our military tech, so I wouldn't be surprised. I would suggest asking first, though. If push comes to shove, if we fly it low enough, it will be screened by the buildings and other ground clutter. Disguising the launch will be tough. Somebody on the airfield is bound to notice."

Mathews mulled that over. "I think you covered all the bases. Work with the drone team to get the Outlaw unloaded and prepped. Do it all inside the hangar. Fewer prying eyes that way. I'll see if I can get us launch clearance from our friend Akeem after I'm through here."

Emily was disappointed that she would not get to stay and hear all the details, but being effectively in charge of the drone detail supporting the team was enough to make her practically skip her way over to the C-17 and get the team started on assembly and checkout of the little drone.

GENERAL MAHIR'S FAMILY WAS AWAY again, and this time Aziz would visit him. The two men spoke privately in Mahir's study while Saqr and M'an were in another room, gathering some supplies the general had obtained for them. This close to achieving his first objective, Aziz should have been nervous being alone with a man not part of his inner circle, but nearness to his objective was heady wine . . . and he did have an HK USP Compact .40 S&W pistol secreted in his thawb.

"What about the perimeter guards?" Aziz asked.

"There will be two, an inner and outer perimeter," Mahir replied. "The outer perimeter will be just low-ranking enlisted men, one on each gate. They know nothing, and each will have one of my junior officers with them who believe as we do. The inner perimeter will consist only of the six men of the king's personal bodyguard and the men we will use tonight."

"How will they be dealt with?" Aziz asked, before looking intently at Mahir and adding, "Violence in the meeting chamber beforehand will not aid our cause."

Mahir looked at the younger man indulgently. "Of course not. The men do not actually attend the meeting. While they wait in the ante-room, they will be served by my chief of staff, Major Najjar."

A knowing smile crossed Aziz's lips. They would be poisoned or shot quietly, of course. There was one thing more to be sure of. "Have you spoken to him?"

"Yes," Mahir replied. "He will take on his new duties in the manner we desire, but to make it official and lessen any outcry, the Allegiance Council must certify it in writing."

"They will," Aziz assured him. "Once they have signed the paper, we will be sure that they cannot refute it publicly."

"Your men are getting the uniforms now?"

"Yes. Is there anything else?"

Mahir smiled. "I am told the American ambassador will be there, but I do not know why."

Aziz's eyes grew wide. "Praise be to Allah! That is perfect. Perhaps the American incited the liberal elements within the Kingdom that killed the king and the members of the Allegiance Council?"

Mahir smiled in a thoroughly sinister way, nodding. "Yes, perhaps he did."

"THE KID JUST DOESN'T WANT to talk." Special Agent Eric Pittman stared through the one-way glass of the interrogation room and studied the young man from United Flight 933. Pittman was of medium height and had dark hair and eyes. He was wearing a suit, a far cry from the more casual uniform of a dark blue FBI T-shirt, tan cotton cargo pants, and black boots he enjoyed wearing during his last assignment at Camp Delta.

Pittman did not fathom Saddam yet. The subject's mannerisms and grooming bespoke some education and intelligence, but he would not say a word. Pittman and Agent Samuels were giving him a break and themselves a chance to observe his mannerisms before they made another run at him. The only other man in the room was a colorless fellow from the FAA. He would interpret anything Saddam said related to aviation.

"Do you want to Mirandize him now?" asked Agent Samuels.

"No. We'll leverage the public safety exception for a few more hours. At least he hasn't asked for a lawyer yet," Pittman replied.

If Saddam asked for a lawyer, they could only hold off reading his Miranda rights for so long under the public safety exception before they were forced to give him his rights. Once they did that, or he had a lawyer in the room, the two FBI men would learn more by talking to a tree.

"Do you guys think he's a hard-core jihadi?" the colorless FAA guy asked.

Pittman glanced at the man sideways. "Use a laptop computer to bring down a plane over the Atlantic and kill nearly 300 people? Yeah, I'd say he's hard-core, just not in the usual sense."

"What do you mean?"

"That Air Force major told us that he saw the kid look around a couple of times while he was fiddling with the laptop. He was also surprised and hesitated when the major confronted him. A serious jihadi bent on martyrdom would have reached for the laptop, not panicked."

"Yeah, well, I for one am glad he did. That major saved a lot of lives."

"Yeah," Pittman agreed.

"Our forensics guys imaged the computer as evidence, and then did a power-on test on board the jet with the flight control computer in test mode. They told the 777 computer that they were at cruise altitude and speed over the Atlantic and then executed the commands he entered on the laptop."

"What happened?" Pittman asked.

"The flight control computer carried out the laptop's commands. It actually froze out the flight controls and the inputs to the flight director and tried to fly the plane into the ocean, at a nasty descent angle, too. Went right through the passenger cabin wireless network and over to the flight control computer without so much as a bit missing."

Pittman was incredulous. "I hope they videotaped it."

"Every bit," the FAA man confirmed. "With three different cameras inside and out. They also had network sniffers running on the wireless and the internal network. Even copied the original configurations of the internal router and flight computer before and after. Boeing and Airbus will be putting out flight safety notices in the next few hours. Anybody flying a jet with the same kind of flight control computer needs to keep their aircrafts grounded until the guys at Honeywell and E-Systems can develop and deploy a software or hardware patch."

"Sounds like a plan. How long will that take?"

The man from the FAA looked resigned. "Two, maybe three weeks."

Pittman was surprised. "Looks like the worldwide traveling public is going to be inconvenienced to say the least."

"Yeah. What's going to happen to the kid?" the FAA man asked.

Pittman managed to look grim and sorrowful at the same time. The young man's life had ended one way or another. "The U.S. Attorney will sort that out, but at the minimum, he'll probably be charged with attempted mass murder, using a weapon of mass destruction, and a few other more minor charges. If he's lucky, he'll spend his life in prison without parole. If not, he'll get the death penalty."

MAJOR NAJJAR HELD THE DOOR, and General Mahir stepped out of the rear of his white Toyota Land Cruiser, the official flags of the Saudi Royal Guard flying from the front bumper. Sunset was an hour away, and Mahir let his eyes roam over the scene before him at the southern gate.

His men were already replacing the current guard shift there and at the other entry points to the north, east, and west, maintaining the outer perimeter. The men moved with purpose but not hastily, weapons slung casually over their shoulders, uniforms impeccably pressed and in order. There was no need to hurry. The entry points to the king's residence in Riyadh, secured for more than a decade since his assumption of the throne, had never been violated.

Mahir had already met with the entire shift to tell them personally how proud the king was of their service, admonishing them to remember that the deliberations of the Allegiance Council were often long and drawn-out affairs.

Not that the guards would hear any of it, of course. More than half a mile separated each of the gates, and the outer, walled perimeter was nearly a mile from the main complex of more than twenty low buildings, pools, and gardens that made up the king's residence.

Mahir smiled, knowing that tonight, those distances would help to ensure the success of their plan.

"Major," Mahir ordered, "have your men follow me, and bring the equipment." Mahir led the way through the south gate, checking the grounds for anything unusual. The king was in his private office across the compound, meeting with the Minister of the Interior, as a prelude to his meeting with the Americans. They would likely conduct the evening Salāt together at dusk when the call to prayer sounded.

Mahir set a brisk pace, not caring that the six men behind him with Najjar carried a nearly 200-pound mil-spec hard case along the paving-stone path leading from the south gate deeper into the compound. Mahir led the small group over the sand-colored paving stones, turning right at the first branch in the path and approaching the conference building. Added to the compound by King Fahd, the single-story, almond-colored building was distinctive due to its distance from the other buildings on the compound, the nearly half-acre of trimmed grass that surrounded it, and the trees that shielded any direct line of sight between it and the other compound buildings.

King Fahd's architects had met all his expectations. Provide a convenient, spacious, and comfortable setting for meetings between the king and his ministers, ambassadors, or invited international guests while maintaining the privacy of his residence. Over the years, King Fahd and his successors had upgraded the conference center with multiple anterooms containing teleconferencing equipment and more energy-efficient lightbulbs, but little else.

As expected, the conference center was unguarded, and Mahir led the group unhesitatingly up the short flight of steps at the main entrance and through the large outer set of double doors. Mahir could hear the men carrying the case breathing heavily as they caught up with him and began to ascend the stairs. The inner doors were already open, and he could see the smaller, final set of double doors to the main conference room.

"Sir?" inquired Najjar, standing at his shoulder.

"Have the men place the device beneath the dais," Mahir answered him. "You know where the access hatch is?"

"Yes. I studied the revised plans. It is fortunate that they made it large enough for our needs."

"Insha'Allah," Mahir reminded him. "It was made large enough for a man because many of the electrical and other cables needed to be hidden from sight. Thanks to Allah, and His foresight, it will serve our needs as well."

Mahir motioned for the major to proceed, and Najjar gestured for the group of six men to follow him. The conference center was essentially a square within a square, with the king's formal conference room encompassing nearly 400 square meters. Surrounding it was a wide, U-shaped main corridor, decorated in deep green and tan, with thick carpets and simple but elegant wall sconces placed every few meters. The outer ring, between the main corridor and the outer walls, held four large conference rooms, two teleconferencing rooms, and large bathrooms for men and women near the main entrance, both decorated in dark woods with gold fixtures and white marble floors.

Najjar crossed the 2-meter-wide main corridor and opened the main doors to the king's formal conference room. It was open and airy, with three massive, white-and-gold marble-sheathed columns along each wall, and white and black marble tiles on the floor. Six crystal chandeliers hung placidly from the high ceiling, bathing the entire central area inside the six columns with bright but soft light.

At the far end was the raised dais and the king's comfortable but simple chair, upholstered and made of wood. In this room, the king held authority, but preferred to exercise it more as a trusted elder amongst the other senior Saudi leaders. All of them were family, and there was certainly no need to try to lord his obvious position over them with an ornate throne or other trappings. The dais was only 30 centimeters high, and that was enough. Meetings with senior ministers or leaders from other countries were conducted in a less formal setting, without the dais and merely a small group of comfortable chairs in its place, but tonight's conversation with the Allegiance Council called for a gentle reminder of the king's authority within the family and the nation.

Najjar stepped on the dais and pulled the king's chair forward a few feet as the six men behind him walked to the left, placing the black mil-spec hard case on the white marble floor.

Mahir watched as they worked. It only took a few minutes. Two of the men opened the latches on the black case, while two others rolled back the rug under the king's chair and used the rings built into the 4-foot-square access hatch beneath it to pry the hatch open. The hatch cut in the marble flooring for access to the power and data cables was directly beneath them, but they ignored it.

The two men working at the dais returned to the case, helping the others to lift the nearly 1-meter-wide and meter-and-a-quarter-long sheet out of the case. The sheet was made of two components: a very thin aluminum sheet that acted as a backing, and a 7-centimeter-thick layer of off-white C-4 plastic explosive. In all, the entire assembly weighed nearly 200 pounds, the aluminum backing curved ever so slightly at one end to create a curl, much like a toboggan, although the curve stopped well short of vertical.

Major Najjar stepped behind them and reached into the box. "Hold it still," he ordered.

The six men balanced the straight end of the sheet on the rear edge of the dais, and the major withdrew his hand from the mil-spec box, holding a silver tubular device attached to a length of wire. He stepped behind the group of men and slid the slim silver tube through a pre-drilled hole in the sheet, pressing it firmly into the C-4. Once it was in place, he removed a slim black box from his pocket and attached the free end of the wires to it.

"Together now," the major ordered, and the men moved in unison to lift the sheet and slowly feed it into the opening in the dais, straight end first. As they fed it into the opening, the aluminum backing rested on the floor, taking the weight so that the men could slide it in deeper as they backed away in pairs. When most of it was inside the dais, the two holding the curled end paused so Najjar could ensure that the slim black box was in position beneath that end. Once he was satisfied, Najjar said, "Place the blocks."

The two men on the right side had already retrieved the angled wooden blocks from the mil-spec crate. One block was passed to a man on the left side of the dais, and under the major's watchful eyes, they placed the angled blocks in the dais beneath the sheet, allowing the two men holding the curled end to settle that part of the sheet securely on the blocks. The explosive sheet now rested at an angle within the dais, tilted up to ensure that the explosive force would blow upward and outward in a lethal cone toward the main entry doors.

Najjar stood and checked the sight lines as the other men set to work closing the hatch, resettling the rug, and putting the king's chair back exactly in the divots its legs made in the carpet. He smiled slightly, imagining the blast wave propagation. The king and his chair would be obliterated first, and the debris and shock wave would travel up and forward, killing the men seated before him and probably blowing out the doors to the main conference chamber as well. Perfect.

"When you are finished here, refresh yourselves quickly in the men's room near the main entrance, and then take your posts," the major told them, latching the mil-spec container himself and hefting it with one hand. The major crossed the room and paused by General Mahir.

"It is finished, praise be to Allah."

The general nodded. "Your men are well drilled. Their posts are outside of the blast zone?"

"Yes. Two men on outer doors of the main entrance, two men on the main doors to this room, and one man each on the side entrances."

"You are sure they will survive?"

"Yes," the major assured him. "The walls around the conference hall are thick to assure soundproofing."

"Good. I will not waste such loyalty. Moreover, they will be impressed with our courage when they see us enter the room with them."

The major shared a knowing smile with his general before walking out of the main entrance. The mil-spec container needed to find its way back into the cargo area of the Land Cruiser.

Mahir did think it was a matter of courage, but he also thought it was a matter of knowing where to be just before he triggered the bomb. The king's private office area occupied the space behind the dais. The clever design of the doors at the top of the upper arms of the "U" leading to the king's private office appeared to be part of the wall, helping to ensure His Majesty's privacy by visually misleading the uninformed among his guests.

He spent just as much time as the young major looking at the plans to this building. The wall separating the dais and the rest of the conference hall from the king's office area was as thick as the other three. Moreover, they would be well behind the blast and therefore safe. He and the major, Aziz, and his two bodyguards would slip through the connecting doors hidden behind the two wooden screens seconds before his finger touched the bomb's trigger.

Mahir took in a deep breath, held it, and breathed out slowly, a satisfied smile coming to his face. Immediately after the explosion, they would all emerge unscathed, praising Allah's beneficence and a timely order from the king to step outside during the council's private deliberations. Then they would guide the Kingdom toward becoming the cornerstone of the new Caliphate.

"MATHEWS LOOKED AROUND THE HANGAR, and then out into the gathering darkness. Everyone on the support team was carrying weapons now, most surreptitiously, but the Wraiths were openly wearing their M9 Berretta 9mm sidearms, carrying them in their black nylon "gunslinger" holsters.

Thompson and the drone team were performing some final checks on the little MQM-170 Outlaw drone just outside the hangar under the watchful eyes of a Saudi Air Force major. The rest of the Wraiths not on guard duty around the hangar edges were taking some time to play cards, watch movies, or play games on their personal tablet computers. A few clustered near the INMARSAT terminal, still waiting in line to make calls home.

Mathews felt naked without the comforting weight of his sidearm and its holster. It would not be proper for him to carry a weapon anywhere near a head of state like the king. Aside from it being considered rude by their Saudi hosts, he would almost certainly be searched by the Royal Guard, and it would cause a diplomatic incident of unprecedented proportions if he were found to be carrying one.

He did, however, have his fully charged cell phone and Bluetooth headset in his pocket, and a black nylon backpack containing two liter-sized bottles of water and the heavy nylon lock bag with the classified AUTUMN FIRE summaries.

"I think so. I've got the reports for the king in here, along with some extra water," Mathews said, hefting the nylon pack. "Where's Johnson?"

"He's in the car," Akeem replied. "Your FBI director called as we were pulling up. It seems that Ambassador Coltrane will not be joining us tonight, and your leadership wanted to give Agent Johnson some last-minute instructions, since he is the senior member of your delegation."

"I see," Mathews told him, chagrined at the ambassador's absence. "Should we postpone this meeting until he's available?"

Akeem shook his head. "No. I spoke to the minister on the way to pick up our FBI friend at his hotel. Your embassy contacted the minister while he was meeting with the king late this afternoon. His Majesty is looking forward to meeting you and hearing the tale of your 'daring mission,' as he called it."

Mathews was not sure how to take Akeem's quote. Was the king being sarcastic or praising him? Well, the best answer was always the truth, wasn't it? "I'll be happy to tell the king about our mission and the reasons we were ordered to undertake it."

"Good, come along, then." Akeem nodded toward the open hangar door, where his white AMG Mercedes sat idling quietly, Johnson visible through the front windshield, phone to his ear.

Mathews started to walk toward the car, and remembered that he owed Akeem something. "Thanks for getting us permission to send up the drone."

Akeem looked at him. "It was no trouble. I can understand your people wishing to have a chance to practice their skills. As long as it remains over the airfield and is unarmed, and our Air Force observer has verified that it is unarmed, we are pleased to allow it."

Mathews noticed Akeem smiled as he said the last part. "I assure you, Akeem, we respect the sovereignty of the Kingdom. I have already instructed my people to cooperate."

There were limits, of course. No mention would be made of the drone's ability to relay video all the way to the CTS, nor would they allow the Saudi officer to inspect the weapons and gear on board the Globemaster. The mission tonight would be pure observation to ensure that they knew as much about base security as the Saudis did.

"That is appreciated, Lieutenant," Akeem responded. "Once the drone is airborne, our officer will return to his duties. We understand that your drone control systems are sensitive. Following its course on radar will satisfy us that it stays over the airfield."

Mathews nodded his understanding and thanks.

"Just remember," Akeem admonished him, "Once it lands, you must seek permission again if you wish to send it aloft again."

"I understand, Akeem. I suspect we'll be leaving after I meet with your king, so that should not be an issue."

Mathews opened the rear door of Akeem's car as their drone pilot, an Air Force major still hoping for a slot in an F-35A squadron, opened up the Outlaw's throttle and sent it down the runway and into the early evening sky. Once it was at 5,000 feet, he put it on automatic pilot and took out his iPad. The drone would bore lazy circles in the sky over the base until he told it to land or it ran out of fuel and crashed. His job was half over for the night.

Before he opened the Kindle software and delved back into the latest *Star Wars* novel, he glanced over at Technical Sergeant Thompson. Not only did the woman manage to fill out a set of ABUs well, but she also obviously knew her job, he thought. The white Mercedes that Mathews had climbed into was plain as day on her screen as it headed out along Riyadh's streets.

CHAPTER 22

THE WHITE MERCEDES APPROACHED THE south gate of the king's palace at a leisurely pace, and after what Mathews thought was an entirely perfunctory visual check of the car's interior by the officer and sole enlisted man on post, along with a few words in Arabic between Akeem and the officer, they were waved through. Mathews was surprised to see that the gate itself was little more than a break in the 12-foot wall that surrounded the compound, with a large sentry box inside the wall on the left, and a simple white wooden barrier with Arabic on it that probably said HALT or something similar.

Mathews thought the limited security absurd, until after they passed through the gate, and he spied the 1-foot-diameter steel circles spaced in a pattern among the paving stones. Hydraulically rammed upward in less than a tenth of a second, each steel cylinder would form an impenetrable vehicle barrier a tenth of a second after one of the sentries pressed a button no doubt hidden in the sentry box. Each one of the steel cylinders could stop a fully laden dump truck dead in its tracks, even at highway speeds. The three offset rows of four just might be able to stop an armored vehicle, too. Mathews shook his head in rueful appreciation for the unobtrusive security measure and his foolishness in assuming the white wooden barrier was all there was.

Once they were through the open gate, Akeem told Johnson and Mathews, "We are to go to the conference building and go in through one of the side entrances. His Majesty would prefer that two Americans not be seen by the members of the Allegiance Council."

"Security seems a bit less than I would have expected," Mathews observed, keen to know if Akeem was aware of any other hidden elements of the king's security.

"This is the home of the king. We do not have the history of violent crime here that you do in your country," Akeem responded. "The biggest concerns we have here are the many well-wishers or those who come with petitions."

That explains the quick inspection of the car, Mathews supposed. "What happens to them?" he asked.

"They are politely told that their remarks will be passed on to the king, and any written petitions are taken and passed to the king's staff. One of his household staff reads them all, and summarizes them. Every few days, His Majesty reviews the summaries. Occasionally, he asks to see the full text of a petition and then responds in some fashion."

Mathews mulled that over. It certainly seemed a little better than sending an e-mail to the White House. You would think the staff probably read it, but he expected that it almost never made it to the president, not even as a summary. At least women could drive and have fuller lives in his country, Mathews thought to himself.

"You never told me what the Allegiance Council is," Johnson said to Akeem.

"It was formed to make the succession proceed more smoothly. When King Fahd died, there was a great disagreement within the family over who should succeed him. The king still holds great sway, of course, and makes the final decision, but the council affords him an opportunity to hear the views of each of the family's twenty-eight different branches."

"That's quite a large family," Mathews observed.

"Yes, it is," Akeem agreed, and then added, "Agent Johnson is already familiar with our culture, Lieutenant, so please pardon me for mentioning it, but please be sure that you do not speak of any family-related matters before the king. Even what you might consider a polite inquiry 'hoping that his wife and children are well' would be considered rude here."

Mathews wondered why, and Johnson filled the gap as Akeem pulled to the side of the paving stone–laid road and parked the car. "Family is an intensely private matter here, spoken of only among other family members."

"Got it," Mathews replied, taking his cue from Akeem and opening the rear door to exit the Mercedes, the locked bag in one hand, and leaving the backpack in the car. The men turned right at the first branch in the path and followed Akeem as he led them 50 meters until the path opened out onto the conference center building and its manicured grounds.

Akeem led them around the building's left side and up a short flight of steps, where a single member of the Royal Guard, a man in his late twenties, stood. A few more words of Arabic between Akeem and the guard, and they were through the side door. Mathews was certain the guard's look at their small group was nothing less than hostile, but he let it pass. He was about to meet the head of a friendly and sometimes allied nation, and it was time to get his mind on what he needed to say.

They followed a middle-aged officer in the Royal Guard down a 6-foot-wide hallway. The guard wore the shoulder braid of the small group of bodyguards who worked directly with the king, Mathews knew. As they turned left inside a door, a sudden thought occurred to him. He reached into his pocket to flip a switch on his phone, and then nudged Johnson, whispering, "Make sure your cell is silenced."

As Johnson checked his phone, Mathews was pleased to see Akeem do the same, although exactly where in his thawb he kept the thing was a question he would save for later.

The three men followed the bodyguard around a sharp right turn and were ushered through a door on the left, into the king's private office. Mathews was only a dozen steps or so from a reigning monarch, and in spite of the fact that the man was not his king, he was a little nervous. The man was still a head of state.

Akeem spoke a few words to the king in Arabic, and King Bandar ibn Faisal ibn Abdul-Aziz al Saud crossed the room to greet him, extending his hand. Minister Ali was already there, standing by his king's side, stern and wary.

"In English from now on, in deference to our guests," the king instructed. Akeem smiled and shook his hand firmly, before turning to introduce Johnson and Mathews.

After handshakes all around, the king said, "Please sit, gentlemen," gesturing toward the small conference table at one end of the office, already laid with fruit, Belgian chocolates, and a crystal jug of water with matching glasses.

Moving to the table gave Mathews a chance to assess the room. It was very similar to what he would have expected in any chief executive's office in the West. Thick neutral-color carpet, dark maple furniture of good quality, many plaques and photos adorning the walls. The framed photos surrounding the conference table showed a much younger version of the king in a flight suit, standing on the boarding ladder of Saudi F-15SA fighters at different times and on different airfields.

Noticing the direction of Mathews' gaze as he seated himself, the king said with a smile, "I was once a fighter pilot. I even trained at your Maxwell Air Force Base long ago."

Mathews settled into the chair next to the king and found himself replying without thinking, a smile on his face, "Well enough to become king one day, it seems."

Akeem's eyes grew wide, and for a second, Johnson was sure Mathews had gone too far since it looked as if the minister was about to jump out of his chair. The king looked at Mathews and then leaned his head back for a short laugh. "I would like to think so, Lieutenant, although there was certainly more to it than that."

Mathews looked sheepish, and responded, "I'm sure there was, sir. Please excuse me."

The king raised his hand. "A guest in my home apologizes for nothing," he said. "Think nothing of it."

Gesturing to the refreshments on the table, he said, "Can I offer you gentlemen water, or fruit perhaps?"

They all politely declined, but the king gently pressed them to at least share in the water since they would be talking at some length, and the men accepted. Then it was time for business.

"Ali tells me you are the man who led the mission into Iran. Tell me of it."

Mathews swallowed and began speaking, covering the mission from the time they stepped aboard the Saudi Air flight until they stepped off the command 747 in Iraq, pausing occasionally to sip a little water when his mouth became dry from the oratory. It took him nearly twenty minutes to tell the tale.

"Extraordinary," the king observed. "You and your men are to be congratulated on your courage and daring."

"Thank you, sir," Mathews replied. "We were just doing our duty. I regret that we were unable to capture this man Aziz. We might have more answers now than we have questions."

The king nodded. "Yes. Your president told me of his concerns about this man Aziz. He also told me that you are carrying some reports for me that explain why your government believed this man responsible." The king shot a mildly stern look at Minister Ali. "I already know that it was an intelligence source we controlled that led your government to believe he was in his house near Tehran."

"Yes, sir, I have the reports," Mathews responded, drawing the heavy nylon lock bag from the floor near his chair and slipping the key in the lock. He withdrew a sheaf of paper from the bag and handed it to the king. His instructions were to bring the papers back with him, and he hoped he would not have to *ask* the king for them back.

Mathews leaned back in his chair and waited as the king read, watching his eyes move from right to left, quickly. To avoid confusion, the AUTUMN FIRE summary reports had been translated into Arabic, although Mathews had the English versions in the bag if he needed to refer to something.

Minutes went by as the king read and then reread the package of material. After the second read-through, he placed them facedown on the table in front of him and rubbed his eyes.

"I can see why your president asked us to aid him, and given the same set of circumstances here in my country, I would likely have done the same."

Minister Ali leaned forward to interrupt, but the king raised his hand, looking directly at Mathews and Johnson alternately. "I am satisfied that the actions we supported were, at the time, reasonable and justified."

Turning his attention to Ali, he said, "I am less satisfied by the conduct of our intelligence services and how what appears to be false information provided by this government to an ally placed the lives of the lieutenant and his men in jeopardy. I will be speaking to the Minister of Intelligence about that tomorrow." Whatever Ali was about to say, he kept to himself. His monarch had just spoken.

The king turned back to Mathews, and slid the Arabic versions of the AUTUMN FIRE reports across to him. "As one military man to another, I hope you can accept my apologies for the poor information that placed you and your people's lives at risk."

Mathews was dumbfounded, but gathered his wits quickly. "I'm certain whatever the error was, sir, it was an honest one." Prodded by instinct, he added, "My only regret is that we were forced to kill six men that night because of that error."

The king nodded. "It is a sad thing, and I will prod our intelligence ministry to avoid such mistakes in the future so that other lives will be spared." Mathews could only nod in agreement as he slid the reports back into his bag, snapping the lock in place.

After a moment's silence, the king spoke again. "I appreciate you gentlemen coming to see me, and I would be pleased to meet your entire team if that would be convenient."

Mathews and the others took the king's first words as a dismissal, and began to rise. Mathews stopped halfway up, surprised by the request. "It would be our pleasure, sir." What else could he say?

"Excellent," the king responded, getting to his feet as the other men backed away to give him a respectful distance. "I will come by tomorrow night. I also understand you are living out of the hangar next to your transport?" The king turned to Ali. "This is not proper for guests of the Kingdom. Please find the lieutenant and his people proper rooms at one of the better hotels."

Ali nodded. "At once, Your Majesty."

"Thank you, sir," Mathews said, appreciating the generosity on behalf of his commandos and the support team. Given his most recent orders from Colonel Simon, he'd save the polite refusal for Akeem's ears after the meeting.

"If you will excuse me, I must attend another meeting. Minister, I would appreciate it if you would remain with me. There are some small matters to attend to during the welcoming portion of the council meeting."

Ali nodded his assent, and after a last round of handshakes, trailed the king out of the office door.

Akeem turned to Johnson and Mathews and smiled broadly. "That went well, my friends." Looking at Mathews he added, "Let me drive you to a hotel. I would also be pleased, as a member of the ministry, to help you acquire the rooms you need for your people quickly."

"About that . . ." Mathews began.

QUITE NATURALLY, MINISTER ALI WALKED into the conference hall behind the king. His Majesty was greeted by subdued applause of the assembled men of the Saud family, which he acknowledged with a smile and a waved thanks. The group of thirty were all in their fifties and sixties, each heading a major branch or tribe within the Al-Saud family. They controlled all the major ministries and critical elements of the government, and all were accountable to the king, but more important, they owed their fealty to the House of Saud. Some were princes, others were governors or members of various academic institutions, but all were members of the Allegiance Council.

Ali looked around as the king spoke with the minister of agriculture. The room was full of men in white thawbs and multicolored keffiyehs, all standing in small knots, telling stories about their youngest children, their wives' concerns, and the latest football scores in between working out deals among their ministries. Their Arabic was flowing and lyrical, and Ali took a few moments to enjoy the ebb and flow of the conversations around him.

The only thing that seemed out of place were the four men in guardsmen uniform clustered near the last pillar on the right side of the dais. Strictly speaking, the meeting was not open to anyone outside the council, but since the formal meeting had not yet begun, and they all wore the uniform of officers in the Royal Guard, they could remain until King Bandar took his seat. Besides, one of the men was a general.

"WHERE IS HE?" AZIZ ASKED. Saqr and M'an stood behind him, uniformed as captains in the Royal Guard. His rank insignia was a major's, of course—far below the level of authority he deserved, but his and the others' insignias served to disguise them all as irrelevant background elements to the council members. Mahir stood serenely, watching the scene, and answered Aziz without turning.

He will be here. His plane landed a few minutes before Bandar entered the hall."

"What about his personal guard?"

"They are being dealt with now."

MAJOR NAJJAR PAUSED, WAITING FOR the last of them—a middle-aged man—to stop gasping for breath. The other three members of the king's personal guard were already on their way to Paradise. Their struggles to breathe stopped a few minutes ago. The major looked at the bowl of half-eaten oranges and decided to leave it where he had placed it on the conference room table. As long as the Royal Guard controlled the access to the conference center, the bodies would not be found.

The major was amazed it had gone so smoothly. Just offer them the fruit, and three of the bodyguards immediately took a piece and began peeling the oranges. The fourth, middle-aged bodyguard needed only the persuasion of the smell and sight of his friends eating the enticing slices to choose one for himself. As the symptoms came on, overwhelming their nervous systems and robbing the hapless men of their strength, the major merely needed to block the only exit from the king's private conference room.

He stepped out of the conference room, closing the door behind him, crossed the interior hallway, and used the door on his left to enter the king's conference room just to the right of the dais, behind the wood screen used to shield the door from prying eyes. Four steps later, he was at Mahir's right side near the rearmost marble pillar.

"It's done," the major whispered.

"There were no problems? No witnesses?"

"None. The neurotoxin worked very well."

Across the hall, there was a slight commotion as another man entered the conference hall. Aziz leaned around Mahir, pleased to see that Crown Prince Abdullah had just entered the room. Nearly as tall as the king, with a neatly trimmed goatee and sharp features, Abdullah strode across the room and shook the king's hand firmly, but without warmth. Abdullah was one of Bandar's nephews, a man the Allegiance Council had felt more qualified to be crown prince until one of Bandar's older sons had gained more experience as the Governor of Riyadh.

"Do it now," Aziz insisted.

"Major," the general ordered.

The major reached into his pocket, grasped the small Motorola GPRS radio, and pressed the transmit button twice. In seconds, six Royal Guards strode purposefully into the room through the main entry doors, brandishing H&K MP-5 submachine guns, and closing the doors behind them. None of the men directly menaced anyone, but they slowly arrayed themselves around the loose group of council members. Mahir was sure that these and the four guarding the perimeter doors would be more than enough to keep this group of older men in check.

"Your Majesty!" Crown Prince Abdullah spoke loudly enough to ensure that he had everyone's attention. "Please sit. General Mahir has kindly consented to ask these loyal sons of Arabia to ensure that we are not disturbed while we discuss the future of the Kingdom."

King Bandar stood in open-mouthed shock, initially at the breach of protocol, and then at the quickly dawning realization that his nephew was staging a coup right in front of his eyes, obviously with the full support of the commander of the Royal Guard.

Although the anger welled in him quickly, he managed to quell it with a supreme force of will, and slowly walk toward the dais and sit. Perhaps this could be settled with words and reason, Bandar thought. If the Royal Guard were truly behind this, many in this room might die . . . if he succumbed to his initial urge to shout Abdullah down.

All eyes were on the king as he walked toward the dais, and Ali seized the opportunity to reach into the hidden pocket of his thawb for his cell phone. Working quickly, and thanking Allah wordlessly that it was still silenced from the earlier meeting, he slid his finger over the touch screen, unlocking it, and double-tapping the spot he thought the phone icon was to redial the last called number. He soon heard the faint sound of the electronic ring, and Ali quickly pushed the button to turn the speaker volume completely down before taking his hand from his thawb, terrified someone might have heard it. A quick glance around showed that everyone was still focused on either the king or Abdullah, watching intently to see what would happen next.

"Please," Abdullah directed the other men, "take seats, my brothers, and keep your hands where we can see them. We will discuss this matter like civilized men. We are not the desert savages many in the West believe us to be."

Ali watched as the small knots of men began to drift toward the upholstered bench seats, arranged in a semicircle around the dais, and seat themselves. Instinctively knowing he should blend with the crowd, Ali moved toward an empty space on one of the seats and sat, praying he did not muffle the phone's microphone or disconnect the call.

MATHEWS WAS SURPRISED THINGS HAD gone so well. He expected the king to question him more closely given Ali's attitude. After a few minutes' thought, he surmised that the king's military service was probably an anomaly within the family, and that might have made him a little more amicable when it came to hearing the story. The AUTUMN FIRE reports undoubtedly served as the best evidence to necessitate the Wraith incursion into Iran. He had never heard of that kind of classified information being shared with a non-U.S. citizen, but Mathews surmised that at the head of state level, candor was the order of the day. Anything less than that was probably considered an unfriendly act when dealing with the head of a friendly nation.

Bringing his thoughts back to the present, he focused on the Riyadh cityscape passing by. "Akeem, which hotel are we going to?"

Akeem glanced in the rearview mirror to catch Mathews' eye. "The Hilton. After living in that hangar for a few days, I think you and your people deserve some nice rooms for a change."

Mathews was about to tell him that the Hilton might be a bit extravagant, since he had no luck explaining to Akeem earlier that the team had been ordered to stay in the hangar for now, when Akeem's cell phone rang through the car speakers.

"Excuse me," Akeem said, looking at the center console display for the caller ID. "The minister is calling. We may need to go back."

Akeem touched a control on the steering wheel to accept the call, and the sound of an Arabic voice filled the car. Akeem kept driving, but did not speak as he listened intently. Mathews leaned to the right in his seat, curious as to why Akeem did not say anything. Johnson was soon staring at him as well from the passenger seat. The voice coming over the speakers kept talking, and still Akeem said nothing.

As he listened, Akeem's eyes grew wide, and he began to slow the car, pulling to the side of the road. Mathews and Johnson were beginning to grow concerned, and Akeem touched another control on the steering wheel. The voice on the speakers stopped, and Akeem spoke quickly in the sudden silence.

"I've muted the microphone in the car. The voice that is speaking is talking about a new direction for the Kingdom, the rightful place of Islam in the world, the need for better security at the Two Holy Mosques, and the poor choices King Bandar had made in maintaining the alliance and friendly relations with the United States and the back-channel dialog with the Israelis."

Johnson looked at him incredulously. "What? Are you sure Ali called you?" The voice started again in the background.

"Yes, the number I have for him is his private cell phone."

"Do you think he's still in the meeting?" Johnson asked.

"I don't know . . ." Akeem trailed off, holding his hand up for silence and concentrating on the voice coming from the speakers in the Mercedes. Mathews leaned forward, more to join the conversation in the front seat than out of any hope of following the conversation. His Arabic was barely good enough for "Good morning."

Suddenly, another voice overrode the first, firm and authoritative, and all three of them recognized it, in spite of the language barrier for Mathews and Johnson. They both looked at Akeem for confirmation.

He nodded. "That's King Bandar. He's telling the other man speaking that what he is doing will damage the Kingdom's credibility with the world. A sudden change in leadership . . ." Akeem trailed off as the first voice overrode the king's, then Akeem's eyes widened.

Mathews prompted him, "What?"

"The king said that a sudden change in leadership like this would not be supported by the council without clear proof of his inability to lead. The first man said that if the council were unwilling to agree with his assessment of the king's leadership abilities, he would be forced to take 'firm measures' to ensure the safety of the Kingdom."

"Holy shit," Mathews breathed.

AZIZ KEPT HIS PLACE IN Mahir's shadow, but he was beginning to grow impatient. One way or the other, the only people walking out of this room alive other than himself, Mahir, and their men was the crown prince. If he could convince the council to sign the decree attesting to Bandar's incompetence, they would leave the king and council members to "adjust" to the situation and then have Mahir trigger the bomb once they were outside of the conference center. With the explosion explained initially as a horrible tragedy and Mahir's appointment as defense minister formalized by morning, Abdullah would be confined under house arrest with carefully chosen Royal Guardsmen, leaving Mahir to carry out Aziz's orders in King Abdullah's name.

Soon thereafter, the explosion would be determined to be the work of Israeli and American agents, and Aziz could begin to extract Arabia from the clutches of America and start aligning its policies more closely with Iran's. In time, his plans for Iran would come to fruition, and the two nations would form the core of the restored Caliphate.

Aziz's thoughts returned from the heady feeling of being so near the completion of the first major step in his plans. Abdullah was still speaking to the council, and Aziz's frustration level rose another notch.

"My brothers," Abdullah continued his plea, "surely you see how the king's close alignment with the West has begun to erode our institutions, threaten our culture and our faith, and expose our people to dangerous ideas!" Abdullah paused for a few seconds to study them. The council members sat silently, observing him closely, their eyes flicking occasionally to the armed men of the Royal Guard. Abdullah saw this and sought to capitalize on it.

"The men of the Royal Guard here in this room are loyal to Arabia, not its misguided ruler! Do you want the women in your household to be exposed to more Western ideas? Already, too many young girls and women continue to seek learning outside of the home. The home is where their duty to their children and husbands rests, where they should be protected by the men in their family from the evils in the world. Too many women in our society claim that they have the right to choose their own husbands rather than obey the wishes of their parents, while also seeking voting rights and jobs."

Many of the council members, who had spoken positively about the societal reforms for women in Saudi Arabia, shifted uncomfortably in their seats, saying nothing.

Abdullah misread that as a sign that they agreed with him and plowed on. "More important, the courts are beginning to 'take judicial notice' of what they term 'modern practices' of law. They have not abandoned Sharia law yet, but I believe that many activist judges in the Kingdom seek only the proper case to begin to make changes. I seek to restore the pride and dignity of our nation! Brothers! I seek to preserve our society and our faith in Allah! I entreat you to turn away from King Bandar and allow him the dignity of retirement."

Abdullah stopped, waiting for their decision. The men of the council stared for a few moments, and a few muttered amongst themselves. Waiting.

"HE'S DOING WHAT?" MATHEWS EXCLAIMED.

Akeem's hands were shaking, and he fought to steady them by gripping the wheel of the Mercedes tightly. "He's trying to convince the council to force King Bandar to abdicate and allow him to be king. He called the Royal Guardsmen in the room 'loyal sons of Arabia,' which implies they are willing to force the issue."

"A coup," Johnson said flatly, not believing it was happening while they listened live on Akeem's car stereo.

Mathews thought quickly. "Akeem, who in your government can intervene to keep King Bandar in power?"

Akeem stared at the red glow of the electronic dashboard display, thinking. "No one. If the Royal Guard is backing the crown prince, there is no one we can turn to. It would take too long to find someone in the National Guard who could be trusted and convince him to intervene. Even Prince Hafaz, the commander of the National Guard, is in there. He sits on the council." Akeem turned to them, stricken by a sudden realization, and added, "It could be over by the time we get someone to act, or they could all be dead if Abdullah chooses to use force."

Mathews exchanged looks with Johnson. The Saudis were allies of the United States. The overthrow of the legitimate government was, strictly speaking, an internal Saudi matter. Unless . . .

"Who are you going to call?" Johnson asked Mathews.

"My CO. That's probably the fastest way to the president."

"Sounds good," Johnson agreed. "I think we need to do a drive-by and assess the external security."

"That's a plan," Mathews agreed, digging out his secure iPhone and unlocking it.

"Akeem," Johnson ordered, "drive back to the king's residence."

Akeem looked at him curiously, and then it fell into place. *May Allah preserve us*, he thought, slipping the car into gear and looking for a break in the traffic to turn around.

In the back seat, the woman in the iPhone announced, "Line is secure."

"This is Wraith Four Six, I have Flash traffic for Apollo."

"Apollo copies, Four Six. Send it." Simon's voice, like Mathews', was flat and steady, with the undercurrent of urgency only trained members of the military or first responders could manage in a sudden crisis.

"Shattered Castle. I say again, Shattered Castle. We have solid indications of an in-progress attempt to overthrow King Bandar. The coup is being conducted by Crown Prince Abdullah and unspecified elements of the Saudi Royal Guard."

Holy shit, Simon thought, then replied, "Four Six, confirm in-progress coup attempt against the Bandar government."

"Affirm, Apollo. We confirm. We're listening to the whole thing."

"You're what?" asked Simon.

Mathews' explanation took less than two minutes, and Simon conference-called him with Cain in CTS to repeat it while Simon briefed General Crane. Five minutes later, the president came on the line.

"Young man, Dr. Owens has just told me what you've reported. Can you confirm this?"

"Yes, sir. Akeem from the Saudi Ministry of the Interior is right here with me; in fact, we are driving past the king's residence now." Mathews glanced out the windows as the walled perimeter slid past the Mercedes' windows.

"See anything?" Mathews asked Johnson.

"Nothing other than the guards on post. Just the way they were when we left."

"Let me talk to Akeem," the president ordered. Mathews reached over the seat and put the phone next to Akeem's shoulder. "Phone for you," he said automatically.

Akeem kept his eyes on the road, his mind only half-believing what seemed to be happening, and took the phone with his right hand.

"Yes."

"Akeem, this is the President of the United States. Do you recognize my voice, by any chance?"

"Actually, I do, sir," Akeem replied, his accent thickening a little and his voice trembling in the stress of the moment. "I accompanied His Majesty to the G8 Summit at Sharm el-Sheikh a few months ago. I recall your speech—it was quite eloquent."

"Thank you, sir." The president paused before continuing, gathering his thoughts for a sudden decision. "Have you heard what my officer told me about the coup?"

"Yes, I heard all of it, Mr. President."

"He learned it from your translation of what you heard from Minister Ali's phone call?"

"Yes."

"Do you agree with his assessment?"

"I do, Mr. President. In fact, since he first called, the crown prince is continuing to make his case to the council."

"You're listening to it now?" the president asked incredulously.

"Yes, sir. Abdullah is still trying to convince them," Akeem responded.

"Have they said anything in response to his proposal?"

"No, Mr. President," Akeem responded, adding, "It is a cultural silence. It means they do not agree, but they are not confronting him openly. I suspect that they are reluctant because of the armed Royal Guardsmen in the room."

"I see," replied the president, thinking. "Do you believe King Bandar and the council can weather the coup?"

"I don't know, Mr. President. I fear for the life of the king and the council. The presence of armed Royal Guardsmen apparently backing Abdullah's claim is particularly frightening."

"I understand." The president paused, long enough for Akeem to turn right in preparation to circle the palace.

"Are you there, sir?" Akeem asked.

"Yes, Akeem. I'm here. Am I correct in assuming that at present, you are the most senior member of the current Saudi government available to me?"

Akeem sensed what was coming, and his left hand gripped the wheel of the Mercedes hard. "Yes, sir. In any event, finding someone more senior whom we can trust, briefing him, and putting him in contact with you might take too much time."

"I understand. Does the government of Saudi Arabia request the assistance of the United States in stopping this attempted coup and protecting the lives of King Bandar and the council members?"

Akeem took a deep breath, praying he was doing the right thing. "Yes, Mr. President."

"I know that was difficult, and I appreciate the courage it took to say it." The president also appreciated the fact that Akeem's request was on tape, and if things went badly, he would be able to explain a U.S. intervention as a formal request from the Saudi government. "We will do everything we can, Akeem, and we would appreciate any assistance you can offer or provide."

"I'll do all I can, Mr. President."

"Thank you. Please give the phone back to my officer."

Akeem moved the phone back over his shoulder so Mathews could grab it.

"Mr. President?"

"Son, your orders are to do everything you can to secure the safety of King Bandar and the council, and see them safely into the hands of loyal internal security forces. Is that clear?"

"Yes, sir."

General Crane chimed in on the conference call, "The rest of his unit is already moving to rendezvous with him now. We're already getting on-site imagery from a small drone orbiting over the nearby military airfield, but its on-station time is limited."

"Good, make sure that video feed is sent to the Situation Room," replied the president. "What's your name, son?"

"Mathews, sir. Lieutenant Shane Mathews."

"Good luck, Lieutenant."

CHAPTER 23

. . . .

MATHEWS WAS SURPRISED THAT ABDULLAH was still talking to the council, making his case, although Johnson's relay of Akeem's translations was describing a situation that appeared to be about to deteriorate. One of the council members had found his courage and had begun to argue with Abdullah. Others also seemed to be defending the king's leadership.

While Mathews and Akeem were talking to the president, General Crane's call to Lieutenant Cochrane got the rest of the Wraiths geared up and headed out toward the residence.

Mathews and Cochrane arranged a quick rendezvous by phone in an empty lot a few hundred yards from the south gate, where Mathews could gear up and do some hasty planning with his team while they looked at the video feed of the south gate from the MQM-170 through their helmet data links. Less than five minutes later, they were ready.

The mission plan was tough. On short notice, infiltrate the palace grounds, then the conference center, and secure the king and the council with no or minimal loss of life. Mathews was proud of how his people took to the mission calmly, even enthusiastically, about being able to save lives. It did not matter to these men and women that these people were not Americans. It did matter that their president and therefore their country had ordered it, and that was enough.

Mathews shook his head once to loosen up, now in the passenger seat of the lead Suburban. They were 50 yards from the palace's south gate, heading north on Al Wadi Street. Mathews glanced at Cochrane. Both men had their helmets, with the enhanced reality displays off for now, but the radio headsets that hung on their ears were unobtrusive enough. They could not afford to spook the two Royal Guardsmen on the gate with the sight of two helmeted men approaching before they were close enough to deal with them. Cochrane kept the white Suburban's speed down and steady. In the rearview mirror, he could see the other half of the team two car lengths back in the second white Suburban, helmets on and ready to deploy if their plan for a quick and quiet penetration of the south gate failed.

"Charlie Six and Apollo, this is Whiskey Four Six. Ready to engage," Mathews said, licking his lips.

"Apollo copies, and good luck," Simon's voice said in his right ear.

From the iPhone's Bluetooth headset in Mathews' left ear, he heard Johnson's quick "Got it" a second later.

"Here we go, guys," Mathews said to Simms and Klein, sitting in the back.

Cochrane hit his blinker, slowed, and turned the Suburban left, crossing the southbound lanes of Al Wadi Street. Mathews visually checked both guardsmen as the Suburban drove up. He saw one man on either side of the vehicle lane at the gate, eyes on the approaching white Suburban. Their positions checked with what the Outlaw UAV had shown them minutes earlier.

Mathews also saw the slung H&K MP-5 submachine guns and the radios clipped to their belts. Right now, the radios were the most dangerous thing those two men carried. If all went well, the guards would never reach them. Timing would be critical here.

Cochrane and Mathews lowered their windows, both waving and smiling at the guards as they stepped closer to the Suburban, following their usual casual procedure. Both guards' eyes went wide simultaneously as their minds registered two obviously Western males, the bulky equipment vests, and the black tactical clothing.

"Hiya!" Mathews exclaimed, ducking left, just before Cochrane ducked right at the prearranged signal. Behind him and Cochrane, Simms and Klein fired. The slim metal darts from the two Taser X4 Defenders crossed the 4-foot distance faster than human reaction time, and both men started to jerk and shake as the electric shock from the guns interfered with the electrical commands from their brains.

Simms and Klein held the triggers for a three count, released them, and then ejected the now-used cartridges from the guns, throwing them and their connecting wires out the open windows. Both guardsmen collapsed on the paving stones, and Cochran quickly drove forward into the compound, dousing the Suburban's lights. The other Wraiths in the second Suburban had "bind and gag" duty, and they followed them in, stopping inside the compound, just beyond the south gate's lighted area.

Mathews donned his helmet quickly, touching one of the controls on the side trigger of the night vision systems. The thickness of the Bluetooth headset in his left ear made the helmet tight on that side, but he could not afford to cut himself off from Johnson's relay of what Akeem was hearing inside the room, and there was no way to patch them into the team's secure radios.

"I can see the path to the conference hall. Pull up and stop," he ordered Cochrane.

Mathews flicked his eyes up and right to see that the video feed from the Outlaw drone over the airbase was still good, but the angle was only showing him the east side of the building.

"Charlie Five, Whiskey Four Six. I can only see half of the building."

"Whiskey Four Six, this is Charlie Five," Thompson's voice came back to him through the helmet speaker. "We've just ordered the Outlaw to climb. The picture should improve."

"Copy," he responded. "Can you show me targets?"

"Negative. No targets in sight. East side of the building looks clear."

"Copy. Call out if you see any movement."

"Roger."

Mathews stepped out of the Suburban cautiously, staying behind the open passenger-side door as the second Suburban, its lights dark, rolled to a stop quietly behind them. The sub-team had made fast work of tying up and gagging the officer and NCO at the south gate.

Mathews studied the immediate area as his team gathered behind him, their suppressed M8s, reactive body armor, and facelessness created by the black helmets making them look as fearsome as they were capable. The last two men, Mellinger and Tate, brought up the rear, carrying a set of three short poles strapped to their backs along with their other equipment.

Mathews quickly scanned down a line of other vehicles across the road, parked along the right shoulder, mostly high-end Mercedes and BMWs, all pointing in the direction of the south gate. The single Land Rover in their midst seemed to be a bit of an anomaly, but there was no doubt in his mind that they were vehicles of the men attending the meeting. All were dark and silent, and there was no sign of anyone nearby.

The team and their vehicles were less than 50 yards from the south gate, at the edge of the paving-stone path heading off to the right and leading to the conference building. Seeing nothing unusual, Mathews waved a hand forward toward the path, confident the other team members could see it with their night vision systems, and led off at a trot. He turned right at the first branch and as the path widened and the conference building came into view, he slowed to a stop, waving his arms to his left and right, wordlessly telling his men to fan out on either side of him.

Mathews could see that the light level around the building was soft and very dim, creating shadows everywhere along the conference building's perimeter and grounds. Mathews thought the lighting was undoubtedly muted by design to create a calming effect on anxious conference participants, but the night vision mode of the helmet's optics was showing him everything in pale greens and blacks. There was no sign of the Royal Guards Mathews had seen earlier on the building's perimeter. They were either dead, or in on the plot and inside the hall now.

The line of trees that shielded the building from direct line of sight of the compound's other buildings made for good cover, and a couple of his people on either side of the path instinctively crouched next to the trees closest to them. Mathews knew that they were dangerously exposed right now, but he would not seek cover unless every man on his team could take it.

Mathews sensed movement in his peripheral vision, and he watched as Mellinger and Tate split off to the left and right, carrying out their part in the mission. They usually worked together as the team's sniper unit, and tonight he expected that their infiltration skills would guarantee at least four of the six rods the team had nicknamed "Super Eyes" would be in place in time. The two men had judged the distances and estimated they would need about four minutes.

"Mathews," Johnson called in his left ear.

"Yes."

"Akeem says things sound like they are getting rough. Bandar just started talking after a couple of council members. The council members just finished speeches supporting Bandar." Johnson paused and Mathews could hear Akeem talking to him.

"Akeem says Bandar is trying to reason with Abdullah, but it doesn't seem to be going well. I think your time is running out."

"Great." Mathews needed four more minutes. Without that, this whole thing could turn into a bloodbath. His eyes flicked to the square of inset video from his helmet's display. The Outlaw was showing him about three-quarters of the building now. Just a few more minutes.

"Charlie Six, Whiskey Four Six, can you do anything for me?"

Cain's voice sounded resigned. "Negative, Whiskey Four Six. We have no assets in range at this time other than the Outlaw. Charlie Five will continue to control Outlaw on-scene and we are continuing to provide the comm links you need. You have to make do with the local assets."

"Copy that, Charlie Six," Mathews replied. He knew the man was disappointed that he could not help them this time. "Not your fault," he added.

BACK IN CTS, CAIN SLAMMED his fist down on his desk in a rare fit of frustration. Everyone looked at him wide-eyed. "Sorry, folks," he said sheepishly, not taking his eyes off the main display showing the Outlaw's video feed. Although they couldn't help directly, the White House was getting the Outlaw's feed through the CTS, and that was better than nothing at all.

In a minute or two, Mathews and his entire team would be visible on the Outlaw's feed. He could already see one of the team members placing the improved PICTURE WINDOW sensors on one side of the building. Once the sensors were in place and activated, CTS could relay that data, too, and more important, Mathews' team would have the edge they needed to prevent the conference hall from being turned into a slaughterhouse. Cain still wished he could do more for them.

* * *

"YOUR VISION FOR THE KINGDOM'S future is a poor one," King Bandar said from his chair, calm steel in his voice. He would not rise to face Abdullah, lest he give the appearance of dealing with a perceived equal.

"I believe that a more modern Saudi Arabia must flower slowly over time, using the advice and shared wisdom of this council, hearing the voice of the people, and implementing changes gradually, with careful consideration of the impacts. You speak of abandoning the friendships and trust we have gained among the nations of the West or the East, going to war with Israel, and deepening our ties with Iran. These things are simply not possible. We would alienate the world by attacking Israel rather than working diplomatically to see a Palestinian homeland secured, and you know as well as I that the majority of the Iranian people do not share the faith with our people."

Abdullah looked away from the king to the council members, shaking his head. Israel would die a quick death, he knew, if both Iranian and Saudi Arabian armed forces worked together. As for the religious questions, Aziz had assured him that the Iranian government was willing to work with him, just not Bandar, no matter the long-standing differences between the Sunni and Shi'a branches of Islam.

Seeing that he was not getting through to Abdullah, but that most of the council members were nodding affirmatively, Bandar continued.

"We must walk the path I have set out, and do it in a way that not only allows us to embrace certain more modern cultural elements, but also demonstrates that our respect and fealty to Islam and our culture does not change. The radical changes you propose will bring war to our world and endanger the citizens of the Kingdom, whom I hold most dear."

"Give him the signal," Aziz insisted quietly to Mahir, his patience with this waiting nearly exhausted.

Mahir let his eyes rove over the seated council members. All were engrossed in the discourse between Bandar and Abdullah. It was beginning to look like the attempt the crown prince had insisted on to create an opportunity for a peaceful change of power was over.

Mahir looked over his shoulder at Aziz and whispered, "Another few minutes. He will be easier to deal with if he comes to the realization himself of how foolish Bandar and the council are. He will mourn them less."

Aziz leaned back and looked at M'an and Saqr meaningfully. Both men nodded, ready for his orders. If Mahir waited much longer, Aziz would take matters more directly into his hands.

MELLINGER CALLED IN, "SET." TWO seconds later, Tate did the same.

Mathews could already see it. The six brand-new PICTURE WINDOW sensors were all in place, spaced equidistantly, and planted in the ground within 2 feet of the conference center's outer walls. Each 4-foot-high aluminum rod, controlled by the encircling electronics package at its base, emitted radio waves in the 2-MHz range. Coupled with an advanced set of signal processors in each base working together via a Bluetooth radio link, they essentially let the team see through the walls of the building. The Wraith Team assaulters called them "Super Eyes."

In seconds, the devices processed and then sent what they were seeing as a stream of high-speed data through a UHF antenna to the Outlaw UAV and the data antennas on each Wraith's combat gear. Every man's vest had a microcomputer attached to it that processed the data stream, extracting a simple, two-dimensional floor diagram, displaying it in the mini-map section of his optics.

On the diagram, the microcomputer placed a small red X marking the presence of "soft tissue" in the room, based on the radio waves reflecting back to the Super Eye sensors at different Doppler shifts for human bodies than for hard walls and other objects. It did not provide a blueprint-like layout, because the field gear did not have the computing power to do so, but now Mathews and his men had a better idea of where people were in the building. It was easy to see the cluster of people in the center area, and from the general arrangement, he could choose some targets if he had to, but he was hoping for a better picture in a few seconds. Thankfully, this set of sensors were the upgraded versions Colonel Simon had Thompson deliver when she joined the team.

THE OUTLAW TOOK THE UHF signal broadcast from the main PICTURE WINDOW sensor, recognized it as a high-priority data stream, and automatically relayed it via the high data rate Ku-band antenna on its back to an orbiting MILSTAR Block III satellite. One second later, the dedicated PICTURE WINDOW signal processor in CTS's equipment rack went to work.

Equipped with twenty-four of the newest Constant Bridge class i9-4550K CPUs running at 5GHz, the powerful signal processor took the incoming data stream from the Outlaw and begin to refine it. In a tenth of a second, it was producing a live, virtual image of what the six sensors were "seeing" through the walls of the building.

"Holy shit, that thing is cool," Cain said.

"Yes, sir," Carmody agreed.

This was the maiden combat use of the upgraded sensors, fresh off the assembly line, and Cain was suitably impressed. In front of him on the drone station's secondary screen was the three-dimensional image of the conference building, appearing as a wireframe rendition. The wireframes were only general representations of more detailed features like walls because the software could not distinguish between a wall and a door or a window, but more important, it now showed blue human-shaped images within that space, in a manner reminiscent of the old TSA body scanners. Although faces weren't distinguishable, a man could be differentiated from a woman by shape—and more important now, Cain could tell which people were holding weapons from the distinctive outlines.

"Tag the armed men and relay it to the Wraiths," he told Carmody. At least they were doing a little more than playing video voyeur on this one now.

"Done," Carmody replied, clicking his mouse on the six men with the guns, and then clicking the update/transmit icon.

"WHISKEY FOUR SIX, CHARLIE SIX, PICTURE WINDOW opened and armed targets identified."

Mathews saw his helmet's display change as ten little red diamonds began hovering in the space over the conference building, surrounding the white squares of the presumed hostages. On the two-dimensional map, most of the red *X* marks he was receiving locally from the Super Eyes turned white, while ten remained red. Mathews did a quick count. Four guards on the inner perimeter and six inside the hall.

"Apollo, Whiskey Four Six. Request weapons free." Tasers were not an option here. If a Taser failed to function for some reason, a team member might be shot, and worse, the sound of any unsuppressed weapons fire might alert the others Tangos in the building, resulting in a bloodbath.

Simon's voice came back immediately. "Weapons free. I repeat, weapons free."

"Whiskey Team, stack on the doors, stand by to open and clear, check your targets."

Mathews and his men broke into their preassigned assault teams, suppressed M8 rifles up and ready. Wainwright joined Mellinger on the left side, while Kegan joined Tate on the right. Mathews and the rest headed for the main entrance and the large double doors, Mathews and Simms on the left, Cochrane and Klein on the right.

"Team 3 ready," Wainwright called in on the left side.

"Team 2 ready," Kegan called in on the right side.

"Team 1 ready," Mathews called out. "Go soft on the inner perimeter. We want to keep stealth as long as possible."

Mathews and Cochrane used their off hands to reach for the door handles, while Simms and Klein moved to stand shoulder to shoulder before the doors, each man's sights set on one of the red diamonds representing the armed guardsman just beyond the doors. Mathews gave them another second to be set, and nodded at Cochrane.

Both men twisted the handles and yanked the doors open. Simms and Klein fired instantly as their targets came into view. Both guardsmen took three silenced rounds to the head and dropped instantly.

Mathews scanned his head left, looking "through" the building at the other two entry points. The red diamonds were gone there, too, his display now showing the paired sets of green diamonds representing the other team members and the white squares of the presumed hostages. The change in symbology told him CTS was still with them, knowing that if this devolved into a close-range firefight, distinguishing the enemies from the friendlies was going to be important.

The team moved quickly into the inner hallway, stacking on the main entry doors to the king's conference room. In seconds, the other four joined them after clearing both sides of the inner hallway, taking positions to hold the doors, or enter the room and back up the assault team if they got bogged down securing the king and the council.

Mathews checked his display again, looking toward the closed inner doors. The other six armed men were arrayed around the group of presumed friendlies.

Mathews called out to Johnson. "Mike, we're ready. What's the situation inside?"

"The king just told Abdullah, 'The radical changes you propose will bring war to our world.' Abdullah is shouting now." Mathews could not hear anything through the apparently soundproof walls as he "looked" through the left of the two double doors. Suddenly, one of the white squares on his display began moving to the right, heading for a small group of four white squares to the right of three red diamonds.

"Mathews! Abdullah just told them that 'if they will not join him in a modern Arabia, then they will be left behind to die with those who cannot rise to see his vision.' Akeem thinks he is going to kill the king and the council members now! Get in there!"

"Team, this is Lead, go loud on entry," Mathews said. "Breach, bang, and clear."

Simms let his M8 assault rifle hang from the attachment points on his combat vest, and came forward with what looked like a small roll of thick, dirty gray tape. Grabbing the free end with one hand, he pressed it against the upper part of the double door, along the seam where the two doors met, then unrolled the tape down the seam, pressing it into place until the 3-foot length ran out, just past the handles.

Simms reached into his pouch, pulled out a timed detonator, pushed it into the line of plastic explosive, and pressed the start button in one smooth motion before returning to his place in the entry line. Five seconds. Behind Mathews, Klein pulled the pin on a nine-banger. Nine flash-bang grenades in one, it would disorient anyone in the room long enough for the team to engage and eliminate the armed guards, while keeping the king safe. Two seconds.

ABDULLAH WALKED TOWARD MAHIR, PASSING the outer ring of armed men, ready to give the order to hold the king and the council incommunicado. Mahir stood straighter, giving every outward indication of a man about to accept an order from his king, continuing the illusion that this man would actually rule the Kingdom. Abdullah grimly nodded at Aziz first, grateful for all of his help. Then he turned his attention to Mahir and opened his mouth to issue his first order as Saudi Arabia's newest king. One second.

THE STRIP OF EXPLOSIVES BLEW the two heavy wood doors inward, splintering the edges and hurling tiny wooden spears 10 feet into the room. Klein did not hesitate and lobbed the nine-banger into the room, its safety spoon flying through the air as the black cylinder bounced and rattled along the marble floor toward the center of the room.

TOO FAR AWAY TO BE affected by the explosion that blew the doors open, M'an and Saqr reacted instantly. They knew Saudi special operations troops had somehow found them. Saqr grabbed Aziz by the shoulders, twisting and pulling him to the floor, while squeezing his eyes shut and trying to cover his ears. M'an dropped down beside them, helping to cover Aziz with his body, squeezing his eyes shut as well, while holding one hand against his right ear and his left ear against Saqr's shoulder.

THE DETONATION OF THE NINE-BANGER was a sudden, rapid series of nine explosions and bright flashes in the large room, temporarily deafening and blinding everyone who hadn't sought cover. As soon as the chain ended, M'an reached for his pistol as he stood, and Saqr began to drag Aziz to his feet. Men in black combat gear, their heads covered by what M'an thought were black motorcycle helmets, were streaming into the room.

MATHEWS ENTERED THE ROOM ON the left side, shoulder to shoulder with Cochrane on the right, the optical systems in their helmets automatically switching to daylight mode in the brightly lit room.

Both men identified three targets painted with red diamonds in front of them holding rifles, and moved deeper into the room at an angle, allowing the other Wraiths to flood in behind them.

Mathews centered his sights on the man closest to him. The nine-banger had done its work, disorienting everyone in the room, but he and the others were starting to recover. The man lifted his rifle, and Mathews' right finger tightened on the trigger of his M8. Three rounds center mass, and the man dropped. He couldn't risk a head shot in the mixed-target environment. On his right, Cochrane fired two three-round bursts, dropping one then another of the targets on his side of the room.

Behind Mathews, Simms identified the target behind the man Mathews had just dropped and fired once, sending three rounds into his heart from a distance of 20 feet. Mellinger was next on the left side, and his burst caught the last Tango in his upper chest, his aim off just a millimeter at that distance.

On the right side, Tate fired at the last Tango, dropping him instantly. The Wraiths stood still, scanning the people in the room over their gun sights, looking for more targets.

M'AN COULD NOT BELIEVE WHAT he was seeing. These men were highly skilled. In seconds, they had eliminated the Royal Guardsmen with ruthless efficiency. Belatedly realizing he was holding a pistol, and inviting instant death, he lowered it to a point behind his thigh but did not drop it. Still suffering from the concussive grenade's effects, Mahir stumbled forward, and Najjar grabbed for him, half-blinded, while fumbling to bring his pistol up. One of the black-clad men to his right stepped forward and without a sound, three red blotches appeared in the center of the major's back and he fell face-first onto the floor.

"Erkud!" Saqr shouted, recognizing the danger as M'an did, grabbing Aziz and starting to half-drag, half-push him toward the door hidden behind the screen.

Mathews watched the body fall and then heard one of the men in the rear shout something and begin dragging a second man backward. Mathews saw the face of the second man and swore. Aziz! Here in the middle of a coup in Saudi Arabia. He recognized him from the grainy passport photo the Saudis had supplied before the team's mission into Iran.

Mathews' mind raced. He could not shoot. They needed Aziz alive and the king needed to be protected. The two—no, three—men disappeared behind a screen to the right of the dais the king sat on, obviously still stunned from the nine-banger.

"Team, this is Lead, secure the king and the council!"

Mathews weaved his way through the knot of stunned older men and around the dead bodies, moving as quickly as he could, knowing he was fouling his men's line of fire and wary of any ambush. He could hear Cochrane ordering Simms and Klein to cover the king and the others to frisk the white thawb-clad council members for weapons.

Mathews reached the screen and peered around it over the sights of his weapon. The three white squares were moving to his right and away from him.

"Right with ya, boss," called Tate as he came up behind Mathews, adhering to the cardinal rule that no Wraith went anywhere alone.

"Copy," Mathews responded. "I think we've got three runners here, and one of them is probably Aziz."

"Aziz from Iran?" Tate asked rhetorically. Wherever Mathews was going, Tate was coming along.

"Affirm," Mathews answered.

At the Wraith base, Simon and Crane looked at each other incredulously. Aziz? In the middle of it all? Jackpot! *If* Mathews and his people could pull it off. Both men wanted to call in and have Mathews confirm, but they knew better than to interrupt now. Crane reached for the phone. Mathews and his team were just as likely to shoot Aziz as capture him at this point, and Crane wanted the president to weigh in.

Mathews moved around the screen and saw the open door gaping into the hallway.

"Oh, shit. XO, Lead. We have a door here. Three runners for sure. One of them is probably our objective from Iran. In pursuit." Matching deed to words, Mathews headed out into the corridor, moving quickly but cautiously, Tate hot on his heels, both men scanning for targets.

"Copy," replied Cochrane. "Do you need backup?"

"Negative. Keep the team with the council and the king. Follow His Majesty's orders explicitly."

"Roger."

Mathews and Tate rounded the last turn in the inner corridor before the damaged main doors, peered around carefully to make sure they were not walking into an ambush, and moved to the entrance, once again peering around it carefully, their helmets automatically shifting back into night vision mode for visibility in the darkness. Mathews could just see the three men sprinting down the stone path toward the south gate.

"Charlie Five! I have three runners, south of the conference building. Track them! Do not lose them! They are hostile!"

"Copy, Charlie Five. We see them. Be advised, Outlaw has less than ten minutes remaining on-station due to fuel state."

Mathews started running, Tate keeping pace with him as the white squares in his optics were replaced by three red diamonds superimposed over the green-and-black shapes of the three running men in their displays. Mathews and Tate were at least 50 yards back, and the trees were in the way, eliminating the potential for a clear shot—not that they could take it. Mathews was breathing heavily by the time they reached the end of the path, tracking his weapon south to see the three red diamonds superimposed over the black Land Rover they had passed earlier.

"Your runners are in the Land Rover," Thompson's voice called out to him over the radio link, as he heard the engine fire up and the tires screech as the driver floored the accelerator to get away.

"Shit! In the Suburban!" Mathews ordered. Both Wraiths ran to the Suburban and hopped in, Tate taking the driver's side so his commander would not be distracted by having to drive.

The Suburban's engine fired instantly, but they lost precious seconds as Tate turned the vehicle in a tight circle to head back toward the south gate and out, turning left onto Al Wadi Street and racing north in the wake of the Land Rover.

"Apollo, this is Whiskey Four Five," Cochrane called over the radio net. "King Bandar is secure. The council members are unharmed but stunned. We have a General Mahir in custody at the request of a Minister Ali."

"Copy that, Four Five. Stay off the net for now while Six is in pursuit."

Mathews was pleased to hear the good news, but wanted more. Capturing Aziz would make tonight's Op even better.

CHAPTER 24

THE LAND ROVER TORE NORTH, M'an at the wheel, Saqr in the back next to Aziz after having unceremoniously shoved him in. M'an was weaving in and out of the light traffic at nearly 100 kilometers an hour, racing to get away from the area as quickly as possible.

Aziz sat in the leather seat, shock rapidly turning to anger. He slammed his fist against the door of the Land Rover repeatedly, screaming out his rage. How had the Saudi security forces known what was happening in that room? They have destroyed everything! He had to flee the country immediately.

Aziz pulled his cell phone out and dialed a number from memory.

"Yes, Sayyid," Zaki answered.

"I want the plane prepared for immediate departure. File a flight plan to Hormuz. We will leave in the next ten minutes."

Zaki was too long in Aziz's service to wonder about the sudden departure. He could file the flight plan by phone and have approval for the flight to Iran in minutes, and the Gulfstream was already fully fueled. "It shall be as you wish, Sayyid."

Aziz killed the connection before telling M'an, "The airport, now! We will leave the country immediately!"

M'an nodded, not daring to take his eyes off the road, still dodging cars.

* * *

"SEE HIM?" MATHEWS INQUIRED.

Tate was having trouble fitting the Suburban in the same gaps the smaller Land Rover was slipping through, primarily because they were closing or shifting before he could get to them. They were more than a half-mile behind the Land Rover according to his helmet readout.

"Yes, I've got them," Tate answered. "What do we do to stop them?"

Mathews thought about that. The street was not too crowded, and if they could get close enough, they could ram the Rover, or possibly shoot out the tires.

"I'm working on that," Mathews told him. "Just get closer."

Tate kept pursuing, exploiting a sudden gap in the traffic with the Suburban's massive V-8 engine to close the gap to within a quarter-mile, when a little blue Vauxhall Vectra suddenly pulled into his lane without warning. Tate swerved hard right to dodge around it, the sound of multiple horns blaring around him.

"SAYYID," SAQR SAID, EYES GLUED to the rear window, drawing his H&K P2000 SK pistol. He just saw the Suburban swerve and accelerate closer to them. "We are being followed."

Aziz turned to look, and saw the massive front grill of the two-ton white Suburban getting closer by the second. Suddenly, a strange rounded shape began to protrude from its passenger-side window. After a moment's confusion and panic, Aziz recognized it as a man's head wearing a black motorcycle helmet. Worse, he could see the stock of a rifle appearing next.

"M'an! Do what you must!" Aziz shouted.

"HOLD THIS THING STEADY," MATHEWS ordered. He was halfway out of the window, using the lower part of his left leg to anchor him by wedging it in between the seat and the center console. The rifle was probably a bad call, its length making it more unwieldy than he expected, and getting it out of the window was taking too long.

"Apollo, this is Four Six! I have the target vehicle in sight. I'm engaging."

* * *

SAQR HAD NO TROUBLE RECOGNIZING the helmeted man as one of the men from the assault team, and the rifle he was trying to get out of the window was a more threatening weapon than either he or M'an were carrying. Saqr leveled his H&K P2000 SK at the helmeted man, aiming through the Land Rover's rear window, and opened fire.

The first round shattered the rear window and went wild, and before Saqr could pull the trigger to fire the second round, M'an reacted to the unexpected gunfire, assuming they were being fired upon and began swerving the Land Rover left and right. Saqr's next three rounds went wild, too.

"TAKING FIRE! TAKING FIRE!" TATE yelled into his helmet radio, seeing the flashes and beginning to slide the huge vehicle back and forth to try to avoid the fire. Mathews almost lost his grip and fell out of the window.

Abandoning his attempt to bring out the rifle, he dropped it on the floor of the Suburban and drew his Berretta, bracing himself by gripping the roof rack with his left hand. They were coming up on one of the large, circular roundabouts. It had a built-up center area landscaped into a small hill. It would be a perfect backstop for his rounds, helping to ensure no innocent Saudis were hit.

Mathews lined up on the weaving Land Rover. He could see the shape of three heads through the night vision mode of his helmet: the driver, the man holding the gun, and the top of the third man's head just behind the rear passenger seat's headrest.

Two bodyguards and one target. Mathews began trying to aim at the driver. They needed the vehicle stopped. His and Tate's body armor would protect them from any small-caliber rounds that hit.

"I have a potential shot at the driver! Taking it!" Mathews announced over the radio link, before seeing the sight picture he wanted and squeezing the trigger twice.

The 9mm rounds from his suppressed M9 Berretta crossed the 20-yard distance in three-hundredths of a second. Mathews knew that firing from a moving vehicle at the occupant of another moving vehicle, when both vehicles were swaying back and forth to avoid fire, was guaranteed to result in a miss. Still, he came close. The first round passed between Saqr and Aziz and struck the "B" pillar in the Land Rover, just to the left of M'an's head, burying itself into the supporting structural steel. The second round passed through the glass in the rear quarter, which deflected it slightly, allowing it to pass over Aziz's head, missing him by a half-inch before striking the center console in the roof, directly above the rearview mirror.

"Four Six, this is Apollo! Cease fire! I repeat, cease fire! NCA wants him captured alive. Disable the vehicle any way you can." Crane's voice was clear in Mathews' ear, its finality unmistaken.

Mathews slid back into the passenger seat, frustrated. In the end, orders were orders, especially when they came from the president.

"Ram him!" Mathews told Tate, reaching for the seat belt and buckling himself in. Tate grabbed his seat belt with one hand and mashed the accelerator to the floor.

AZIZ LOOKED UP AT THE bullet hole in the Land Rover's roof, and blanched. These Saudi fools almost killed him. "M'an! Get us out of here, now!"

M'an had felt the impacts of the faceless commando's bullets around him, and then Saqr fired six more shots before the slide locked open on an empty magazine. M'an thought Saqr's shots were probably going wild anyway, and their current circumstances were untenable. It was only a matter of time before the entire Saudi police force began to hunt them.

M'an had them past the huge roundabout and back on the two dual carriageways running north and south. The road was slowly curving to the right and they would reach King Khalid Road in another mile or two. He knew he had to act now.

M'an turned the wheel sharply to the left, launching the Land Rover up over the median strip and into the oncoming southbound lanes, trusting Allah to preserve them. Cars scattered before them, some left, some right.

Mathews watched the Land Rover sail over the median strip and veer into the oncoming traffic, weaving a little, but mostly forging a path between the oncoming cars that moved right and left to clear a path. "Stay in these lanes! Pace him!" Mathews ordered Tate. This would not end well for the Land Rover, Mathews thought. Any moment, the driver's luck was going to run out.

MATHEWS WATCHED THE LAND ROVER sail over the median strip and veer into the oncoming traffic, weaving a little, but mostly forging a path between the oncoming cars who moved right and left to clear a path. "Stay in these lanes! Pace him!" Mathews ordered Tate. This would not end well, Mathews thought. Any moment, the Land Rover driver's luck was going to run out.

M'AN SAW THE RED MUSTANG GT Premium coming toward him and not moving out of the way. It must be some young Saudi with his new toy, he thought. M'an dodged right, the Mustang went left; M'an slid back to the left, and the Mustang went right. They were still heading directly for each other. M'an put his faith in Allah and held his current path. The Mustang driver took a hard left at the last second, hoping to make a sharp enough turn to avoid M'an if he turned right again. It was a good idea, except that the Mustang driver lost control as he panicked, mashing his foot on the accelerator instead of the brake.

The Mustang vaulted up over the concrete edge of the median strip then across the grass strip at 70 kilometers an hour. Tate saw the car coming and moved the wheel to avoid it. Too late.

The Mustang speared the Suburban just behind the big off-roader's center of gravity. The Mustang pirouetted past as the energy it imparted to the rear end of the Suburban caused the massive SUV to lurch drunkenly to one side and its tires to slip. The Suburban began to rotate counterclockwise, allowing the Mustang to barrel on and crash into the roadside, while the Suburban, past its equilibrium point, rolled onto its right side, skidding and sliding into the median and stopping with its nose pointing toward the oncoming traffic.

Mathews and Tate bounced around a bit, but when the Suburban stopped moving, they were still securely strapped into their seats. After shaking off the initial disorientation, Mathews asked Tate, "You okay?"

"Yes, sir," an exasperated Tate responded. "The son of a bitch is getting away!"

Mathews was just as frustrated but held it in check. "Let's get out of here, Chief. We can't catch the bastard from inside a beached whale."

Both men reached for their Emerson CQC-15 combat knives and began sawing at the seat belts. In seconds, the razor-sharp blades had sliced through the heavy nylon belts. Tate stood on the center console, smashed through the driver's-side window with the butt of his M9, then climbed up onto the vehicle's side. A small crowd was gathering, mostly from the cars stacking up at a standstill behind them. Some of the gawkers were pointing and chattering excitedly about Tate's battle gear and mildly odd motorcycle helmet.

Tate reached down to help Mathews out of the damaged vehicle. Once Mathews was on the roof of the vehicle, he stood and looked north. The three red diamonds were still out there, and Mathews could see the range numbers scrolling up rapidly. The video feed from the Outlaw was somehow wrong, too. The angle seemed too low. Worse yet, he could hear sirens close behind him.

"Charlie Five, stay with the target. Our vehicle is out of commission."

"Negative, sir. The Outlaw is flying on fumes. Less than four minutes left before the pilot has to land it."

"Shit!" Mathews exclaimed. "How long before you can relaunch?"

There was a pause and Mathews was thinking about calling in his question again when Thompson came back on the link. "Fifteen minutes at least, Four Six."

Dammit! Mathews was fit to be tied, and the sirens were getting closer. He glanced behind him and saw three green-and-white police cars, lights flashing, working their way through the stopped cars. In minutes, he would be facing armed police officers from a friendly country and would be forced to surrender.

"Charlie Six, is there anything you can do?"

"Negative, Four Six. We're out of options here."

Mathews heard the cars stop behind him and a stream of insistent Arabic behind him, no doubt directed at him and Tate.

"Stand easy, Chief," he ordered Tate.

"Roger that, sir," Tate replied, lifting his hands in the air.

"Johnson, we need some help over here."

"We're coming, Shane. We can see the lights. Don't do anything sudden. Akeem will talk to them when we are on-scene."

"Copy." Mathews turned slowly, keeping his hands well away from his body, and found four Saudi police officers standing near the Suburban, looking up at him and Tate, their hands on their holstered sidearms. In the distance, he thought he could see the lights of Akeem's Mercedes coming up the right shoulder.

"Apollo, Whiskey Four Six. We're going to lose him. Call the Saudis and get them to go after this guy."

SEEING THAT THE NORTHBOUND TRAFFIC had vanished due to the accident; M'an crossed back over into the northbound lanes of King Khalid Street, driving north for nearly half a mile. Then he saw the road signs for Highway 522 and made a sudden decision. He turned right, heading up the on-ramp to the superhighway. Soon they were heading east at more than 120 kilometers an hour.

"DAMMIT," EMILY SAID. "CAN'T WE refuel it any faster?"

"No dice," the lieutenant in charge of the support detail told her. "The pump we have for the gas is burned out. We'll have to do it manually after the engine cools for five minutes. Otherwise, the fuel might ignite and we'll have an explosion. We can't risk it."

She shook her head and keyed the microphone on the radio link. "Charlie Six, Apollo, this is Charlie Five. The Outlaw is going off-station now for landing and refueling. We're going to lose contact. Target vehicle is now heading east on Highway 522."

M'AN STAYED ON 522 FOR another 2 miles, checking his mirrors for any sign of pursuit or for the Saudi police. He saw two cruisers heading west, but neither one attempted to turn and follow him. He had to assume that would not last long. Another half-mile slipped by and he took the next exit. King Fahd Road ran northwest across the cityscape. M'an pressed the accelerator closer to the carpet, and the damaged Land Rover accelerated past 130 kilometers an hour.

M'an checked the road signs. Six miles to Prince Salmʌn Road. He pressed the accelerator down another inch.

IT TOOK AKEEM AND JOHNSON nearly five minutes of concerted effort to explain to the police officers on-scene that Mathews and Tate were not terrorists attempting to attack the Holy Cities or part of an imminent invasion of the Kingdom; that they had, in fact, just saved the king's life and were honored guests in the Kingdom. Even then, it took a call to their watch commander before the officers would allow the two commandos to retrieve their rifles from the crashed Suburban and speak to Akeem.

"Can you get a description of the car out?" Mathews asked. "They need to be stopped while they are still in Riyadh."

Akeem shook his head ruefully. "I've already given it to them. They insist that their watch commander take my statement personally and decide what to do."

Mathews looked at Akeem, confused and annoyed.

Akeem continued, "You must understand, my friend. I am a senior member of the Minister of the Interior's staff. They"---he gestured at the officers—"are concerned that if they accept my statement and act incorrectly, they will get in trouble and bring shame on their families. They must wait for their senior officer."

Mathews had heard of some of the Saudi cultural differences during his Special Forces orientations to different areas of the world, but this was ridiculous. He knew getting mad and venting at Akeem would not help; in fact, it would only confirm that he was an ignorant American. Akeem knew there was an urgency, but he also knew he could not make this go any faster.

"I understand. What about the minister?" Mathews asked, barely controlled exasperation evident in his voice.

Akeem understood Mathews' frustration with Saudi bureaucratic procedure and did his best to placate him, but he knew that what he had to tell him would not achieve that goal. "I called him twice. After your assault, he hung the phone up, and I can only assume he hasn't turned the ringer back on."

Mathews shook his head. That bastard Aziz was getting farther away every minute.

M'AN TURNED RIGHT THROUGH THE gate near the general aviation aircraft ramp at King Khalid Airport and moved as close as he could to the Gulfstream 550. He could see Zaki and the new copilot through the cockpit windows, illuminated by the flight deck lights and the instrument glow. The right engine was already turning, its distinctive whine steady and promising escape.

M'an parked the Land Rover alongside the aircraft with the passenger-side doors closest to the boarding stairs. Saqr exited the back and held the door for Aziz, who stumbled out of the rear compartment and then stood, looking around the airfield, expecting to see the blue lights of Saudi police or military vehicles.

Saqr touched his elbow, drawing an immediate look of pure anger. "Forgive me, Sayyid, but we must leave now before the security forces have the time they need to find us."

Aziz looked at Saqr, the clear logic of his words penetrating the rage filling his brain. Without a word, he gathered himself and strode purposefully to the waiting jet. He climbed the stairs in a pace he hoped was measured, but quick. Once he was inside the cabin, he turned to look at Zaki through the open cockpit door.

"Take off immediately." Aziz's tone and the fierce look on his face brooked no argument, and Zaki wasted no time closing the cockpit door, before turning to his copilot.

"Start number one now. I'll get taxi clearance. We'll run the takeoff checklist during the taxi."

"Khalid ground, this is Gulfstream EP-FAS, requesting immediate taxi for south departure." Zaki heard engine number one growl to life, and automatically checked the gauges. Everything was in the green. He reached down and released the parking brake, hands on the throttles.

"Gulfstream EP-FAS, cleared to taxi via Charlie and Echo to One Five-Left, position and hold."

Zaki had the throttles moving before the ground controller finished speaking. Five anxious minutes later, following the blue lamps that defined the taxiways at night, the Gulfstream was sitting at the end of the 4,000-meter runway.

"Khalid Tower, Gulfstream EP-FAS, ready to go, Runway One Five Left."

"Gulfstream EP-FAS, wind is 5 knots at one two zero, clear for take-off."

Zaki advanced the throttles to their stops, feeling the thrust of the engines press him back in his seat. "EP-FAS rolling."

AZIZ SAT IN THE LEATHER chair in his private cabin, watching as the lights of Riyadh fell away in the darkness. So close. He inhaled and let out a breath of frustration. How had they known? Perhaps the king had some sort of panic device on him? One of the other council members, perhaps? Who were those black-clad soldiers? The Emergency Force from Saudi General Security? They often trained with some of the best special forces units in the world, *but how had they known?* Mahir had said nothing of an Emergency Force assault unit nearby. Had Mahir betrayed him? If so, he would meet a horrible death as soon as possible.

Aziz leaned back in his chair and closed his eyes. The shock of the sudden end to his plan was nearly overwhelming. He had planned for so long since his father's death to restore the Caliphate. Using Saudi Arabia as a puppet state, much as the Taliban had served the old al-Qaeda's needs, and aligning its foreign policy more closely to Iran's would have been able to blunt Western involvement in the Middle East.

Taking a few months to insinuate properly trained and prepared men like M'an and Saqr on Abdullah and Mahir's staffs would have neutralized them both and left Aziz as the power behind the throne.

Aziz shook his head in tired frustration. Now he must begin again. Restoring the Caliphate would still be accomplished; he would simply need to choose another country to work from within. In any event, it would not take years this time, only a few days to put things in motion. Regretfully, he realized he could not return to Saudi Arabia openly, but he still had his contacts there and enough of his wealth to ensure that he would have influence.

Such is Allah's will, he realized, with a slow nod. Allah was testing him to ensure that he had the leadership skills necessary to build and maintain the new Caliphate. Did not Mohammed, peace be upon him, suffer trials throughout his life, even though he was Allah's final messenger? In any event, Aziz had hurt America greatly during his preparations, and that in itself was pleasing and helpful to the worldwide jihad.

Aziz rose from his chair, removed his shoes and socks, and moved to the basin, drawing water for the Wudu. When properly cleansed, he retrieved the finely woven prayer mat from the side cupboard and arranged it neatly on the cabin floor, before he stood facing the tail of the aircraft, as the Kabbah was now behind the Gulfstream, and began Salāt.

Aziz knew without any doubt that it was proper to offer prayers of thanks to Allah for His sometimes harsh but needed lessons. As he began the second raka'ah, the Gulfstream passed out of Saudi Arabian airspace and into the Persian Gulf.

"FOUR SIX, WHAT DO YOU want us to do? The Outlaw is refueled and ready."

Mathews knew the horse had fled, but there was still a security perimeter to monitor. "Go ahead and get it airborne. Scan the surrounding area and keep an eye out for anything that might look like the target vehicle. Maybe we can give the Saudis a hand finding him."

"Copy that," she replied.

Mathews, Johnson, and Akeem were standing in the rear of the first conference room immediately to the left of the conference building's main entrance, a few paces down the inner hall from the now-blown-open doors to the king's conference room. The rest of the Wraiths were spread throughout the room, standing around the main table or clustered in groups of three or four, all with an eye on the door. Most of them were standing between Mathews' small group in the rear of the room and the conference room's single doorway. Two of the Wraiths, Simms and Kegan, had taken it upon themselves to stand post just inside the open door. All the men had removed their helmets, now that the need for immediate action was over, and placed them on the central conference table.

Mathews heard the heated Arabic voices just down the hall and ignored them. Akeem had told him earlier that the members of the Allegiance Council were debating the fate of Crown Prince Abdullah, and their discussions were of no concern to Mathews. His attention was focused on providing the after-action report to General Crane and Colonel Simon over his secure iPhone, while the president and Cain listened in.

"That's about it, sir. After the Mustang ran into us and the Suburban rolled, we were unable to continue the pursuit."

"The target?" Crane asked.

"The Outlaw lost track of the Land Rover when it descended for landing. We passed a description on to the Saudi police with Akeem's help, and they've put out their equivalent of a 'be on the lookout' to every officer in Riyadh."

"Were any Saudi nationals hurt?" asked the president.

Mathews closed his eyes, and chose to ask a question rather than answer the president's question without requesting further clarification. "At the accident scene, sir?"

"Yes."

"No, sir," Mathews replied, "at least not seriously. The only Saudi national hurt was the driver of the Mustang. He's got a bloody nose and probably a concussion, but he was walking and talking to the police officers on-scene before they released Tate and me into Akeem's custody."

"I see. General Crane, King Bandar is on the line for me now. I'll be back to you."

"I'll be standing by, Mr. President," Crane told him, before Mathews heard the click of the White House dropping off the secure conference line.

"Four Six?"

Crane reverted to Mathews' call sign, signifying that with the president gone, it was time for a more candid military conversation.

"Copy, Apollo," replied Mathews.

"How many Tangos did you neutralize?"

"Four on the exterior perimeter, six in the room itself. All were either a direct threat to my command or the precious cargo." In this case, the precious cargo included King Bandar and the council.

"Copy that, Four Six. As far as I'm concerned, Bravo Zulu to you and your team. I'll back your actions with the C-in-C."

Mathews was grateful for the general's support and his appreciation of Team Four's efforts, but ten members of the king's personal guard were still dead, and Bandar might be expressing his displeasure about that to the president now.

Mathews' pause gave Cain a chance to chime in. "What do you think of the Saudis' chances of catching him?"

Mathews looked sidelong at Akeem, choosing his words carefully before answering. "I'm sure they will do their best, sir, but I think too much time may have elapsed between the crash during our pursuit, the Outlaw going off-station, and the time the Saudis were able to get the word out."

"Copy that," Cain replied. "I'll start getting things moving at this end. We'll see what we can do to pick up the trail."

Crane started to say something but was interrupted by Mathews. A Saudi man, resplendent in his Saudi Royal Guard uniform, was standing at the entrance to the conference room. He was Mathews' height, with olive skin, dark eyes, a thick but well-trimmed goatee, and a serious face women no doubt found appealing. The tan shoulder boards his uniform displayed were those of a brigadier general.

Mathews lowered his voice a bit, "Sorry, General, a Saudi general officer just arrived. I need to go." Mathews barely heard Crane's assent before he disconnected the call.

Mathews walked over to the new arrival, Akeem and Johnson in tow. Two steps toward the man, Mathews voiced an order, "Team! Attention on deck!" The Wraiths ceased their conversation and stood at attention, all eyes on the newcomer, a few of the more nervous team members glad that the position of attention allowed them to keep their hands near or on their weapons. This man was a senior officer of an allied government, and Mathews knew that showing the correct military courtesy was not just proper, but in this case might also help ensure that he and his people were treated as the professionals they were. In offering respect, he hoped to engender it from their hosts as a hedge against any fallout from their actions tonight.

Mathews need not have bothered. Once Mathews was standing before him, Brigadier General Salim ibn Nasab ibn Tariq al-Shabab grasped him firmly by the shoulders and leaned forward to deliver the three kisses on the cheek common amongst close friends and family in the Middle East.

"Lieutenant Mathews," Salim said in slightly accented English, relief in his voice, "I am very grateful to you and your men for protecting His Majesty from Abdullah and my predecessor's attempt at usurping his throne."

Mathews, initially startled when the general reached for him, had just managed not to reach for the Emerson CQC-15 knife resting in the sheath in the small of his back. To give himself a few seconds, he called over his shoulder, "At ease," and the Wraiths relaxed their posture of attention, but stayed alert, listening to the conversation.

"We are pleased to be of service to your nation and glad that the king and his council are unharmed. May I ask who you are, sir?"

The general smiled broadly. "I am Salim."

"It's good to meet you, General," Mathews said, extending his hand in the more traditional Western greeting.

Salim gladly reached out to shake Mathews' hand, but shook his head, the smile still in place. "No, my friend. I am Salim to you and your men." He waved with his free hand to encompass the whole team. "You and your officers have served tonight as members of the Royal Guard, placing your lives at risk for our leader and his government. I am pleased to speak to all of you as friends."

Mathews was embarrassed slightly by what he thought was effusive praise, but thought this also might be the time to get some questions answered.

"Thank you, Salim. Can you tell me how the search for the man we know as Aziz is going?"

Salim shook his head. "I do not have any news to share. Our police forces are watching for the car you described, and I have ordered two officers I trust to work directly with the national police force and the Interior Ministry."

"I see," Mathews replied. "I hope you can catch him quickly. My government has many questions for him."

"We will do all we can," Salim assured him.

"I know that you will. My executive officer," Mathews said, gesturing in the direction of Cochrane, "found a remote trigger on the officer we captured. Do you know what it activates?"

Salim's face turned grave. "Yes. I threatened to press the button while he remained alone in the conference hall. My predecessor told me a bomb lay beneath the dais. Our experts have defused it, and it is being taken away as evidence."

Mathews was stunned that the Saudis had not ordered the evacuation of the building, but arguing that now was a moot point. Something else Salim said caught his attention, anyway.

"Your predecessor?"

Salim's smile returned, but he lowered his head modestly as he spoke. "Yes. His Majesty has appointed me the new head of the Royal Guard. I am honored by his confidence in me."

"Congratulations," Mathews said, reaching out to take his hand again. "I'm sure King Bandar will be safe in your hands."

"I will do all I can to serve him." Salim looked away, hearing the voices down the hall grow silent. "It seems that the council is finished deliberating."

"About what?" Mathews inquired.

Salim looked at him. "A new crown prince is required. Abdullah was formally removed from that post shortly after my men and I arrived at Minister Ali's summons. He called us as soon as your men had secured their safety."

"I should thank you," Mathews told him. "Lieutenant Cochrane said some of your men were very surprised to see him and our team surrounding the king."

Salim laughed outright. "Indeed they were. A group of unknown, heavily armed men standing around the king, all wearing black helmets? I think the only thing that kept my men from opening fire immediately was that your men were directly between the king and the guardsmen. I was pleased to help them remain calm. Especially when your lieutenant removed his helmet to identify himself. 'American Special Forces!' he said. My men are still wondering how it was you came to be there."

The implication that he also was wondering was not lost on Mathews. "I'm afraid that is something King Bandar will have to tell you."

"He will not," Salim said jovially. "I already asked him." After a moment's consideration, Salim chose to let his curiosity go unfulfilled. "Truly, it is of no matter. I shall simply thank Allah that you were."

Another guardsman came to the door of the conference room and said something quickly in Arabic to Salim. Salim nodded to the man and turned to Mathews.

"His Majesty wishes to speak to you and your men. Please keep your weapons and equipment with you. For your bravery and actions tonight, His Majesty has ordered that you and your men be considered trusted members of the Royal Guard."

Mathews and the Wraiths followed Salim outside to board the Suburbans, a new black model replacing the one Mathews and Tate had crashed. General Salim and his Royal Guardsmen formed up as escorts in powerful black Land Rovers in front of and behind them, and the small four-vehicle convoy drove deeper into the compound that formed the king's residence.

They advanced nearly a full mile into the compound, passing huge stands of palm and other trees surrounding areas of green grass and fountains interspersed among the low one- and two-story buildings that housed who knew what. Mathews knew that the king was wealthy, not just because of his nation's oil wealth, but because the Saud family had held power in the country for decades now. The last article he read quoted the king's wealth at something more than thirty billion dollars. As they approached his quarters, Mathews mused that King Bandar obviously spent a little of it on this small house.

The vehicle convoy rolled to a halt in front of a two-story building with wide front steps and landscaping that included no less than four fountains spaced across the front lawn. The architecture was quintessentially Arabian, of course, and there were at least fifty uniformed Royal Guardsmen standing at posts scattered all along the front of the house. The four-vehicle convoy pulled up behind a larger six-vehicle convoy of four BMW 7 Series limousines with a leading and trailing Land Rover. Each vehicle in the larger group had two or three guardsmen in attendance, and Mathews could see the wisps of smoke from some of the tailpipes. The engines were running.

Mathews waited until he saw Salim exit the lead Land Rover and wave, and then he alighted from the Suburban, leaving his rifle behind. The rest of Team Four exited the two Suburbans and stood in a loose group before the steps, their eyes automatically roving over the grounds, seeing the guards and likely looking for good cover positions, just in case.

"This way, my friends," Salim encouraged them, walking up the short but wide expanse of steps toward the building. Mathews led the way for his men, stopping alongside Salim under a broad portico formed by the overhang of the second floor.

"What's going on?" Mathews asked Salim.

"His Majesty wants to thank you and your men," Salim responded.

Mathews barely had time to order the Wraiths to form a straight line on him when the doors to the building opened and King Bandar strode into view. Mathews saw a flash of long, twin staircases behind him before the doors shut and the king and his retinue of two aides and four guardsmen were upon him. He expected the guardsmen to be anxiously concerned that the Wraiths, for the most part, still carried their rifles, but their eyes stayed focused beyond the small group of commandos. Clearly they were not perceived to be a threat.

"Lieutenant. I am very grateful to you and your men for saving my life tonight," Bandar told him, taking Mathews' hand and shaking it with both of his.

Mathews found himself acting instinctively again. "We were pleased to help an ally in need, Your Majesty. I deeply regret that we were forced to kill ten of your Guard."

Bandar looked deeply into his eyes. "I see that is so, and I must tell you it proves to me that you are as honorable a man as you are a capable warrior. Please do not think on it. Those men in the hall chose to join Mahir's folly and they paid for it with their lives. I am sure Allah will be merciful with them. For my part, I will speak to their families and tell them that they died in my service, without going into the specifics. I will not add to the pain of their wives and children. I will also see to it that their survivors are looked after."

"That is kind of you, sir," Mathews said, impressed. "If I may ask, how will you deal with the public knowledge of our participation in this?"

Bandar smiled. "What public knowledge?" It took a second for Mathews to catch on and smile in acknowledgment, but the king explained anyway. "What happened in my home is *my* concern and my concern alone. My Guard is sworn to protect the House of Saud, and will remain silent.

"The only information released publicly will be that 'a misguided officer of the Royal Guard' attempted to attack the king and that General Salim and a handpicked team of Royal Guard and Emergency Force personnel stopped the attack, resulting in the regrettable deaths of some of my guardsmen. The dead men will be thought of and buried as heroes, and General Mahir will be tried under Sharia law quickly and punished appropriately." The king thought briefly, and added with a smile, "As they say in some of your movies, 'you were never here.'"

"Yes, sir," Mathews replied. "That would be best for both of our nations."

Bandar nodded. "I'm glad you agree. Your president and I reached the same conclusion a few minutes ago."

"Have your police forces captured Aziz yet?"

Bandar shook his head. "No. The airport police at King Fahd International found the Land Rover a few minutes ago. They are conducting a thorough search of the airport now, but there is no sign of him. The officials at the airport tell me that there have been several departures in the last two hours. Any and all information we discover will be shared with you and your government." The king looked over his shoulder, holding out a hand to one of his aides, "Colonel?"

The man who stepped forward was in his early forties, with closely cropped hair and a clean-shaven face, wearing the uniform of the Saudi National Guard, which Mathews knew was the standing army of the Kingdom.

"This is Colonel Alem, my military aide. He is now your direct contact with me, and your Agent Johnson will continue to work with Ali's aide, Akeem." Mathews offered his hand and exchanged greetings with the colonel, whose English was easily as good as Salim's.

"Alem will see to it that you and all your people are given secure hotel rooms near the airfield to rest and refresh yourselves. If there is anything you need, just ask Alem and he will see to it that it is done for you in my name." Bandar looked up and down the line of men to Mathews left and said loudly, "You and your support team are honored guests in the Kingdom, and we shall look after you as we would anyone who is a guest in our home."

Bandar reached out to take Mathews' hand again. "Please excuse me, but I must return to the conference hall and meet with the council. I must approve the selection of the new crown prince."

The king released Mathews' hand and made a pass down the line of Wraiths, shaking hands and thanking each man for his courage and bravery, before heading down the steps toward the waiting convoy for the short trip back to the conference hall.

After getting Colonel Alem's cell phone number, Mathews and the Wraiths, very pleased with the king's praise and respect, boarded the Suburbans for the trip back to the airfield.

CHAPTER 25

THE HEAT IN THE CABIN, even this deep into the night, and smell of jet fuel was almost overwhelming, but Aziz refused to deplane and wait in the nearby lounge while Zaki oversaw the refueling at Bandar Abbas International Airport. The jet was parked in the small private aviation section of the airport, which was used mainly for high-ranking Iranian military and civilian leadership.

The plane's Iranian registration number and the fact that no one but a government official or wealthy man could afford such a thing gave them, in an odd way, a form of invisibility. In Iran, the common man did not pay too close attention to the comings and goings of the rich or senior clerics. It was a good way to vanish mysteriously in the night.

M'an and Saqr stayed near the front of the jet, hands on their weapons, out of sight of anyone on the airfield. They had even drawn all the window shades after landing to eliminate the possibility of anyone seeing inside the jet.

Remaining on board also served one other purpose. They did not need to report themselves to Iranian customs or immigration, since they were still technically "in transit." Aziz had friends in the Iranian government, but for now, he would prefer not to involve them. He would find a way to keep his father's dream alive without involving his friends in Iran. They were best left in place, and uninvolved until needed.

Aziz took out the special cell phone and dialed.

"Yes." Repin was sitting in front of his computer, another football game on in the background, monitoring the news websites for the first signs of the coup in Saudi Arabia.

"Things have not gone well."

Repin was surprised. "Oh?" he asked, inviting explanation but not requesting it.

"Yes. You will need to put the plans you had ready on hold."

"All right," Repin responded.

"I'm going to need you to support me in another way until I can implement the alternate plan we discussed."

"I may need some time to arrange whatever you need done."

Aziz's voice hardened. "You will do whatever I ask, when I need it done. I have given you a great deal of money to place your skills at my disposal, and I will see that investment properly leveraged, or you will not receive the remainder of your payment."

Repin frowned. First, the sudden "do-it-in-twenty-four-hours" orders and now a complete derailment of the remaining plans to support the coup. Sudden changes to established plans did not generally go well. "I'm listening," Repin replied, annoyed at Aziz's financial hold over him.

Aziz spent ten minutes outlining what he needed, and Repin listened. "It will take about a week to arrange," Repin told him when he was through.

"Sooner."

"Not possible. It will take time to get the people we need in place. Contacting them and getting them there will take three to four days. If you want them to be effective, they need a night's rest and then a day or two to become familiar with the targets."

Aziz wanted to argue, but the man made sense. "All right. One week." He broke the connection and dialed another number on his personal phone.

"Yes, Sayyid," answered the captain of the *Saladin*.

"Be prepared to sail by dawn. Go to my winter home," Aziz ordered.

"Insha'Allah."

Aziz hung up and put the phone on the pull-down desk before him. He would need the *Saladin*, and if it did not arrive safely, the captain would pay with his life.

Aziz heard footsteps on the boarding stairs, and M'an stood, blocking the view from the entry to Aziz, his hand gripping his H&K P2000 SK.

Zaki breezed into the cabin, bringing the oily smell of Jet-A in with him. "We are fully fueled, Sayyid. Where do you wish to go?"

Aziz could see the sky lightening in the east. As dawn broke, he had intended to pray in the private mosque on the grounds of the king's compound in Saudi Arabia, as the de facto, behind-the-scenes leader of Saudi Arabia.

He would have been a true and proper custodian of the Two Holy Mosques. The holy sites would have been cleansed of cripples and the sick, of all who were not true and righteous Muslims. People who sought only peace with the so-called People of the Book, or wanted to talk with the infidels who threatened Islam rather than kill them for Allah and to protect the faith, had no place in Aziz's world or Kingdom. This was especially true of those who lived among the infidels in the West or in Europe, for they would not rise up and kill to protect Islam. They chose, of their own free will, to live among the infidels, send their children to infidel schools, and claim that Muslims could coexist peacefully in mixed communities, in an atmosphere of mutual respect. Aziz knew them from his father's teachings to be fools and likely apostates, those who claimed to believe in Allah but did not.

Once he came to power—and he would come to power—those who did not understand the true nature of Islam would pay for their sins. They would never be allowed into the restored Caliphate, never be allowed to worship within the Holy Mosques, or be allowed entry into the country to conduct the Hajj. They would remain outside the great nation he would build and dedicate to his beloved mentor.

Aziz's eyes never left the window, still seeing the dawn approach and knowing that his fight was not yet finished. "To my winter house," he finally answered. "Once we are there, I shall tell you what to do next."

"Yes, Sayyid."

MATHEWS, THE WRAITHS, AND THE support team were clustered around the INMARSAT terminal in the hangar, waiting for the call General Crane had told Mathews to expect, the huge C-17 looming over them in the first light of a new day. The Outlaw drone had landed a half hour ago and Thompson had helped the support team put it back into the belly of the Globemaster III transport.

In spite of the early hour and the lack of sleep, everyone was smiling and seemed relaxed. They had saved the life of an allied leader and preserved his government. The Wraiths knew that the Kingdom was very different from their own nation—women's rights and the rule of law were decidedly alien to what they knew, and their way of thinking— but they had performed their duty and obeyed the orders of their commander in chief, likely saving hundreds if not thousands of innocent lives through pure happenstance.

Mathews looked around to see the vehicles and men of the Saudi National Guard a hundred yards or so from the hangar. Colonel Alem had provided them at Mathews' request, just before Akeem and Johnson had left. Akeem was heading home to his family, giving Johnson a lift to his hotel on the way, and as a special treat, letting Johnson drive his Mercedes.

Mathews looked down as Sergeant Thompson wormed her way closer to the terminal.

"I wish you had some weapons on the Outlaw," he told her with a smile.

"Me too, sir," she answered, "but I think our Saudi friends would have been pretty pissed if the president would have allowed us to shoot."

Mathews shook his head, smiling a little wider. "Not today, they wouldn't have. The king loves us."

She knew there was an explanation for that, but before she could ask for it, the operator at the INMARSAT terminal held up his hand. Maybe when this was over, she could make another call back home. She missed the sound of Jerry's and Jeff's voices, and they could be proud of what she helped with tonight . . . even though she could never tell them about it.

The operator had rigged up a loudspeaker so everyone could hear, and gave Mathews the telephone-like handset. "Stand behind the loudspeaker, sir, or you'll fry us with the feedback," he told Mathews.

Mathews stepped around the rack, and for good measure, the operator moved the speaker a little closer to the crowd. The Wraiths and the support team numbered nearly thirty, and they all gathered a little closer. Mathews had already told them who was going to call.

"General Crane, this is Mathews. We're all here, sir, and you're on speaker."

"Copy that. Stand by."

"Mathews, can you and your people hear me?" asked the president.

"Yes, sir. You're on speaker, sir, and all of my people are here."

"Good. I wanted to thank you all for a job well done tonight. You have single-handedly participated in preempting a coup that would have toppled a friendly government and created untold problems for your nation in the middle of a crisis. Each one of you is a credit to your service and to your nation."

The president paused, and Mathews saw his people's faces light up from the president's praise. "Lauded by the president" would look good in all their yearly evaluations, he thought, weariness bringing out a little cynicism born of the inevitable paperwork that came with being an officer in the U.S. military.

The president continued. "As a result of your actions tonight, I am hereby directing that every member of this deployed unit be promoted one pay grade, effective immediately."

The whoops and hollers and cheering went on for a minute or two, and Mathews held down the transmit button on the handset so the president could hear the effect of what he had said. When it died down, Mathews said, "Thank you, Mr. President. As you just heard, we're all very grateful."

"You and your people have earned it, Lieutenant Commander Mathews. Well done."

Mathews let the idea of his own promotion sink in. In concentrating on letting the president hear his people's joy, he had neglected to remember that he had also just been rewarded.

"Thank you again, sir."

"You're welcome. As you are all no doubt aware, with increased rank in the military comes increased responsibility. As such, I have new orders for you, and since General Crane is on the line, we'll consider the chain of command to be properly respected. Mr. Cain, I'm told you and the people in CTS are listening in as well."

"We're here, Mr. President," Cain interjected.

"Good, the orders I'm about to issue affect your organization as well."

"Lieutenant Commander Mathews, Wraith Team Four is hereby ordered to locate, track, isolate, capture, and, if needed, kill the man we know as Aziz. His appearance in Saudi Arabia in the midst of an attempted coup, coupled with his apparent involvement in the attacks on our nation, have convinced me that he is a clear and present danger to the United States of America. Are those orders clear?"

Mathews did not hesitate. "Yes, sir. They are clear, sir."

"Very well. Then I will drop off the line and let you, the general, and Mr. Cain get back to work. Good luck to all of you."

There was a click on the line as the White House dropped off. General Crane wasted no time.

"Mathews, you and your people are probably dog tired after tonight. We'll keep this brief and you can get some sleep. Cain and his people have been coordinating with the various intelligence agencies and they are continuing to build the intelligence package on your target. David?"

Cain started talking without missing a beat. "Right now, we're hoping for additional information from the Saudis' interrogation of Mahir and Abdullah. FBI is still working the financial angle, but with little results. The CIA, DIA, and NSA are adding manpower to their efforts. We hope to have some actionable intelligence for you in the next day or so. Any questions?"

Mathews looked around the terminal and saw only tired, smiling faces, with eyes a little bleary from a lack of sleep, but shining with an eagerness to get started on their new mission. Questions would wait for now.

"Negative. Not at this time," Mathews replied.

"Copy. One last thing before we clear the line. Your target now has a codename—FALSE PROPHET, and this operation will be known as SWIFT JUSTICE."

Mathews smiled. "Copy that."

Crane added, "That's all we have for you for now, Lieutenant Commander. You and your people get some rest. You'll be hearing from us soon."

The link went dead and Mathews came around the terminal to stand in front of his people. "First of all, congratulations, everyone." The smiles widened, and a few of the people closest to him clapped him on the shoulder congratulating him as well.

"All right," he continued, "everyone grab your personal gear and load up. King Bandar has arranged for us to have an entire floor in the Sheraton nearby. Everybody can crash, the Saudi National Guard will be guarding the floor. Get a solid eight hours or more if you can, and something to eat. Starting tomorrow night, the hunt is on."

Tom Wither

served his country for more than 25 years as a member of the Air Force's Intelligence, Surveillance, and Reconnaissance Agency and its predecessor organizations. He served on active duty as an intelligence analyst at various overseas locations and is a veteran of the Persian Gulf War. He has been awarded the Meritorious Service Medal, three Air Force Commendation Medals, and three Air Force Achievement Medals. In addition to his graduate-level IT/Computer Security education, Tom holds professional certifications from the NSA as an Intelligence Analyst, and the Director of National Intelligence as an Intelligence Community Officer. He lives near Baltimore. *Autumn Fire* is his second book.